BOOKS BY FREDA BRIGHT

INFIDELITIES

INFIDELITIES

FREDA BRIGHT

New York ATHENEUM 1986

This novel is a work of fiction. Any references to historical events; to real people, living or dead; or to real locales are intended only to give the fiction a setting in historical reality. Other names, characters, and incidents either are the product of the author's imagination or are used fictitiously, and their resemblance, if any, to real-life counterparts is entirely coincidental.

Library of Congress Cataloging-in-Publication Data

Bright, Freda, ———
    Infidelities.

    I. Title.
PS3552.R462515   1986   813'.54   86–47673
ISBN 0–689–11797–3

Published simultaneously in Canada by Collier Macmillan Canada, Inc.
Composition by Heritage Printers, Inc., Charlotte, North Carolina
Manufactured by Fairfield Graphics, Fairfield, Pennsylvania
Designed by Harry Ford
First Edition

To Carole Abel

"A second chance—*that's* the delusion. There never was to be but one. We work in the dark—we do what we can—we give what we have."

HENRY JAMES, *The Middle Years*

PART ONE

1

"MAKE A WISH," SETH SAID.

Annie studied the expanse of chocolate frosting and pink sugar candles.

Enough cake for an army, she thought, although there were just the two of them. That, of course, was vintage Seth, who believed enough was never as good as a feast. And the number of candles could start a conflagration. Thirty, to be precise. Hard to believe she was actually thirty.

No matter. It happened to the best people. It had happened to Seth a couple of years ago and he'd survived, hadn't he? Survived and flourished.

Instinctively, she reached across the table for his hand and squeezed it. He squeezed back.

"Come on, sweetie, make a wish. But remember the first rule of wishing," he cautioned. "You have to blow them out all in one go, or your wish won't come true."

"Rank superstition." She borrowed his favorite epithet.

"Established fact. You have it on the highest scientific authority."

"And whose would that be?"

"My own, of course!"

She laughed. "In that case, I'll make it a good one."

She leaned back to survey the situation.

Thirty candles in one breath. That called for good lungs, but those she had. You didn't spend the last fifteen years belting out high C's without developing ample lung power. The problem was . . .

3

what to wish for? What was missing from her life? For a moment, her mind went blank.

To ask for something monumental—world peace, an end to famine—that would be pretentious, let alone hopeless. She should stick to what was feasible.

On the other hand, she wasn't going to settle for small fry: two tickets to *La Cage aux Folles*, say, or good weather over the weekend. They were trifles unworthy of the occasion.

She was suddenly conscious of standing on the threshold of a new and significant chapter of her life, looking at a decade from the prime cut, the time when singers hit their stride. And women too, according to both Balzac and *Harper's Bazaar*. In any event, a watershed birthday, which surely entitled her to ask for something substantial.

There must be a list somewhere, a cosmic shopping list entitled *What to Ask For in Life*. If so, the first entry would be

HEALTH.

But why wish for what you already have? She'd always been in fighting trim, even before it became fashionable. The sum total added up to a strong, resilient body, furnished with top-quality ingredients, all in perfect working order. Anyhow, it was observable fact that musicians live practically forever. Seth had a theory about it (he had theories about most things), claiming they got such a charge out of what they were doing, they simply refused to pack it in. So much for health. She moved to the next item on the list.

WEALTH.

A perfectly good wish, as wishes go. There had been times when she might have asked for nothing better than to hit the lottery—even a modest win would have done. Times when they'd barely been able to face the first of the month. But happily those days were over. While Seth's salary wasn't stretching as far as they had hoped—New York prices were obscene—nonetheless, for the first time in their lives together, the heat was off. She could walk into a department store any day of the week and buy a VCR or a good wool suit without throwing the family budget into cardiac arrest. Besides, if all went as Seth hoped, they might be on their way to sizable income indeed, what he fondly called big bucks. Be that as it may, they were worry-free, which was reasonably as much as one could ask for.

4

BEAUTY, then.

In theory, that had to be every woman's wish since the dawn of time. In fact, she couldn't picture herself with any other face than the one that stared back at her from the mirror every morning. For better or worse, that face was hers and she quite liked it. Most people considered her attractive. Striking, even. Good figure, nice strong features, an infectious smile, and the kind of coloring that fashion writers termed "vivid": near-black hair, fair skin and emerald eyes.

A perfectionist might carp that the cheekbones were too broad or the nose too long, but she couldn't have cared less. And if the purpose of beauty was pleasing your man, then she was as beautiful as she had to be.

So much for life's baubles, she thought. Now for the big ones.

MARRIAGE.

Still blissful after nine solid years, thank you very much.

LOVE.

Ah . . . love! What life would be without it, she couldn't fathom, but thank God she had more than her share. Who needed petty flirtations, casual rolls in the hay to boost the ego? Not her. She was in the midst of a terrific love affair this very moment, absorbing and passionate—albeit the man in question was her husband. She glanced at Seth in the flickering candlelight. Sweetly sexy as ever—and beyond that quite possibly the nicest, brightest, most loyal, most affectionate of men. Not that he didn't have his faults. Impatience was one of them and right now he was fidgeting slightly, drumming his fingers, waiting for her to get on with it and make that wish.

OK OK . . . Next on the list.

ROMANCE.

(See MARRIAGE.)

SEX. HAPPINESS. INTIMACY. AFFECTION.

(Also see MARRIAGE.)

FRIENDS.

They'd left dozens upon dozens back in Galveston, but there was no reason they wouldn't find plenty of replacements once they settled in. They were a pleasant, sociable couple.

SUCCESS.

The magic word.

For Seth, it had virtually arrived in the shape of his new job at

Medi-Tekk. He believed himself close to a breakthrough. For herself, it didn't matter quite that much anymore; certainly she didn't
ache for it the way she had at twenty, when she wanted to write her
name across the sky. And yet it was conceivable that even now, as she
hovered over the candles, she might be on the brink of a major
career. Never had she been in better voice and at last she was in the
city where everything happened. God bless New York!

So here she was, virtually at the end of her shopping list, every
major item ticked off with a resounding check.

A sudden wave of happiness surged through her, followed by an
equally sudden wave of fear. Had life given her too much? Spoiled
her unfairly? Happiness was so fragile. The Greeks talked of
hubris—the insolence of asking for more than one's due—and the
gods had a way of visiting terrible trials upon the greedy and overly
arrogant. Perhaps the prudent thing would be to wish only that
nothing might ever change. Here she was, married to a man she
adored. Living—at last—in the city she loved. Heading—she could
feel it in her bones—into the mainstream of the great and glittering
world.

"Come on, darling. Hurry up," Seth urged, "before the candles
go out."

There was only one thing left to wish for, a wish for both of
them, a wish almost as old as their love.

"I wish . . ." she whispered and drew in a lungful of air.

"You mustn't tell." Seth put a finger to his lips. "That's Rule
Number Two."

She nodded and shut her eyes, squeezing them tight for a moment. When she opened them they were moist with tears.

I wish—the words formed silently in her mind—*I wish for a child*.

Then with one glorious burst of breath, Annie Sayre Petersen
extinguished every last candle.

Success, ran a current definition, is having all your calls returned.

If so, Seth Petersen growled to himself in the deafening silence,
I must be a resounding flop.

With a sigh, he squeezed his rangy six-foot-three frame into the
leather depths of the shiny new Execu-Chair, adjusted the baseball cap that had been his trademark on every job since Harvard,

crossed his long legs on the desk top and surveyed his realm.

Fresh fresh fresh. Everything was fresh from his freshly ironed khaki pants to the bright white of his freshly painted office to the glittering island across the river fresh in the clean morning light. He crossed his legs again, folded his arms and waited for the phone to ring.

Goddam! He eyed the instrument with distaste. Should he try the son of a bitch again? That would make it the tenth time this week. And the week was young.

Seth's face, usually so animated, was now dark and troubled in repose. There was puzzlement in the restless gray eyes, a worried wrinkle to the brow, an uncharacteristic grimness in the set of the lips.

He lifted up the phone, put it down again undialed.

In his old job he would have waltzed into his boss's office without fanfare and said, "Tarky, I want to see you." But this wasn't Texas, as the view of the Manhattan skyline confirmed, and Dr. Gerald Marriner was proving himself the most inaccessible of men.

At any given moment, according to his private secretary, the noted director of Medi-Tekk was in Boston, in Washington, in conference, out to lunch. Anywhere, in short, except on the other end of the line. The fact that this information was delivered in the cajoling singsong of a nursemaid accustomed to dealing with unruly three-year-olds did little to mollify Seth's unease.

True, he had seen Marriner briefly at the weekly review meetings and the great man had duly smiled, cocked an ear, clapped Seth on the back once or twice and exuded total charm. Marriner was a master of the gracious word and the quick departure. But that gladsome charm, Seth was quick to note, was on offer to everyone. In the more vital areas, those involving an actual outlay of time and attention, the director could be as elusive as quicksilver.

What the hell had Seth been hired for? he wondered. Why had they smoked him out of his lab at U. of Texas, bribed him with money and title, lured him with promises of staff and equipment and unequaled opportunity, tantalized him with visions of working closely with one of the finest minds in medicine? Why had they moved him two thousand miles at considerable expense if no one was interested in what he was doing?

He had half a mind to get on the next plane to Galveston and

7

ask Tarkowsky for his old job back, except that Annie would have conniptions and Medi-Tekk could conceivably sue him for breach of contract.

Moreover, Texas might not want him back.

"Going for the big bucks, are you?" Tarkowsky had said when Seth gave his notice, and the temperature had plunged to absolute zero. "I thought you were in this field because you wanted to make a contribution. My mistake. However, if money's that important to you, you may as well go, because you're not going to find it here."

And before Seth could break in to explain that money was not the only motivating factor, indeed not even the most vital, Robert Tarkowsky had turned his back on him in a manner that precluded all possibility of a reply and stalked out of the room.

Stung, Seth had beat a hasty retreat to Mark Wilkins' office, the news of his leaving still sitting heavy in his vitals. From Mark, at least, he could expect a sympathetic reception.

"Why, you sly old thing!" Mark's jaw had dropped. "Moving to Medi-Tekk! I didn't even know you were on the prowl."

"I wasn't," Seth said. "They came to me. It seems that Gerald Marriner read that piece of mine in *Southwest Medical Review* and next thing I knew, their recruiter made me the proverbial offer you can't refuse."

"What'll you be working on?"

"Same as here. The project! The thing is"—he could confide in Mark. For the past two years they had shared not only lab space, but also a large measure of the gripes and gossip that came with the territory—"the thing is, Tarky made me feel like a traitor. Just turned his back on me, like I'd sold out for silver or been caught in bed with his wife. Is that what you think too, Mark? Be honest. I'd like a second opinion."

"Of course he feels betrayed," Mark said. "Frankly, so do I. What else could it be but money. Why, I ask you, would any man in his right mind want to give up the cultural riches of Galveston, to say nothing of the privilege of working for the great Robert Tarkowsky, if not out of avarice? And the worst of it is, you'll have to live in New York. I grieve for you, fella. There ain't nothin' there unless you're one of those quiche-eating wine-slurping pansies. No country music. No good ole boys. No oil slicks. Nothing but theater, opera, ballet . . ." Mark shook his head sadly.

"Art galleries, Szechuan restaurants"—Seth picked up the refrain—"jazz joints, concert halls, bagels and lox, the Mets, the Nets, the Jets . . ."

"The Rockettes . . ."

"Greenwich Village, Fifth Avenue, Yankee Stadium. Yessiree, New York's an absolute wasteland. Why, I bet those hicks up north have never even seen a wet T-shirt contest . . . you know— the kind they have at Sully's Bar and Grill every Saturday, where they hose down the girls before they dance. Personally, I've always considered that particular art form to be Texas's unique contribution to the American heritage. Mark, baby, I love ya!"

Both men laughed.

"Now seriously . . ." Seth said.

"Seriously, you'd be a schmuck not to take it. Don't let Tarkowsky get you down is my advice. He's just pissed off about losing the best research associate he's ever had. And to Gerald Marriner yet. Insult to injury."

"How so?" Seth was puzzled.

"Trouble with you, Seth, is you don't pay enough attention to politics. It's notorious that he and Marriner have been feuding for years, battling to see who can rack up the most Brownie points and collect the Nobel Prize. They don't even shake hands at international conferences. So not only is Tarky losing your services, but he's losing you to his fiercest competitor. You know what they call you around here, Seth? 'Golden Hands.' The man with the magic touch. No doubt about it, you pull off experiments that have everyone else stymied . . ."

Seth acknowledged the tribute with a modest nod. It was true enough.

"Plus," Mark continued, "Medi-Tekk will be getting the benefit of all that lovely data you'll be taking with you . . ."

"I walk out of here empty-handed," Seth protested.

"But not empty-headed. Let's face it—you've got most of Tarky's trade secrets neatly stowed in that commodious brain of yours."

"A good deal of that is my work, too, you know." Seth bridled at the implication.

"I know . . . I know. And I'm not criticizing. Except you can't blame Tarky for seeing your defection as a stab in the back. But that's his problem, not yours. Scruples aside, I should think it's kind of flattering, being fought over by the two giants in the field. Listen, Seth, if I were in your shoes I'd be off like a shot, as would every other guy in this department. Of course, you don't have tenure in private industry, but security is for babies, right? And Christ, all those sweet bucks . . ."

"It's not the money," Seth broke in. "It's the opportunity. And the independence. You know, the more I look around, the more it strikes me: private corporations are where the cutting edge is these days. They've got the drive, the dough, the technology. They're giving scientists plenty of scope. They know how to cut through red tape, so you don't have to spend half your time groveling for grants. Look at Humana—the job they did with the artificial heart. Or Genentech, or the big pharmaceuticals. Those guys are doing pioneer work. As far as I'm concerned, good science is good science wherever you choose to do it. And Medi-Tekk's as good as they come. Jesus, the staff they've got, the equipment! And I'll be heading up my own projects, following my own line of inquiry . . ."

"Please!" Mark put out an admonitory hand. "You're preaching to the converted. It's a fantastic outfit, from all reports. But what I really want to know is . . . are they giving you stock options?"

"Well, yes . . . based upon performance," Seth dragged out. "But it's not—"

". . . it's not the money!" Mark chimed in unison. "How many times are you going to say that? For Chrissakes, stop apologizing!"

"You're right," Seth replied. "You work in academia long enough and you get brainwashed. You're supposed to feel guilty about wanting to earn a decent living. There's that notion that you can't do good and do well simultaneously. Tarkowsky seems to think that your true scientist should be in it for love only, like unpublished poets, or monks who've taken a vow of poverty. But as my father used to say, it's as easy to marry a rich girl as a poor girl. And since I didn't marry a rich girl, it's about time I started making a living wage for the sixty hours a week I put in."

"Speaking of wives, I imagine Annie's over the moon about moving to New York."

"Need you ask?" Seth grinned. "She wasn't made for the provinces and vice versa. Galveston may be big league in medical research, but by her lights it's bush league in most other departments."

"Yeah, Kay's not crazy about it here, either. But it must be worse for your wife. What does an opera singer do in a city that has yet to recover from the death of Elvis Presley?"

Seth laughed. "Absolutely right. A classical musician's got to be crazy to try and make a career in this town. Too bad Annie never got the hang of real country music."

"Sure, she should've learned to play the *gee*tar . . . you know, one of those twelve-string electric jobbies with the mother-of-pearl inlay. Then she might have got herself a job at Sully's Bar and Grill. Singing backup for the wet T-shirt contests."

The image had made Seth laugh. Annie with her luxurious voice, her aristocratic style and presence, in her long black crepe concert dress, stepping out before a barroom full of oil-field roustabouts and singing "There's a Little Box of Pine on the 7:29," or maybe "Hound Dog" with Mozartean grace and flourishes.

"Yes," he'd murmured. "Annie's very happy we're moving to New York. And so am I. I expect to do good things up there."

"Well, congratulations." Mark clapped him on the shoulder. "You're making the right move, and it looks to me as if you're making it for all the right reasons. Do us proud and—oh yeah . . . one more thing?"

"Yes?"

"Swiss banks," Mark whispered behind the back of his hand. "Put all that beautiful bread into Swiss banks. They say numbered accounts are the best."

Seth jabbed him playfully in the ribs, then left.

But it wasn't the money that had been the decisive factor. Nor was it even the professional challenge. And though he would never dream of confessing it to Mark, he was going to New York to pay off a long-standing debt. He owed it to Annie, pure and simple.

Seth Petersen had been raised to achieve.

The only son of a prosperous automobile dealer, he was reared in a house of mock-Tudor splendor, complete with three-car garage and swimming pool in one of Cleveland's leafier suburbs. But fortune had blessed him in other ways than the material, and from the cradle on he possessed an uncanny knack for doing everything right.

He earned the right grades, pleased the right teachers, made the right friends, won all the prizes the Cleveland school system had to offer, played passable baseball and a mean game of tennis. Moreover, he managed it all with apparent ease and grace. Then at a scant sixteen he was accepted at Harvard.

His parents were beside themselves with joy. To Wally Petersen, whose only education had been the traditional college of hard knocks, there was no doubt but that his son would become a doctor—a *rich* and *successful* doctor at that, the two words being synonymous in his mind. Over the years, he had made a great deal of money selling Cadillacs to physicians, and he held the medical profession in a respect that bordered upon awe.

"Go for the M.D.," he constantly urged Seth. "You couldn't do better. You'll be respected, live well. I've got customers who buy a new model every year for their practice and a second one just for their wives."

"I should become a doctor so you can sell me a Caddy?"

"Become a doctor and I'll *give* you a Caddy—a brand-new Fleetwood the day you finish medical school. And that's a promise."

Seth soared through four years of Harvard as effortlessly as he had Roosevelt High, duly entered the university's medical school and was on his way to claiming his Cadillac Fleetwood when he fell in love with what was to become his life's work. Without further ado, he transferred out of med school to pursue an advanced degree in biochemistry.

For Wally Petersen, Seth's decision came as a blow. He had set his heart on having a physician in the family, and this change of direction was unfathomable.

"I'll still be a doctor," Seth reasoned, "only a Ph.D., not an M.D.," but Wally wasn't buying it. To him, a proper doctor had patients and belonged to a country club.

"What kind of life is that? A chemist, a man who sticks powders into pills or manufactures soap flakes? Seth, you could be a respected surgeon, a credit to your community."

"I'm not going to be a pair of hands, Dad," Seth explained. "That's not the kind of chemistry I mean."

Bio was the Greek word for life, and the biological sciences dealt with the very building blocks of all life on earth. It was in the laboratory, not the hospital—Seth grew eloquent—where you might find the answers to the most profound, most provocative questions nature had to pose. " 'To see the world in a grain of sand,' " he quoted Blake.

Moreover, he was temperamentally suited for the work. He loved the complexity, the subtlety, the sheer sophistication of research; it offered him an intellectual challenge that had gone unsatisfied in med school. In fact, he had never cared much for clinical stuff, he now confessed. The human factor kept getting in the way of what he wanted to do. "You wind up wasting your time listening to patients bitching about hospital food, whereas in research you're inquiring into fundamental truths. That's right"— the phrase struck him as telling—"fundamental truths. I'll still be working in medicine, if that's any consolation. Still trying to conquer disease. After all, Louis Pasteur wasn't a physician. Or Ehrlich, or any number of the breakthrough scientists whose discoveries changed the history of medicine. And that's what I hope to do too in one way or another. You'll be proud of me yet, Dad, I promise."

Wally Petersen looked at his son with wounded eyes. Researchers didn't drive Caddies or live in twenty-room homes in Shaker Heights. That was Mr. Petersen's fundamental truth.

"So with all your talent, all your gifts"—Wally's sigh bespoke a deep disappointment—"you're going to hole up in some college lab looking through a microscope. And make peanuts. You're big-league stubborn, that's what you are. I hope you realize what you're giving up."

Seth did. He accepted, but not without a twinge, the fact that he would probably never live as his father, barring some lucky fluke. When he swam it would be in other people's pools; when he played tennis, other people's courts. "I'll be a model of downward mobility." He smiled wryly. "The American Dream in reverse. But at least I'll be happy in my work."

There was no open break between them—father and son loved each other too much for that—and after lengthy discussion, Wally reluctantly accepted the change of circumstance.

The promised Cadillac was never to materialize, which suited

Seth fine. He would have looked like a damn fool driving a Fleet-wood on a researcher's salary.

Seth didn't regret the shift in career. Clearly it was the work he was born for. Yet he could never quite rid himself of the notion that his father saw him as a failure, a talented son who dropped out of med school because he couldn't keep the pace.

After Harvard, Seth had taken on a series of research projects, distinguishing himself in each, and had risen quickly and seamlessly through the ranks. No question but that his career would continue its irresistible thrust, and the Medi-Tekk offer, though decidedly a plum, was in its way inevitable. He had long felt himself earmarked for a special fate and, though not a particularly introspective man, was quite aware that nearly everything he wanted out of life had come to him without a struggle.

Everything except, of course, Annie. But that was another story.

So here he was at ten thirty on a sunny Wednesday morning feeling like the Invisible Man. He'd give Marriner another few minutes before trying again.

Down the corridor the coffee wagon tinkled. Damn those temps! They were never on hand to run the simplest errands.

Seth was fumbling for change when the door opened and—lo and behold—two steaming mugs on a tray made their appearance followed by a curly-haired young man in a seersucker suit.

"Seth Petersen? I understand you're the new kid on the block. I thought we might coffee it up for a bit. My name's Dr. Gene Leavitt. Immunology. Yale. Stanford. I just got back from a trip to Japan."

Even as he spoke his bright restless eyes darted about the room with the avidity of an auctioneer at an estate appraisal.

The brashness of the introduction took Seth by storm.

Doctor indeed. Everybody in this place had a doctorate in something or other. Seth for one never used the title; at his level it was a redundancy. However, since his visitor was so young (at a bet, early twenties), perhaps the novelty had yet to wear off.

New York manners, Seth supposed. Not that it mattered. Leavitt apparently meant well, and with friendly overtures at such a premium, Seth was willing to overlook a great deal.

"Glad to meet you, Gene." Seth took a coffee from the tray, wondering if he was expected to give his academic credentials in return. "Have a seat, and by all means let's, um, coffee it up."

"Maybe you'd want to grab us a couple of doughnuts before the coffee wagon goes. Cinnamon, if they've got it. If not, the jelly's OK."

Seth stared for a second. Never before had he been requisitioned to carry groceries, but what the hell—he reasoned—every lab had its own code of courtesies, its rituals. Presumably this was standard procedure here: You buy coffee, I spring for doughnuts. For the dozenth time, Seth was conscious of being in a foreign country whose mores he had yet to learn.

"Right, Gene. Cinnamon it is. Meanwhile, make yourself at home."

He went for the doughnuts, returning a few minutes later to discover Leavitt riffling through the correspondence on his desk.

For a moment, Seth froze in the doorway, then swallowing a spike of rage, said softly, "If you're curious about my work, Gene, why don't you simply ask me?"

He had hoped to surprise the younger man, to wring a shame-faced apology for such egregious conduct, but apparently Leavitt operated from a different moral base, for he looked up, sublimely unembarrassed, and gave a quick smile. "Sure, bud. Always interested in talking to the competition. You're working on the Project Omega, I see. Me too, only from a different angle."

They sparred lightly for the next half hour. Despite the shabby incident over the papers, Seth found himself unwinding. It was a pleasure to talk about his work, especially to someone as bright and perceptive as Gene. To give the man his due, he had a brain like a steel trap, absorbing everything and offering in return the occasional unexpected insight. Not much in the humor department, Seth concluded, but a stimulating guy, and it was hard not to feel a grudging respect for him. To be so young and so fucking smart! Had Seth been equally obnoxious at that age, or was it a symptom of the time and place? Probably the latter.

In any event, Gene offered something Seth had been aching to know—a candid summation of who was who in the local pecking order. To hear Leavitt describe it, the company was a Machiavellian web of intrigue, with plots and counterplots multiplying with the speed of laboratory mice.

"You gotta fight your way up in this organization, although it looks to me like they've been treating you pretty good," he remarked. "How's your assistant working out . . . that Pakistani?"

"Chandra? She's terrific."

"I'll say terrific." Gene described a generous S curve with both hands. "I usually think of Asian girls as flat-chested . . ."

"I meant . . . terrific on the job." Despite himself, Seth laughed. "The technicians are pretty good, too. But what do you have to do to get decent secretarial help? I've had nothing but temps."

"Yeah." Gene nodded. "It's hard to get girls to come out here. This is Long Island City, after all, not Manhattan. Competent secretaries don't want to spend that extra travel time. And when you get here, no place to lunch, no place to shop. I used to gripe about the commute, fuckin' waste of time, but now I subscribe to the Princeton Seminar Series. You know, they're these teaching cassettes, you put 'em in your Blaupunkt when you're stuck in traffic and you can use that time to bone up on current management techniques. This morning's cassette was on decision making."

Seth squinted at Gene to see if his leg was being pulled, but the young man's expression was stolid as ever.

"Tell me something, Gene . . . If your time is so precious, how come you're wasting it on me?"

It was said as a joke, but Gene considered the question solemnly.

"Like I told you, I was curious about your work." He swept the crumbs of his doughnut into the wastebasket, then rose and looked Seth straight in the eye.

"You're never gonna make it with those mice, you know."

"I beg your pardon?"

"With all due respect, Petersen"—this in a tone singularly devoid of any respect—"you may be doing fuck-all elegant research, but it's got nothin' to do with nothin'. And don't tell me what great results you're getting in mice. Mice aren't people, and the disease in mice isn't the same as it is in people. You're going sixty on a dead-end street."

Seth repressed an urge to grab him by the collar and shove facts down his throat. Leavitt, he realized, was approaching the problem from a different direction; he had a vested interest to protect. In any event, Seth had no wish to start an office feud, preferring to believe himself above such pettiness.

"Have it your way, Gene," he said, but he couldn't resist a retaliatory twist of the knife. "Although presumably Gerald Marriner values my work a good deal more highly. I didn't ask to come to this party, you know. I was invited . . . practically dragooned."

Gene chewed this over. "You were with Tarkowsky down in Texas, weren't you?"

"I was his right-hand man. We did good things together."

Gene offered a tight quick smile. "That's why you were hired, bubbeleh. Corporate games." And when Seth scowled, his adversary's smile grew wider. "It's not so much that Gerald's hot about your coming to Medi-Tekk, don't you see? He just wanted to take you away from Tarkowsky. Welcome to the snake pit."

"I don't believe this place!"

Seth came home early that night in a stew of disgust, kicked the door shut, growled at the cat, sprawled across the length of the sofa, his head in Annie's lap, the very picture of a man in need of every form of comfort—moral and physical.

"And it isn't just Leavitt, either. He's just a bit crasser than the rest of 'em. Or you could say, more honest. You work there and you get the feeling that the battle isn't between us and the goddam disease. It's between Medi-Tekk and every other lab in the country. Code-naming the projects, for Chrissakes, in case somebody overhears you talking in a bar. To me it's infantile, but OK, I can understand it. There are megabucks involved, patents . . . all that garbage. But what beats me is the atmosphere within the company. No camaraderie, no kidding around. The only thing that would raise a laugh in that joint is someone breaking their ass on a banana peel. Talk of pressure cookers . . . Jesus! It's every project director for himself, to see who can grab the biggest bonus, the most stock, who's gonna be Gerald Marriner's fair-haired boy. There's a line in the Annual Report" —he made a wry face—" 'We foster a spirit of healthy competition.' Whoever wrote that gets the Pulitzer Prize for understatement. Dog eat dog is more like it. Well, I'm as competitive as the next man" (more so, Annie had always thought) "but there are limits! You know what the real sickness is there? Not the fucking disease . . ." He continued his litany while Annie listened with a sinking heart.

She was stunned by the swiftness of Seth's disillusion. Comfort she could offer—kisses, drinks and reassurance—but solutions were beyond her ken. For the thousands of times she had been a willing audience to his "home is the warrior" recital of each day's woes and wonders—and it was a pattern as old as their marriage—lately she recognized a new element in his tone. New York bitching, she had come to think of it, going beyond the usual gripes and minor gossip to convey an anger, an anxiety so profound it frightened her.

Here they were, their fourth home in nine years, ink scarcely dry on the lease on their Greenwich Village apartment (and, modest as it was with its tiny kitchen—"Nobody cooks in New York," the agent had said—yes, even with all its shortcomings, they'd had to beg and borrow the key money just to move in); here they were with furniture just arrived, with their lives still in transit; here they were barely a month in the city she had dreamed about for years, and now, to judge by Seth's complaints, they might conceivably be pulling up stakes tomorrow. It was all she could do to smother a heartfelt groan, for herself as much as for him. Never had she seen him so driven, so petty and backbiting in his appraisals. Frustration did not sit well upon Seth Petersen.

Which would be worse, she deliberated: to resettle in yet another provincial city or to stay on here with a husband grown daily more embittered?

"Well, Seth," she commented when he finally ran out of breath, "I don't know what to say. Why don't you wait a bit, stick it out another couple of months, then if you still feel the same way . . . quit. You can always look for something else in New York . . ."

"Doing what . . . driving a cab? I'm a specialist, dammit!"

". . . or find another job elsewhere. You don't like the lab, you don't like the people. Well, if that's how you feel, then maybe the simplest thing to do is quit . . ."

"Quit!" Seth roared. "What the hell kind of talk is that? Quit, my ass. Oh, wouldn't Leavitt like that! Wouldn't that bastard Tarkowsky! Wouldn't they all! Dammit, I came here to do a job no matter what the boy genius from Stanford thinks. He practically called me a pawn, Annie . . . sneaky little creep! Well, don't you worry, baby, I'm going to come up roses on this one if I have to bust my balls to do it."

Annie jerked his head from her lap and got to her feet.

"Fine," she snapped. "Just don't bust everything else up in the attempt. I'm going to start getting dinner."

With a click of the heels, she flounced out of the room.

A moment later he followed her into the kitchen, puzzled, then perched himself on a stepladder while she rooted about in the refrigerator.

"Annie?"

Her answer was to slam a couple of lamb chops on the counter with a murderous thunk.

"Not you too, Annie!"

She started pounding fresh basil in a wooden mortar with a vigorous intensity.

"Talk to me, Annie. Jesus, I'm beginning to feel I'm the object of a universal conspiracy. What have I done to deserve the treatment?"

Above the thud thud thud of the pestle, her voice throbbed low and dangerous.

"You talk like a Mafia hit man, that's what. This one's an asshole, that one's a bitch . . . You used to be able to express yourself in terms other than basic barnyard. Well, I don't need this, Seth. Either quit the job or quit grousing. Either way, I expect you to behave like a human being."

At her reproof, he grew thoughtful.

"I'm sorry, Annie. Let's forget it."

She turned to him with narrowed eyes, but sitting there, he seemed suddenly drained of all anger.

"Sorry what? Sorry you took the job?" she asked.

He considered that. "I'm sorry to bring all this shit home with me and then dump it onto you. I'm under such pressure there, it's hard to leave it all behind me when I walk out the door."

"Well," she admitted, "I'm sorry I snapped. Do you want to discuss it?"

"I thought we *were* discussing it . . ."

"Nope. That was a monologue, not a conversation. You know

19

whatever happens, I'm behind you, but I'd like to know . . . Do you feel you have to stick it out here for some kind of macho reason? Because if you're going to become a total workaholic, a permanent malcontent . . . if it's going to louse up our marriage"—her voice trembled—"well, then, the job is costing more than it's paying."

"Bless you, Annie." He swung up behind her where she stood at the sink and encircled her in his arms. "You are such an island of sanity in this crazy ocean. You're right, of course. Absolutely right. Don't worry. I'll work it out somehow, short of homicide, because I sure as hell don't want it eating into us. Anyhow, I promise to keep my beefs to myself from now on. You have my word on it. My God . . . if I didn't have you . . ." He nuzzled her neck. "Mmmm . . . you smell delicious. What is that stuff you've got on?"

"Basil. I'm making pesto . . ."

"No, I mean the perfume."

"It's called Obsession," came the tart reply. "They named it after research scientists."

She refused to be sweet-talked out of making her point.

"Christ." He laughed softly in her ear. "Minced basil and Obsession." He dipped his finger into the fragrant blend of herbs, then licked it up. "Mmmm . . . That's a dynamite combination. I think we may have discovered the new yuppie aphrodisiac."

Certainly it was having that effect upon him, for she could feel him, suddenly grown hard and hungry, pressing into the small of her back. He reached around her in an encompassing embrace, and there was urgency in his whisper.

"Let's go to bed, darling. Let's forget all our woes and go to bed. Right this very second."

"Seth, it's only five o'clock." She wiped her hands on a dish towel. "At least let me finish up with the cooking."

"Listen!" He insinuated a hand under her T-shirt, enfolding her breasts. "If you don't wrap it up, I'm gonna eat it here."

Despite herself, she felt the warm familiar prickles of desire. How easy it was for Seth to trigger her responses, how well he knew the workings of her body.

"Don't tease," she said warily.

"Goddam, Annie, I'm not teasing. I need you . . . and never more than now."

It was impossible to stay angry with Seth, not as long as his hands were on her flesh, his mouth brushing against her ear saying the words she never tired of hearing.

"I love you very much, Annie," he murmured in a voice from which all bitterness had fallen away. "As long as I have you, I have everything."

She turned and kissed him with a need as powerful as his own. "Yes . . . let's go to bed and make babies."

Now, lying content in his arms, listening to the muffled hum of voices from the street beyond, she watched the rise and fall of his breath with fascination.

No matter what else, they had the gift of making each other happy, and should the day ever come when they couldn't settle their disputes in the act of love, then she would know their marriage was over.

How good they were together, how expert and responsive— like seasoned ballet dancers displaying their skill in a magnificent yet eternally varied pas de deux. With a lingering thrill of pleasure, she recalled the rhythmic thrust of his body, the powerful thighs locking her tight in a relentless embrace. In their lovemaking to-day there had been an element part sensual, part savage, heightened, perhaps, by the pressures of recent days. For if Seth was her home, her shelter, her haven in an uncertain world, then she was his as well.

With catlike contentment, she surveyed his sleeping body: the powerful chest, the firm arms, the loving hands. The last warm ribbons of sunlight trickled through the venetian blinds, covering his torso in golden stripes.

My golden boy, she mused. Half consciously she placed her hand between her legs. It came away moist and warm. Perhaps even now as she lay beside him, the miracle of life had already begun. Let it be this time, she wished, and if the intensity of their love was any measure, how could she not be pregnant! It wasn't fair!

Dear God, let it be this time! Having a baby would make all the difference. Not that Seth ever reproached her, but she knew he wanted it as much as she. He needed something—they both did— beyond the relentless thrust of career, career, career. What was the point of building nests, dreaming dreams, if at the end of the day there were just the two of you? Hell, what was the point of getting married?

She looked around the room with its scant pride of treasured possessions. Everything here—the furniture, the knickknacks, the bits and pieces of their lives together—spoke of stopgap. Two people marking time, waiting for the measure of their lives to begin.

"So do without the second bedroom," the real estate agent chided when they complained about New York rents. "For a couple like you, that's a luxury."

But they had always had the extra bedroom, waiting to be filled, and they would have it here, no matter what the cost.

"We plan to have a family." Annie had smiled at the agent, and Seth had concurred with an eager hum.

True, the room was hardly bigger than a closet and at the moment contained no cargo more precious than old books and winter clothes, but it could be fixed up in no time. Oh yes indeed. Plenty big and bright enough for a new baby. Of course she'd want to do it up. Some pretty wallpaper—a nice bouncy pattern. Floral maybe, or cheerful animals. Yes, definitely animals. She'd seen some cute stuff at Bloomingdale's, with Beatrix Potter illustrations in lovely pastels. Do as well for a boy as for a girl. A pretty paper, then, and they'd want a chest of drawers, maybe one of those lovely Boston rockers. Seth's father had promised them the fanciest nursery furniture money could buy. "A Cadillac of cribs" had been his words. Except where would they put big items? After all, you had to leave yourself space to move around in. Of course, if you placed the dresser by the door and had the crib facing the window where it would catch the morning sun . . .

Annie shut her eyes and wished the ache away. Yes, maybe this time. After a while, she got up and threw on a robe. "Are you hungry, Seth? Should I start dinner?"

His answer was to grunt and sink into a deeper sleep.

Poor lamb. She sighed and went into the kitchen.

"Well, Max?" Their cat, reprehensible beast, was perched atop the counter smacking his lips with a satisfied leer. "You might have had the decency to leave a chop for me."

* * *

Despite his good intentions, the next few weeks did little to ease the tension. In short order, one of Seth's technicians quit, claiming he was being driven too hard, while Seth himself fired another for refusing to show up on a Sunday afternoon.

"Oh, come on," Annie said. "Give the guy a break. Even God doesn't work on Sundays, as someone I used to know once said."

"Yeah . . . well, God never worked for Medi-Tekk."

Annie tended to shrug it off. Lack of dedication among the junior staff was one of Seth's oldest complaints, dating back to the early days of their marriage.

"I never ask anyone to do anything I wouldn't do," ran Seth's refrain, usually followed with "so I wound up doing it myself." But was it reasonable to ask paid hands to share his unrelenting drive?

If Seth went it alone oftener than most researchers in his position, Annie suspected this was by choice. He was loath to delegate even routine chores, convinced—for the most part correctly—that no one else could handle detail so well.

The only member of his staff who met his standards was his assistant, Chandra Patel.

"Lord knows what I'll do when she peels off . . . ! She's so devoted. Wonderful with the animals, too. But the problem is she'll have to go back to Pakistan once her visa expires."

Seth planned to appeal to the immigration authorities on her behalf. If he could prove she was irreplaceable, they might be convinced to award her the coveted green card, entitling her to stay on indefinitely.

Annie was curious about this paragon of hard work and virtue. "Is she attractive?"

Seth shrugged. "I don't think so . . . just well endowed. The thing is . . . don't get upset Annie, but I suspect she has a bit of a schoolgirl crush on me. Lonely, probably. And her English isn't that hot. Not that it matters, and Lord knows I wouldn't do anything to encourage her, but I believe it gives her that extra bit of incentive."

"Maybe you should hire nothing but nubile young ladies from Third World countries," Annie twitted. "At least you'd get the kind of loyalty you like."

Should she worry about her husband's being the idol of a lonely,

23

homesick girl, albeit one with an opulent figure? Knowing Seth, she decided the answer was no. If Seth ever were to have an affair, which she deemed unlikely, it would certainly not be with a co-worker. He valued the division between his private life and his career far too dearly to get involved with any young assistant, no matter how adoring.

One evening he came home practically hugging himself with glee.

"Good day at Black Rock?" Annie inquired.

"Not for Herr Professor Doktor Gene Leavitt it wasn't," Seth smirked, and recounted with blatant pleasure how a much-touted project of his pet rival had gone right down the tubes.

Annie listened to him, arms akimbo, eyes narrowed.

"You are something!" she marveled. "I never thought the day would come when you'd be crowing over something like that. Come off it, Seth. What's good for the lab is good for everyone, including—I should imagine—the patients. After all, you guys are supposed to be fighting disease . . . not each other, remember?"

"Whose side are you on, for Chrissakes?" He was glowering.

But later that evening he confessed she was right. "You get so crazy up there, you tend to forget what the research is all about. This business with Leavitt . . . I can't believe I reacted on such an infantile level, gloating like that. He could well have been on the brink of a truly significant advance. Oh, I don't know." He sighed. "Sometimes you lose all perspective as to the whole point of medical research."

In fact, Annie recognized, the real world of pain and suffering was as remote as Mars from the everyday concerns of the staff at the lab. Researchers were, in their way, much like bank tellers who handled precious currency in such vast amounts and with such frequency that it had no meaning in any other context; thus a man might deal with millions and come home and quibble about the price of a hamburger. In her experience, most of Seth's colleagues maintained a considerable distance from the patients they were purportedly trying to aid; and though she liked to think of Seth as perhaps more idealistic than many of his brethren, she didn't make him out to be a professional saint. It was the intellectual challenge of the work and his own highly developed competitive instincts, rather than the humanitarian aspects, that drew him and

kept him so absorbed. Still, it pleased her that the ultimate bene-
ficiary was the world at large.

When people asked exactly what it was Seth did, she would
answer, "My husband is looking for a cure for multiple sclerosis."
Inevitably, their response was a murmured "How wonderful!"

His adversary was a notoriously tragic disease: cruel, crippling,
striking down its victims in the prime of life, as incurable as it
was unpredictable. Yet over recent years, it had earned a reputation in scientific jargon for being "sexy," which is to say that
exciting advances were looming on the horizon and a man might
make a reputation therein. Around the world, top labs were giving
it time and money, for, with its 250,000 victims in the U.S. alone,
the disease was prevalent enough to constitute a "market" in commercial terms.

"Sure," Seth once said, "I could apply myself to lassa fever, say,
or something equally out-of-the-way, and the research would be
just as fascinating. Problem is, no one would want to fund it."

So, MS it was, and very impressive it sounded. "A terrible af-
fliction," Annie would say, "but my husband is very hopeful that
someday a cure will be found."

All this certainly sounded a good deal more uplifting than saying
his work was actually confined to an obscure disease in a particular strain of mice. For, to add to the complications inherent in
all medical research, there was the problem that multiple sclerosis
did not exist in laboratory animals. Seth's work, therefore, was
centered upon a related disorder known as EAE. EAE had been
developed exclusively for the purpose of providing scientists with
test situations. It was akin to, but not identical with, MS in humans.
However, it provided the medical world with significant opportunities for research, and it was Seth's contention that the conquest
of the one disease would lead to the conquest of the other.

Soon after the Leavitt fiasco, his optimism returned, accompanied by an incredible burst of energy. Gradually he stopped
griping about the interoffice competition, although not about his
personal staff, with the exception of the much touted Chandra. To
Annie's vast relief, he appeared, for the first time since joining
Medi-Tekk, to be actually happy.

Most nights he would come home (and those homecomings
grew later and later) more buoyant than tired, too wound up to

sleep, in a near euphoric state. He would start pulling scraps of paper out of every pocket, notes to himself, observations, reminders of things to be done on the morrow. A couple of nights he didn't come home at all. To Annie it was a familiar pattern, a symptom that he was hot on the trail.

"What is it, my birthday?" he asked when she handed him a new electric shaver.

"Take it to the lab. And use it! If you're going to sleep at the place, the least you could do is look reasonably reputable in the morning."

His prime source of annoyance seemed to be that the day was only twenty-four hours long. Had Annie not known him better, she might have ascribed his mood to booze or drugs. But Seth being Seth, she recognized this particular form of intoxication for what it was: the joy of creativity.

"I'm on to something, babe," he told Annie, eyes sparkling, fingers dancing with excitement. "Something big. I think I just might be at the edge of a breakthrough."

❦

Among local brokers, the place was known as Horror House, and Vi Hagerty rarely showed it to prospects. Why bother? The property had been on the market for donkey's years, a gingerbread pile of crumbling Victoriana that would never find a buyer. Simply to trudge through the rooms was a form of punishment.

But today, she took an exquisite pleasure in showing it to Mrs. Mayhew.

"Baronial, I think you'd call it," Vi said with the straightest of faces. "Honest-to-God baronial. Of course, very few people have the personal style to live like that these days . . ."

Mrs. Mayhew's beady eyes flickered greedily.

Nouveau riche, Vi thought, although who was she to talk, herself having been *old-eau* poor all her life. Although not if she could swing this sale. One helluva commission that would be.

"You know, this house belonged to a very distinguished local family," she crooned (*distinguished largely for its lousy taste in heating contractors*), "and it was built by one of the finest architects of the time, um . . ." She fumbled in her memory for an appropriate name. ". . . Stamford Weitz."

26

No, "Weitz" didn't sound correct. It had a funny ring to it. Worse yet, it sounded Jewish, which in this case was probably a major tactical error, Mrs. Mayhew having made it abundantly clear that she had little tolerance for Jews. Or Catholics. Or Poles. Or Italians. Or Hispanics. Or what she slyly referred to as "people of the Negro persuasion." In fact, the whole day had been spent traipsing around in search of a neighborhood that would meet her standard for racial purity, which was—Vi gathered—on a par with entry applications for the Ku Klux Klan. At half a dozen points during the day, Vi had been ready to haul off and sock her; outwardly she managed to maintain a professional smile.

Think commission, she kept telling herself, and hoped that phony Weitz credit wouldn't prove a booboo. However Mayhew didn't pick up on it, too bemused, probably, by visions of herself posed in front of the fireplace being photographed for the Montclair *Times.*

Mind you, Vi Hagerty was as honest as the next person, provided the next person wasn't a saint. However, a little discreet exaggeration never hurt a sale, and Vi moved swiftly into high gear, touting the virtues of what had to be the county's biggest white elephant.

To Vi's astonishment the pitch was working. Within twenty minutes, Mayhew began talking mortgage and taxes and closing costs.

They were on their way out when Mayhew paused for a last look, then peered into the windows of the house next door. "What kind of people live there, do you know? The right kind?"

Something snapped inside Vi. How in God's name did she know who lived there? What was she expected to do . . . run a blood test on everyone on the block?

"Abyssinians," she said. It was a stupid answer to a stupid question, but Mayhew jumped as though goosed.

"Are you serious?" The fat face was dead white.

Suddenly, the irritations that had been building all afternoon got the better of Vi. The hell with the sale. The hell with the commission. Above all, the hell with Mrs. Lilywhite Mayhew. Vi smiled her toothiest smile.

"Yes, ma'am. That house is the property of the Abyssinian Black Baptist Church. Of course, they're not actually Abyssinians, more

27

from Harlem and Newark is my guess. Practically every night, they come here for the prayer meetings—hundreds of 'em." The Mayhew jaw dropped another inch, the eyes filled with abject terror. "And when they get going, why, you can hear it from miles around. It is something, let me tell you . . . that singing and dancing and stomping and shouting. Why, it's all you can do to keep your foot from tapping. You can say what you like about black folk, Mrs. Mayhew, but you gotta hand it to them . . . they sure do have rhythm."

By then, however, Vi was talking to air, for Mrs. Mayhew was halfway down the street, running as if the hounds of hell were at her back.

Vi was still laughing a half hour later, back at the office.

"You should have seen the look on her face," she told Sherm Walters. "I thought I was gonna have a basket case on my hands."

"Are you nuts?" Sherm shook his head in astonishment. "You just smart-assed your way out of a six-thousand-dollar commission. Try and remember that you're a woman with a kid to support."

"Yeah, I know . . ." Vi wiped the tears from her eyes and suppressed a final giggle. "It was a dumb thing to do, and I'll probably die in the poorhouse, same way I grew up, but I can't grovel to people like that. Listen, babe, I spent the first sixteen years of my life being told do this, don't do that. Well, what's the point of being independent, if you can't speak your mind every now and then? You know something? If I had to spend another afternoon with that Mayhew dame, I'd do it again. What the hell, it was worth it."

"I don't understand you, Vi," Sherm said. "Sometimes, you're your own worst enemy."

In fact he understood her very well. They'd been colleagues, friends and—more recently—lovers, and it was precisely this gutsiness that he found so endearing. For better or worse, Vi called the shots as she saw them, and Sherm, who knew her story, respected her for it.

"I'm a bastard," she'd told Sherm when they'd first met. It was a literal description. She had been born unwanted and raised unloved in the drearier reaches of Brooklyn. The strict discipline and gray anonymity of St. Theresa's Home for Catholic Children had provided her with an elegant handwriting, a dread of regimentation and a firm resolve never again to take orders from anyone. The day she turned seventeen, she left without looking back.

All things considered, she'd come a long way in the dozen years that followed, and freedom was still fresh enough in her mind for her to derive an illicit thrill from the simplest things: sleeping in the nude or watching television at 3 A.M., both practices firmly denied her in childhood. And if, in the assertion of her independence, she occasionally thumbed her nose at the smug and the smarmy or sent a Mrs. Mayhew into terminal shock, hell, wasn't that what freedom was all about?

On those occasions, Sherm threw up his hands. You don't tell Vi what to do, he realized long ago. You don't tell her she's pigheaded, gauche or just plain wrong. You simply sit back and let her roll over you like a force of nature.

Within the office they were known as Laurel and Hardy, and though the description was fanciful, it nonetheless conveyed the sense of absurdity people had when seeing them together. Physically, they were an odd couple: Sherm, big and lumbering, with the comfortable look of an outsized teddy bear; and Vi, a scant hundred pounds of greased lightning, her tough wiry frame topped by a burst of short curly hair that was twice as blond and bright as nature intended.

"Well, what's done's done." She sighed. "The sale would have probably fallen through anyhow. No bank would be dumb enough to lend money on that property. Christ"—she kicked a desk drawer shut with an exasperated clang—"there's another day shot to hell. What're you doing for dinner, Sherm? You wanna come home and eat crow with me and Noonie? Or anyhow, spaghetti and meatballs?"

"Sure, I'll provide the beer."

"Beer, my ass." Vi laughed. "After what I did today, the least I deserve is a bottle of Chivas Regal."

"A guy came into the playground today looking for me," Noonie said when they were finishing dinner.

"What do you mean?" Vi stopped in mid-mouthful. "What guy?"

"I dunno." Noonie shrugged. At nine, he was a cut-down version of his mother, minus the blond hair, plus steel-rimmed glasses that gave an owlish cast to his countenance. "Some guy. But he was looking for me OK. He asked if I was James Noonan Winfield."

Vi shot an alarmed look across the table at Sherm. Creeps, the look said. This world is full of creeps and weirdos.

"Did he . . . um, did he touch you or anything, honey?"

"Nah." Noonie giggled. "I did what you said. I told him my dad is a killer cop and he should just piss off."

Vi swallowed her spaghetti in a big gulp.

"And . . . ?"

"And that was it, Mom. He got into this silver car and drove away. It was one of those Porches."

"What on earth are you talking about?"

"I think he means a Porsche," Sherm translated, then turned back to the boy. "One of those fancy little sports cars, right? Jesus, that's forty thousand bucks' worth of motor. Did you really tell him to 'piss off,' Noonie?"

Noonie gave an enthusiastic nod.

"Honestly, Vi, is that the kind of language you should be teaching the kid?"

"It worked, didn't it?" she said triumphantly. "The guy pissed off."

"I won't grace that with an answer. Come on, sport." Sherm got up from the table. "Help me clear away and I'll beat you at checkers."

Noonie smacked his lips gleefully. "Like you did last time when I took you three to nothing?"

"Three to one," Sherm corrected, "and I let you win."

"Yeah yeah bushwah!"

"Noonie!" Vi barked.

"What's wrong with bushwah? It's not as if I said bullsh—"

"Noonie," she cut him off. Much as she hated to admit it, Sherm was right. The kid had the vocabulary of a longshoreman, which was certainly nothing to boast about. And yet . . .

And yet, the shock value of his language notwithstanding, there was about him a certain feistiness, a peculiar self-reliance, that made her quiver with pride. He was what she had raised him to be, and by her lights she'd done one sweet job of it.

Sherm meant well, of course. Everyone did: the good samaritans, the social workers, the schoolmarms intent on advising her about the fine points of parenthood. And excellent advice it was concerning what boys that age should wear, say, eat, think. But she preferred her own judgments.

Pity the poor single mother—the world seemed to be saying—so foolish, so ill-equipped for life that she didn't even have the savvy to hang on to her man! If husbands were good for nothing else (and it was Vi's theory that they were good for very little indeed), at least they scored high marks for getting the establishment off your back.

Not that she had anything against men—she glanced to where Sherm and Noonie were huddled over the game board. In fact, she was feeling pretty romantic tonight. Romantic? Horny was more like it.

"Noonie, bedtime!" she announced the moment the game was over, then followed him into his room. To Sherm, she whispered en route, "Ten minutes, lover," and he knew enough to be patient.

She and Noonie had a nightly ritual. Prime time, she called it, a part of the day that belonged to them alone. She would sit on the side of Noonie's bed, just the two of them, to share a quiet final wrap-up before lights out. When he was small, she used to read to him—*Robin Hood*, *Tom Swift*, the stories she had missed when she was a kid—but now he had reached an age when they could really talk, she to him as much as vice versa.

She waited till he was settled in, then asked softly, "This man in the schoolyard, what did he look like?"

Noonie squirmed. "Just some guy. Hair. Nose. Eyes. Ears."

"Was he young . . . old?"

"Oldish, I guess. About your age."

"Gee, thanks, fella!" She felt a chill of premonition. "If he comes again . . ." She hesitated. Feisty the boy might be, and full of beans, but he was so young . . . so very vulnerable. "If he comes again, holler for the cops."

They chattered for a while about pleasanter matters, then Vi leaned over to brush his cheeks with her lips.

He put his skinny arms around her.

"G'night, Vi."

"Good night, Noonie, and don't let the bedbugs bite."

31

"I'll bite back," came the time-honored reply.

The living room was empty when she returned.

"Sherm?" she called softly. "Sherm, you still here?"

Dead silence. She looked around puzzled, but there was no sign of him. Then—

"Me Tarzan, you Jane!" The pantry door burst open. With a fierce jungle yell, Sherm leaped out, clad only in tiger-striped boxer shorts, wielding a banana.

"Ugh ugh ugh ugh!" He loped across the room in a simian crouch, grunting as he went, head lowered, arms flailing, as Vi doubled over helpless with laughter.

"Tarzan want Jane"—he suddenly lunged at her, tearing off the buttons of her blouse with a single swipe.

"Jane great knockers." His free hand groped at her breast, and a moment later he had her pinioned on the floor, face down. "Jane great ass."

Oh, Jesus, she thought, wiggling out of her jeans. *This is going to be wild.* Even better than last week, when they'd come home from seeing *Rambo* and she'd got the idea of smearing him all over with coconut oil. That had been sensational. Only trouble, she'd had to throw the sheets away afterwards.

At last, she lay naked beneath him on the floor, the rough nap of the rug against her breasts, making her nipples turn hard. Down her back she could feel something smooth and firm slowly tracking the spiny path of flesh that led to her buttocks. In another second . . .

"For Chrissakes, Tarzan. Will you put down that banana? Damned if I'm gonna be fucked by a piece of fruit."

"Tarzan better than a banana." Sherm ripped off his shorts.

"Show me," she gasped with pleasure. "Come on, you big ape . . . show me!"

It was an hour before they wore each other out and finally stumbled into bed.

"Jesus, Sherm, you really are something." She nuzzled his cheek. "How about a little Scotch before we turn in? You want to get us a drink, lover?"

He went into the kitchen and returned with the bottle of Chivas and a couple of glasses.

"Ah, this is the life." Vi settled back with a contented sigh.

"It could be like this all the time, babe," Sherm said. "All you've gotta do is marry me."

"Thanks a lot, Sherm . . . but, like I keep telling you, I don't want a husband. We've been all through that at least a dozen times. I love you. You're a terrific guy and a hero in the sack, but I don't want to be chained . . . to you, to anybody. Don't take it personally."

"Just because your first husband was a shit . . ."

"Don't spoil it, babe." She shut him up with kisses.

"And Noonie, Vi? He needs a father. He's a great kid, but he could use a little discipline."

"Spare me the discipline stuff. I had discipline up to my eyeballs when I was his age. I don't want him turning into a goddam robot . . ."

"You didn't turn into a robot, Vi."

"But what a struggle." She finished her drink and snuggled into his arms. "Let's drop it for now. You know Columbus Day weekend's coming. They'll be closing the marinas pretty soon, so why don't we go sailing down in Cape May? Last chance. What do you say, doll?"

He had introduced her to sailing a few months earlier, and now she lived for the sport. Some day, maybe, when she'd pulled off a few good deals, she'd get herself a boat of her own. Nothing fancy, maybe a little catamaran, twelve, fifteen feet . . . but big enough for her and Noonie.

And possibly Sherm, too, if he chose to come along.

She woke earlier than usual the next morning and had breakfast with Noonie.

"Come on, ducks, I'm gonna walk you to school."

"Ah . . . Maw . . ." he protested. "You're treating me like a baby."

"I just want to see if that creep is still hanging around."

But the man in the playground had vanished, never to appear there again.

The following week, he made himself known.

33

2

ONE OF ANNIE'S FIRST STEPS AFTER SETTLING IN WAS TO LOOK up her closest friend from the old days. If anybody knew what was what and who was who, it had to be Lainie Carpenter. Lainie of the flashing eyes and stunning presence and unlimited promise.

She found her living in a fifth-floor walkup on Columbus Avenue, handsome as ever if a bit more weary around the eyes, dressed with a flair—dashing scarves and clunky jewelry—that bespoke theatrical savvy. By contrast, Annie felt provincial.

"We were such a talented bunch at the Conservatory," she said as Lainie opened a bottle of wine. "You especially. That Rosina you did in senior year! I still get chills thinking of it." It had been Annie's private conviction that if any one of them had been destined for the top, Lainie would surely have been that one.

"Ah, schooldays," Lainie reminisced, "when we were going to eat the world for breakfast. And here I am in a lousy West Side brownstone, still bedding down on secondhand furniture. This is one tough town, let me tell you."

"But now you're at the Met . . ."

"Oh, the Met!" Lainie laughed. "I'm a step above the chorus, basically. *Enter peasant girl with basket.* That's my cue."

Over drinks, the past was resuscitated, examined, disposed of. Then began the even pleasanter task of catching up on gossip: who had gone to Cincinnati as second oboe, who was teaching piano in Springfield, who was singing at weddings and bar mitzvahs on Long Island, who had chucked it all and gone into the dry-cleaning business. The defeats were many, the triumphs few. "By comparison, I've done pretty well," Lainie conceded. "At least I'm working steady, which is more than you can say for half our class."

Five years ago, she'd been accepted into the bottom rung of the Metropolitan. "Nothing much so far," she explained, "mostly those little garbagey roles you find at the bottom of the program. Vignettes, they call 'em to be charitable. But things are starting to look up. I've got my fingers crossed that I'll get a chance to do some supporting roles next season, hopefully a Suzuki, a Micaela. OK, it's not top billing, but at least I should get curtain calls and maybe some reviews out of it. And what have you been doing with yourself in Texas? Besides being happy in love, I mean. Is there any kind of musical life in Galveston?"

Annie laughed. "You're looking at it. I was the mainstay of the cultural scene, such as it was. There's no opera company where we were, but I did everything else. Church services, *Messiah* every Christmas and Easter till it was coming out of my ears, women's clubs, weddings, even—would you believe?—some Gilbert and Sullivan. But there was no real competition down there, no first-rate artists. It's very isolating, musically. I can't tell you how glad I am to be in New York, back in the mainstream. I walk around Lincoln Center in a daze. Of course, I'll be starting almost from scratch. I've already started looking for church work, but I still have my sights set on opera. What I need now, though, is a coach. It's been so long. Who's the best in town?"

"Liadoff-Grey. Best in New York. Best in the world."

Annie blinked with surprise.

Natasha Liadoff-Grey. It was a name out of the history books, resonant with echoes of the Bolshoi and La Scala. The famous Madame Natasha, guiding genius behind many of the greatest voices of the century.

"I had no idea she was still alive, let alone teaching."

"Very much so. The question is, if she'll take you on. She has her pick, as you can imagine. She won't take students without an audition, and there's no guarantee she'll take you even then."

"Well, maybe I'll sing for her anyhow. At the very least, she can tell me if I'm crazy to even try to get back in after all these years. I used to think of it a lot down in Texas, but I don't know . . . maybe it was all a pipe dream."

35

Hearing the fate of old classmates had left Annie with mixed feelings. On the one hand, no one in their ranks had had a soaring success, which was ominous when you started figuring out the probabilities. On the upside, however, was the fact that most of the truly determined were still left in the field. Second oboists become first oboists. Peasant girls become Suzukis, perhaps even Madama Butterflys one day. That afforded consolation.

In any event, she was still reasonably young. Most singers didn't hit their stride, either musically or physically, until thirty-five or so, in which case Annie hadn't fallen so far behind. It was really a question of talent. Talent and will.

"Yes," Annie repeated. "I'd like to audition for her just to know whether there's any hope for a serious career."

"She'll tell you 'No,' of course." Lainie grinned. "She'll tell you to chuck it all, throw in the towel. That's standard procedure with the old witch. Whenever anyone asks her if they should pursue a career in music, she always tells 'em to forget it. Her reasoning is, if they can be discouraged that easily, they don't have what it takes to be professional. And if they've really got the stuff, then whatever she says won't make a damn bit of difference. So be prepared to be dumped on. The acid test of how good she thinks you really are is whether she's willing to take you on as a student. She doesn't waste her time on people unless they have the makings of a major career."

"Interesting," Annie brooded.

"And even if she does take you on," Lainie added, "Madame Natasha doesn't come cheap."

"How bad?"

Lainie told her. Annie winced.

"That's fierce." Then she laughed. "My mother could never see the point of singing lessons. She used to say, God gave you a voice free. You shouldn't have to pay for it."

"Yeah . . . well, your mother never met Madame Natasha."

"And Madame Natasha never met my mother."

�

"Sing?" Jeanette Sayre had said. "Well, of course you can sing, Annie. Nobody's stopping you. Get married and you can sing to your babies. But you have to realize I'm in no position to send you to study at the Conservatory and even if I were"—her voice turned edgy—"that is hardly the kind of life I'd want a daughter of mine to lead. Musicians, painters, writers . . . it's just an excuse for loafing. You're seventeen, Annie, and it's time you made something of yourself. Go to secretarial school, learn shorthand, bookkeeping. That way, when worst comes to worst, at least you'll have a skill to fall back on."

An otherwise well-meaning woman, Mrs. Sayre became heated on all matters pertaining to art and artists, in unwitting accord with Hermann Goering's dictum: "Whenever I hear the word 'culture' I reach for my gun."

It was a prejudice born of experience. The daughter of an old Maine whaling family, she had, in the teeth of common sense and parental judgment, married a raffish painter of seascapes, gone to live with him in the resort town of Larmouthport, sacrificed name and position and any claim to the family fortune, only to be widowed before she was thirty.

In addition to a basement full of unsalable canvases, Frank Sayre had left her with two young children and barely enough money to cover his bills at the local art supply store.

For Jeanette, her husband's death was tantamount to desertion. "He had no right," she would say on occasion. No right to die young, to die poor. No right to send his widow scrambling for a living in a lonely seaside town, for if Larmouthport's resources were meager, Jeanette's were even more so.

Coming as she did from a family where women were not expected to carry briefcases, she had no skills, no aptitudes. Eventually, she found work in a firm that sold athletic goods by mail, rising to the rank of head bookkeeper. "It may not be 'artistic,'" she would pronounce, narrow-lipped, "but at least it's steady."

The years of struggle had filled her with a profound pessimism coupled with a distrust of the bohemian life. To sing, to paint, to dance, to flutter brilliantly on the surface of life was nothing but a flight from responsibility. Work was meant to be a form of punishment, otherwise it would be known as play. Ergo, there was something suspect about those who enjoyed it.

The ultimate safe harbor, she believed, was marriage to a professional man. Barring that, the ability to type sixty words a minute.

"Look at Linda." She would point to Annie's older sister as a model of sensible behavior. Linda had learned a skill, become a secretary, then surpassed herself by marrying an engineer from MIT. She was currently raising children and basset hounds in Silicon Valley.

"Now, you may not find Len the most exciting man in the world"—and, indeed, Annie didn't—"but he is a provider, and Linda's one lucky girl to have him. You'll find you can't go through life without a safety net."

That Annie sang, that she possessed—admittedly—a lovely clear soprano voice and an unerring ear, was beside the point. Life was a serious business, ambition a trap, and one must always be prepared for the worst.

It was a vision—grim and fearful—that Annie could not accept. But she could escape. For if grand passions and noble deeds existed nowhere else, if ever there were dashing heroes and fair damsels in distress, they existed in the make-believe of opera. It was an enchanted world. And although Annie had never seen an actual opera, she was totally caught up in its mystique.

A tall dreamy girl, she turned her green eyes inward, proceeded to bury herself in books and recordings from the library. The high spot of her week was the Saturday broadcast from the Metropolitan Opera. Then she would lie on her bed, the music flowing over her, to live vicariously through each starring role.

Why be Antonia Sayre of Larmouthport, Maine, when she might be a pagan princess or a gypsy or a Parisian courtesan? The real world paled alongside the fantasy.

She followed the careers of the divas with awed fascination. Their lives were as colorful as their roles. Chief among her objects of worship was that most *assoluta* of all prima donnas, Maria Callas. Such a life that woman led! The music. The jewels. The glamour. The acclaim. The tragedy of love betrayed. Given opportunity, Annie could have killed Ari Onassis for having abandoned the divine Maria to marry Jackie Kennedy instead. The man deserved no less. And what a third act dénouement that would have made!

Become a secretary? Settle for a prudent marriage? Not as long as there was breath in her body.

"My goal," she wrote in her high school yearbook, "is to be a player in the great game of life."

If the phraseology was pompous, the sentiment was sincere. She ached passionately to be admired, to be heard, to hobnob with the great and gifted. Above all, to put as much distance as possible—emotional and real—between herself and her mother's house with its flaking gray paint and smell of disappointment.

So Annie sang. She sang at school assemblies, at Fourth of July picnics, at football rallies, and every Sunday at the Congregational church, where Grace Peach, the choir mistress, taught her the finer points of the craft.

She sang "Oh Promise Me" in the auditorium the day her class graduated from high school. Everyone agreed it was one of the highlights of the afternoon, and the glow of their approval merely confirmed her desire.

"I've definitely decided," she announced that evening. "I'm going to Boston to study music. Please, Mother, don't argue. Someday maybe I'll be a famous opera star."

For three hours, Jeanette pleaded, prayed, wept, and threatened, all to no avail; Annie would not be forestalled.

"Mom, I'm leaving"—her resolve shone clearly in her eyes—"with or without your blessing. I'm going to go to the Conservatory if I have to scrub floors to pay for it. I won't ask you for anything."

Her mother bowed to the inevitable. "But who knows?" Jeanette consoled herself. "Perhaps you'll get yourself a husband there. A doctor or an engineer. The city is full of eligible men."

"Mo-ther!"

As it had for the past hundred years, Boston in the seventies swarmed with students, crackled with energy, played paradise to the young and the gifted.

Had Annie chosen to use the city as a marriage bureau, she might indeed have had her pick of future providers, but she refused even to entertain the possibility. She had come to make waves.

The Conservatory hit her like a shower of ice water.

For her first lesson with the renowned Julian Baer, she was determined to impress him with one of opera's grandest arias. A small, saturnine man with tufts of hair sprouting from his nose and a vestigial Dutch accent, he enjoyed a reputation for terrifying novices. She would show him she didn't scare easily.

"*Vissi d'arte*"—she let loose with Tosca's magnificent credo— "I lived for art, I lived for love," endowing each note with the heartrending vibrato that she and Miss Peach had often sweated over.

For a moment, Baer was silent. Speechless, Annie thought. That final throaty sob used to bring tears to Miss Peach's eye every time.

"Where did you learn to sing like that?" he said at last.

"With Miss Grace Peach of Larmouthport, Maine."

"And your Italian? Whom have we to thank for that?"

"My next-door neighbor, Mrs. Antonelli."

"I see. Well, now"—his face was long and grave—"I want you to forget everything you know about singing. More than that, I want you to unlearn all the accumulated wisdom of the Larmouthport musical community. There was none. Dear girl, you don't even know how to breathe!"

"I've been breathing all my life!" She went scarlet with humiliation. "Good Lord . . . was it that bad?"

To her chagrin, he burst out laughing. "It was absolutely horrendous. However, you have a voice of sorts and a certain native musical intelligence. If you're willing to work hard and listen hard, we might yet make a singer out of you."

"Will I ever become . . . an opera star?" she asked him in a frightened whisper.

"An opera star! Ho ho ho!" He rubbed his hands at the joke of it. "You won't be anything until you first become a musician."

It was one thing, clearly, to be the darling of Larmouthport High, quite another to compete in this most musical of cities with the best and brightest from all over the country. She had had no idea the field was so full of prodigies, wunderkinds, students trained to professionalism almost from birth.

Every day was a reminder of how little she knew, how much there was to learn. She refused to be discouraged. Nonetheless, she was realist enough to trim her expectations, to know that she wouldn't walk out of the Conservatory and right onto stage center of the Met. Talent was the cheapest of all commodities, and the chance of actually achieving stardom was statistically a wild improbability. Still, she owed it to herself to make the most of her gifts. And after a while, the music—not the fantasy—became the real reward.

For three years she poured all her energies into her work.

There were lessons in solfeggio and voice production and piano and ensemble, in theory and harmony and history of music. There were master classes, French classes, Italian classes, German classes. There was a limitless repertoire to be discovered: English madrigals, Bach cantatas, Brahms lieder, the smoky songs of Debussy and Ravel. Once over the initial shock of her ignorance, Annie surrendered herself totally to the new life.

She loved the hum and hubbub of the Conservatory, where music bulged from every room. Simply to stroll down the corridors, gleaning snatches of pianists' scales and string quartets and the occasional brass choir, was her idea of bliss. The sound of an oboe giving an A filled her with delicious expectation.

In fact, however, she rarely strolled, her usual pace being a frantic rush from classroom to rehearsal hall to job. For if her days were hectic, her evenings were even more so. Her first week in Boston, she found work waitressing in a busy hamburger house. It was hell on the feet, but her meals were free and the tips were excellent.

Home was a high narrow room in an aging brownstone off Kenmore Square, with nothing to commend itself except a low rent. The windows were dark with a hundred years of city grime, the furniture vintage Salvation Army, but it served Annie's purpose: a place to flop and vocalize.

Most nights, she would return to it past midnight and fall into bed exhausted, music running through her head, customers still shouting orders in her dreams, only to wake at dawn to the jangle of the alarm clock and begin another day of the same routine. Her leisure hours were hardly less frenetic. There were always concerts to be heard, rehearsals to be attended, repertoire to be devoured, to say nothing of the important pleasures of sharing pizzas and shoptalk with other students. The school thus provided her not only with an education, but also with a self-contained social life into the bargain.

To Annie, such an existence seemed perfectly natural. All her friends lived as she did, music students being a notoriously clannish group. Like mafiosi, they had their own jokes, their own jargon and a beleaguered feeling that the rest of the world didn't really understand them.

"We're all nuts," said Jay Appleton. "Who else would practice six hours a day, then relax by playing chamber music all night?"

He was the young pianist to whom she lost her virginity early in her junior year.

"Let's sublimate our music and make love instead," he had said at the end of a particularly gratifying practice session, and they had wound up in bed with Mahler going full blast on the stereo. It was the first of several affairs with fellow students, for sex—like everything else in life—came from within the circle. It was fun, enjoyable and emotionally undemanding, but in truth, merely an extension of student life. What mattered most was singing.

Thus, little by little Annie shed the label of aficionado, of amateur, and slowly began to earn the title of artist.

That there was a Boston beyond the confines of the practice rooms and the Bagel Burger, a Boston of politics and sports and law and medicine and business and banking and industry—all that was of very little moment. She had spent three years totally immersed in her craft and expected to spend the next thirty the same way. She barely read the newspapers, except for the music reviews.

Then, one warm September evening at the start of her final year, the world, the great world, which has a way of intruding on the most reluctant recluse, knocked at her door as she was singing.

She put down her music and opened the door.

And there he was.

3

"YES?" SHE ASKED.

He stood in the door, his large loose frame blocking out the meager light in the hallway, a baseball cap perched across his head at an improbable angle. From the look of him—the furrowed brow, the set of his jaw, the gray eyes narrowed behind horn-rimmed glasses—she knew exactly what had brought him.

One more complaint and the landlady would throw her out on her ear. Defensively, Annie smiled her most ingratiating smile.

"I know what you're going to say." She clasped her hands imploringly. "You're going to say my music is driving you mad. You can't work. You can't sleep. And you'd be absolutely right in thinking I'm wildly inconsiderate, except that I had no idea it was so late . . ."

For a moment he seemed at a loss for words, his grievance having been so thoroughly preempted. His face softened.

"I hate to sound like a Philistine"—he sighed—"and as a rule it doesn't bother me, but . . . well, your voice *does* carry." He fidgeted, clearly unhappy about causing her distress. "It's just that I was finding it hard to concentrate."

"Please, I understand. It's part of the curse . . ."

"Par for the course?"

"No, the curse." She smiled. "The one that says all of us musicians are bound to go through life as pariahs bearing an infinite burden of guilt."

"God forbid that I should add to your load." He smiled back. "Maybe if you just shut your windows and I shut mine."

She nodded, but he made no move to go.

"What was that you were singing, by the way?"

"A song by Berlioz."

He continued to stand there with a quizzical expression, as though waiting for the last piece of a puzzle to fall in place.

" 'Le Spectre de la Rose,' " she added. "That's the title of the song."

"Never heard of it." He shrugged. "Or him. Pretty, though."

There was nothing more to be said on either side, but he seemed reluctant to go, leaning in the doorway, looking at her, and then beyond into the near darkness of the room.

"You've got a light bulb missing over the sink."

She followed his gaze to the high gloomy ceiling.

"I know. I've been meaning to replace it."

"If it's too high for you to reach, I'll be happy to do it for you. Got an extra bulb around?"

It was then that she noticed his hands. Wonderful, capable hands, large and powerful with long fingers that looked as though they might do anything they chose to: pilot a plane through a thunderstorm, control a runaway horse. Yet for all their strength, there was a delicacy about them, in the subtlety of gesture, in the carefully tended nails. She could as easily picture those hands holding a newborn baby. Doctor's hands? she wondered.

He changed the light bulb, then without being asked began fixing the drip in the faucet that had been driving her crazy for months.

"Anything else, ma'am? Locks repaired . . . toilets fixed? I do everything but slice bagels. Too hazardous."

"You're not a professional handyman, are you?" she teased.

"Nope. Wish I were. I'd make a fortune. Just a poor student— like everyone else in this town."

He gave the kitchen faucet a final twist and she asked him if he'd like a cup of coffee.

"Sure would." He grinned. "That's what I was angling for."

She put on the kettle, got out the Nescafé, scoured the shelves for an enamel mug that looked sufficiently clean for company, all the while aware that he was following her motions with quick and curious eyes. She should be anxious, she supposed, remembering her mother's admonitions about letting strange men into her room.

Doctor's hands? They could just as well be strangler's hands, albeit a very attractive strangler.

"What are you studying? Sorry, but I'm out of cream and sugar." She poured the coffee out quickly, hoping he wouldn't notice the ring around the cup. Housekeeping never was her forte.

He considered. "If I tell you what I do, you'll fall asleep. It has that effect on girls."

"Let me guess . . . you're a medical student?"

He blinked with surprise. "No, but close. I'm getting my master's in biochemistry."

"Oh dear. I'm afraid this is going to be the end of all intelligent discourse between us. You just managed to combine the only two subjects I ever almost flunked. To me chemistry is being in the tenth grade and blowing things up, whereas bio is eleventh grade and cutting things up. Frogs." She clutched her stomach. "Yecch! Is that what you guys do . . . cut up frogs?"

"Mice and rats as well." He laughed. "But it's OK. I washed my hands before coming here. Actually, biochem is just my hobby, only don't tell them that at Harvard. My real aim in life is to pitch southpaw for the Red Sox." He clasped his hands in a mock windup and lobbed an imaginary ball through the window over the sink. "Strike! And how about you? What name am I to look for on the posters at Lincoln Center when you're rich and famous?"

"Antonia Sayre, only everybody calls me Annie."

"And I'm Seth Petersen." He offered her a formal handshake. "With an *e*, Norwegian style. I live over there"—he gestured— "right across the courtyard. I had a helluva time figuring out which window the singing was coming from. I've never known a music student before."

"We're an exotic species." She laughed.

"To me, certainly. Is it a nice life? Do you enjoy it?"

"What a funny question. Yes, I think it's terrific. Work and pleasure all rolled into one, and there aren't too many careers you can say that of. What about you? Seriously, I don't have a clue what a biochemist does, other than being nasty to frogs, I mean."

"I inquire into the fundamental questions of life."

"Such as . . . ?"

"Such as"—he swallowed off his coffee—"will you have dinner with me Friday night?"

45

His request took her by surprise.

"Well, actually I work Fridays up until midnight . . ." Did she want to go out with him? She wasn't sure. From their few minutes of casual conversation, it seemed unlikely they had much in common.

"Saturday," he persisted.

". . . and all day Saturday, then I have tickets to the symphony in the evening."

"Very well," he said. "It's settled. Sunday. Even God doesn't work on Sunday. Neither do I and neither should you. I'll pick you up at noon and we'll go to Fenway Park, or if the weather's lousy, take in the Fine Arts. Are you a Red Sox fan, by the way?"

"I don't know fact one about baseball."

"I'll teach you. Guarantee you'll love it straight off. Then afterward, we'll go for dinner. How does Maison Robert hit you? I'm told they've just hired a new chef."

Annie shook her head. "I've heard it's terribly—"

She was about to say "expensive," but he broke in, "Unless you don't care for *nouvelle cuisine.*"

"I don't know that I've ever eaten it."

"Well, we'll give it a try. At any rate, it makes a nice change from the usual *boeuf bourguignon.* And then, let's see, we could go dancing at Jason's . . ."

"I don't dance." She was beginning to find the conversation embarrassing, a list of her ignorances and inadequacies. "I really don't think you'd find me much fun on a date like that. I'm sorry."

He frowned. "You don't follow baseball, you don't eat, you don't dance . . ."

"Musicians never dance," she explained. "It's like . . . well, like a code of honor. You see, we believe music exists for no other purpose than to be listened to . . ."

"That may be true of Bach, but I don't know about disco. Listen," he said. "You want to be an artist? Well, how in God's name can you be an artist unless you experience life to the full . . . its ecstasy, its glory, its passion, its heartbreak? And believe me, you don't know what heartbreak is until you start following the Red Sox. For that matter, you don't know what agony is until you've had your toes mashed to a pulp at Jason's, but I'll try and be careful. Say you'll come, Annie. Please do."

She answered the entreaty in his eyes with a tentative nod.

"Terrific!" His smacked his lips in triumph. "And now, before I leave, I'll ask you one more favor."

"More coffee?"

He shook his head. "I'd like you to sing to me. The same piece you were singing when I came. Who'd you say wrote it . . . Berlioz?" He folded his hands on the table with an air of expectation.

"But the neighbors . . .?"

"I'm the neighbors. Remember?"

She didn't dance or follow baseball, but there was one area where she could lead from strength. She had an unaccountable urge to impress him, to appear on her own ground as a person of dignity and merit and consequence, even in old jeans and a T-shirt. "Very well," she said. As though in a concert hall, she stepped into the middle of the room, drew herself up to full height, thick dark hair falling loose to her shoulders, poised and proud. She captured his eye. And sang.

Oh, but there was magic in the air that night. She had never been in lovelier voice, the long gossamer lines of the music spinning out, slow and sensual, enveloping him in silken threads as he sat at the kitchen table, entranced and immobile. He was watching even more than listening, she could tell, studying her face, her mouth, with an intensity that was almost palpable.

The last notes of the song hung heavy in the summer air, and she stood motionless, unbreathing, until at last he broke the silence.

"Beautiful," he whispered. And, flushed with pleasure, Annie knew the accolade was as much for the singer as the song.

Later—much, much later—he would tell her he had fallen in love with her at that moment. "You brought poetry into my life." But at the time he merely asked the most prosaic of questions.

"And the words . . . what do they mean?"

"It's from a poem by Gautier. The singer is the ghost of a rose, a rose that has given its life so that a young girl might have a corsage to wear to a ball. That night, as the girl lies sleeping, the perfume of the rose comes back to haunt her. 'Your white breast was my tomb,' the ghost murmurs, 'and where I died, a poet has written with a kiss, Here lies a rose that kings themselves might envy.' "

"Thank you," he said softly. "I'll see you Sunday at noon."

47

* * *

He arrived on the stroke of twelve, with a solitary rose in one hand, a leather-bound edition of Gautier poems in the other, and in his eyes, a look of joyous expectation.

Even long after, she could recall every detail of that day, of that night, with a clarity that defied the warp of memory.

It had rained and they had gone to the museum.

"We'll look at pictures," he said and they walked down the long, silent galleries—French, Italian, the gilded luxuriances of the Renaissance—her heels clacking on the marble, seeing and not seeing, more aware of each other than of the paintings. He paused before a Flemish Venus, naked and rosily opulent in a rococo frame.

"She has green eyes, too." Seth smiled, then placed his hands on Annie's shoulders and kissed her lips.

It was just a kiss, nothing more. Yet suddenly, the sexual chemistry between them exploded. Annie trembled. As Venus watched with greedy eyes, she kissed him back hungrily. In the quiet gallery, the flutter of heart and pulse were almost audible. At the far end, the museum guard made clucking noises.

"Just jealous," a breathless Seth murmured in her ear, for he had felt it too—that swift and sudden kindling of desire. Long after, Annie would remember that first moment they touched as pure magic, but at the time it was agonizing. The rest of the day was a charade, to be endured until they could decently go home and make love.

Somehow they survived the afternoon with small talk and little courtesies, as though they were anything other than two people who were—quite simply—dying to go to bed with each other.

They even got as far as the restaurant, with no overt acknowledgment of what was on their minds. After due consultation with the waiter, Seth ordered. Salmon mousse, pressed duck, an excellent bottle of wine. All to be accompanied with the requisite chatter.

"Do you like Woody Allen movies?" *I ache for your touch.*

"Yes, very much." *And I for yours. God, yes!*

"Did you see *Sleeper?*" *I can't survive another hour.*

The salmon arrived, pink and moist on a bed of radicchio.

"You're not eating." Seth wiped a bead of sweat from his brow.

"Neither are you."

They sat for another few minutes, lost in each other's presence.

"Aren't you hungry?" he asked.

She crimsoned. Not for food.

He caught his breath, then gave a short crisp laugh.

"What the hell are we doing here, Annie? Waiter . . .?"

Ten minutes later, they were in his apartment, ravenously un-dressing each other in a desperate need to see, to feel, to touch. The bed was strewn with books and papers. Their coupling must have been unplanned, she realized. As spontaneous for him as for her. The idea pleased her.

In the light of his desk lamp, she stood before him, flesh glowing, nipples erect, clothed only in the glow of his approval.

"My God!" His voice was rich with anticipated pleasure. "Oh Annie . . . you're so beautiful."

His hands ran the length of her body, turning skin to silk—those magnificent hands, defining her breasts, sculpting her thighs. Artist's hands, creating desire wherever they went with the light tender caresses.

She laughed for sheer pleasure, and suddenly they were tumbling on the bed—papers strewing, books rattling to the floor as they clung to each other mouth to mouth, belly to belly, heart against heart. At last, she could bear it no longer.

"Now," she cried, her voice thick with hunger. "Oh Seth, I want you now."

Then firm and fierce he entered her—his proud strong body en-veloping her, absorbing her until she no longer knew where he ended and she began. Silently, ritually, he moved within her, each rhyth-mic thrust pushing the world farther away. There was only the touch of him, his passion and warmth and taste. Then, as she hovered at the blind edge of orgasm, he pulled himself upright leaning his weight up on his hands. Every tendon, every sinew was poised for the moment of fulfillment. For an instant he held still and devoured her with eyes. "Oh Annie," he groaned, "I . . . want to see your face."

And then they were one.

Later, lying in his arms, sweated and happy, she said, "I don't know what came over me . . . that terrible urgency." Then she laughed. "After all, we have all night."

He propped himself up on one elbow and smiled down at her.

"Longer than that, love." His face was radiant. "Much, much longer than that."

Within a week they were virtually living together in his apartment. Within a month, she could hardly envision what her life had been before Seth. No one had ever suited her so well.

Those strong hands that had captivated her the night they met, those hands were infinitely wonderful when they caressed her cheek or stroked her breast or smoothed her hair. His touch was balm.

"Move in," he urged her. "Give up that pesthole of yours and move in."

Yet she continued to maintain the little room on Chester Street, surely an extravagance considering her circumstances, as a symbol of her hard-won freedom. It was too soon to commit herself to anything larger than a marvelous affair. Moreover his life had a shape and dynamic very different from her own.

"I think I'm in love!" she confided to Lainie Carpenter.

"Think? You're not sure?"

"Reasonably sure." She hesitated. "But not a word to anyone. I don't want to look like I'm fishing for a commitment. One thing I can tell you, though . . . he's like nobody I've ever met."

Nor was he.

To say that Seth was smart and sexy and made her laugh would be to understate the case. Seth was cut from a different cloth.

At twenty-three, he seemed already possessed of a deep, hard core of wisdom, a certainty about where he was going and how.

Annie had a drama coach who often talked of "star quality"—a special aura that couldn't be learned, a gift reserved for the chosen few. Annie doubted that she herself had it, but she recognized it instantly in Seth, with his zesty love of life and boundless optimism.

He exuded confidence and a profound sense of inner security. *Maybe, ought to, should, would*—this kind of vagueness had no place in his vocabulary.

Seth knew. Moreover, he knew that he knew. And what he didn't know, he made it his business to find out. It never ceased to astonish her that he could chat as gracefully with Cambridge academics or Annie's Conservatory friends as with the elderly Jamaican woman who came to clean for him once a week.

She had hitherto assumed that a first-class brain was inevitably accompanied by second-class everything else, but Seth defied the rules. He was fun to be with, quicksilver company, flexible and often impulsive, and she could never predict quite where his nimble mind would alight. He spoke almost as quickly as he thought—hands jabbing, eyes bright with enthusiasm, head thrust forward to impart a greater intimacy to his words—always eager to share some delicious morsel of information, be it the origin of chess or the decline of movie westerns or the sexual habits of penguins or why toast falls butter side down or how the Renaissance masters mixed their paints.

"How do you know all that?" Annie asked him one evening after he had talked down a pugnacious army captain in a Boston bar. "About the Russian front in World War II?"

"Read it somewhere and it stuck," he said. "I have a retentive memory. It's just a knack, the way some people have perfect pitch."

Now, for Annie's sake, he set about acquainting himself with music.

"Tell me all about singing," he said on their first date. "Where do you produce the tone from? How do you project your voice to the back of the hall?"

His questions were shrewd and pragmatic, largely concerned with the physical aspects of her craft, and she could see him filing away data as rapidly as she answered.

"Are you really interested in all this?" She paused in the midst of a technical explanation.

He grinned. "I'm interested in you, and that amounts to the same thing. Besides, there's a long-standing affinity between science and music. Einstein played the fiddle, after all."

"By all reports, very badly." Annie laughed. "There's an old story of his playing sonatas with Artur Rubinstein, and Rubinstein stops in the middle of a piece and says, 'What's the matter, Albert? Can't you count? *One . . . two . . . three . . . four!*' "

Seth duly laughed, but his curiosity persisted.

Once, after a concert, Annie remarked that at a certain point the performance had "caught fire."

"What exactly do you mean, 'caught fire'?" he wanted to know.

"It . . . well . . . um . . ." Annie rolled her eyes, shook her head, floundered for words. "It . . . uh, caught fire, became magic, touched the soul, if that doesn't sound awfully pretentious. I can't define it any more precisely than that. You know, Seth, not everything in life is measurable in concrete terms."

"Uh huh . . ." He considered. "I accept that. But tell me, Annie, what exactly do you mean by 'soul'?"

She looked at him, relieved to see that he was joking.

On the other hand, he was definitely not joking when he caught her reading her horoscope in *Cosmopolitan*.

"You don't honestly believe that shit!" He was appalled.

Her horoscope having just advised her to avoid arguments in the early part of the month, she shut the magazine, marking her place with her finger.

"Of course I don't believe it."

"Then why do you waste your time on it?"

"It's fun, that's all. Come on, Seth, confess. Aren't you curious as to how you Libras are going to do this month?"

"As predicted by *Cosmo*?" he replied. "My God! How primitive can you get! You know, if there's anything I can't stomach, it's rank superstition. I'm a scientist, remember?"

"OK, OK," she said mildly.

A few days later, they were having dinner in Chinatown. When the waiter brought dessert, Annie said nothing as Seth routinely picked up his fortune cookie, crumbled it and began unraveling the message.

Then "Gotcha!" she yelled.

He reared back, startled.

"If there's anything I can't abide," she said, "it's rank superstition. You're not going to admit you read fortune cookies, are you?"

Seth froze for a moment, then burst out laughing.

"Touché, as the fencer said when the other guy cut his head off. I had that coming. Still"—the incident left him looking foolish, not a stance he enjoyed—"you have to admit, if any medium does exist for divining the future, it most probably is the fortune cookie . . . so Oriental, so inscrutable . . ."

"So—" Annie giggled. It was a nice change, being one up. "So . . . what does it say? Stop horsing around and open it."

"It says"—he crumpled the paper sliver and pointedly dropped it in his tea unread—"'Never try to pull a fast one on Annie Sayre.'"

He made no secret of his adoration. They spent every free moment together. Most nights, he would meet her at the Bagel Burger and walk her home. Whenever she appeared in student concerts, he rounded up a couple of dozen Harvard friends, positioning them at strategic locations where their applause would sound the loudest and the longest. "We're your fan club," he declared, "and I'm the number one member.

In return, she was hugely proud of him. It delighted her beyond measure that of everyone he knew—the intellectuals, the scientists, the Harvard elite—he was happiest in her company. She only wished she were better equipped to share some of his professional interests.

"Don't let it trouble you," he assured her. "I keep work and life separate." Dedicated but not obsessed was how he described himself. "Besides, I spend the whole day with what you might call like-minded people. I'll be damned if I'll spend my nights with them too. I'd much rather spend my nights with you."

They had been one evening to the Brattle Street Theatre, watching old Flash Gordon serials in revival. For two hours, the screen trembled with high camp as rockets and death rays and Art Deco spaceships battled it out in grainy black and white. Seth had watched transfixed.

Later, in a Cambridge wine bar, he hoisted a glass of burgundy. "Here's to Flash. He fought the good fight. You know, all through the movie I kept thinking about monoclonal antibodies."

"About what?" Annie cocked her head.

"Monoclonal antibodies. You remember that scene where Flash tries to save Planet Earth from the evil Emperor Ming with those customized rockets? Well, it's like a metaphor for what's happening these days in science. And incredible things are happening, Annie. Stuff nobody imagined even a year or two ago."

"With . . . um, monochromal . . ."

"Monoclonals," he said. "Now picture this." Seth grabbed a dish of pretzels and tumbled them out. "This table is Planet Earth, or—to put it another way—it's the human body. Let's make it yours, Annie. Such a lovely body, great legs . . . But that's beside the point. The important thing to remember is this beautiful body is in a constant state of siege."

"From subway mashers?" Annie giggled.

"Worse than mashers. All the evil forces of the universe, the

53

minions of Ming just waiting to get in. You have to do everything in your power to protect yourself. But fortunately you have at your disposal this fleet of spaceships, otherwise known as antibodies, still otherwise known as pretzels. These are the good guys, the Flash Gordons, so to speak. And it's an enormous fleet, Annie. Tens of thousands of different models, all sizes and shapes, each model armed with a different kind of weapon. Day and night, they're on the job, cruising up and down the bloodstream on the prowl for any hostile invaders. This one is looking for tumor cells, that one is into clap. Of course, this hunt is going on on a microscopic scale, you understand. Figure a million or so of these mothers on the head of a pin. And now from outer space"—he reached over to the next table for a bowl of Cheezits and scattered them among the pretzels—"come the invaders."

"Aaah. The evil minions of Ming."

"Not all of 'em evil. This guy, for instance—" He picked up a Cheezit, studied it and ate it. "Mmmm . . . delicious. He was just a friendly visitor popping in for a chat. Whereas this one might well be a killer. The trick is, you see, to be able to distinguish friend from foe. Only after you've identified the enemy can you exterminate him. I'm simplifying enormously, of course, but you get the idea."

"Well, yes," said Annie, "but with your ten thousand varieties, how do the good guys know which invaders to go for? I gather it wouldn't be much help for a tumor pretzel, say, to go hammer and tongs against a Cheezit that's got Asian flu."

"No it wouldn't." Seth smiled. "And that's the beauty of the thing, the immense subtlety of this invisible war. Each of our guardian ships is fitted out with its own type of key, just as each of the invaders has its own type of keyhole. Once the key is in the lock, then the battle is joined. It's an epic struggle, Annie. It dwarfs every other kind of war in history, and it's been going on for millions of years with no respite. On the whole we've waged it quite successfully, which is how come the human race has survived. Most of the time, the invading body is found out and fought off by its matching antibody. The key fits the lock. Flash conquers Ming. And we can all go about our business, which is playing baseball and singing Berlioz. But sometimes, Annie, our antibodies don't come to the rescue. Maybe we don't possess the right ones. Or maybe we just don't have enough of them in stock. Too many Mings striking out and too few Flash Gordons to defend. When that happens, the victory belongs to Ming."

"And the patient dies of cancer, right?"

"Could be cancer, or any number of presumably incurable diseases. Those are the locks for which we haven't found the key. *Yet!* But suppose we could *make* the key, Annie? Manufacture exactly the weapon that we need in each case? It's one of the oldest pipe dreams in medicine, only now, with monoclonal antibodies, it could be a reality. We can conceive of a whole new armory in the war against disease."

"Go ahead," Annie said. "I'm following you."

Seth furrowed his brow. "Let's say what I'm looking for doesn't exist in nature, but it became technically possible to create it in the lab. I could engineer a totally new kind of antibody, by fusing different types of cells, perhaps cells from different species. It would be a hybrid, so to speak, a custom-made model designed for a specific function. I might want to arm it with a poison warhead or maybe a radioactive bomb. I could structure it any number of ways before sending it into the body to do battle. Only unlike today's chemotherapy, I won't be shooting poison into the whole system. This baby will be so smart, so specific that he'll go exactly where I direct and nowhere else. But of course, that's just one cell and I would need these new antibodies in vast quantities. What's more, each one would have to be perfect, identical to all the others. Do you know what cloning is, Annie?"

Well, that she did know. It was all the rage in horror movies this year.

"It's being able to duplicate a living thing, isn't it?"

"That's right. And being able to do it endlessly, each individual cell genetically identical. And now, we see the possibility of cloning these hybrid cells. We can, theoretically, make a continuous culture of them. Manufacture them like Kellogg's makes corn flakes. Of course, at this point the field is in its infancy, there's hardly even any literature on it. But the implications—" Suddenly his voice shook. "Oh, Annie! the implications are stupendous—for conquering disease, for birth defects, for diagnostic techniques, for almost every branch of medicine." His eyes ranged over the mess of crumbs and pretzels. "All I can say is—the sky's the limit. Just now I put it all to you in comic-strip terms, but that was only to give you an inkling. You know, pet, science isn't what you think it is, all cut-and-dried, putting one foot after another in a well-defined course, marching from A to B to C. Most of the time you're stumbling about in an unlit, uncharted country, with roads leading off in every direction, confusing, full of will-o'-the-wisps and false trails. That's the agony of it, but that's the thrill of it, too. Because there are times when the only way to break through is to take a leap in the dark." The words appeared to hold some special significance. "Yes, a leap in the dark, that moment when you follow instinct as much as judgment."

"You make it sound like an art form," she said.

"It's my art form. In any event, I've pretty much decided that's where I want to be the next few years—in monoclonal antibodies. My God!" His eyes left the tabletop battlefield and ventured far away. His voice shrunk to an awed whisper. "My God . . . a man could make his mark in this field!"

She had never seen him so self-absorbed.

"I thought"—she smiled—"that the object was to relieve human suffering."

"Why, of course, darling." His gaze whipped back. "That goes without saying. But you have to realize, I'm ambitious for myself as well. I'll be damned if I'm going to be just another pair of hands in a lab. I don't even care that much about money. Hell, if I did I would have stuck it out at med school. I want . . ." He paused. "I want my name to stand for something. I want to feel that my life has made a difference to the world. You can understand that, can't you?"

She could indeed. It was what she had always wanted for herself. And while she couldn't foretell her own success with any certainty, she was in no doubt about his. Without question, Seth Petersen would one day be a name to conjure with.

The following week she went into a print shop and had them make up a bumper sticker.

I BRAKE FOR MONOCLONAL ANTIBODIES it read.

He kept it on his Honda for years.

If he had taken the mystery out of his work a bit, the question of how he lived, what he lived on, continued to bemuse Annie.

"I'm the poor son of a rich father," he told her, and much of the time he was as short of cash as the next student. Yet his income was subject to wild fluctuations, and every now and then he would come up with amazing propositions.

"I'm flush this week, sweetie. What say we fly to New York tomorrow and see a show?"

She never knew whether they would feast on lobsters at Jimmy's Harborside or settle for takeout pizzas followed by a stroll along the Esplanade. In theory they split food expenses. In actuality he deemed it ridiculous to split the cost of junk food and out of the question that she share the cost of a luxury dinner. He let her buy him coffee every now and then, and that was it.

A few weeks before Christmas, Seth presented her with a magnificent bracelet, an inch-wide band of brushed gold.

"Is this my Christmas present?" She was taken aback. It had to cost a fortune.

"Nope. Just a present present. I was passing by Shreve Crump this afternoon when I saw it in the window, and it was saying, 'Buy me, buy me.' "

"But Seth . . . ! You mustn't . . . I couldn't!" The thing was too big and too beautiful. She handed it back to him. "I couldn't possibly accept such a gift. It's much too expensive."

"Of course it's expenisve. That's part of its charm. I thought it would look terrific with that black wool dress you wear when you sing concerts."

She felt a frisson of alarm.

"It's so extravagant, Seth. You can't possibly afford such things. Are you"—the idea struck her—"are you playing the horses?"

"No way!" he replied. "That's a sucker's game. The track takes so much of the money off the top, the odds are stacked against you from the start. Anyhow, figuring the horses takes too much time. Fact is, I won at poker the other night." He grinned. "Over fifteen hundred dollars in a friendly little hi-lo game with a bunch of doctors from the Peter Bent."

"You're kidding!"

"The hell I am." The grin was even broader. "Listen, those guys are loaded, screwing patients left and right for crazy fees, so why shouldn't they spread the wealth a bit and underwrite a poor scholar?"

57

"You make it sound as if they were giving you a research grant!" His attitude upset her. He could as easily have lost, and they would have been broke for a month. He was a student, after all—not Jimmy the Greek or some character out of Damon Runyon! But what really rankled was that during those same hours when she'd been hoisting trays and mopping tables for a few lousy dollars, Seth had been playing around with such vast sums. It belittled all her efforts.

And yet she could hardly suppress a thrill of pride. Damn him! He really was so much smarter than everyone else!

"Why do you play at those stakes?" She was curious.

"For money!" Her question surprised him. "Why else? I don't do it that often, maybe a couple of times a month . . ."

"But suppose you lost . . ."

"I don't lose. Believe me, honey, I know what I'm doing. If I didn't come out ahead consistently, I'd quit the game."

"But such big money, Seth! Why should you take such a risk?"

"Life is risk, Annie. Science is risk. Everything is risk. You cross Copley Square at rush hour and you're defying the gods . . ."

"You cross Copley Square because you have to, to get to the other side. Besides, that's acceptable risk . . ."

"And so is this, Annie. I need the money."

She looked at him hard-eyed.

"For what? To buy me gold bracelets? No way. I never asked you for anything. Come on, Seth . . . you're just rationalizing."

"OK," he conceded. "It's not just the money. Truth is, I play because I like it, and I'm damn good at it. To me, it's the game with everything—mystery, drama, excitement, bluff. You're betting on yourself with every card, betting that you've got more smarts, more balls than every other guy at the table. And when you win, well, then you've proved you were right. And you know me, Annie. I love to win. Don't begrudge me the adventure. Besides, these guys can afford it. What's fifteen hundred bucks to a plastic surgeon? It's a fee for doing a nose job, that's all. Play money. And if I didn't win it, it would simply wind up on the back of some doctor's fat wife or on a bar bill at the country club. I'd much rather it wound up on your wrist as this bracelet. Please accept it, darling. Besides, I can't take it back. You see I've had it engraved."

She held the golden circle up to the light. On the inside, in precise tiny script ran the legend: "To Annie from *Le Spectre de la Rose.*"

"Oh Seth . . ." She looked at him with love and dismay. "What am I to do with you!"

He picked up the bracelet and closed the clasp around her wrist. "Be happy with me. That's all I ask."

She was happy with him. It sometimes frightened her how happy, for her joy was muted by the knowledge that their affair would end with the academic year.

Then Seth would go his way and she would go hers. He had already applied for various fellowships, although he had his heart set on a doctoral program at Oak Ridge, Tennessee. As for Annie, she wavered between trying her luck in New York and spending the last of her savings on a one-way ticket to Germany. Professor Baer urged her on the latter course. On her behalf, he had sent a tape to an old friend in the provincial town of Gelsenkirchen, with the result that Annie had been promised an apprenticeship upon graduation.

Seth took this development with a vinegar face.

"I looked the place up," he told her the following day, "and it's a mining town, a cruddy Ruhr Valley mining town, population under 400,000. Jesus, if it's coal slag you want, you may as well go to Altoona, Pennsylvania. We'd be in the same country at least."

"Except Altoona doesn't have an opera company and Gelsenkirchen does. You know, Seth, that's how a lot of American singers get their start, working in Germany. Every self-respecting town has an opera house." But even as she spoke, she could see he was hurt. He seemed to have taken it as a personal rejection. "I'm sorry," seh added, "and I'll be sorry to leave, but I have to think of my career."

"What have they offered you?"

"Money? A bare living."

"I presumed that. I meant, what kind of parts? Will you be singing feature roles?"

"Not at first. I'd probably start off as a utility singer . . ."

"Is that like a utility infielder? No place in the starting lineup, they just drag you out to do all the little odd jobs?"

"Something like that." She bit her lips. It wasn't like him to be so caustic. "My hope, of course, is that within a couple of years, I'll

59

get more substantial roles, maybe even the occasional lead. It's a terrific opportunity, plus of course . . . The thing is, Seth, it's living in Europe. I've dreamt of going there ever since I was a kid. I grant you, Gelsenkirchen isn't much, but it's the first step. It's a chance to sing, to learn, to travel . . . London . . . Paris . . ."

"I have traveled much in Concord," Seth snapped.

"What's that supposed to mean?"

"Henry Thoreau. It was his way of saying you can learn and grow and experience life without—"

"Without ever leaving home! Great! If that were my attitude, I'd still be in Larmouthport, learning double-entry bookkeeping, just like my mother. And then"—she tried to win him over with a smile—"I'd never have met you."

He made an effort to return her smile, but his eyes were unhappy. "Well . . ." He shook his head slowly. "What can I say? You're a free agent . . ."

That she was, and she intended to continue as one. Several times in the past couple of months, she sensed that Seth was on the brink of proposing. All signs were pointing in that direction: his growing involvement, the lavish presents, the way he showed her off to his friends. And from his circle of friends, male and female, she was given to understand that she was on to a very good thing. "Seth's quite a catch," a woman friend from his med school days told her bluntly. "And I should know. I spent two years trying to catch him."

Yet the thought of marriage made her nervous. Much as she cared for Seth, much as she hated the thought of losing him, he wasn't part of her plan. And marriage wasn't part of her plan. Maybe when she was thirty and had established herself, or when she was thirty and had failed. Then there would be time enough. But for the present, it was out of the question. To marry now would be an admission that her mother was right, that her aspirations were nothing but a pastime. Pride, if nothing else, would keep her single for the next several years.

As for her coming separation from Seth, she did her best not to think of it. It hurt too much. He would settle down in academia, she would lead her own nomadic life and that would be the end of it. In the meanwhile, they had a few precious months left. It added poignance to their lovemaking.

* * *

One blustery April morning, she was in a top-floor practice room when every alarm bell in the Conservatory went off.

"Fire," someone shouted in the hall. "Everybody out onto Huntington Avenue."

Annie spurted into the corridor, tore down the staircase. Five minutes later the entire staff and student body had achieved the safety of the streets, most of them breathless, many still clutching their instruments. In the distance, the fire trucks were screaming their way to the scene.

Arms clutched against the cold, Annie stood on the pavement scanning the facade anxiously for licks of flame, plumes of smoke. Suddenly someone poked her in the back.

"Seth!" She was astonished to find him here. To judge by his appearance—collar open, face flushed—he must have been running, too. Had he heard the alarm from ten blocks away and come to her rescue?

"My God, Seth, you must be psychic. There's a fire somewhere in the Conservatory!"

He put his lips to her ear. "I'm the fire, Annie." His eyes were bright, his voice strained but exuberant. "I'm on fire to see you."

He seized her elbow and began fast-walking her away down a side street with a sense of urgency. His words had made no sense; if anything they rang a different kind of alarm. Annie twisted her head to see what was happening, but there were still no flames, no smoke. Nothing but pandemonium.

"Seth!" She felt a premonitory quiver.

But he continued pulling her, tugging her until they were out of sight of school and crowds.

"All clear!" He stopped, gathered his breath, then burst into a yard-wide grin.

"It's Oak Ridge, baby! I got the fellowship! They called me ten minutes ago with the news. They'd like me down there June first, I can plunge right in. Isn't that fantastic? I just had to tell you and I didn't know where the hell you were . . . which class . . ."

"So!" She broke loose from his grip. "So you just decided to walk into the Conservatory and pull the fire alarm. Is that it?"

61

He could barely keep from laughing. "It was disgraceful of me, I know . . ." But there was no remorse in his eyes, only exultation. "Here, love, take my jacket before you freeze to death."

"I don't want your goddam jacket." She was shaking with rage and cold. "You may think this is all very funny, but what you've done is absolutely criminal. Criminal! You could go to jail . . ."

"Oh, come on, Annie." His tone betrayed surprise. "At worst, it was a dumb prank. Don't make a federal case out of it. I thought you'd be . . . well, flattered."

"You honestly did? How little you know me!" She began to weep out of sheer vexation. "How dare you be so high-handed? Who are you to reorder the lives and plans of hundreds of people, total strangers, because you couldn't wait till I get home at four o'clock? I'm glad you got your fellowship, Seth, but that doesn't give you the right—"

"Oh, Annie. You're taking the whole business far too seriously. Come on." He reached into her handbag and fished out a handkerchief. "Now, dry your eyes and see if you can listen without getting mad. The reason I did this—OK! dumb impulsive criminal unforgivable thing—the reason was, I want you to marry me. Today. Next week . . . as soon as City Hall can get it together. Then we can go down to Oak Ridge and live like real people. Granted, the first couple of years might be a little hard, but once I've got my doctorate . . . Oh, fuck it all, Annie! Stop looking like I just raped a convent full of nuns. I love you. I want to marry you. I want us to be together for always. And where's the crime in that?"

She was too dumbstruck even to shape an answer.

"Look . . . you don't believe me? You think it's some kind of joke? Would you prefer if I got down on my knees right here on the street? If that'll make it official, OK . . . I'll get down on my knees . . ."

"Please . . ." The image of him kneeling on the dank pavement helped her find her voice. "We can't talk about this here."

"I agree. Let's go home and hash it out in comfort over a bottle of wine."

Her reply was a vehement shake of the head.

She knew him, knew herself. Once there, he would coddle her, cater to her, cup her face with those strong supple hands, kiss her eyes and they would wind up in bed, making love. That was the worst place to have this kind of discussion, making this kind of decision. Instead, she settled for the back booth of a coffee shop thick with the odor of bacon grease.

"Not another word." Her hands clasped tight under the table. "Please don't say anything more about marriage. I've been dreading this moment for ages, Seth. I hoped you wouldn't ask me because then I wouldn't have to answer. I never expected to get so involved, to have it take over my life." She made a concerted effort not to cry. That would be disastrous. "It's not that I don't care for you. You know I do, but I have a responsibility to myself, to my work. I've made plans . . ."

"Plans can be changed," he implored. "I'm only going to Tennessee for a couple of years. Once I'm established, I'll look for a job someplace compatible where you can pursue your own goals . . ."

"It's no good, Seth. Oak Ridge or anywhere. Our lives don't fit."

"How can you talk such rubbish!" He pounded the table in exasperation. "We've been together nonstop since September, we love each other, we're good to and for each other, and absolutely terrific in bed. So how can you say our lives don't fit?"

"Because I don't want to end up as just another suburban housewife and that's what'll happen. I'd be miserable, I'd make you miserable . . ."

Her words had a sobering effect.

"You'll never be just a housewife, Annie, nor would I want you to. Whatever happens, you'll still be my unique wonderful Annie . . . a musician, an artist. That won't change. Now, before you give me your final answer, let me tell you what you can expect from me."

He would be a good husband, he promised, faithful and loving. He came from a long line of good husbands and intended in this wise, if in no other, to follow his father's example. He would care for her, provide for her, do everything in his power to make her happy. He had every expectation of success in his field, and if it was unlikely he would ever be rich, it was even more so that she should ever go without. The closeness that they had shared this past year would be just a prelude to the rest of their lives. All she had to do was . . .

"Come with me! Come with me in June."

"You make it sound so simple, but you don't seem to realize . . . you're asking me to give up everything! My career, my dreams, everything I've worked for . . ."

"No!" He was emphatic. "All I'm asking is that you put it on hold. Just for a few years, baby, just until I've made my name."

"And what about *my* name? What about Gelsenkirchen . . . ?

"I have no answer to that," he admitted. "Believe me, Annie, it's even harder to find great research opportunities than it is to find towns that have opera houses. If you could only wait. The fact is, you can sing anywhere. OK, not opera, but there are always choirs, churches. You can sing all by yourself, for that matter, and still make music. But without a first-class lab, I'm helpless. I have to go where the facilities are. I wish it were different, that I could come with you to Gelsenkirchen and we both could have what we want, but there's nothing there for me. I even toyed with the idea of commuting, flying out for long weekends just to be with you, but expense aside, that's just fantasizing. The thing is, I want more of you—not less." He spread his hands with a sigh of acceptance. "Those are the realities, I'm afraid."

Within her everything was warring, emotions raging at each other, pulling her in a dozen different directions. It was so unfair, so cruel that he should put her on the spot like this. Why couldn't he leave well enough alone? To answer as she must would take all her courage. Yes, courage, because one part of her wanted to be with him so desperately, even to marry him, that it might indeed have been the world well lost for love. She hadn't known that until now.

"Would you like time to think it over?" he said softly.

But there was nothing to reflect on. Painful though it was, she knew her duty. Anything less than a firm clear "No" would be a denial of everything she'd struggled to achieve.

"I'm sorry, Seth." She fought back the familiar impulse to turn to him—of all people—to seek comfort and advice. He always knew what to do. "I'm sorry beyond words, but the answer is no. I don't want to marry and God knows I don't want to move to Tennessee. I don't want"—her voice broke—"to nip my career in the bud, without even giving it my best shot. You have no right to ask me to make such a sacrifice. Why can't we just go on as we were for the next two months, loving each other, enjoying each other, and forget today ever happened? Can't we at least have that?"

He sat very still for what seemed like eternity, then waved to the waitress for the check.

"I don't see the point of it." He began fumbling in his pockets for change, fishing out a selection of quarters and dimes. "We're going nowhere. You've made that quite clear, and no purpose is served by prolonging the agony. I'll pack up your things and drop them off some time tomorrow. You can leave my key in the mailbox. I wish you luck, Annie. Luck and success."

He left a pile of coins on the table and was gone.

She couldn't believe it. Couldn't believe it even when a neatly tied package containing everything of hers—clothes, makeup, library books, records, pencils, even Tampax (Seth was nothing if not thorough)—appeared on her threshold next morning. The collection was so inclusive it bespoke an act of exorcism. Proof that she was out of his system once and for all.

Impossible! He would never walk away, never give her up that easily. He prized winning too much.

Certain though she was of having done the right thing, she was even more certain he would try to win her back. There would be notes, trinkets, love letters, a barrage of phone calls. And one day there would be Seth himself standing at her doorstep with an armful of blooms and a penitent smile. Roses of course. *Le spectre de la rose* come to haunt her and prevail.

She knew him and accordingly began girding herself against the inevitable onslaught. Oh, she had an arsenal of reasons, powerful ones, new ones each morning, reasons without number as to why marriage was a total impossibility. And she would need them all, need every device and tactic in the repertory to keep him at bay, for Seth could be enormously persuasive. For days she dreaded each ring of the phone, trembled with every step in the hallway.

The calls never came.

Nor the flowers. Nor the expected letter in which Seth would plead and explain and redefine at length. Oh, how that man dearly loved logic. And dearly loved having the last word. An abrupt "good luck" in a coffee shop could hardly suffice; there had been no true finality about it.

But nothing broke the silence.

As April turned into May, the possibility that she might never see him again slowly began to take root.

Never.

It was an unfathomable concept. Never again in this year, in this century. Never—as long as she lived.

For weeks, she had avoided turning down his street, afraid of meeting him by chance, seeing him woebegone and solitary. Now she avoided it for fear of seeing him with someone else, happy and absorbed. He was an ardent and gregarious man, not given to lost causes.

Gradually, his absence came to fill every space in her life even more completely than his presence had done. The scene in the coffee shop replayed itself ad infinitum on the screen of her memory.

Had she really been so brusque in her refusal? What insult had he offered? He had proposed marriage, surely an honorable estate, promised love and warmth and intimacy, and she had bulldozed over him without a second thought. And now when she replayed that last meeting, she would alter the dialogue, modify the outcome. Her answers became less hidebound, more loving. The prospect of marriage became less outlandish. Far less outlandish than the prospect of never seeing him again.

She took to peering through her courtyard window, to see if there was a light in his room. Was he home? Was he alone? Was he out?

The room was dark almost every evening now. And it was only a matter of time until the day came when she might look toward his window and find an unfamiliar silhouette.

"I'm sick." She wept in Lainie Carpenter's arms. "I'm sick from missing him."

"Ye gods, Annie . . ." Lainie, who hadn't seen her in nearly a week, was shocked at her appearance. "Listen, kid, you better shape up pronto if you're going to make final exams."

"I can't sing," Annie complained. Her throat was locked tight with tension, anxiety. The head tones were ugly, the timbre forced and shrill. Singing hurt.

"Try a mixture of honey, aspirin and lukewarm herbal tea," her friend prescribed. "C'mon. I'll brew you up a batch."

But the problem wasn't just physical, Annie told her. She seemed to have no defense these days against the emotional content of the music. A simple Schubert song reduced her to tears.

"*Du bist die Ruh* . . ." she began. It was impossible to continue.

"Oh, wow!" Lainie put down the kettle. "That's out of my class. I don't have remedies for broken hearts."

But Seth could fix a broken heart, Annie thought. Seth could fix everything.

"It's almost six weeks since he left," she wailed. "I can't just trot off to Germany without seeing him. You know, last night I tried to recall what color his eyes are . . . whether they're hazel or gray, and I couldn't remember exactly. But I don't want to forget him. It's so final . . . like death. I never thought he'd leave without saying good-bye. How could he do this to me? He said he loved me."

"Maybe he's just cutting his losses, Annie. It sounds like you came down on him pretty hard."

"I guess I did." Annie swiped her cheek with the back of her hand. "Good God, I can't stop crying. Tell me, Lainie"—she tried to make light of it—"do people ever die of love?"

"Only in opera," came the rejoinder.

It was the last week in May and the weather had turned suddenly sultry, warm as that summer night they met.

For two days there had been no light in his room, no discernible activity, but late one afternoon she saw movement behind the net curtains, a shadow so tall and spare it had to be his.

She would see him. Bury her pride and her pain and go see him, because she couldn't endure his leaving on such an unfinished note.

For the better part of an hour she tried and retried every item in her meager wardrobe, flinging garments left and right. Silk was too dressy—he would think she'd come begging. Jeans were too plain. Should she look sexy? Or bold? Or was pathos the best note to strike? At last she pulled on a simple black jersey turtleneck and skirt. He liked her in black. Moreover it seemed appropriate, the color of mourning.

Twilight was setting in by the time she knocked at his door. Inside the radio was blasting out Bruce Springsteen. An omen. He never played rock music when she was there. Suppose—the sweat began streaming down her breasts, clinging to her jersey—suppose he wasn't alone. Love in the afternoon. Their favorite pastime. She waited in an agony of fear.

Then there he was—standing in the doorway with a look of

67

troubled surprise. Gray eyes, they were. How could she not have remembered? She'd never seen that plaid shirt, though. Must be new for the trip. He seemed thinner, almost gaunt, she realized with a rush of adrenaline. Yes, he had missed her too. He had suffered.

"Hello, Annie," he said softly.

Behind him the room was bare except for packing cases, denuded of all warmth and personality. Dark patches on the wall mocked the places where his lovely Japanese prints used to hang. Yes, his departure was imminent.

"I came to say good-bye, Seth," she managed to breathe.

"Good-bye?" His voice was firm but not unkind. "I thought we said our good-byes at the Burlington Coffee Shop."

"We said a lot of things there . . ." she blurted. "Or at least I did. May I come in?"

For a split second he hesitated, then gestured her to the sofa. "I'd offer you some coffee, but as you can see everything's stowed. I may have a beer around somewhere . . ."

She shook her head no. In the next room, a stack of freshly pressed shirts, piles of clean socks and linen lay atop the bed, awaiting their place in an empty suitcase. Seth and she had made love on that bed times without number.

"When are you off?" she shouted above the music.

"Tomorrow. Driving down." He switched off the radio.

She expected him to sit beside her, ply her with questions. *And you, Annie, when are you leaving? How are you doing? You're looking great. You're looking lousy.* More likely the latter.

Instead, he straddled a hard-back chair at the far end of the room, folded his arms across the top and waited for her to speak.

"I want to know why you never called me," she said at last.

His answer was a shrug.

"Don't I deserve some kind of an explanation, Seth! Didn't you miss me? Didn't you ever think of my feelings?"

And there they were, the tears she had struggled to hold back, hot and unconstrained. Surely now he would come to her, comfort her, take her in his arms, but he merely sat there looking ineffably sad.

"Annie," he said when she finished wiping her eyes, "if it makes you feel better, I've thought of you every waking moment. I've made love to you a hundred times in my dreams. God"—he shook his head in wonder—"the things I've done to you in my dreams! So don't fear you're forgotten. But I've also remembered something you said that day. You said I had no right to ask you to give up so much, to sacrifice your chance to go to Europe. No right. That stuck in my mind.

"Don't you think, Annie, I could have got you back these past weeks? I could have made you say yes. What would it have taken? Love? Flattery? Persistence? I could have wooed the bejeezus out of you, swept you off your feet so hard you wouldn't know what hit you. But I didn't want it, I didn't want to bludgeon you into submission. So we'd get married and then what? A year from now, ten years from now, you would say to me, 'I could've been this, I could've been that . . .' " He gave a bitter laugh. "I don't want you ever to claim that I wore you down, sweet-talked you into marriage. That I made you act against your best judgment. Not only would you hate me; I'd hate myself. I'd have it on my conscience that I waylaid your dreams. And I didn't have that right. Only you have that right. And there's something else, too. You know, Annie, you've never really been open with me . . ."

She was thunderstruck. "I don't know what you mean!"

"Don't you? Even when we were in bed, there was always a part of you holding back . . . cool, uncommitted. Was it the best part? Probably, but I suppose I'll never know. Yet I felt it was a conscious decision. What were you afraid of . . . that you'd lose control? Or was it simply that you didn't care that much? How come, Annie, you never once told me that you loved me?"

"Oh, Seth!'

"You never did. Not in so many words."

He rested his chin on his hands with an air of finality.

In a sudden shaft of anguish, she knew what he said was true. She had rationed, scanted, withheld. For all the intensity of their sexual exchanges, for all the laughter and passion shared, she was listening always to a persistent inner monitor, a tiny nagging voice advising caution. Only so far, it had dictated. So far and no farther.

Now Seth was moving beyond her realm. In the fading light, in the echo of the half-empty room he seemed already to be retreating into an untouchable distance. She was losing him. Losing him . . .

The monitor fell silent.

"I love you, Seth." She mouthed the words.

And then stood up and declared them aloud.

"I love you."

He jerked his head up.

"I love you," she repeated, "but I have to know . . . do you still want to marry me?"

"That's not the question."

She shook her head, confused. And then . . .

"The question *is*"—she smiled in swift comprehension—"do *I* want to marry *you?*"

For the choice had to be hers. That was his meaning. Only Annie had the right to make such a decision. Only she had the authority to surrender her career.

He would woo her no more, pursue her no longer. The quest was over, had ended that day in the coffee shop, and now it was she who must come to him. But come to him without any qualms, without doubts or second guessing. Fully. Freely. There could be no looking back.

She crossed the room to where he sat, took his hands and placed them on her cheeks.

"My darling Seth"—she kissed his open palm—"I want to marry you more than anything else in the world."

The moment she said it, she knew it was true.

He lifted his head, radiant, then swooped her into his arms.

"Oh, Annie! My sweet girl. You'll never regret it. I swear to you, I'll make it up to you one day. You have my word."

They made love amid the sweet-scented piles of linen, her dark hair spread against the white of his shirts, bodies damp against the crispness of the starch.

His touch, real and present, erased the memory of pain, and under the opium of his kisses, beneath the enveloping thrust of his body, all other dreams were vanquished.

She traced his flesh with her fingers, discovering every hollow, every bone, the line of his brow, the heft of his thigh as for the first time. "I'd almost forgotten how you felt," she murmured.

Later, lying in each other's arms, content and replete, they chatted, exchanged endearments, made plans, furnished rooms as yet unseen, named children yet to be conceived.

"Did you know," she wondered, "that I would come back to you?"

"Naturally I hoped," he said, "but how could I know?"

In the dark she could not see his exultant smile.

"Come on, Annie. Try and get some sleep."

Instead they made love yet again.

Dawn found them red-eyed and happy.

"I guess you should start packing, lovey," he said.

"I guess I should." She paused, then spoke her mind.

"I've given up a great deal for you, Seth. You know that. Now I'd like you to give up something for me."

"Anything!" He was surprised. "That is, anything within reason."

"I want you to give up playing poker. Don't laugh. I'm perfectly serious. We'll be living on a pittance down there. I'm not like you, Seth. I'm not a plunger. If I felt you were risking every penny we have in some high-stakes game, I wouldn't be able to sleep nights . . ."

"No poker means no more gold bracelets," he teased.

"I've got a lifetime's supply. Promise me," she urged. "Promise me you won't gamble anymore."

He promised.

But Seth Petersen had just come off the first great gamble of his life. He had gambled on her love. And he had won.

That their union, founded as it was on tears and anguish, should be successful was a constant source of wonder to her. Quite simply, they suited each other. A physiologist friend of theirs attributed it to a fortuitous mesh of right-brain and left-brain personalities, a description Annie rejected out of hand. Why try to analyze love? Some things in life were better left a mystery. And by the time a year had passed, she couldn't recall what life had been like before Seth.

However, marriage was hardly a full-time occupation for a woman of her drive and energy, and even had Annie chosen to become one of "the ladies who lunch," their circumstances wouldn't have permitted it. Seth's grant might be enough to hold one body and soul together. It was hardly sufficient for two.

Every day, she set aside three hours for intensive practicing, determined not to let her voice lapse.

When she could, she sang professionally. When she couldn't, she worried about money.

Before long practicality outweighed her long-term prejudice. She learned to type and take shorthand ("My mother should see me now," she'd say ruefully) and found secretarial work in whichever town Seth's nomadic career managed to land them. Some of the jobs were amusing, some dull. But they were all, they both agreed, stop-gap measures against the day when her husband would be established and she would be free to resume her true career.

And to have children. That too was part of the dream.

At first, they postponed parenthood until Seth finished his doctorate, but as soon as he began to earn a living they decided the time was ripe. However, Annie's body refused to comply.

There was nothing wrong, the gynecologist assured her, with either of them. "You're still shy of thirty," he there-there'd her. "You've plenty of fertile years ahead. Try not to be anxious."

Every new year brought fresh hopes; every month brought fresh disappointments.

At Christmas, her in-laws would descend upon them for a whirlwind visit, highlighted by Wally Petersen's quest for the best restaurants, the most lavish entertainments in town. Inevitably, the night before their departure, Wally would take her aside.

"So, Annie?" he would begin with an expectant smile.

"So, Wally?" She would smile back, although she knew perfectly well what was on his mind.

"So, my girl"—he would put an arm around her—"so when are you kids going to give us a *real* Christmas present?"

He meant no unkindness, but the question always pierced her to the core. When indeed?

To Annie, it was a source of nagging anxiety. Why was life so unjust? Everywhere you looked, women were bearing children—single women, simple women, hapless teenagers and aging matriarchs on the brink of menopause. And here were the Petersens with everything to offer, remaining inexplicably childless. It just wasn't fair.

One day Seth brought home a magnificent Himalayan cat. "This proud imperious beast," he announced, "is named Maximilian the Third with a pedigree as long as your arm." Annie couldn't help wondering if he had meant it by way of consolation.

Two weeks later, she opened their American Express invoice.

"Five hundred dollars for a cat!" She was outraged. "My God, Seth, no wonder we're always broke!"

"Quality costs," was Seth's response.

She had half a mind to return Maximilian or at least put it up for sale, but by then he had already embezzled his way into her affection. He was an exceedingly lovely creature, with long silky hair and startling blue eyes. Yet for all his aristocratic bearing and pedigree, the cat had a penchant for escaping at every opportunity, to be found after hours of searching in some disreputable alley, filthy and sated, with a mouthful of feathers. "A born predator," Seth had said. They wound up renaming it Runaway Max. Not that names mattered, for the cat never answered when called.

"Some pal you proved to be," she would chastise him occasionally, but, blood feasts and all, Runaway Max would have to do until a baby came along. In the interim, she and Seth adjusted themselves to their childless state.

Seth was deceptive (she came to realize) in the facade he presented to the world. Ostensibly genial and easygoing, there lay beneath his bonhomie a deep reserve, a fear of letting strangers get too close. He had friends but no true intimates. Annie alone was the exception. Only she was permitted to glimpse him with his guard down, his disappointments visible. He viewed the rest of the world in direct competition.

They had been one night at a party of academics, eating overripe brie and drinking jug wine when their host had proposed a parlor game.

"There are two kinds of people in this world . . ." Ricky Naismith posited. Each guest in turn was required to complete the definition according to his own lights. The object was to be either witty or profound.

"Those who read Proust in the original," said the insufferable Laura Davies, "and those who don't."

"Those who buy suits wholesale," Bernie Kahn contributed, "and then there are *goyim*."

There was a can-you-top-this atmosphere in the room, which made each successive effort more difficult.

"There are two kinds of people," Annie volunteered. "Those who divide the world into two kinds of people and those who don't."

When it came around to Seth, he bowed out with a graceful sweep of the hand. "In deference to my wife," he said, "because I couldn't possibly improve upon her definition."

But driving home that night, he remarked, "What an asshole game that was of Naismith's. Christ! Save me from the company of scholars."

"Come on, Seth," she twitted him. "Your problem was you just couldn't think of a good enough comeback."

"Are you kidding?" He turned to look at her with an almost somber expression. "There are only two kinds of people in this world, Annie. *Us*"—he put his hand on her knee—"and *them*!"

It was true.

For better or worse, Annie and Seth Petersen had grown into a closed corporation. And Annie fervently hoped it was for better.

She left Lainie Carpenter's brownstone in an unsettled mood.

Summer had turned to fall and the chill in the air, as much as her reunion lunch, brought back the long-forgotten mood of schooldays.

To call Madame Natasha or not to? She couldn't decide. There was risk in entrusting her ego to a total stranger. Years of being a good-sized fish in a small talent pool made her dread the possibility of a rebuff. This wouldn't be singing for friends or private parties. This was, as Seth might have put it, the big leagues.

She would do nothing until she discussed it with him, the money alone being a powerful factor. Meanwhile, she had the whole afternoon ahead of her. Go to a museum? Catch a movie? Visit friends? But as yet she knew hardly anyone in the city.

On Central Park West, the cabs were cruising, hungry for fares, and on impulse she flagged one down. Seth was always urging her to visit the lab, and today seemed as good a day as any. She would take him by surprise. Catch him in his habitat.

4

"WHAT A DUMP!"

Vi cast a critical eye over the scruffy anteroom with its bark-cloth walls and ailing aspidistra. Even the magazine rack, populated by a lone copy of a year-old *Newsweek*, exuded an air of defeat. Honestly, she asked herself, could any guy who couldn't even afford to renew his magazine subscription be accounted a competent attorney?

But Sherm had said he was competent. Or had he said compassionate? Yes, that was it.

"Dom's a real sweetheart. He did my divorce completely without tears, and I think you'll find him very understanding. Also," Sherm had added, "he won't charge you an arm and a leg."

Price certainly was a factor. Still, by Vi's lights, this place didn't even look like a proper lawyer's office, and she had ample grounds for comparison, having once worked at Wall Street's very finest blue-chip firm—an office where power was made visible in Chippendale and marble. Slater Blaney! Now, that was a law firm for you. They had genuine Renoirs in their anteroom, not year-old *Newsweeks*.

True, she didn't require a top honcho from the corporate bar to handle what was surely a straw in the wind. A case? What case! That son of a bitch couldn't possibly be serious! Yet she would have wished Dom Tarantino's office provided something more in terms of moral support.

She shoved the magazine back into the rack and turned the waiting minutes to pleasanter thoughts.

Oh, but that had been a marvelous week down on Cape May. They'd chartered a twenty-seven-foot Catalina, cruised the coast down to Newport News, feasting on lobsters and soft-shelled crabs and pretending they didn't have to grub for a living.

"You ought to be in the business," the marina operator had told her. "You're a natural sailor."

Of course it was hustle ("The guy probably wants to sell you a boat," Sherm twitted), but there was truth in it too.

Vi didn't believe in magic or fairy tales or even the possibility of mystic experience, but put her out on a sailboat and she was transported into another existence. Then a latent streak of poetry would surface and the rest of the world fell away. There was fascination in the infinite patterns of the whitecaps, peace in the silences. It was a world beaten pure of all imperfections, clean and shining, free at last from the buzz of traffic, the jangling of phones, the niggling of clients, the dealing of deals. Nothing but the whoosh of white sails and the scent of the sea.

She shut her eyes and let the remembered sun beat down upon her face. Someday . . . someday . . .

"Mrs. Hagerty?" Her reverie was broken by a rotund little man with a half dozen wisps of black hair brushed hopefully across a balding scalp. The effect was comical, yet somehow endearing. He had a gentle smile.

"I'm Dom Tarantino. Sorry to have kept you waiting."

He ushered her into his sanctum, a room larger but no more prepossessing than the outer quarters, swept a pile of papers off the top of his desk and steepled his fingers.

Vi needed nothing more than a "What seems to be the problem?" before she was off, spewing out her story in a torrential downpour.

"Well!" She caught her breath. "He can't do that, can he? He can't come out of the woodwork after all these years and give me this shit about having 'claims'?"

"May I see the letter?"

Lips pursed, she gave it over. There were three much-fingered pages typed on the luxurious bond of Slater Blaney. Dictated, she pointed out, as though to give it official clout. Her immediate instinct had been to ignore it, to throw it in the garbage half unread. But that would simply be hiding out from reality, for where one letter had found her, others soon could follow. By now, of course, she

could have recited it by heart, at least the pertinent passages, stripped
of legal whys and wherefores.

"Dear Viola" (that was a lie right there; she had never been dear
to him) . . . "nine years since I saw you last" (by whose choice,
might she ask?) . . . "before I even had a chance to see my child"
(which he had steadfastly denied was his) . . . "your unexplained departure followed by the resumption of your single name" (put that
way, it sounded as though she had been hiding) . . . "located you
through private detectives" (sneak!) . . . "I am now happily married" (well, bully for you, buddy) . . . "not blessed with children"
(oh, she could smell the next one coming!) . . . "natural curiosity"
(and then here it came—the part that had Vi gritting her teeth every
time she thought about it):

"He says here," Dom Tarantino read aloud, " 'I was appalled to
see the condition both of his clothing and his person—' "

"Yeah yeah . . ." Vi interrupted. " 'His sneakers were full of holes,
his shirt badly stained, hair unclean and uncut, thereby giving the
lad the general appearance of a charity waif.' Jesus! Anybody who
lived with a nine-year-old kid knows that there's no way you can
keep 'em looking in one piece. And his hair was clean . . . !"

" 'And further,' " Dom read on, " 'the language he employed is
totally unacceptable in one so young . . .' " Dom lip-synced the next
couple of lines, his eyebrows forming inverted V's. He looked up
at Vi.

"Does your son really say things like that?"

Vi sighed. "Only when strange men come on to him in play-
grounds. OK, I admit Noonie gets a little foul-mouthed sometimes,
probably comes of watching too much TV. But it doesn't mean anything. He's really the sweetest kid in the world . . . and bright!"

" 'Considering,' " Dom droned on, " 'the obvious financial hard-
ships you bear and the vast opportunities I am able to offer our
boy . . .' " He finished the letter and put down his glasses.

"It looks as if your Mr. Ross Winfield intends to sue for joint
custody."

"What I want to know"—Vi's hands turned sweaty—"is, he
doesn't stand a chance, does he? My God, I had to bludgeon the
bastard into marrying me."

"Well, Ms. Hagerty . . . or do you prefer to be called Mrs.?"

"I prefer Vi."

"Well, Vi. To go by what we have here, your ex seems to be making an interesting case. The drift of it is that, having given birth to this baby, you deserted the father summarily, before the man even had a chance to see his own child. Here"—he poked through the letter to find the pertinent phrase—"where he talks about 'depriving me of my parental rights.' Could be he's laying the groundwork to a claim of kidnapping."

"You've got to be joking!" Vi turned white. "It wasn't like that at all. Dear God, it was nothing like that."

"Then tell me," Dom urged, "just how it was."

She was nineteen and working in the secretarial pool of Slater Blaney when she first met Ross Winfield. Though but a few years older, and just as new to the firm, he was already enlisted in the ranks of hierarchy. At Slater Blaney, the world divided sharply into two classes: aristocrats (meaning lawyers) and peasants, comprising everyone else. For whereas Vi, as her narrow-lipped supervisor kept reminding her, was but another pair of hands, Ross was a princely associate, on the rise in that most prestigious and stuffy of law firms. Tall and broad-shouldered, with a shock of ginger hair, he looked as though he stepped from the pages of *Gentleman's Quarterly* by way of Vic Tanney. "Chewy" was how the girls in the pool described him.

Company protocol dictated that he and Vi should get no closer than the length of a stenography pad; sexual chemistry dictated otherwise.

Within twenty-four hours of their first encounter, the two had embarked on an affair that would make them lunchtime familiars of every hotel room south of Times Square.

Wow! Vi would think as she made her way back to the office wobbly-kneed. *You could almost see the smoke rise.*

He never brought her back to his apartment. God forbid his roommate, a fellow lawyer, should find out he had broken the firm's unwritten law.

"They don't approve of fraternizing."

"Fraternizing!" she teased. "I thought that was when you had sex with your brother."

78

She offered another word for their association, alliterative if rather cruder.

Ross laughed. "You are so gross."

"And don't you love it!"

Yet there was, she told herself, more to their relationship than the mere exchange of bodily fluids. She was crazy about him, totally besotted. However could she not be? For Ross was bright, ambitious, with the kind of hustle she admired. In a vulnerable moment, he confessed to having grown up in a dusty corner of Queens, where his father ran a dry-cleaning shop.

"I knew it," she crowed. "You're just like me! You're a street guy at heart."

"*Was*," Ross emphasized. "That Queens stuff is definitely past tense. And if you tell anyone, I'll have your head on a platter. It took me three years of speech therapy to obliterate the scars."

His favorite pastime—other than making love—was to spread out on the bed, hands clasped behind his head, and fantasize about the day he'd make partner.

"You know what those guys pull down? Maybe half a million dollars a year. They meet everybody, get invited everywhere. I figure six and a half more years in the salt mines . . ."

And then—he kissed his fingers into the air—that glorious mañana when he would have the Park Avenue penthouse, the summer home in the Hamptons, the Maserati, the Dunhill suits.

Indeed it made a very pretty picture, and Vi was not above sharing it, although she never told him so. Not that she really saw herself as a conventional lawyer's wife, but then they weren't a conventional couple.

They were two of a kind, or so she believed.

The day she told him she was pregnant, that particular illusion came to an end.

"I'm going to have a baby." She had picked her moment carefully, catching him in a mellow mood.

His eyes narrowed to slits.

"Oh no you're not." His voice was cold steel. Ross Winfield had given an order.

Vi had been prepared for shock, anger and puzzlement, followed sooner or later by cuddles and an eventual accommodation. Surely all those hot words murmured in the sweat of passion had some meaning, conveyed some promise of love. She had not been prepared for this abrupt dismissal.

Ross got out of bed and pulled on his shorts.

She couldn't believe her eyes. He was behaving as though she were invisible. Until that moment she had dithered over whether to press him for marriage or consent to an abortion, but the arrogance of his tone and the sight of him coolly sorting out his clothes filled her with a courage born of desperation.

"I'm a Catholic, you know," she said flatly. "Abortion is a mortal sin."

"So is premarital sex. So if it's your soul you're worried about, you're a little late in the day."

He put on shirt, trousers, socks, shoes, flicked an invisible speck off the jacket of his pinstripe suit. And in that gesture, she saw herself being discarded as indifferently as a bit of lint. She was a temporary blemish on the surface of his existence, a minor nuisance, nothing more.

Speechless with grief, she watched as he adjusted the length of his cuffs, knotted his tie and submitted to a brief inspection in the mirror. Immaculate. Ross nodded approvingly at the reflection, then turned to go. She was powerless to stop him.

"I'm sorry, Vi. I wish you no harm. But this business of yours . . . it has nothing to do with me."

Within her, something snapped. Naked as Eve, she jumped out of bed and pasted herself against the door. He would have to knock her down or peel her off before he could escape.

"You're standing in my face, Vi," he hissed. "Now move . . . before I really get nasty." His fists clenched and unclenched in white-knuckled impatience.

For one terrified moment she thought he would strike her. The itch was there, visible. With his heft, with those powerful muscles she had nuzzled and fawned over, he could break her in half. Oh, God, she could see the headlines . . .

No, not headlines. She was too insignificant a person for that. But certainly a story on page three of the *Post*.

For if she was insignificant, Ross Winfield was not!

Her desperation gave her the courage she required.

"Touch me," she said, "and I'll scream."

"Are you crazy . . . ?" He reached to push her aside.

"One finger on me, I'll scream my head off. And boy, won't the papers lap that up! WALL STREET LAWYER ASSAULTS NUDE IN TIMES SQUARE HOTEL. Jesus, they'll love it at Slater Blaney."

His eyes blazed, and in their depths, she could read a murderous rage. If looks could kill, she was a dead women. It was a glimpse into Ross Winfield's soul she would never forget.

Pure hatred, followed a moment later by a flicker of doubt. Then one of fear, of incipient panic. Would she do it? the eyes asked. Was Vi crazy enough?

He hesitated, then expelled a weary sigh.

"Come on, be reasonable, Vi. Why drag both our names through the mud? It's just stupid. Frankly, I don't know what you expected. We had a couple of laughs, a few funsy rolls in the hay. I got the impression you enjoyed 'em pretty much. Let's face it, you weren't exactly a dewey-eyed virgin when we met . . ."

"No, but I wasn't a whore!" she spat out.

"Look . . ." He backed into the room and sat down cautiously at the edge of the bed. Clearly, she was going to take some doing. "Put on your clothes and we can talk it over."

"Uh uh . . ." She shook her head. Her nakedness was a decided asset. Any moment she could scream her way into notoriety. "No clothes. And I'm being perfectly reasonable. Now, what concrete suggestions do you have to offer?"

"Well . . ." He rooted about for a cigarette. He was uncertain, groping to find the right tone. When he did, his voice was clear and firm, an announcement that he intended to end this nonsense and regain the upper hand. "Well, Vi, I really don't owe you anything. We had an equitable arrangement, but not an exclusive one. For all I know you may have been screwing half the men in the office. No, no, I'm afraid you can't lay this one off on me."

"It's yours," she hissed. "You know damn well it's yours."

Ross shook his head. "I deny it categorically. And if you're thinking paternity suit, forget it. That went out with Charlie Chaplin. However, I might consider—on purely compassionate grounds, mind you—advancing you a sum of money . . . let's call it an interest-free loan. A thousand dollars seems about right on the proviso that you sign a paper declaring me free of all obligation, either moral, legal or financial. I can draw the agreement up this afternoon. You can have

81

your money tomorrow. I would advise you to have the abortion and maybe treat yourself to a little vacation on what's left over. Of course, you're free to spend it as you choose. Considering I have no reason to believe I'm the father of your child, if indeed there is a child, I consider that a generous offer." He crossed his arms with a clear expectation of financial haggling, followed by a coming to terms. But Vi was in no bargaining mood.

"I repeat . . . I am not a whore. I don't take money in return for my favors. And from you especially, I wouldn't take a lousy dime."

He scrutinized her with a puzzled expression.

"Then what do you want if not money?"

"I want you to marry me."

His answer was an incredulous laugh.

"That's right," she repeated. "I want you to marry me and give our baby your name."

"*Me*." He choked down his laughter. "Marry *you*! That's the damnedest thing I ever heard of. Jesus, I can just visualize you at a dinner party for the partner's wives. Little Miss Nobody from Nowhere breaking bread and caviar with the Aldriches and the Van Cortlandts and the Slaters. And for an encore you drink up the finger bowl. No way, babe. Believe me, if and when I marry, it's going to be somebody who looks right for the part. Christ, my bachelorhood is one of my biggest assets. Now come to your senses, girl. We've had some good times together, nothing more . . ."

But in her way, Vi had come to her senses. She had read enough cheap fiction to know that she was in that most classic predicament, and Lord knows he had said everything he could to humiliate her, to remind her of her worthlessness.

And yet, in her life she had never belonged to anyone, never had anyone who belonged to her. Men were shits and Judases from whom one could expect nothing but a kick in the teeth.

But a baby, a child of her own—that was another matter. A child would be her own flesh and blood, someone to be loved without qualms, a possession, a part of herself no one could take away. Yes, she would have her baby. After nineteen years in the wilderness, Vi Hagerty would finally have "family."

Not, however, a bastard like herself, condemned to grow up with the stink of illegitimacy upon it. God forbid. Hers would be a proper child born into wedlock and bearing its father's name.

How alarmed Ross had been when she had threatened to make that scene at the door, scared his tight little world might be coming to an end. What had worked once could work again, now that she knew which button to push.

"OK, Ross, this is how it is. If you don't marry me within a week, I am personally going to everyone who's anyone at Slater Blaney . . . all your precious Aldriches and Van Cortlandts and old man Slater himself—oh, that pillar of high-class society. Yes sir, I'm going to see these dudes and tell 'em that you've been scoring off me lunch hours in every crummy hotel from here to the Battery. Well, buddy, you may be right about paternity suits, but out of court? . . . Forget it. Because there's nothing would frost those old boys more than knowing you've been screwing around below the salt. And that's not the worst of it. You've been doin' it with a kid . . . an ignorant kid. I'm only nineteen years old, after all. A teenager!"

She suddenly widened her big blue eyes and assumed her most virginal expression, and, petite as she was, she looked more like fifteen than nineteen.

" 'Oh, sir,' " she mouthed, " 'where I grew up in the orphanage, the nuns never told me there were men like him. Why, the things he did to me . . .' Believe me, toots, once I go into my act at Slater Blaney, you can kiss good-bye to your ever making partner. Partner, my ass. Chances are they'll can you then and there. Moral turpentine, or whatever you lawyers call it. Now"—she drew a breath—"this is the deal I can offer."

They would marry with neither fuss nor fanfare and never see each other again. No one at Slater Blaney need ever know. After the birth of the baby, she would file for divorce and that would be the end of their connection. As for money, she absolved him of all responsibility, now or ever, and would sign a statement to that effect. All she asked was his name on a birth certificate. And if he wanted to save his career, he had better comply.

In a silent contest of wills, they stared at each other with undisguised hatred. Ross was the first to avert his eyes.

"And now"—Vi rose—"it's time I got dressed. I'll make the wedding arrangements."

Ross's answer was a mute nod.

She had done it, had brazened it out magnificently. Never for a moment had he seen the depth of her fear, the raw throb of her pain. Throughout, the facade had remained in tact. But the moment he left, she fell down on the bed utterly devastated and wept uptil there didn't seem to be a teardrop left in the world.

They were married the following week by a justice of the peace in White Plains. Unthinkingly, they both wore black. It seemed to suit the occasion.

"And that," she told Dom Tarantino, "was the last time I laid eyes on Mr. Ross Winfield, Esquire."

She had quit her job, moved to New Jersey and begun a second existence. The day Noonie was born was the proudest of her life. Little Miss Nobody from Nowhere she may have been, a flyspeck in Ross's spotless world, but she had produced this perfect, wonderful child. From the moment she first held the baby, red-faced and squalling, and pressed him to her body, the months of doubt fell away. Her decision had been the right one.

Not that the succeeding years had been easy. Anything but. Yet she had managed to support them both without taking a penny's worth of welfare, not even when times were toughest, because "I'll be damned if anyone'll call me a charity case." Gradually, she'd fought her way up from near destitution, saved, scrimped, gone to night school, learned the ABC's of real estate. Six months ago, she'd earned her broker's license. It was the second proudest moment of her life.

Now, at last, she could look forward to a measure of financial security for both her and Noonie. Life was going so right.

"And then this!"

She began to tremble uncontrollably.

"I mean, that boy is my life," she cried out. "I'm sorry." She looked down upon her shaking hands and gripped them tight. "This whole business has knocked the bejeezus out of me. I'm OK now."

"Sure?" Dom poured her a glass of water.

"Sure." She mustered a stricken smile.

Now the lawyer leaned back and tugged his ear thoughtfully.

"I wouldn't get overanxious if I were you. Winfield may not be serious. Could be he's just sending up a trial balloon."

"Oh," Vi said, "he's serious. I know his tone. And what the hell . . . I guess if his wife can't have children, then Noonie is all the little Winfields he's ever going to have. Ross can be one tough cookie. Besides, he's probably never forgiven me for what happened in that hotel room."

"Well, you're a tough cookie too," Dom assured her. "Offhand I would say there's nothing to worry about. You've been a responsible mother, there's no question about your competence to raise the child . . ."

"And Noonie's foul mouth and sloppy sneakers . . . ?"

Dom shrugged. "Doesn't amount to a hill of beans."

"Or the fact that I've . . . well, I haven't exactly been a vestry virgin . . . I mean there have been guys . . . And"—the thought struck her—"if Winfield's hiring private detectives, he could probably try to show I'm unfit. I wouldn't put it past him."

"Have you ever been in trouble with the police?"

She shook her head no.

"Then I doubt that would be a factor. These are enlightened times."

Vi breathed a sigh of relief.

"However," Dom continued, "there has been a tendency lately for the courts to award joint custody if the nonresident parent puts up a fight, and it might be realistic of you to consider it. Especially where, I gather, he's a pretty hot-shot lawyer himself. And you certainly can't deprive him of visiting rights. After all, the man has established a suitable home, I would presume a very prosperous one. And there is, as you've ensured, no question of paternity. Suppose the boy were to spend the occasional weekend or holiday with his father . . . would that be such a disaster?"

"To me it would," Vi snapped. "I hate that man and everything he stands for. Cold-blooded . . . social-climbing. And my God, so successful. He's a partner now, he says. He drives a Porsche. Well, I don't want Noonie making comparisons between what Ross has to offer and what I have. Ross is rich, powerful. Kids that age . . . you can dazzle 'em with a ride in a fancy sports car or a couple of dips in the swimming pool. Where does that leave me? Listen . . . I don't want that man having equal say in how Noonie is raised or what kind of school he goes to. I don't want the bastard even to have access. Noonie's mine!"

"Ouch!" The lawyer pursed his lips. "You're making it tough for me. However, let's start out on the assumption that Winfield won't pursue the matter. I'll write him a tactful letter and stall for time."

"Yeah," Vi said doubtfully. She got up to go, feeling ineffably depressed. "Stall him as long as you can. Tell me, Dom, would it make any difference if I were married?"

"How do you mean?"

"Well, you were saying Ross can offer him a suitable home. If I were married to someone substantial, if I had a proper house and the boy had a proper stepfather, would that help? I mean if worst came to worst and that bastard tried to get joint custody."

"Oh, I trust it won't come to court, Vi."

"But if it did?"

"It wouldn't hurt."

She offered Dom her hand.

"Thanks, hon." She smiled. "I know you're gonna do your best."

She left the office thinking maybe Sherm was right. Maybe the boy did need a father—as long as that father wasn't Ross Winfield.

5

MEDI-TEKK INC. WAS A LOW BOXY STRUCTURE OF GLASS AND cinder block, indistinguishable in a landscape of factories and warehouses. The place looked, Annie thought, as though it had been run up by a child with building blocks on a rainy afternoon. The effect was neither sinister (as she had somehow anticipated) nor prestigious. A far cry certainly from the high-tech design of the logo and letterhead that declared the company's state-of-the art image to the world.

Obtaining access, however, required a bit more muscle. First you had to identify yourself to get past the outer gate.

"You looking for somebody?" The guard had unwelcoming eyes.

"I'm here to see Seth Petersen."

He punched a series of numbers into the computer, then frowned. "Dr. Petersen isn't expecting anyone."

"I'm his wife." Annie stuck her head out of the cab. "He asked me to pop around any time. I wasn't aware I needed an appointment."

The guard made a phone call lasting several minutes before pressing the buzzer that allowed the taxi to pass.

Once inside the lobby, closed-circuit television took over, monitoring her every movement. Should one manage to elude the electronic eye, there was still a uniformed guard to cope with.

Medi-Tekk, clearly, was not a place that encouraged the casual visitor, and for a moment Annie was tempted to call it quits. But a few minutes later, Seth himself strode into the lobby at a brisk pace, coat half-unbuttoned. He looked harried.

"Hello, darling." He pecked her cheek. "This is a surprise."

Annie flushed. "It looks as if I've caught you at a bad time."

Seth hesitated for an instant, then grinned. "No worse than any other. Welcome to the madhouse. It's OK, Sam"—he nodded to the guard. "I'm just going to show my wife around. Although you'll have to sign in, love. Same procedure for everybody."

A moment later, she was being ushered into the elevator, then down a series of immaculate corridors into a small bright office.

"I was rather hoping you could give me the grand tour." She smiled. "Aren't I going to get the chance to meet the whole gruesome cast of characters in the flesh after everything I've heard?"

"Sure, if you like. In a bit." He took her coat, then asked the girl in the outer office to bring them some coffee and hold his calls. "But what brings you out here on such a gorgeous day? I thought you were having lunch with your girl friend. Is something up?"

"Oh dear. I thought I had an open invitation." How well Seth knew her. He had sensed that she had come with something on her mind. "But yes, actually. I would like to talk something over with you, although it can certainly wait until you get home."

"That could be pretty late. Meanwhile you're here . . . I'm here." Seth settled into his chair. "So . . . what seems to be the problem?"

She was about to recount the details of her lunch with Lainie when the door opened to admit a dark-haired woman in her early twenties. Even the shapeless lab coat couldn't disguise the voluptuousness of the body beneath it. With a sense of unease, Annie took in the black hair, the lustrous eyes, the youthful bloom of olive skin.

"I'm sorry, Seth." The newcomer appeared startled. "I didn't realize you had company. But . . . I had something to ask you."

Seth motioned her in. "Annie darling, I'd like you to meet Chandra Patel, of whom you've heard me speak so often. Chandra, this is my wife."

Did Annie imagine it, or was the girl miffed at finding her there? If so, she quickly regained her equanimity.

"How do you do, Mrs. Petersen." Chandra smiled, displaying tiny white teeth, then gave Annie a businesslike shake. Close up, she reeked of a musky perfume. "If I can just borrow your husband for a minute."

Without further ado, she began a low-pitched dissertation filled

88

with jargon, peppered with questions. Even had Annie been able to catch every word, it would have meant nothing, for the matter under discussion appeared to be highly technical. From time to time, Seth nodded or mumbled something in return. Certainly there was nothing untoward in the girl's behavior.

And yet, their tête-à-tête disturbed Annie. She felt that Chandra was staging a power display for her benefit, establishing a beachhead, as it were, and staking her claim.

Look, these professional hummings seemed to declare. *Look how intimately Seth and I can communicate on matters from which you are totally excluded. In this place, at this time*—each bob of Chandra's head made the statement—*I am the insider and you the intruder.* The conversation lasted only five minutes, and at its end, Seth waved a hand of good-natured dismissal.

"You can handle it yourself, Chandra." He smiled at her. "I have every confidence."

"Thank you." The girl glowed. "Good-bye, Mrs. Petersen. So charmed to have met you." She brushed Annie on her way out, time enough for another whiff of perfume.

"That's a very pretty girl," she remarked when the door closed. For a moment, she submitted to a twinge of jealousy.

"If you say so." Seth shrugged. "And now"—he settled himself behind his desk—"tell me what you've been up to."

He heard Annie out—or so it seemed to her—with only half an ear, doodling on a scratch pad as she spoke. "I *do* have your attention, don't I?" she asked at one point.

"Undivided." He put down the pencil. "There's this ancient Russian lady who is the world's greatest vocal coach . . ."

"If she'll accept me," Annie cautioned. "And then of course, there's the question of money."

She named the fee, expecting a protest, but Seth made no comment.

"It's practically our entire household budget," she temporized. "Perhaps I'll sit on it for a while."

"Sit on it!" he burst out. "Ye gods, didn't you do enough sitting down south? What do you think, Annie . . . that opportunity is going to come knocking at your door while you sit tight? No, ma'am. You have to go out there and grab it."

"But the expense . . ."

"Fuck the expense! What's money for if not to buy us the things we want? For Chrissakes, Annie . . . seize the day."

Not for the first time, she envied Seth his knack for swift, decisive action. Instead she waffled. "I need time to think it through."

"You spend too much time thinking." Seth resumed his doodling. "What's the worst that can happen? She won't love you? Your feelings will be hurt? If you can't stand up to a rejection, you shouldn't go for an operatic career."

"Maybe I shouldn't. It was so easy when we were in Texas," she said wryly. "I could rationalize and say—well, of course if I hadn't been bogged down here, I might have been this, that and the other thing. I might have been a world-class artist. Sure . . . why not? Because there's no problem hanging on to your illusions, as long as you're never put to the test. And then, of course"—her voice trembled—"I thought we'd have children, and then I wouldn't need any alibis . . ."

"I hear what you're saying, Annie," Seth broke in softly. "You're saying that you're afraid. Well, sweetie, who the hell isn't, from time to time? But I'll be damned if I'm going to let you cop out. Not after we've come this far. Could be you're another Maria Callas. Or maybe you're just a good, run-of-the-mill soprano. I'm no judge, but surely you owe it to yourself to find out whether you've got the makings. Go audition for the woman, Annie. She either takes you on or she doesn't. It's that simple."

"Suppose she doesn't?" Annie projected. "Suppose I bomb out?"

"Suppose you do? It's not the end of the world. Jesus, Annie, if I felt like that, I'd have thrown in the sponge years ago. Nobody bats a thousand, not in baseball, not in music or science, anything that really matters. If what's-her-name turns you down, you'll find someone else. I'm sure there are plenty of terrific coaches in New York."

"I don't know." A wave of anxiety engulfed her. "I have such mixed feelings about entering the fray after this time. Especially after seeing Lainie. She was the best of us, there she is ten years on and scuffling. You're right, Seth . . . it is scary, and I'm not sure I have the stomach for it." She stopped suddenly. "Funny, I wanted it all—children and career, now it looks like I may not be getting any of it. Sometimes I feel . . . oh, I don't know—paralyzed. Like one of your mice. Give me time, Seth. I want to think about it some more."

Seth studied her for a moment, then got up. "Come on, love, I'll show you around the joint."

He took her through his lab, which looked like every other lab she'd ever seen with its array of sinks and glassware and centrifuges, showed her the conference room, the computer mainframe. Security was paramount. Doors opened to coded passwords. Elaborate disposal systems flushed away dangerous waste. Each floor possessed its own document shredder, lest trade secrets fall into unauthorized hands.

Not a cozy place, Annie decided.

En route, Seth introduced her to those of his co-workers they happened upon. He was polite if somewhat perfunctory, but Annie found the encounters fascinating. At last she could put faces to the names Seth talked about. As she smiled and shook hands she remembered his private assessments.

There was the bright-eyed, wispy-haired Dorrie Metzger ("she's totally into cocaine"); the sleek and smiling Jeff Burns ("the prototypical corporate suck-up"); René Legros fresh from the Sorbonne ("an ego that spans two continents"); the black-bearded Hal Milius ("that psychopath"); and ultimately, Seth's favorite bête noire, Gene Leavitt.

"Pleased to meetcha." Leavitt shifted an unlit cigar from one side of his mouth to the other while giving Annie a skeptical once-over. "I didn't know Seth was married."

How dare the man! Annie's gorge rose. How dare he make such a gratuitous remark, insinuating that Seth was passing himself off as a bachelor? She turned on her heels and walked away.

For the rest, however, Seth's co-workers appeared an unremarkable lot: no snarling Mengeles or Dr. Frankensteins among them. Yet she was sensitive to the mood of the place, somber and sterile, with its undercurrent of nervous tension.

Seth buzzed for the elevator. "I'm taking you to the basement, where the animals are kept." There was pride in his voice. "I'd like to show you my mice."

Instinctively Annie recoiled.

She understood the need for experimental animals. In theory it was inarguable, people being more important than animals. In any discussion with antivivisectionists, she would fly to Seth's defense.

"My husband is trying to relieve the world's suffering, not add to it," she would argue. "As it happens, he's fond of animals. We keep a cat ourselves, you know."

But despite the rationale, the actual business repelled her.

Once, early in their marriage, she had gone to visit him in the labs, when, from behind a door marked NO ENTRY, the heartrending howl of an animal made her freeze in her tracks. Curiosity overcame prudence. Like Bluebeard's wife, she opened the door to find more than she had reckoned on.

The room was a preview of hell, packed with caged dogs of every size and breed, twitching, writhing, in varying degrees of suffering and consciousness. Most of the dogs had plastic inserts in their skulls. Others were catheterized. A pure-bred cocker with a head full of electrodes looked at Annie with imploring eyes.

A technician shouted and shooed her out, but not before Annie had become violently sick. For months after, the sound of their howls, the pain in their eyes, had turned her dreams into nightmares.

"I'm sorry you had to see that," Seth had said at the time. "They've been doing tests on pain, unpleasant but highly productive. Those are stray dogs, you know, not anyone's pets. If they weren't here, they'd have been put down by now."

But they must have been somebody's pets at some time, must have known love and caresses. She had never gone back to that lab again.

But today, Seth took her hand. "We're only going to look at some mice, Annie. And I promise you won't see any blood and gore. In fact, you might be pleasantly surprised."

He inserted a coded card into a slot. The door swung open.

She followed him into a long low room lined with portable glass cages, each housing a small number of mice in varying stages of health, from the lively to the twitching to the decidedly moribund. The only sound was the white hum of the air conditioning and the click of her heels on the tile flooring. Mercifully, mice don't howl.

There must have been a hundred cages in all. She fought down a residual desire to avert her eyes until they were well out of here. But that was unfair to Seth. They're only mice, she told herself, hardly better than vermin.

"Are these all yours, Seth?"

He nodded. "Yup, I keep my animals separate." He stopped before a cage, checking its label. "Here we go . . . SP Lot 31-B."

With one easy sweep he pulled it off the shelf and placed it on a trestle table, motioning Annie to a seat on the bench.

"Take a look, love. What do you think?"

In the cage, a dozen mice, brown-coated and pink-nosed, were skittering about, upset by the abruptness of the move, but otherwise looking hardly different from the mice she used to trap in the garage back in Galveston. Of course, she knew, these weren't house mice, but valuable hybrids, one of the many hundreds of special strains, each bred generation after generation for a single useful talent: in Seth's case, their ability to contract his experimental disease.

Seth reached in through an opening at the top and picked one up, holding it in the palm of his hand.

"OK, baby." He stroked the smooth fur gently with his thumb. "Calm down. No one's going to hurt you."

The captive creature responded with a series of barely audible squeaks.

Out of sheer relief, Annie gave a nervous giggle. Thank God there were to be no horror shows.

"You look like Lennie in *Of Mice and Men*." She moved in for a closer look. "He's kind of cute," she admitted, "if you're into mice."

"Cute!" Seth laughed. "Come on, you can do better than that. Where are your descriptive powers, Annie?"

"Well, healthy, as far as I can see. Certainly very skittish."

As if to confirm her judgment, the mouse nearly bolted out of Seth's hand.

"OK, fella," He slipped the creature back into the cage. "That's it for the day. Yup . . . a very peppy animal."

Annie looked at her Seth's face. It was transfigured. She sucked in her breath.

"You don't mean to tell me that mouse was suffering from EAE! Incredible. He didn't appear the least bit paralytic. In fact, he looked like he could go a few rounds with Runaway Max."

Seth returned the cage to its shelf, then sat down beside her on the bench.

"It's almost too good to be true." He glanced up to the ceiling, where a television eye was installed, then instinctively lowered his voice to a whisper.

"I began a new treatment on this batch a few weeks ago, a slightly different formulation in the antibodies, very delicate . . . very elegant stuff. But my God, the results have been startling. I'm not talking remission, either. I'm talking the actual reversal of paralysis. Of course, it's early days yet, but . . ."

"Have you told Marriner yet?" She couldn't help but echo the thrill in his voice.

He nodded slowly. "I will, darling. I sure as shit will. I'm not sitting on this one. Anyhow"—he got up—"I have a lot of work to do today, so if you don't mind, I'll call you a cab."

He kissed her, then glanced up at the monitor and winked.

"Are we on television?" Annie laughed.

"Uh huh . . . but that's OK." He patted her rump. "No one ever watches the damn thing."

On the taxi ride back to Manhattan her mood was ambivalent, anxiety mixed with exhilaration. About her own career she was hesitant; a lot of hard thinking lay ahead. Her concern of the moment was with Seth's.

Wonderful if this was really the long-awaited breakthrough. No one deserved success more. Yet despite his optimism, despite the evidence of her eyes, she was infected with a faint sense of dread. Suppose it was a dud? What if this turned into yet one more occasion for disappointment and heartbreak? She had seen it happen time and again: high hopes dashed, promising experiments gone awry. It was a familiar last act.

Nobody bats a thousand, as he had reminded her earlier, and scientists especially seemed to score distressingly low, defeats outnumbering triumphs with grim regularity. Yet it was hard not to admire Seth's resilience, his drive.

Have more confidence, he said, as though it were a commodity you picked off the shelf like a bag of sugar. But that self-belief came easily to Seth. He had been raised in optimism, she to a heritage of caution.

Doubts assailed her. Had she married Seth, she wondered, to avoid any chance of falling smack on her face in Germany? If so, it was an unconscious decision. That last night in Boston, she felt that love had conquered all; but love could be used as a crutch, a flight from the struggle. Perhaps she had taken the easy way out.

Nor was Seth's baseball analogy lost on her. Nobody batted a thousand, but a great many people batted zero. The way not to lose was simply not to play the game at all. Of course, as Seth would have pointed out, you couldn't win that way either.

She arrived home still undecided about the wisdom of submitting herself and her talents to the scrutiny of Madame Natasha. It had been a mistake to broach the subject to Seth. Poor Seth! He had enough on his plate already.

Let sleeping dreams lie, her heart seemed to caution. One success in the family will be quite enough. Maybe her mother was right after all. With luck, Annie would sing to her babies.

He came home very late the following night with a look of total exhaustion.

"Nope, no dinner." He flung himself down on the sofa. "But be an angel, will you, and bring me a king-sized Scotch. Better yet, how about having one with me?"

She returned a few minutes later, drinks in hand, to find him fishing through his pockets, pulling out bits of paper here and there, straightening the crumpled scraps out on the surface of the cocktail table.

"Ah, here we are," he said when she sat down. "OK, you have an appointment with this Liadoff-Grey a week from Tuesday. You should be there at noon. That's . . . um"—he squinted at his handwriting—"at the Osborne, Fifty-seventh Street corner of Seventh."

"Seth!" Annie's eyes opened in wonder.

"She says bring your own accompanist. OK." He straightened out another chit. "I called Juilliard and they recommended this Israeli fellow, he's a student there, but apparently with a lot of experience working with singers. Young man's name is Ari Ben-Ilan and he sounded pleasant enough on the phone. He'll be here tomorrow at ten. Now about pianos . . . Steinway says they have plenty of instruments for rent, although I don't see how you're going to be able to squeeze a grand in here. But an upright, certainly. Yup, we could move the TV into the bedroom and put it up against that wall. They started to give me an argument about delivery dates, but I told 'em it was a rush. Anyhow, they can have a piano here next week. But first, of course, you'll have to go and try 'em out. I think it might be a good idea if you take Ben-Ilan up there with you tomorrow morning, and the two of you could pick a good one ... Now, somewhere in here I've got the name of a couple of other accompanists just in case this Ari guy doesn't work out ..."

But Seth never got to finish his sentence, for Annie was suddenly in his arms, the tears streaming down her cheeks with abandon.

"I can't believe you." She wept with happiness. "I can't believe how wonderful you are!"

"Oh, come on, Annie!" Seth was pleased and slightly embarrassed. "All I did was make a few phone calls. You're the one who's going to do the work. You just needed a little shove." Then he put his arms around her for a mammoth hug. "It'll be good, darling. I can feel it in my bones."

They clung together, kissing, rocking gently, in a closeness too perfect to be marred by speech. At last Annie disentangled herself.

"Wow!" She wiped her eyes. "Do I ever need that drink!"

Already her mind was racing through the repertoire, culling music from here and there that would show her to the greatest advantage. Smart thing would be to open with something pure and uncluttered, a little Schubert perhaps. Then maybe a good solid chunk of Verdi, since Madame Natasha was the expert on Italian opera. "Pace Pace" ... or better yet, the Willow Song from *Otello*. Yes, the Willow. Suited her voice perfectly. Trick was, getting the right tempo ... most singers tended to drag, but she didn't feel that was in character with Desdemona. She'd have to talk it over with this accompanist ...

Seth watched her for a few minutes with a bemused smile. Then he broke her reverie. "Anyhow, that was *your* day. Now, would you like to hear about *my* day?"

"I'm sorry." She jerked herself back into the present. "I was just ... well, let's say you took me by storm. Juilliard ... Steinway ... my God, you must have been on the phone all day! Did you manage to get any work done?"

"Did I ever! You know, after I finished making those calls, it hit me: Here I am, taking a few basic steps to promote your career, being the dynamic executive, so to speak, not because I don't think you're perfectly capable, but because you needed that extra little push. Who doesn't have doubts, Annie? But with all that noise, what was I doing for myself? Nothing! Zilch. Sitting around like a plain girl at a prom, waiting for Mr. Wonderful to descend from Olympus and maybe . . . just *maybe* ask me to dance. What crap! I could grow old waiting. Old and bitter. Well, Annie, I decided it was time to take my own advice. I figured, what have I got to lose . . . my job? Better that than lose my self-respect. Bold measures." He grinned. "There comes a time when nothing less will do."

Every Friday afternoon, the dozen members of the Plans Board, under the direction of Gerald Marriner, clustered around the oval cherrywood table in the fourth floor conference room to chart the future of Medi-Tekk. It was here, Seth said, where the white coats and the three-piece suits got together. "Because the fact is, sweetie, the MBAs carry as much clout in that room as the Ph.Ds. More maybe, this place owing as much to venture capital as to science."

It was at these confidential sessions of top management that priorities were thrashed out, funds allocated or brutally cut, promotions approved, dismissals agreed upon, power manifested in its various forms.

You only appeared by invitation, Seth told her, if the board members had specific questions that needed answering. As a matter of policy, their deliberations were secret.

"Well," Seth told Annie, "I figured it was time I made my move."

Shortly after five, when he was certain all the principals were assembled, he had simply barged into the room with a great slamming of oaken doors, bearing two cages of mice. A bomb might have gone off more quietly.

"Gentlemen," he announced to the astonished board members, "if you refuse to hear me out, I shall simply let these mice loose into the conference room and be done with the lot of you." There was a horrified gasp.

"However"—he smiled graciously—"if you will allow me five

minutes, I will show you something that will warm your hearts as scientists and, I would hope, as stockholders too."

At the far end of the table, Gerald Marriner surveyed him with unflappable calm.

"Go ahead, Seth." He nodded. "Tell us what this is all about."

At that moment, Seth felt as though he had won a reprieve from the electric chair.

"I can tell you now, Annie. I was a lot scareder than I sounded. You, me, Runaway Max . . . I had visions of us all out on the street."

Gently, he placed both cages in the center of the table, taking care not to scratch the antique gloss.

Both sets of mice, he explained, had been injected with the experimental disease simultaneously. In the first cage were the control mice, animals in which the disease had been allowed to develop untreated. "Already one has died. The survivors, as you can see for yourself, are weak, paralytic, in other words, normal symptoms. However, in this cage—" The hush was total now, all eyes on the busy scurrying rodents, who, like Seth, were nervous in these unfamiliar surroundings.

He said nothing more. Merely stepped back to let his specimens make his point more eloquently than any words could have done. Marriner himself was the first to respond. As Seth had done the day before, he reached into the cage and held up a sample animal for closer inspection.

"He was thunderstruck, Annie. I don't know how else to put it to you. I swear the man looked as though he'd just seen the face of God."

And then it was pandemonium. For over two hours, the board had Seth on the carpet questioning each step of the procedure mercilessly. How? When? Through what techniques? The board didn't miss a trick, determined to find any catch if one existed.

"I tell you, I haven't been taken over the coals like that since I did my orals."

"And . . ." Annie said breathlessly. "And then what?"

"And then what?" he echoed gleefully. "Isn't that enough for one day? You know, ducks, this is just the first step down the path. We're looking at seven years, assuming all goes well, until FG-75 hits the market."

"FG-75!" she explained. "Is that what you're calling the substance? Sounds more like an airplane to me."

"You're close. The actual moniker runs about three hundred syllables, you could grow old just getting your tongue around it. We needed a working name for quick reference. Well, I thought about it a while and decided, what the hell . . . I'd pick a name that wouldn't mean a damn thing to anyone but us two. Strictly private. The FG, Annie . . . and if you tell anyone I'll never speak to you again"—he chuckled—"the FG stands for Flash Gordon."

Annie burst out laughing. "And the 75 is the year that we met. Oh, Seth, you are an absolute lunatic and I love you."

He poured them both another round of Scotch.

"Of course, at some point a marketing director or medical copywriter or whoever will brainstorm to come up with a commercial name for the trademark. Something catchy and suitably highsounding. But first . . ."

There was an exhaustive procedure that must be followed before the drug gained approval by the FDA.

The process began with preclinical and animal testing which had only now commenced. Then came Phase One. This was the initial clinical test performed on a group of human subjects, numbering between ten and twenty. Should Phase One prove effective, they proceeded to Phase Two, this time involving some two hundred patients. Barring adverse reaction, they proceeded to Phase Three, enlisting even greater numbers. Only after all these clinical trials were completed and evaluated would they enter the final stage.

At this point, accompanied by perhaps a hundred thousand pages of documentation, Medi-Tekk would file its application for newdrug approval. The review would take two years, during which the Food and Drug Administration would scrutinize the data, poke for holes, perform their own exhaustive tests on every aspect of the drug. At last, the agency handed down its ruling. Your formulation could be *approved* (in which case you were in business); *approvable* (subject to certain limitations); or it could be rejected out of hand.

About one drug in a hundred met the FDA's exacting standards for approval, yet in his heart, Seth believed his "baby" would be that one.

"Of course"—he grinned—"I'll be an old man of forty by then."

"In the meanwhile . . ."

"In the meanwhile—" He clinked her glass, then placed his own back on the table, too excited even to drink. "This really ought to be champagne. Sweetheart!" Unable to suppress his jubilation for even one second more, Seth jumped to his feet, clasped his hands above his head in the time-honored manner of champions.

"You're looking at the new Golden Boy of Medi-Tekk."

PART
TWO

I

STOCKHOLM WAS BITTER ON THIS DECEMBER DAY. THE SUN HAD set by three o'clock, such sun as there had been, and the darkness merely added to the intensity of the cold.

But here inside the vast hall, everything was brilliance and warmth.

From his post in the elegantly appointed anteroom, he could only hear, not see, the vast crowd that filled the hall, yet the hum of the audience wrote its own description. They were happy. Excited. As was he.

Suddenly the world fell silent. Then, a fanfare of trumpets announced that the king himself had entered the hall, followed by the royal family and their retinue. He could hear the whoosh as two thousand spectators, resplendent in evening dress and jewels, arose as one to pay homage.

His Majesty must have taken his seat.

Once more the trumpets broadcast their clarion call. The grand march began.

At last! He adjusted his tie more to quiet the trembling of his hands than for any other reason, then took his place in what must surely be the most elite line of men and women ever assembled.

They began their progress through the portals onto the stage, two by two, moving with measured step across the rich carpeting to where a row of red-velvet chairs stood empty and expectant. On the stage great banks of white mums and carnations added their sweet scent to the mingle of expensive perfumes.

He entered. And now, it was the king himself who rose in homage.

Smoothly, flawlessly, for each moment of the evening had been carefully rehearsed, he took his place in the front row of chairs, then searched the festooned loge to where his wife would be sitting.

There she was, magnificent in cerulean velvet and diamonds, a clutch of sable round her throat. Amid the dazzle of the chandeliers, he found her eyes, her lips. Never had she looked more radiant.

Proud of you, that beautiful mouth seemed to say. *My darling, I am so wonderfully proud of you.*

There were the speeches, of course, the traditional protocol, all the pomp and ceremony for which the occasion was famous, while the television cameras recorded the ritual for posterity. Then Dr. Bjorgsson of the Karolinska Institute addressed the hall. In Swedish, of course, but beyond doubt the speech included Alfred Nobel's own ringing words: *to those who shall have conferred the greatest benefit on mankind.*

Now it was time to rise, step forward. In but a moment the royal hand itself would place the precious gold medallion into his own.

Now. Now! His heart fluttered in ecstasy. Now they were calling his name. Gerald . . . Gerald . . .

"Gerald." A small, firm hand shook his shoulder. "Gerald, wake up. We have guests coming in twenty minutes and you're not even dressed."

"I wasn't asleep." He stirred in the depths of the armchair. "Just thinking . . ."

"Woolgathering is more like it." Margot laughed. "Anyhow, they'll be here at eight. What do you think?" She spun around for his approval. "Do I look all right?"

His eyes lit with admiration. "Fabulous, darling . . . as always."

"I didn't want to wear anything too elaborate." She smoothed down the soft fullness of the Valentino skirt, as simple as it was expensive. "I don't want to make the wife feel uncomfortable. And you did say, I should be extra nice to them, didn't you, darling? Now, while I have no objection to your being casual too, I do draw the line at your greeting them in a dressing gown. Come on, Gerald, get ready."

He pulled himself to his feet. Lord, he was tired. These last few weeks had been grueling.

"Are we eating here or dining out, Margot?"

"Out. I thought we'd have a drink here to warm up, then I've made reservations at Windows on the World. Out-of-towners always seem to enjoy the view. Texans did you say they were, darling? Yes, I think a little Manhattan glitter should be a refreshing change after all that flatland. I have a mental picture of Stetsons and cowboy boots for him, and for her, all sequins and teased hair. Maybe I should get gussied up after all."

"You've been watching 'Dallas,' I can tell." Gerald laughed. "However, I don't think the Petersens qualify for authentic Texas. He's from the midwest by way of Harvard, very well spoken, and the wife—I believe—sings. I couldn't say about the teased hair, but knowing Seth, I doubt it."

"Right!" She planted a kiss on his nose. "I'll go down and see about drinks."

He watched her leave with a whoosh of silk, then sat down in the armchair again. Women . . . he smiled fondly. They always assumed it took a full hour to get dressed. He could rest a few minutes more.

For a moment he shut his eyes and permitted himself the luxury of that daydream recaptured. Stockholm. The prize. The immortality.

It was a dream that had nourished him in his youth, in those dark days when he had been a fighter pilot in Korea, in those lean years when he had been going through Johns Hopkins on the GI Bill. The first years on the faculty at Yale.

The hope of becoming a Nobel laureate had not seemed so fanciful then, when all the world was singing his praises. When he was winning more prizes than he had shelf room for, breaking every university record for achievement. "Not bad," he was fond of saying, "for a bricklayer's son." He had felt himself at the edge of the ultimate dream.

By the time he was thirty, he had published papers without number, important papers that set the standards of research within his discipline. At thirty-five he enjoyed that consummate award of the American establishment, election to the Academy of Sciences, one of its youngest members ever. And the years between then and now were just so many more chapters in one of the most brilliant careers of a generation. The directorship of Medi-Tekk. The Lasker Award. The Presidential Citation. And marriage to one of the world's most beautiful women.

To say that Gerald Marriner was a failure was patently absurd. He had virtually everything a man his age could desire. In England, his wife assured him, his merits would have earned him a knighthood.

His writings were read and quoted everywhere. He was a superb administrator, the idol of his staff as he had once been the idol of his students, on the board of half a dozen institutions, the friend and confidant of presidents and celebrities alike.

Through his wife he had wealth beyond avarice; through the happy chemistry of her beauty and his own accomplishments, he had arrived at a secure niche in American society. He went everywhere, knew everyone.

What more, then, could this man—this cultured, witty man, surrounded as he was by friends and admirers, blessed with all the gifts and graces of his time—what more could he possibly ask for?

Only this. Only the small priceless gold medallion in its leather case and the immortality that prize conferred. To enter the history books alongside that great roster of laureates—Pavlov, Curie, Fleming, Crick, Watson; to change the face of medicine and be remembered as a benefactor to mankind: surely not even sainthood provided a higher reward. With every atom of his being, he longed to have his name pass into common currency, linked forever with some great and tangible boon.

Mention Curie, and the man in the street would think of the blessings of radium. Say Fleming, and the world nodded a thankful "penicillin." Say Dr. Gerald Marriner, and the response that came to mind was, "Oh, isn't he the fellow who married Margot Trent?"

Yet even before he'd met his wife, well before he turned forty, he'd begun to despair of ever joining the immortals. With every passing year, hope diminished.

Science is a young man's game, he knew, and the great creative breakthroughs come—often as not—in that first dazzling flush of youth. Einstein was twenty-two when he formulated the theory of relativity, James Watson shy of thirty when he confounded the world by breaking the DNA code.

As the clock ran out, Gerald Marriner inwardly acknowledged he would never join their numbers. That much had been clear to him twenty years ago. For all his brilliance, despite the mountain of published papers, the growing list of honors, he lacked that divine surge of creativity that marks the titan.

A splendid organizer, yes. An administrator second to none. A man with a genius for discerning merit in the works of others. Yet somewhere along the line, the creative juices had run dry. Or perhaps they had never existed.

Thus the time had come to pack away the dream, forget it, pretend it didn't matter. Gerald accepted his limitations, for he liked to think himself a realist, far too pragmatic to spend his life waiting for a train that would never arrive.

And then, but a week ago, this brash young man from Texas, all youth and hot passion, had charged into his life to the sound of distant trumpets. Broken in without so much as a by-your-leave and commanded Gerald to dust off the ancient dream and live with it once more.

Oh, what a glorious moment that had been, for all of Petersen's outrageous behavior. Threatening to set loose his pack of mice on a roomful of middle-aged gentlemen, indeed. Such gall! Gerald could hardly recall the incident without shaking his head. Such style, too!

Yes, it had been a dazzling bit of hocus-pocus. But the evidence was there, despite the shock of presentation, and he recognized its importance in a blinding flash.

In retrospect, he could kick himself for having neglected Seth Petersen all these months. What would it have been to answer the phone calls, invite the man around for drinks? True, he scanned Petersen's weekly reports, and of late they had shown some promise. In fact, he'd been meaning to look in on the lad one of these days, but the truth was Gerald had never been fully committed to that particular line of research. Gene Leavitt had convinced him it wasn't fruitful, and Leavitt was a gifted young man.

However, there was yet time to make amends, and with Margot at his side, he would soon have the Petersens eating out of his hand. Moreover, he liked the fellow.

The little brass carriage clock chimed quarter past eight.

Gerald Marriner put on a jacket and a smile and went downstairs to greet his guests.

On an East Side block lined with million-dollar brownstones, the Marriner residence appeared neither more bumptious nor more modest than its neighbors. Appearances deceived.

Stepping inside, Annie took one look at the vast center hall, with its vistas of rooms leading into rooms leading into rooms, and concluded that the facade had concealed not a mere million-dollar brownstone, but at least three such run together. A mid-city mansion, complete with ballroom and book-lined library. Who thought such things existed anymore?

A divinely elegant Englishman in full regalia, looking more like an earl than a butler, had answered the door, satisfied himself as to the visitors' identity, then proceeded to relieve Annie of her coat. She handed it over with a wry smile. Was that a raised eyebrow cracking the aristocratic reserve? Had he spotted the Loehmann label? The subway tokens jingling in the pocket? Surely such a magnificent creature had never before sullied his craft by handling such an unprepossessing garment. But his aplomb was superb.

Without further comment, he ushered them down a broad marble hall into a spacious sitting room where a wood fire crackled. Annie seated herself cautiously at the edge of a sofa piled high with needlepoint cushions and looked about her wide-eyed. For all its size, the room radiated warmth and intimacy. And expenditure without restraint.

Great bowls of cut flowers mingled with the scent of woodsmoke. Family pictures brightened the inlaid tables. The walls glistened with Italian paintings in rich gilded frames.

The moment they were alone, she whispered to Seth, "My God, I don't believe my eyes. Have we stumbled into Xanadu? Or is this what we can normally expect when your next raise comes through?"

But the joke fell flat, for this display of naked wealth was awesome. It went beyond the trappings of mere success into the realm of fantasy, bearing no relation to any world that Annie knew. The image came to mind of Renaissance princes, or of the great robber barons of a century ago, mindlessly accumulating their piles of treasure.

Had Gerald Marriner, in his experiments at Medi-Tekk, stumbled upon the secret that scientists had pursued throughout the Middle Ages, found the philosopher's stone that transmutes base substance into gold? Or had she and Seth come to the wrong place? She rubbed her eyes in disbelief.

"Did you expect anything like this, Seth?"

But her husband was too bemused to answer, intent upon a small but lovely painting of Madonna and Child in a gold rococo frame. He finally stood back and sighed. "That's a Veronese. Imagine . . . owning a Veronese! And that's a Titian."

Annie looked to him for enlightenment.

"Did you expect . . . *this*, Seth?" she repeated.

Seth shook his head. "It's not Marriner, I don't think. It must belong to his wife."

"Who is she . . . a Rothschild? A Rockefeller?"

He suddenly smiled. "I thought you knew. I must have mentioned it at some point. Gerald Marriner is married to . . ."

His voice suddenly dropped to nothingness, for across the expanse of Kirgiz came the most beautiful woman Annie had ever seen.

Garbo? Elizabeth Taylor? Certainly here was beauty of that order, that throat-catching, breath-taking quality that defied comparison with mere mortals. Annie had never before seen it in the flesh. Hair of spun gold, falling simply to the shoulders, Grecian nose, skin translucent as alabaster, luminous eyes of gentian violet. Above all, a kind of incandescence that made you believe the woman might glow in the dark.

Age? Who could tell? Perhaps thirty, perhaps forty, not that it mattered, for such beauty passed the test of timelessness. No. More, Annie decided as this splendid creature came toward them, arms outstretched. Probably nearer fifty.

And now their hostess reached out with a hand for each of her guests, gathering them to her with a sunburst of a smile.

"Annie . . . Seth"—the voice was warm, musical, with the trace of an English accent. "I'm so glad you could come. So terribly glad to meet you after all that Gerald has said."

Annie returned the gentle squeeze of the hand, all the while scouring her memory. *Where do I know her from?* But where *could* she have known her from! In what conceivable situation might she have encountered such a dazzlingly wealthy, dazzlingly beautiful personage—and not remember?

Only on the screen. Yes, that must be it—why thoughts of Garbo and Taylor had sprung to mind. Suddenly, Annie evoked a fleeting image of her hostess in a green bejeweled gown, head thrust back to highlight the long classic throat, the glistening bosom, a golden chalice at her lips . . .

What the hell was the name of that movie? One of those lavish ducats-and-doublets costume dramas it had been, the kind they'd stopped making years ago, boring and expensive, and if you were the least bit high when you watched them, you fell over laughing. Only Annie had fallen asleep instead, she recalled, having caught the first twenty minutes on TV not too long ago.

"Mrs. Marriner . . ."

"Please call me Margot."

Margot what? The name of an English river, wasn't it? Avon? Thames? Ah! now she remembered. That actress who'd snared herself a Greek tycoon.

"You're Margot Trent, aren't you?" The discovery delighted her. What fun tonight promised to be. She had come expecting to be locked into (or more likely, left out of) an evening filled with scientific shoptalk and stumbled into a fugitive from a far more glamorous world. "Of course! I saw you in"—she started to say "an old movie," but that might sound insulting—"in . . . a movie on the 'Late Show' just recently."

Margot rolled her eyes. "*Lucrezia Borgia*! My God, that horror. I still remember the lines . . ."

A butler came in bearing champagne in tulip glasses. Margot waited for her guests to be served, then picked up a glass of bubbly, hoisting it with the same gesture Annie recalled from the movie, then intoned in a mock-sultry whisper: " 'Tonight, my prince, you dine at the Borgias. For you, there will be no tomorrow.' Oh my!" She threw back her head and laughed. "They don't write lines like that any more . . . thank God! I keep telling Gerald we should buy up all the existing prints and destroy them in a huge auto-da-fé, but he says we should put them in a time capsule instead."

"I enjoyed it," Annie lied. "Anyhow, I'm awfully happy to meet you, and frankly—rather relieved you're a civilian. So am I."

"A civilian?"

"Well, that's my term for it. What I meant is, that you're outside the science world, unlike most people we spend time with. You know, I don't believe I've ever met a movie actress before."

"Not an actress." Margot dismissed the notion with a wave of the hand. "Never that. I couldn't act my way out of a paper bag, as they say. What I did, essentially, was stand around in a lot of very heavy garments, with my waist pinched in and my boobs pushed up, trying to remember inane lines of script."

"Now now," Seth intervened. "You're being overly modest. If you refuse to accept the term 'movie actress,' then we shall simply have to say 'movie star.' That much is indisputable."

"How very flattering you are. But yes," Margot considered. "I would acknowledge the word 'star,' although that's really not much of an occupation. Lassie was a star too, you may recall. In any case, I'm pretty much of neither at the moment . . . haven't made a film in thirty years. Ah!" She turned round, the radiant smile growing even more radiant. "Here's Gerald. Well, darling, I foretold you'd be late and so you are."

Seth had prepared Annie for this meeting with considerable fanfare. "He's slick, but I like him. I think you will too."

His early doubts, his feelings of rage and neglect, the long list of unanswered phone calls: all were forgiven now, swept away in the warmth of the older man's enthusiastic patronage. They worked together, lunched together, played squash on occasion. "He treats me like a son," Seth commented. "Besides, the man is really brilliant!" And that, Annie knew, was her husband's highest accolade.

The object of this newfound adulation was a stocky, balding man, with the appearance of a tweedy household Buddha: bright brown eyes beneath a rough hedge of eyebrows, amiable smile, full rounded cheeks that shook when he laughed. His comfortable girth attested to a long-term affection for the good life.

"The famous Annie! Forgive me." He kissed her hand with a gallant flourish. "But I'd nodded off upstairs. Your husband works me too hard at the lab. He's a hard man to keep up with . . . absolute slave driver."

Annie let out a whoop of laughter. Yes, she was going to like the Marriners, husband and wife. She felt it in her bones. His voice was soothing, comforting even as he made small talk, like a country doctor making house calls among friends. He was a physician, Annie reminded herself, as well as a researcher; perhaps that accounted for his air of quiet authority.

The evening passed in a glorious haze. Champagne. Limousines. A table a hundred stories high above Manhattan. Beluga caviar. Breast of guinea hen. A classic Château Lafite. "The world at your feet," Seth toasted her. Then brandies in big snifters at the Carlyle, as Bobbie Short drove away the midnight chill with his music.

Of course the men huddled together, talking shop for much of the evening. That was to be expected. But Margot and she had hit it off from the first. The older woman appeared immensely sympathetic.

"I understand you sing, Annie. Jazz? Musical theater?"

"Opera, actually."

"Aah." Margot sighed and furrowed the perfect brow. "Now, let me think . . . whom do I know that you should meet? Well, Jimmy Levine, of course. And Lenny, but he's out of town . . . Polo Brüning will be in New York next month. I could throw a little dinner for you . . ."

Annie raised an admonitory hand. The thought of her being suddenly thrust into the company of the director of the Metropolitan Opera or the renowned Polonius von Brüning filled her with alarm. It was decidedly premature.

"Good Lord, Margot. I have a lot of work to do before I'd be ready for the heavyweights. Actually," she confided, "I'm auditioning next week for one of the great vocal coaches. Madame Liadoff-Grey."

Margot didn't know the name, but accepted Annie's appraisal.

"Good luck on the day, although you sound a trifle apprehensive."

"I am, a little," Annie admitted. "Does it show?"

"Only to a fellow survivor of auditionitis. There's one malady our lads at Medi-Tekk never really looked into. Excruciatingly painful! I used to suffer from it myself when I was your age. One of the ten dozen reasons I gave up trying to act. But learn from my experience . . ." She leaned forward and placed her hand on Annie's wrist. "The anticipation is always worse than the reality. Promise me you'll let me know how everything turns out and then we can have either a celebratory lunch or a consolation dinner, whichever is appropriate."

The night ended in the small hours, but not before further outings had been planned—a theater foursome, a Sunday brunch date, a shopping excursion ("just the two of us") insisted upon by Margot to see what Adolfo had up his couturier sleeve. It was past three when the Petersens returned to their apartment.

"Bushed!" Seth fell on the bed with his shoes on. In fact, he was far too wound up to sleep.

"Have a good time, love?" He stretched out, hands clasped behind his head, while Annie took off her makeup.

"Terrific! The view...the food. The company. The whole thing. And I particularly like Margot. Not at all snobby or stand-offish. Hardly what you'd expect from a movie star."

"Mmmm..." Seth hummed absentmindedly. "That Château Lafite was superb, although I had my reservations about the raspberry soufflé. Could have been tarter. You know what I was thinking...? Of that last night we spent in Texas. Our farewell bash, remember? All the barbecue you could eat."

The night before their departure, Mark Wilkins had thrown a Texas-style feast for the Petersens, outdoors with trestle tables, beer kegs and a whole side of beef. The entire department had showed up—from typists and technicians to full professors and their wives. The only holdout had been Robert Tarkowsky.

"I can't believe he won't come!"

"Me neither," Annie had said. "There's nothing so awful as a big man being petty. You worked so closely with him, you'd think he'd be proud of you..."

"Well, screw it. He's not going to spoil our last night in Texas."

Tarkowsky aside, it had proved to be the kind of occasion every ego deserves at least once in a lifetime.

How sweet the air had been that night, brilliant with stars, thick with the scent of magnolias, the sound of laughter. Seth had drunk it all in shamelessly: the booze, the bonhomie, the bad jokes and good wishes.

Toward midnight the mood had grown sentimental as the final round of toasts began, wavering between the frankly envious and the tearful. "There is a time and tide in the affairs of men..." Jack Regan had misquoted. "You're gonna knock their socks off in New York," Mark had predicted. And then, Jerry Lynch had clapped his hands for attention. "Let's hear it for the Petersens. Texas Medical's gift to the world!"—upon which he had grabbed a guitar and launched into a lusty rendition of "The Eyes of Texas Are Upon You." The song concluded with a round of applause and the inevitable cry of "Speech, speech."

Seth had raised his beer mug, surveyed the crowd with the satisfying awareness that almost every professional there would cheerfully have given eye teeth, right arms and most other expendable parts of the anatomy for the opportunity that now was his. Looked again to see if Tarkowsky had shown up by any chance, then addressed the sea of smiling faces.

"It's a great honor," he'd begun, "an extraordinary privilege to be singled out by destiny . . ." He paused to take the measure of his friends. "Yes, singled out by destiny, tapped on the shoulder by a kindly fate"—no, that son of a bitch Tarkowsky hadn't come—"to be chosen, unique among men for the fulfillment of a dream I have cherished since I was a small boy in Cleveland. Soon I hope to realize the aspirations that saw me through dark days in Harvard, Oak Ridge, Atlanta, here in Galveston . . . as I set forth tomorrow to embrace the goal of a lifetime—to go to the greatest city in America"—at the end of the table, Annie was doubled up in laughter. She knew his style—"to assume my rightful place . . . as third-string relief pitcher for the New York Yankees."

And everyone had roared.

Singled out by destiny.

Now, lying in their Village apartment, the buzz of great wine still in his head, the phrase recurred. For the hundredth time Seth shaped the thoughts he had left unvoiced that night.

He was going to New York to show them all: Tarkowsky, Mark Wilkins, the lot of them. To prove to his father that he was something more than a med school dropout. To show his wife that he was worthy of her sacrifice. Above all, to confirm to himself that he indeed had been singled out by destiny for a remarkable and glorious fate. To write his name across the sky.

"Seth!" Annie began tugging at his shoes. "Come on. Get undressed and get into bed. You're a million miles away."

"No . . ." He leaned up and kissed her full on the mouth. "Not quite a million."

For Gerald Marriner was not the only one that night to nourish the dream of Stockholm.

❄

"Talk of menial labor . . . Wow! could I use a drink!"

Vi Hagerty dumped an armful of packages on the floor of the booth and collapsed on the tufted plastic bench.

"Manual labor, hon. Menial means you're a servant." Crystal Klein wiggled her considerable form into the seat across from her friend. "You sure do mangle the language."

"Well, I feel like a servant. Why didn't you tell me this was such hard work?"

"You want outlet prices, you do outlet shopping. Macy's . . . Saks . . . you can have 'em. I'll take Secaucus any time. Same labels, same goods. Listen, we've accomplished a helluva lot today. Ask me, you saved close to a hundred bucks on the suit alone. Beading costs a fortune."

"You don't think it's too dressy for a city hall wedding? It's a real kelly green."

"Could be worse." Crystal laughed. "You could wear white."

"Me in white? You've gotta be joking."

Yet the truth was that tough-talking gum-chewing street-smart worldly-wise wasn't-born-yesterday Viola Hagerty felt like an honest-to-God bride for the first time in her life. Go figure.

When she'd asked Sherm if his offer of marriage was still open, his answer had been to sweep her high into the air with a triumphant shout of "Whoopee!"—and she had yet to come down to earth.

Extraordinary how a single word could change her life, a single gesture brush away all her fears. From her newfound perch with his strong arms around her, it was hard to remember how frightened she'd been of marriage, of actually tying the knot.

"Tying the noose," she used to call it and Sherm had to put it down to yet another unfortunate collision course between Vi and the language. But that was exactly what she'd meant—until that very moment when he hollered *Whoopee.*

Whoopee indeed. She could tell from the joy in his voice, from the sudden surge in her heart, that she was writing herself a ticket to paradise. The orphanage, the years of struggle, the men who'd used her and abused her, that scary two-in-the-morning panic when she didn't know where her life was heading: all that was behind her. Routed by love. Disposed of, once and for all.

She and Sherm were entering a fresh new world and who knows where it might lead. Already they were talking about children, about whether to go Scandinavian modern in the living room, and should they spring for Fortunoff silver or settle for prudent stainless?

A host of considerations that had never entered Vi's mind now filled it with a buoyant sense of expectation.

Practical souls might think her foolish, splurging on new clothes for the benefit of the man she'd been sleeping with for nearly a year. Maybe so, but Vi yearned to come to her Sherm brand-new and sparkling. Right out of the package, like fresh bread or the wardrobe that lay beside her, nestled in tissue.

On the jukebox, Madonna belted out her latest hit. "Like a Virgin." Vi smiled. That was how she felt, for the first time in her life. Like a goddam virgin.

The drinks came.

"To men, God bless 'em." She clinked glasses with Crystal.

"To business," Crystal reminded. "We want to get this stuff done this afternoon."

"Right." Vi fished in her bag for the list of "must have's," then stifled a yawn. "Although frankly I'm ready to call it a day. Don't know about you, toots, but I'm absolutely wiped out. Financially and physically! OK, let's see. Suit . . . blouse . . . we decided to do without the hat, right . . . ?" The letters were blurry, hard to make out. "Here, Crystal, you check 'em off. Jesus, I'm too woozy even to read."

Crystal pulled out her glasses and began ticking off items from the list.

"Handbag . . . yup, we did that. Gloves . . . What's this item? Teddies. You have two down on the list, you only got one."

"Yeah!" Vi smiled at the memory of that purchase. Spidery black lace, imported from France, sexy as they come. Just feeling the play of the satin beneath her fingers had been enough to turn her on. Wait till Sherm got a load of that number. He'd go bananas. Her bet was he'd have it off her in ten seconds flat.

"Yup," she repeated, "I think one will do."

"That one will," Crystal replied with a wink.

Vi had the decency to blush before signaling the waitress for another round of drinks.

"And make 'em doubles," she added. "I need all the strength I can get. This shopping takes the life's blood right out of you."

"Back to work." Crystal resumed her recitation. "I think we're OK on underwear, bras and all that stuff. This is getting to be quite a trousseau. Pantyhose . . . half slips . . . Oh shit! You know what we forgot? We forgot shoes."

"Jesus," Vi groaned. "Can't we leave it? My legs are ready to give out."

"Leave it? For when, honey? The wedding's three days away and you're not going out there the barefoot bride, not if I have any say in the matter. Look, we'll finish our drinks, nip right across the mall to Foot Fetish. They have nice things there . . . Delman seconds, Charles Jourdan . . . The whole business won't take more than fifteen minutes and then you're done. Meanwhile, relax, enjoy your drink. How does it feel, getting married again after all these years? You happy, Vi?"

"I'm embarrassed to tell you how happy." She looked for some wood to knock but the table was marbleized Formica. "And a little bit scared too. All that pressure I've been under since my ex decided to surface. But yeah . . . I feel real good about Sherm. And he'll be terrific to Noonie . . ."

"And will he be terrific to you?" Crystal wanted to know. "Because that's the bottom line. I hope you're not marrying the guy just for the boy's sake."

Vi shook her head thoughtfully.

"Funny. At first I thought I was. It was the last straw that broke the camel's back, you might say. But truth is, I wouldn't pull a number on Sherm. It's just not in me to use people like that. Anyhow, I still intend to keep on trucking with the real estate, pull my own weight whether we have a family or not. The thing is, I've got kind of used to paying my way, and I hate the thought of being dependent, even on Sherm. Anyhow, he wouldn't want it, either. Can you see me as a clinging violet? Just as soon be poison ivy. By the way, did I tell you what the company is doing for us?" She brightened. "Well, we looked at this house over in Bloomfield, a cute little ranch split-level with a carport. Sherm's dying we should buy it and me too, kind of. You know something? It'll be the first time in my adult life I ever lived in anything but a dinky apartment. Well, the long and short of it is, Orson Realty says we can have it without paying the broker's commission. That's their wedding present to us. It's like wholesale. So . . ." She laughed. "I'm getting my trousseau wholesale. Our house wholesale. Even our wedding breakfast wholesale, thanks to you. You're a doll."

Crystal looked embarrassed.

"Listen, if it were up to me alone, I'd let you guys have the run of the restaurant for zip. But I'm only the manager of the Purple Parrot, not the boss."

"Thanks again . . ." Vi began, but Crystal cut her off. "We'd better get a move on, presuming you still plan to get married in the foreseeable future."

"Drinks on me." Vi slapped three ten-dollar bills on the table. "Now let's get those shoes off our back."

She wove out of the bar on unsteady legs. Never should have had that second double.

They were thin, strappy, gorgeous silver leather with three-inch heels and open toes. "Higher," she told the salesman when he brought out the initial offerings. "I want stiletto heels yea high and then some."

Now she wriggled her feet in satisfaction. Say what you will, those Italian spikes did wonderful things for her ankles, the shape of her legs. Best legs in the Garden State, Sherm liked to say. At least for a short person.

"Stop admiring yourself, honey, and stand on 'em, if possible," Crystal said. "See how they feel when you walk around."

Vi staggered to her feet. The shoes made her feel about ten feet tall, but damn! they were hard to negotiate.

The salesman was watching her, arms folded. Drunk as a skunk, his expression seemed to say.

Maybe she was a little tipsy at that.

"They look good," Crystal commented doubtfully, "but not awfully comfortable. Can you manage? Sunday's going to be a long day."

"Fine. Just fine," Vi mumbled.

She tottered over to the mirror for a reassuring glance and looked down, concentrating on the spot where her feet were supposed to be. All she saw was a silver blur.

Vi rubbed her eyes, frightened and confused. Nothing seemed right, nothing was as it should be. Not her, not the room. From a distance, she heard Crystal calling—jumbled words that made no sense.

And then the ground rushed up to hit her.

"You OK?" Crystal helped her into a chair. "Jesus, you're lucky you didn't break anything."

Terrible. Terrible. She wanted to sit in that chair forever.

"Help me home," she finally got out. "And let me sleep it off. I'll be OK tomorrow."

But after a long night of pain and panic, she knew it wasn't the booze at all.

As soon as dawn broke, she called Sherm.

"Come get me to a hospital," she said, "without disturbing Noonie."

"What's the matter, babe?" His voice was thick with sleep.

Dry-mouthed, she framed an answer. Even to her own ears, the words sounded incredible.

"I can't walk."

2

"LIKE A MUSEUM." ARI BEN-ILAN LOOKED ABOUT THE STUDIO WHILE
Annie fidgeted and smoothed down her skirt for the dozenth
time and sucked furiously on eucalyptus pastilles.

"Like a walk into the past," Ari mused, "including the piano."

Her new accompanist was a hearty Israeli, short and stocky with
a booming voice more suited to tracts of desert space than to this
overheated studio with its heavy velvet drapes and massive furniture. For all its size, the room appeared cluttered, almost cloistered.
There were outcroppings of plush and mahogany that bordered
upon the monumental, a nine-foot Bechstein grand that looked as
though it had seen fifty years of service, towering glass-fronted
bookcases crammed with scores and librettos, Afghan hangings,
Persian carpets, a large and ugly marble bust of what Annie presumed to be a czarist notable. The only concession to modernity
was the acoustic tile of the ceiling. But it was the long wall behind
the piano that drew Ari's attention, for it was covered with hundreds of photographs—some recent, some in fading sepia tone, all
duly autographed and fulsomely inscribed in half a dozen lan-
guages by the great, the near great and the almost forgotten.

While Annie focused on the tension in her throat, Ari was making
a tour of inspection.

"Toscanini . . . Galli-Curci . . . Rosa Ponselle . . . Callas! The old
lady knew everybody. I'm impressed."

"Shhh!" Annie put a finger to her lips and mouthed "She might
hear you."

"Hear that I'm calling her an old lady?" He bellowed with laughter. "But she must know she's an old lady."

Ari's own ebullient youth and gusto seemed to preclude all sensitivity. Except at the piano, Annie thought. Once those stubby fingers settled in on the keys, Ari would turn psychic. There was no need to spell anything out, to explain what it was she sought. A word, even a nod would suffice. Sometimes not even that much. Like the tenderest of lovers, Ari would respond to her every subtle shift of tone and mood and tempo. It never failed to amaze her that a man could be so intuitive when it came to music, so crude when it came to women.

Their first morning together, she and Ari had gone to Steinway to choose a piano. No sooner were they alone in one of the showrooms than Ari made a grab at her breasts.

"You've got to be kidding!" She'd jumped back in disbelief.

"All right . . . all right." Ari raised his hands in a gesture of surrender. "Some ladies like a little fooling around. You don't. I'm sorry."

"But . . . but . . ." she spluttered, "you knew I was a married woman. Why . . . it was my husband who made the arrangements."

He laughed the matter off without the feeblest apology. "I thought you were maybe just a bored lonely housewife looking for fun. It happens." Without further ado, he ripped off a cascade of arpeggios, followed by a few simple chords. "Nice piano. This one I like." He played the opening phrase of a Schubert song. "See if it suits."

Cheeks still burning with embarrassment, Annie launched into "Die Forelle" with trepidation. Could she trust the man to keep his mitts firmly on the keyboard? But by the time the song was over, the incident had been wiped clean.

It was, she told Seth afterwards, musical love at first sight and the beginning of a solid friendship. If it pleased Ari to fancy himself a Don Juan, flirting with everything in skirts, that was his privilege. Their own relation was based on matters more profound.

She soon came to think of him as a younger brother as well as the ideal accompanist.

For the next two weeks, they lived in each other's pockets—smartening up repertoire, learning new music, arguing to the point of exhaustion about the finer interpretive points.

Today, in the studio of Madame Natasha Liadoff-Grey, she would learn if that unrelenting work was to bear fruit.

On the stroke of eleven, the door to an adjacent chamber opened and out popped an improbably tiny woman in a floral print dress, the feet in carpet slippers, wrists jingling with bangle bracelets, long crimson nails, the whole unlikely vision topped by an explosion of Day-Glo orange hair.

Was it a fright wig, Annie wondered, or an amateur dye job gone amok? The former, she supposed, for no reputable manufacturer would have the effrontery to put such a hair color on the market. Had it not been for the eyes—raven black and fiercely intelligent—the effect would have been comic. Instead, it was intimidating.

"So!" The little woman shuffled across the room, seated herself dead center on a red-velvet sofa, crossed her arms stoutly and fixed those shrewd black eyes upon Annie.

"So," she repeated. "Sing."

Annie sang. She sang Gluck. Handel. Snippets of Mozart. Bits of Beethoven. Verdi. Sometimes she was permitted to continue to the end; more often, she was cut short after a half dozen bars with an imperious "Next."

The experience was new to Annie. She had come prepared to cope with criticism and nit-picking. This brusque lack of interest threw her off balance. Only Ari, so firm and supportive at the piano, seemed unflappable.

After a half hour of what Annie mentally termed the third degree, Madame Natasha said, "Thank you, Mr. Pianist. You play very well."

Ari answered in what sounded like Russian, and for the first time that morning, the old woman actually smiled. She addressed him in the same language, and they chattered amiably for a few minutes while Annie waited in an agony of suspense.

"OK." Ari patted Annie on the shoulder. "I go now. She wants you to stay and talk."

Madame rang a velvet bell pull. A moment later, a Jamaican woman entered with a samovar and two tiny porcelain cups on a brass tray.

"So . . . Antonia Sayre Petersen." She waved Annie into a chair.

"You will take some tea with me, please?"

It was only then that Annie realized that her mouth was as dry as her hands were sweaty, and thanked God that the ordeal was over.

"Yes," she breathed. "I would like that very much."

"Now ... my young friend, will you tell me what roles have you studied?"

Annie did, but not before downing three cups of tea. As she heard herself out, it struck her as an impressive list, beginning with Mozart and moving up through the next hundred years.

"And as for Puccini, well, I can sing Mimi and Butterfly and I've been working on Manon Lescaut."

"Don't you know Tosca?" The orange hair bobbled in surprise.

What a question. Annie knew it, of course, inside out. Knew every role, every word, every note of music.

"I know it," Annie said, "but it's not in my repertoire."

"Oh?" The eyebrows shot up. "Why is that? I think the role lies very well for your voice."

Annie paused to consider her explanation. Of all operas, *Tosca* was imbued with a special meaning, a particular challenge. Even now, after the passage of a dozen years, she still winced at the memory of singing the "Vissi d'arte" for Professor Baer and making a thorough fool of herself. How cocky she had been at seventeen, how fearless and ignorant. At thirty she knew better. At the least, she knew how little she knew.

"I don't sing it," Annie replied, "because I don't understand the depths of her character ... I can't quite grasp what makes her tick."

"Oh?" The eyebrows steepened further. "My dear girl, if singers only sang the roles they thoroughly understood, half the opera stages of the world would be empty. What is it you don't understand about Tosca? She is all woman ... every woman ... passionate, tender, jealous ..."

"Inconsistent," Annie finished the sentence, and then regretted the remark. Even to her own ears, it sounded flip.

"Indeed!" Madame rubbed her hands with a gleeful air of expectation. "You will have the goodness to explain."

Annie gathered her breath and her thoughts. What was there to say about Tosca that had not already been said? What could she add to the lore that was significant?

She would be the first to admit that most opera plots were absurd, if not downright loony. As for the heroines, they were made of either cardboard or spun sugar. And even while they carried on singing, the craziest things happened to them. *Rigoletto*, for instance, where Gilda had the misfortune of being accidentally kidnapped by her own father. Or Manon, the Parisian courtesan exiled to the deserts of Louisiana. "But there are no deserts in Louisiana," Seth protested. Oh, the endless mistaken identities, mad scenes, forced marriages, the discoveries of long-lost brothers, children, fathers. Any playwright who ventured to fob off such plots would be strung up on the spot.

Yet in opera these extravagances were the norm. You checked your sense of reality in the cloakroom, along with your coat and hat, and entered ready to weep over the fate of Druid priestesses and Ethiopian slaves.

Was *Tosca* inconsistent? Probably. If so, what did it matter?

Yet to Annie, it did. Of all the major roles, it was the one she identified with most closely. For one thing, Tosca—like Annie herself—was a singer. For another . . .

"I see Tosca," Annie clarified her thoughts, "as a modern woman. I wouldn't be surprised to run into her on the street or backstage at Carnegie Hall. To me, she's real, made of flesh and blood. Most opera heroines are passive, foolish, fragile. Victims or martyrs, so to speak. Silly virgins who fall in love at first glance and go mad when things don't turn out right, or else the kind of women who can't wait to sacrifice themselves out of sheer nobility. But Tosca! Ah, she's something else. She strikes me as very much a contemporary woman. Independent. Professional. A success in her own right. That's the excitement of the role—and the contradiction. On the one hand, she's assured, glamorous, living openly with her lover. That took some doing back in 1800 when the action opens . . ."

"The play itself was written long after," Madame reminded her.

"Yes. Nearly a hundred years after," Annie broke in. "Which makes it even more remarkable. It appeared in Victorian times, when prudery was rampant and respectable folk believed that a woman's place was in the home. As for love outside of marriage, one lapse was enough to mark you as an outcast. But not our Tosca. She's neither apologetic nor guilt-ridden."

Madame smiled, and Annie sensed that her analysis, as much as her singing, was to be a crucial part of the audition. Was there a mind attached to the voice, Madame wanted to know, a critical intelligence brought to bear?

"That's the Tosca I admire," Annie continued, "the one I can identify with. But there's the other Tosca . . . irrational, jealous, behaving like a jealous shopgirl. And that Tosca bothers me. I'll accept artistic temperament, but her behavior is absurd. A woman of her ability wouldn't carry on like that. It doesn't make sense."

"Why not?"

"Let's assume we're dealing with real people," Annie pressed on. "Here is a successful career woman having an affair with a terrific guy. And Mario is terrific—he's talented, passionate, politically aware. They're consenting adults. She comes to visit Mario in a church where he's painting a mural. And what does she see? The girl in the painting has blue eyes. Tosca's eyes are black. Now, you and I might say, 'Big Deal.' But not Tosca! Right away, this sophisticated woman of the world flies into a tantrum. No intelligent woman would behave like that, unless she's putting on an act."

"Have you never been jealous?" Madame asked.

The question stopped Annie in her tracks. For if she, in one way, was Tosca, then in another way, Seth was Mario—creative, buoyant, full of light and brilliance.

"No . . . I suppose I haven't."

She tried to be honest with herself. Was she jealous of the women Seth worked with? Of Chandra? Of course not. Just mildly irritated. "Anyhow," she continued, "I certainly wouldn't make a scene with so little justification. Tosca loves this man! How can she love him unless she trusts him? And if she really believes he's lying to her, that he'd betray so casually, be so brazen as to paint his mistress on the walls of a church—how could she possibly love him? No, Madame Natasha, it's ridiculous. She's behaving like a prima donna."

Madame laughed. "But she is a prima donna. Please continue. This is fascinating."

"OK. Now, enter the Baron Scarpia. He's evil incarnate. I could picture him in our century wearing a Gestapo uniform." Involuntarily she shuddered. "A vile man, our Scarpia, yearning to possess Tosca, to debase her. Naturally she despises him. Yet when this

125

snake . . . this villain starts hinting that Mario is deceiving her, she snaps at the bait. Why? Why should Tosca take the word of this lecherous beast rather than trust the man she loves?"

"Perhaps," Madame suggested, "she's secretly attracted to Scarpia. There are woman who are drawn to the dark side of life."

"Not normal women," Annie said. "Certainly not our Tosca. She may be liberated, but she's not promiscuous. She's totally committed to Mario. In fact, I'm rather puzzled as to why Tosca and Mario never got married in the first place."

"Married!" Madame Natasha was thunderstruck. "Our lovers married! The thought never occurred to me. Or to them apparently," she added with a laugh.

"But why not?" Annie persisted. "Tosca and Mario love each other, there are no impediments. Why didn't they ever get married and settle down, long before the curtain ever rose on Act I?"

"Well . . ." Madame rang for the maid to clear away the tea. "This has been most instructive. I can't say, my dear, whether you have given me any new insights into Tosca, but you have certainly told me a great deal about yourself."

She crossed the room to an ormolu desk and riffled through a red leather notebook.

"Tuesday and Friday mornings at nine, I am free. But if you come earlier, we have a little more time. Arrive prepared to sing Tosca, Act I." The idea afforded her amusement. "The jealousy scene, if you please."

Annie was halfway down 57th Street when the realization hit her. Madame had never told her not to hope, had never said Nay. She had not trampled dreams, squashed her ambitions. Had simply accepted her on the spot in defiance of everything that Lainie had foretold.

In detail, Annie tried to recall that long wall of photographs. Ponselle . . . Galli-Curci . . . Callas. Perhaps one day her own likeness would find its place in that gallery. *To the beloved teacher who made my success possible. Antonia Petersen.*

She walked all the way home to the Village without ever touching the ground.

[*Infidelities*]

The shortest list in the world, Margot Marriner believed, was the list of those items money couldn't buy.

Outside of life eternal, it purchased everything truly worthwhile. The cliché about money not buying happiness had always struck Margot as balderdash. Money counts and is counted. And if it didn't make you happy, you were probably one of those malcontents whom nothing could satisfy, not even poverty.

She herself had been born neither rich nor poor, the daughter of a history don at Oxford. The scholastic ambience may have had its rewards, but it hardly provided the clothes, the travel, all the larger amenities to which a girl of Margot's beauty was entitled.

Those needs that the Trent family had failed to supply at birth, Kir Allegorio filled handsomely two dozen years later.

Poor Kir! ugly as sin, standing yea-high to her shoulder in his stocking feet, his complexion a dermatologist's delight. More frog than prince, truth to be told. She still remembered him fondly as the Wart.

Not a bad man, actually. In some ways not a man at all, despite the fearsome reputation. The name was adopted. The nationality as well, for Kir was not—as the press had burbled—"a Greek tycoon of fabulous wealth," but a dour, swarthy dwarfish creature of Albanian extraction who had made his first few millions at seventeen running guns to Mideast terrorists and acquired a second, even greater fortune years later on the bourses of Paris and Hong Kong.

He was a gentleman of sixty when he spotted Margot in a cinematic costume drama. Promptly he set about meeting and marrying her. For this woman possessed all the attributes required of Kir's wife. She was a splendid vehicle for parading his wealth, his collection of Renaissance jewels and—above all—his purported virility.

They never shared the same bedroom except in other people's homes, and then cohabited merely for display. The arrangement suited both of them admirably. Half a dozen years into their marriage, Kir had the bad taste to drop dead in a seamy male brothel in Istanbul, the good taste to leave Margot his fortune intact. She would always remember him with gratitude.

Shortly after, she married again—not for money, this time, but for fun and the possession of an ancient title. Should the need to impress ever arise, she could still call herself La Contessa della Mezzacielo e Romana. The marriage was as brief as the title was long, il Conte proving a consummate swine. She considered herself lucky to be rid of the man for a paltry million dollars' cash.

Margot waited until she was forty to marry a third time, and this time for love.

Dear sweet adoring Gerald. She sometimes felt he deserved someone better, less shopworn. Someone less given to infidelity. Personally, she considered theirs a successful marriage. Her adulteries were incidental, bearing not at all on her feelings for Gerald. Yet time and again, her affairs had broken his heart.

If only her husband could understand how ephemeral they were. How little they had to do with him. Yet in typical male fashion, Gerald viewed each lapse as the mark of his own inadequacy.

"I can resist anything"—she paraphrased Oscar Wilde—"except flirtation."

Even as a child she had but wanted to be wanted. It later became her life's work. She loved nothing better than to pursue the elaborate trembling ritual of thrust and parry, retreat and advance, of whispered promises and stolen hours that marked the progress of every love affair. To see the light of admiration in a lover's eye.

It hardly mattered that this elaborate game of hearts often ended in the briefest of couplings. The act of sex was secondary; it was in the act of conquest that Margot found bliss.

But no more.

Those days of enchantment were gone. And if she stayed faithful to Gerald now, it was not out of guilt or repentance, but from a lack of alternatives. For what men were there left so chivalrous, so nearsighted that Margot could still kindle desire in them?

At forty there had been suitors by the hundreds. At fifty, still candidates galore. But she was sixty now. An elegant, chic, extraordinarily good-looking sixty, to be sure, nonetheless simply too ancient to elicit the unbounded adoration of men.

Except from Gerald. Only in his eyes did her beauty gleam undimmed. How could she not be grateful? Thus Gerald had finally prevailed. Her only hope now was that there remained still time enough to compensate him for the agonies already endured. One could do worse, she reflected, than share the final curtain with a man of such quality, such resonance. Such constancy! For Margot knew no one would ever again love her quite so much.

On balance, she could review her years with satisfaction. Her fortune had been well spent. It had allowed her to maintain her beauty, her health, her half dozen homes, her friends, her position in society, and a shrewd grasp of all that went on within the world. Why be book smart, Margot concluded, when one could purchase the produce of other people's minds with either warm smiles or cold cash?

Charm had been the currency with which she paid for much-wanted enlightenment earlier that week in the office of Dr. Egon Reiner. They were old friends, sometime lovers, and she had no qualms about calling in her debts.

"Now, my sweet"—she tapped his wrist gently—"what have you been hiding from me? Why has Gerald been visiting you these past couple of months?"

When Egon claimed the privilege of professional confidentiality, Margot had simply hooted.

"No, my darling. I shan't let you off the hook like this. You owe me half your practice, my pet. Beside, I have eyes. I can see there's something wrong and you're going to tell me exactly what."

She had noticed changes in her husband's behavior recently, subtle but damning. He had taken up jogging for one thing, grossly out of character for such a sedentary man. Even more conclusive was the fact that Gerald, the bon vivant who adored the richest of foods, the headiest of wines, the man who had flown the Atlantic in pursuit of the perfect *paté Strasbourgois aux truffes*—her Gerald! of all people had taken to nibbling carrots and watching his cholesterol intake.

"Just being sensible, my dear," he'd told Margot, who naturally hadn't believed a word of it.

"When a man gives up Godiva chocolates, something is seriously wrong. And now this!" She pushed an empty prescription bottle across the desk. "This with your name on it. It proves something, doesn't it?"

"It proves you shouldn't be snooping around in your husband's medicine cabinet."

Margot took a wild stab. She had no notion what the stuff on the label translated as, but her instincts were not to be denied.

"Heart? High blood pressure?" And when Egon refused to answer, she fixed her magnificent eyes upon his. "Come on, my darling. Tell me. I'll be the proverbial sphinx. He'll never know I know, he'll never know you told me. But I love the man and I have a right to the truth. It *is* his heart." She was certain of it now. "I can see it in your silence. His father died of a coronary. There's a history of it in the family, so you won't be betraying a trust."

"I don't want to alarm you, Margot."

"You're alarming me now." She felt a jab of fear. Egon was being so close-mouthed, so solemn. "And you're only making it worse by keeping me in the dark. Please, darling, I beg of you."

As so many lovers before him, he could deny Margot nothing. Moreover he felt it was as well she should know. Before the hour was out, she had wrung from him all the details of Gerald's illness, all except the most crucial one.

"You know I can't answer that," Egon said. "Nobody can ever predict just how long. He could collapse today. He could live another few years. I couldn't possibly commit myself to an answer. It depends . . ."

"On what, Egon? Please . . ." She began to weep. "You've virtually given my husband a death sentence. Don't start playing games now."

"As I said, it depends. On how well he looks after himself, his mental state, peace of mind. His work is terribly stressful, as you well know . . ."

"Gerald's life would be meaningless without it."

"And of course a great deal depends on you, Margot."

"Then tell me . . . what should I do? All that matters to me now is his welfare."

"It's what you shouldn't do," came the guarded answer. "Don't . . ."

He halted, at a temporary loss for words.

Don't betray him yet again, she could read in the doctor's eyes. *Don't add more insult to an injured heart.*

"Don't . . . cause Gerald any unnecessary anxiety," he said lamely.

But Margot had guessed his meaning.

She wiped her eyes and opened her bag to inspect the ravages.

"You needn't worry, darling." Her tiny mirror revealed a face suddenly grown old. A fresh layer of lipstick hardly helped. Margot snapped the compact shut and looked up at Egon with an ironic smile.

"I don't think I have it in me to cause anyone much anxiety these days."

"Beautiful lady"—came the gallant answer—"you still do. You always will."

"Thank you, even for saying so."

That was Monday. For the next few days she had kept her own counsel, had been gay, charming, determined that no hint of her discovery might reach Gerald. In fact, Margot had embarked on the finest acting job of her career for a husband who, she knew from bitter experience, was not easily deceived.

But she could not shake the sense of urgency. If Gerald was ever to be happy, it must be now. If he was ever to achieve his goals, it must be soon.

Secretive though he may have been concerning the nature of his armchair fantasies, he hadn't fooled her for a moment. Margot could read him like a primer: his need for fame, his hunger for public recognition. He should have been an actor—poor lamb!—not a scientist.

Of course he yearned for the Nobel Prize. What man in his position did not? Had it been possible, she would have bought it for him, with price no object, like the Learjet she had given him last Christmas.

But, reluctantly, she had to enter the gold medal in that brief list of items not for sale.

It was monstrous, really. Especially now, when his collaboration with young Petersen was such that he had reason to hope.

Granted it was early days, but given time their efforts would surely attract the attention of the Nobel committee. Instinctively, Margot sensed that the men were engaged in significant work, the sort that made headlines and heroes.

Yet due recognition might take years, nor could the experts in Stockholm be hustled. It struck her as unlikely that Gerald would live long enough to collect the prize, no matter how richly deserved.

But if that honor lay beyond his grasp, there were other, more immediate rewards. There was fame. Glory. The esteem of a worshipful public. Margot knew from experience how to light the quick blaze of celebrity. Very well. What Gerald wouldn't do—out of ethical considerations or a misplaced sense of propriety—Margot would do for him. Tonight. Over an elegant dinner.

She opened her wardrobe thoughtfully and drew out a long shaft of sequins, dazzling in a rich midnight blue. Strone Guthrie had always liked her in that color. No, she corrected herself. Strone no longer, but Lord Guthrie, as of the Queen's last birthday. An earl, no less (Margot had to smile), a peer of the realm—this son of the Glasgow slums. The old blowhard!

But earl or no, press lord or no, she had always known just how to play him.

By tomorrow morning, Margot determined, Gerald Marriner would be front-page news.

※

Shit piss and corruption.

Ward Daniels rolled over the supine body next to him on the bed and reached over to where the phone was screaming a premature reveille. Not even 6 A.M. He grimaced and grabbed for the offending instrument with a second round of curses.

Sleeping late and in your own bed was one of the prerogatives of magazine work, he had been led to believe. Beat newspaper reporting hands down.

"No more fleabag hotels," the editor of *Worldnews* had promised, when they were courting him. "No more Delhi belly or scorpions in your suitcase or trying to find a shot of bourbon in downtown Tehran. You'll be living like a human being for a change."

And after fifteen years of covering savagery in Viet Nam and loony toons in Ayatollah country and then that bloodbath out in Lebanon, it was the one part of the offer he couldn't refuse. He was forty now, getting too old to have gunfire served up with breakfast every morning. Time to stop skirmishing with death and start living. Time to get a little money in the bank.

One story a month was all the magazine asked, and Ward pretty much picked his subjects. That last piece he did on corruption in the aircraft industry looked like it might earn him another Pulitzer. And the beauty of it all was that this new career could

132

pretty much be packed down in the hours from nine to five. Leaving the other hours available for pastimes, like whatever-the-name-was that belonged to the adjacent body.

So who the fuck was trying to rouse him out of bed while the sun itself was still catching up on its ZZZZZ's?

"You got the wrong number," he growled into the phone, while what's-her-name rolled over and began to snore. A pillow hog, this one. A blanket snatcher. She'd have to go. Ward tried to replace the phone.

"I've got the right number, laddie." The Scottish burr sounded bright and chipper, ready for business. "It's Guthrie here."

As if there could be two voices like that in the world. The Flying Scotsman himself. Did the man never sleep, Ward wondered? Probably not. That's how come Strone Guthrie managed to turn black-and-white newsprint into lots of long green. That and the refusal ever to take no for an answer.

"There'll be a story in all my papers, this morning," the peer continued, "about a major medical breakthrough . . ."

" 'S nice," Ward mumbled. Man Bites Dog. Dog Contracts Rabies. Go bother somebody else at this hour.

". . . and I want you to follow it up with a magazine piece. Human interest. Young doctor, old doctor, working hand-in-glove to conquer disease, the romance of science, the miracle of modern research, hope for grinding humanity . . . Wring the withers. You know how."

Ward shook his head, trying to defuzz his mind. Why the hell should Guthrie himself be handing out story assignments as if he were some junior editor instead of the great panjandrum of the popular press? He must have a personal interest in it somewhere.

"I think, Lord Guthrie, you have got the wrong number after all. I'm not a science writer . . ."

"Don't want a science writer. Want the best man for the job, big by-liner, Pulitzer person." His early years writing headlines for one of Britain's saucier dailies had left Guthrie with a love of cheap alliteration. "Someone who can make a story sing and that's you. So do it, laddie, nice upbeat confirmation about the wonder of life, the rewards of hard work . . . in time for the March issue . . . which means you should start on it today. My secretary will be sending a messenger over to you with all the details so you can get an early start. Oh yes, another point to remember. One of these chappies is married to a dear friend of mine. Margot Trent . . . lovely woman. I'd like her to be happy with the results."

And before Ward could utter an outraged No, the great man had rung off.

Terrific!

Ward grabbed a sizable chunk of the blanket back off the bed hog, wrapped it about his skinny shoulders and tried to settle in for another hour's sleep, but the phone call had hit a nerve.

You don't say no to Strone Guthrie, not if you wanted to stay in business. And yet! Ward Daniels was a quester, a seeker to whom the truth was holy, goddammit, and the pursuit of truth the most noble of professions. In short, he was a journalist—not some two-bit flack squeezing sweet dollops of publicity out of a verbal pastry tube. Not one of your Madison Avenue "wordsmiths" whose cutesy paeans were on sale to the highest bidder. He was a man with certain standards to maintain—in ideas if not in women—and he should have put his virtue where his mouth is and told old Guthrie to jack off.

Of all the sweet idiocies! Ward marveled. Here was Strone Guthrie—the Earl of Fleet Street, the Titan of Tripe, the most powerful opinion shaper in the world, a man who commanded a couple of hundred newspapers, a dozen magazines, TV and radio stations by the score, a man who could make premiers and presidents, break them as well—the great Guthrie!—asking to have a routine news story custom-tailored to please some aging bimbo. This Margot Trent must be fantastic in bed. Even so!

By Ward Daniels' lights, such behavior was unfathomable. How could any man with even a modicum of self-respect let a woman get her mitts into him like that? It's not as if they were different, one from the other.

He looked at his current bedmate with mild curiosity.

Technically, Goethe was in error when he said at night all cats are gray. This one was redheaded, it so happened. But on the whole that crafty old Faustian had it right. There was nothing much to choose between one woman and another. They were all fitted out with the same protuberances, given minor variations in shape and size. The same orifices, too.

Only the names were different, like it used to say on those police shows, to protect the innocent. But there were no innocent among these bimbos. And the names became indistinguishable after a while.

134

This one, for instance. Miss Pillow Hog. He remembered picking her up at Gallagher's last evening, buying her a few drinks, taking her home and screwing her roundly, but that was all he remembered.

She was just a woman. No name. Generic. Like that no-name brand toilet paper you bought at Safeway. The idea amused him.

Generic Woman.

"Hey, Gennie." He nudged her awake. "You'll have to get your sweet little ass out of here by seven o'clock. I got a lot of work to do this morning."

"The name's Irene," she murmured, half asleep.

"Sure thing." He patted her rump routinely.

But they were all Gennies to him.

3

MIRACLE CURE FOR MS?
Medi-Tekk Docs in Big Breakthrough

"WILL YOU ANSWER THIS ONE, HONEY?" SETH GROANED. "Tell 'em they got the wrong goddam number or something. Let me at least have my coffee in peace."

"Bureau of Internal Revenue," Annie crooned into the mouthpiece. "Thank you for holding. We will have a tax inspector available in just a moment."

She waited for the ensuing click, then left the phone off the hook.

She sighed. "Well, at least they spelled your name correctly in the story."

"What the hell got into Margot, jumping the gun like that?" Seth rapped the offending article with his knuckles. "Here, where it says 'plan to begin clinical applications within the year.' Jesus!"

He shook his head in wonderment, but Annie couldn't resist the notion that deep down Seth was pleased with this turn of events. In fact, the first call they'd had that morning—after Margot's, alerting them to the story—had been Seth's father ringing up from Cleveland, ready to pop his buttons by the sound of his voice.

"Some reporter feller from the *Plain Dealer* saw a story on the wire service . . . called to ask if it was the same Seth Petersen he went to school with. I told him—Yup! that's my boy."

But within the hour, other calls began coming through.

136

"You don't know me," a timid voice would posit, "but I've had MS since I was a teenager . . ."

Or—"I read the story in the *Sun* and I have a daughter in a wheelchair . . ."

Or worst of all—"Please, Dr. Petersen, don't hang up on me. I beg of you."

And still they came: sad calls, desperate calls, voices that begged, cajoled, fawned, demanded. Some of the callers had been hungry for nothing more than information. Most of them were hungry for the "miracle cure." Like volunteers for the first civilian rocket to the moon, each unknown petitioner pleaded to be put at the head of the list.

"There *is* no list," Seth had finally barked, at which the woman at the other end had burst into tears. Now he simply refused to get further involved.

"I think we'll have to have the number changed." Annie shrugged. "Although who can blame 'em, poor souls? Still"—she brightened—"I gather the story is reasonably accurate, and it's nice to think you're offering hope."

"Offering hope is one thing. Promising miracles is another. That was very unfortunate phrasing. Besides which, the accepted procedure is to publish first, and let the scientific community arrive at their own evaluation. Anyhow, the boss's wife is not the proper person to blow the corporate horn, let alone the New York *Daily Sun*. I wouldn't be surprised if we wind up with the SEC breathing down our necks."

"The Securities and Exchange Commission?" Annie frowned. "Why should they get involved?"

"Because this kind of publicity sounds very much like stock touting, which isn't exactly considered ethical. The kind of thing where insiders make a killing. Speaking of which . . . ! Boy, by the end of the trading today on Wall Street, we're going to look very, very rich—at least on paper."

"And that's bad?" Annie grinned. The previous week Seth had been rewarded for his role with a sizable block of shares in Medi-Tekk and an option to purchase even more. In conjunction with Seth's walloping raise, the Petersens considered themselves well off indeed. Now, however, with a quick jump in the market, who could say what they'd be worth?

"No," Seth conceded. "Not bad. Anyhow"—he gulped down his coffee and grabbed his jacket—"I'm off to the lab. If you see Margot today, try and get a reading on what she thought she was doing. See you later."

He pecked Annie on the cheek and headed into the hall to return within a matter of seconds.

"Omigod!" He was pale. "Would you believe! There's someone outside the door just waiting to pounce . . . old lady in a wheelchair. Looks like she brought her lunch. Must have picked our address out of the phone book. Shit! Where do I go from here? Damned if I'm going to be a prisoner in my own kitchen."

"Price of fame and fortune." Annie sighed. Although Lord knows, she didn't want their front step besieged by the lame and the halt. "Maybe if you spoke to her . . ."

"And said what, Annie? Should I do an Oral Roberts number just like on television . . . a little soul, a little sermon and then the laying on of hands? Faith healer? Hell . . . I'm not even a physician! I couldn't prescribe a high colonic, let alone some nonexistent wonder drug. I'm sorry for the lady, but I've got some rights too, privacy among 'em."

He finally made his escape by climbing out the kitchen window and beating a low-profile retreat over the ash cans to Sheridan Square.

"Leave the phone off the hook," were his last words, "and don't talk to anyone you don't know."

"I tell you, Margot, in some ways it's wonderful, but in others it's a nightmare." Annie unwound over tea and Amaretto biscuits in her friend's Chinese sitting room. "I suppose you're used to the glare of publicity, but this morning came as quite a shock to us."

"I'm sorry, lamb!" Margot patted her hand. "It'll blow over pretty soon, and of course you should never never never have your phone number where every crank and creep can get hold of it."

"If it were just the phone calls . . ." Annie nibbled on a macaroon. "OK, I can fix that, but we've got total strangers camping on our doorstep."

Margot frowned. She had visited the Petersens at home and didn't approve.

"You people don't belong in Greenwich Village," she stated now with assurance. "It's so marginal . . . not at all smart. And that place of yours is far too small. How in God's name do you practice there? It's a basement!"

Annie smiled. By Margot's standards, anything less spacious than the Frick Museum was unfit for human habitation.

"A garden apartment is what the broker called it."

"Darling, I know what gardens are, and three ash cans and a dying aspidistra do not constitute a proper garden. What do you pay for that place anyhow?"

"Sixteen hundred," Annie said hesitantly.

Margot didn't know if it was a lot or a little, but she could tell that Annie felt it was a lot.

"Outrageous," she clucked. "Absolutely outrageous to pay that kind of money for a hole in the wall. You know, Medi-Tekk has a lovely courtesy flat just a few blocks from here up on Park."

No, Medi-Tekk did not. Margot Marriner did. She had bought it years ago, a spacious penthouse reserved for romantic assignations. A place where one might be discreetly indiscreet in luxury and style.

Only there would be no such assignations anymore. Those charming rooms, with their handsome details and panoramic views, were sitting idle and unloved.

She scanned Annie's troubled face with near-maternal affection. Yes, it would be pleasant having the Petersens so near by, convenient for Gerald as well. As for herself—Margot smothered an inner ache— Annie might become the daughter the Marriners had never had. Someone to shop with, fuss over, help along with her career.

Right! Margot's mind was made up with a near-audible click. She'd put the furniture in storage, have the closets cleaned out . . .

"You could move in right after Christmas." She settled the matter with a brisk clap of her hands. "In fact, I insist."

Arguing was useless, Annie discovered, as had so many of Margot's friends before her. The woman was addicted to having her way.

"But I'd have to know what the carrying charges are, see the place. Discuss it with Seth. He may not want to go for more rent."

Oh, bother the rent! Margot was tempted to say, but she suspected that Annie didn't care to be the recipient of special favors, a peculiarity of that rockbound New England temperament. No, Margot intuited correctly, rather a woman who preferred to think she was paying her way.

"It's fifteen hundred something, I believe, I'll have my secretary check it—and much, much better value than what you have. Eighteenth floor, a pretty little terrace, as I recall, just in case you really want to garden. Two bedrooms and a maid's room. Good neighborhood, nice schools. I know you and Seth are planning to have children. It's the perfect location. And, of course, the building has doormen . . . concierge . . . the usual flunkies, so you won't have the walking wounded squatting at your door. We'll pop in tomorrow so you can see it, decide what you want to do. I know a wonderful decorator, Binkie Lewis. Roaring faggot of course, but exquisite taste. For me he charges half price. For you, maybe less. I'll work on him. Oh, darling—" She squeezed Annie's hand and gave her glorious smile. "We are going to have such fun!"

Annie grinned back. Margot's prescription sounded marvelous. The fairy godmother. It was then that she remembered Seth's injunction.

"I must ask you one thing, though . . ."

"Mmmmm," Margot purred. "Anything but my age . . ."

"Why you dropped the bombshell to Lord Guthrie the way you did." She hesitated, then added softly, "Seth didn't believe it was quite proper, informing the press that way. Was it an oversight, Margot, just a slip of the tongue or what?"

Margot recouped her hand and examined her perfect manicure.

"No, darling," she said at last. "I may not be a card-carrying intellectual but I'm not quite stupid either, and this is strictly between you and me." She leaned forward, a priestess confiding some dazzling secret to a novitiate. "It's what they want, you know," she whispered. "And I tell you this in absolute confidence."

Annie felt a tremor of unease. "I don't quite understand."

"Fame . . . glory. It's what our men want, why they're playing the game in the first place." Before Annie had a chance to protest, Margot barreled on: "They want to be loved, admired, want their words of wisdom treated like gospel—not just by us, but by everyone. They want rooms to fall silent when they walk through the door. Followed by a round of applause."

"But they're not actresses or opera singers," Annie broke in. "They're dedicated scientists."

"They're men, darling. At heart no different from the rest of the breed. I know whereof I speak, Annie. I've made a lifetime's work of studying the male of the species. They're programmed to win, at least the good ones are, and I for one understand it. I've had my share of success, my face for the world to see, so to speak, and I don't belittle the motive. There's something irresistible about being the idol of strangers, let alone the envy of your peers. I've known it. I can tell you it's pure bliss. But our husbands, poor lambs, are bound by all these archaic conventions, medieval oaths, that kind of thing. Why, they could wait forever before they get their due. Now, what's the point of the competition, I ask you, if you're not seen to have actually won?"

"Ideals ... knowledge ..."

"Fiddlesticks! You mean to tell me Seth isn't happy as a clam about today's story? Of course he is. Or will be, once he gets used to it. Gerald, too. You may be sure he made a point of pretending to chide me for speaking out of turn. Said all the things that your husband must have said. Premature ... irresponsible ... lah-de-dah-de-dah. But Gerald, happily, could put it down to my having been an actress, which of course is all very convenient. Because it's perfectly proper for a shoddy little actress to seek publicity, part of the profession, if you will."

Annie brooded for a moment. There was no denying the truth in much of what Margot had said. She divined that one of the sources of Seth's surface irritation was a fear of admitting to himself how delighted he really was.

"In other words," she said thoughtfully, "you feel you were doing them a favor."

"Sometimes," Margot said, "we have to do for them what they won't do for themselves. Now ..." She leaned back and scrutinized Annie with a camera's unsparing eye. "To more important matters. When are you going to get rid of those dreary twin sets and pearls and start dressing like a woman to be reckoned with? Colors ... drama ... that's what your wardrobe cries out for. Today's the day, love. New life ... new looks. First, I'm taking you down to Bergdorf's for some basic training. And believe me, no one knows more about clothes than Mama Margot. Then, Ferragamo for shoes.

Then, I'll make an appointment for you with my man Enzo—let him show you how to minimize noses, maximize eyes . . . the whole business. Man's a genius. Then Klinger's for skin, Kenneth for hair and don't tell me no. You owe it to me, darling, let alone to yourself and Seth. After all, say what you will about my little tête-à-tête with Strone Guthrie, it must have earned you both a fortune on the stock market."

Within the week, Annie had joined the ranks of New Yorkers who never dine at home, with the occasional exception of late-night takeout. Who had time to cook? Or energy? Or inclination?

These days, their kitchen rarely held anything more than a couple of microwave dinners, a few odd jars of gourmet delicacies to wash down drinks with, and a supply of catfood for Runaway Max.

Lunch was something to be grabbed on the run—a bolted sandwich stolen between rehearsals, appointments, drama classes; a hot dog and soda from the vendor outside of Carnegie Hall. Occasionally, when she could squeeze the time, a salad with Margot at Le Touquet.

Dinners were invariably social.

Each morning, she and Seth would make appointments with each other, like two busy executives on the run.

"Meet you at the theater. Don't worry if I miss the first act."

Or, "If I can't make cocktails at the Bereks', then I'll catch you up at Jay and Tina's. Save me some champagne."

A kiss. A shout of "Taxi" and they were on their separate ways.

Never in their lives had the Petersens known so many diverse and exciting people. There was Annie's new circle from the operatic world, a wealth of scientists eager for Seth's favor. There were the dozens of fresh faces—writers, diplomats, sportsmen, bankers—that they met at the Marriners' glittering parties and musicales.

"Sing for my guests, darling," Margot urged her one night. "There are a lot of somebodies here this evening."

And now the Petersens, too, were becoming somebodies, the people other people wished to meet.

One evening Annie and Seth had dinner with Ward Daniels at the Palm, which she deemed a singular honor.

"I wept over your dispatches from Beirut," she told him with untrammeled admiration.

He was a slight, dark man, foxy-faced, with circumflex eyebrows and a tendency to sniff when something caught his interest. Annie found it difficult to equate his mordant humor with the prose that had moved her to tears. She could hardly wait to see what he would write about her husband.

"Seth's going to be featured in a story in *Worldnews*." She phoned first her mother, then her sister in California. It was all she could do to keep from crowing. "An in-depth interview. Terrific, huh? And there's going to be a piece in *Fortune*, too." She felt herself the proudest woman in the world.

For though the public reaction had not quite been unanimous (there were plenty of scientists, of doctors in the field, advising caution and a large grain of salt), nonetheless the broader verdict was in. Seth had become, in his way, a hero, a celebrity of the finest sort. There was no longer the need to explain who he was, what he did, try to proselytize his efforts to acquaintances.

"You're quite a brilliant couple," a U.N. official remarked upon being introduced.

"We?" Annie queried. The kudos were usually reserved for Seth.

"I heard you sing at the Marriners' last month. Wonderful Puccini. Are we going to get a chance to hear you on stage before long?"

Annie crossed her fingers.

She had already joined an opera workshop and would soon get a chance to test her roles in action.

"There's a helluva lot more to opera than singing," she reminded Seth. There was an art, equal to the art of vocalizing, in commanding the stage, in revealing the depths of characters through body language and gait and gesture and diction.

Opera was the most brutal form of theater, she felt, making demands that mere actresses never had to cope with. It was tough enough to produce tears and laughter at will. Still more difficult to dominate the stage when you were lying horizontal on your deathbed. Virtually impossible to simulate the throes of love when your leading man hardly came up to your shoulder.

These were problems enough, as any actress could testify, without having to produce beautiful sounds into the bargain. In perfect tune, if you please. While keeping one eye on the conductor.

Annie knew she could sing, but could she act?

In this, as in so much else, Margot sprang to the rescue. Despite the claim that her own career was based upon nothing more than superb décolletage, she had a firm, hard sense of the craft. Over long afternoons in her spacious drawing room, she would furnish Annie with the tricks of the trade. How to take a fall without injury. What to do when you're being upstaged. How to make a full turn when you're wearing a train. Makeup tips. Costume secrets. Practical hints to keep from blinking in the spotlight.

Shortly before Christmas Annie made her New York debut singing the Countess in a workshop production of *Figaro*. The production was—to put it kindly—off off off Broadway, held in an aging theater on the Lower East Side that had once played host to Yiddish drama. But the stage was large and the acoustics splendid.

There would be no critics present. The audience consisted largely of friends, family, musicians, talent scouts, coaches and opera fans for whom the price of a ticket at the Met was too high.

"It went well," a flushed and breathless Annie said to Madame Natasha when the curtain fell, to which Madame answered with a sage nod. As for Seth, he was over the moon with pride.

"That's my wife." He collared perfect strangers in the crush backstage. "Isn't she terrific? Wasn't she wonderful?"

In fact she had been very, very good indeed.

No question but that the Petersens were, by all contemporary standards, a very brilliant couple indeed.

"I'm a layman." Ward Daniels settled into a chair in Seth's office and pulled out a stenographer's pad. "And I'm writing for laymen. People who don't know which end of a microscope is up. So let's keep it simple. I know that 'multiple' means 'many' and from my high school Latin I could figure out that 'sclerosis' means 'scar.' Beyond that I'm a total ignoramus. What is multiple sclerosis?"

The pencil hovered over the page ready to dart.

"It's almost easier to tell you what it's not. It's not contagious. It's not lethal. It's not inherited. It's not preventable. It's not predictable."

"Fine. Now tell me what it is." Ward waited.
Seth drew a deep breath and began.

Picture—he said—your body as a vast and complex telephone system, capable of making thousands of connections, both internal connections and links to the outside world. All this is commanded by a central switchboard: your brain.

The brain gives an order—for instance, "raise your right leg"— the way a switchboard might effect a call from New York to San Francisco. Then, like an electronic impulse down a telephone wire, that message is transmitted through the body, bypassing certain junctions, making necessary connections, till it arrives at the proper terminal. Head to toe, the operation takes about one-fiftieth of a second. The system's working. You raise your right leg. Mission accomplished.

Just as telephone wires have protective insulation to keep messages from going astray, so do the nerves of the body. This insulation is called a myelin sheath. Should this vital myelin coating wear away or be destroyed, the underlying nerves become exposed, and messages no longer reach their destination. In short, the brain may give orders, but without the myelin sheath to keep them in place, the body won't obey. These electronic impulses spill out, willy-nilly, bumping up against each other, at worst creating a massive short circuit. The result could be anything from a mild tingle to severe paralysis.

"In other words," Ward commented, "it's as if you've dialed San Francisco and your call never got beyond Chicago."

"Or never got anywhere at all," Seth added. "You've reached a dead end." This would apply to both conscious and unconscious movements. The more damaged the myelin, the more devastating the effects.

"What causes it?" Ward wanted to know.

Seth splayed his hands out. "Your guess is as good as mine. The most recent thinking is that it's viral in origin. But it could be caused by something in the environment, or some undetermined flaw in the genetic makeup of the victims. We really don't know. From every angle, it's a frustrating disease to deal with. Mysterious in origin . . . unpredictable in its course. There are theories galore, and plenty of data as well. The trouble is they don't necessarily add up."

"For instance?"

"For instance, white people contract it with greater frequency than Asians, northerners more often than southerners, women more than men. You know, we call it MS for short"—he shook his head— "like the name of that women's magazine. There's a certain irony in the nickname, because MS tends to strike women in the prime of their lives. Mostly between fifteen and fifty. Why they're singled out beats me.

"What happens, essentially, is that normally benign white blood cells—we call them helper T cells—leave their usual stations, invade the brain and the spinal cord, where they have no business going. They then attack the myelin sheaths. It's as if your own body turned upon itself, for no discernible reason. Outside forces aren't the enemy, what you're living through is a kind of rebellion from within. That of course makes it extremely difficult to treat without resorting to dangerous measures. Immunosuppressive drugs, for instance. In cancer, of course, this kind of chemotherapy is quite common. In the battle to destroy the cancer cells, healthy cells are also destroyed in vast numbers. Not only are the side effects terrible; technically the patient is being poisoned. That's acceptable in dealing with certain cancers, where the risk of death from the disease is greater and far more immediate than the risk of death from the treatment. But it's unacceptable in MS. An MS patient can live on for many, many years, even when the disease is severe. Of course the quality of that life is another matter. Sometimes there are spontaneous remissions, but it is a degenerative disease. In its latter stages, MS patients may have to face paralysis, blindness, an inability to control bodily functions . . ." Unwittingly, Seth shuddered. "It's a pretty grim picture on the whole."

"And you can offer them hope?" Ward asked.

"The experiments have been with mice, mind you," came the cautious reply. "What we've done here is develop a substance, an antibody that singles out these errant T cells and stops them in their tracks, prevents them from attacking the myelin sheath. The results . . . well, the first time I saw them, I could hardly believe my eyes. Damn close to incredible. Out of a dozen mice injected with FG-75, we've had total success with all but one, and even that one is still alive. We've actually managed to reverse paralysis in some of the specimens, within a remarkably brief span of time. Whereas the control mice, the ones that were given the disease but not the treatment, were either dead or severely paralyzed within the same period."

"And how do these results translate into human terms?"

But before Seth had a chance to answer, Gerald Marriner bustled in, all smiles and geniality.

"Dr. Petersen's too modest to make a commitment." Gerald beamed at Ward. "But I can tell you from my own vaster experience. We're very, very optimistic indeed. Yes"—he paused—"and you can quote me on this. I think a cure is just around the corner."

❧

"No!" Vi stared at Dr. Browning in shocked disbelief. "You can't tell me I have an incurable disease! I can't believe it! I won't believe it! Why me, for God's sake . . . why me!"

From the moment Sherm had brought her to Jersey State General, gray with panic, she had found herself thrust into a waking nightmare. The spasms, the keening aches, awful though they were, remained within the range of endurance. And Vi had never been the one to holler Uncle, at least not in front of onlookers.

But when the pain subsided, in its wake had come something far more terrible: an icy-fingered dread, a blackness of the mind and soul that set the stage for unimaginable terrors. For three days she had hovered in an anguished limbo, not knowing what was wrong or why.

"There is nothing worse," she pleaded with Dr. Browning, "than being left in the dark."

"I'll try not to keep you there," he had promised.

Repeatedly, she told herself she could cope with anything, once she knew what was going on. She was tough, resilient, and anyhow,

147

doctors these days could cure just about everything. Everything except the common cold. She even made feeble jokes about it to the night nurse, but it was whistling in the dark.

Whoever said that ignorance was bliss had never spent three days undergoing high-tech neurological testing.

When Dr. Browning first reviewed her medical history, he had asked her a question that seemed to come out of left field, resurrecting a long-forgotten incident.

Shortly after Noonie was born, she had gone with her new baby to live in a shabby furnished room in Jersey City.

"It was cheap, and I was nearly broke. And if that wasn't bad enough, suddenly," she remembered, "out of a clear blue sky, I began getting these terrible pains. It was my eyes. I thought I was going blind . . . trouble seeing. Hurt like hell, too. God, it was awful and I was so scared . . ."

Scared she wouldn't be able to fend for herself and her child. Scared of being nineteen and nearly friendless. Scared, above all, that some nosy health official, some visiting nurse would stumble on her plight and take Noonie away. Put him in an institution.

For nearly two months she lived in abject terror, venturing out of the room only for basic needs, holed up like a cornered animal till the last of her money had nearly run out. And then:

"Then, overnight it just went away . . . vanished," she told Dr. Browning. "The pain . . . the eye trouble. I just figured it was some kind of anxiety attack. What do they call it . . . postparting depression?"

Browning murmured something noncommittal, then ordered a battery of tests.

Now sitting by her bedside, he told her, "It's conclusive, I'm sorry to say. You have multiple sclerosis. You had your first attack after your baby was born, only it wasn't diagnosed at that time. You had your second attack last Thursday. This time, I regret, there's no question. The neurological tests confirm it beyond doubt."

He told her the ABC's of her ailment, described the path the disease was likely to take, and as he spoke she knew she had erred.

Ignorance *was* bliss. Or if not bliss, at least better than this terrible certainty now being thrust upon her slight, trembling frame.

"But why me?" she tried to keep the despair out of her voice. "Why me, of all people?"

Outrageous. She refused to let this happen to her. No way. Why, any moment, Noonie would come by and give her a Class A pinch or maybe a shove, followed by a "C'mon, Ma. Get moving. I'm gonna be late for school." And she would open her eyes, rub away the sleep, and this strange man with the soft smile and the funny balding fringe would be gone. She blinked. Blinked fast again, but he was still there. Still talking. Still making these absurd and incredible claims.

"Oh, we'll get you up on your feet, Vi." Damned if he didn't sound almost cheery. "As soon as possible. In fact, I'm going to put you to work starting today. It might take a few weeks, but there's no reason you shouldn't be able to manage quite well with canes, once you get the hang of it." He began outlining a course of physiotherapy, chatted on about gait training, the merits of diet and exercise, while Vi listened without taking in a word.

"No, goddammit!" she broke in on his monologue and began pounding his thighs with her fist. "There has got to be a cure. Don't tell me canes. Don't tell me gait training, whatever that is. What am I, a horse or something? For Chrissakes"—the words tore out of her—"you guys are transplanting hearts, kidneys, all that crap. You're keeping human vegetables alive on all kinds of million-dollar machines. And you're telling me all I can do is go to cripple classes? I don't believe it."

He waited until her wrath had run its course—a kind and feeling man who had heard it all before too many times.

"I wish I could tell you something else, but I'd be lying to you, offering you false hope. That's the greatest enemy there is—unfounded hope—because it'll break your heart every time. Vi, it hurts me every time I tell a patient this, but you'll have to learn to live with the disease . . . to conquer it"—he tapped the side of his forehead—"in here. Because that's the only place you can ever really lick it. And that's where the toughest struggle will be. Not in your legs . . . but in your spirit.

"You know, there are plenty of doctors who'll make you all kinds of promises. Plenty of panaceas. How does cobra venom hit you? We've got some self-styled healers who'll be happy to shoot you up with the stuff. Trouble is, the snake oil doesn't work. Or would you like to blow a few thousand dollars being bombarded by hyperbaric oxygen? It'll lighten your head and your wallet simultaneously. Now, if you were a mouse, Vi, we might be able to offer you some help. There have been some interesting developments, just recently, at a hot-shot lab in New York. But you're not a mouse. Besides which, it's too early to say. Any real benefits will be years down the road. Then again, maybe they won't. Don't count on it. Count on yourself instead. You're going to have to find that place," he said softly, "that lies between false hope and despair. It's a place called reality—and that's where you'll be spending the rest of your life."

She couldn't sleep that night. By dint of repetition, Dr. Browning's truths had begun to settle in. It was no use waiting to wake out of the nightmare. The nightmare was here to stay. And as she lay in the darkness, amidst sleeping strangers, the hollow clang of hospital corridors breaking the night silence, it was hard not to succumbing to panic.

In the dim night light, she looked down over the shape of her body beneath the sheets. That body was a stranger. How well she had treated it. How much she had enjoyed it—and so had a lot of other people too. Until tonight, she had viewed it as an instrument of pleasure, something to be proud of. The best legs in the Garden State, to quote Sherm. It was a body that had seen some pretty good service. And, ultimately, it had betrayed her.

For all these years, despite all those fondlings and caresses, beneath the cute clothes and perfumed skin, that same body was playing host to a silent secret enemy, a sleeping predator. Even as she laughed and made love and cooked brownies, this malevolent stranger was lying in ambush waiting to strike. Waiting for a time when her world looked perfect. And then felled her with a single vicious blow. It was too much, too cruel to be borne.

Noonie!

What would happen to him when Ross found out? This was all Winfield needed to screw her in court. Compassion had never been his strong point, and she could see him gleefully adding MS to his arsenal of weapons. Could she keep Ross from finding out?

More immediate, could she keep Sherm in the dark as well?
Should she?

Her wedding day had come and gone and she had yet to face him.
Given this knowledge, would he marry her? And what if he didn't?

His love had never been more important than in this time of
crisis. For if she had to face the question of what would become of
Noonie, she must also come to terms with what would become of
her. The time might come, indeed it might not even be distant,
when she would be unable to function in even basic ways.

The moment dawn broke, she called Crystal.

"Don't say a word to Sherm about anything," she pleaded. "Come
and see me this afternoon. I have to talk."

"Oh, lovey!" Crystal Klein pressed Vi to her ample bosom. "Life
really sucks sometimes, doesn't it?"

Vi shut her eyes and lay there unmoving, encompassed by her
friend's broad comforting arms, wishing she might hide from the
world forever.

"Oh, God, Crystal . . ." She finally disentangled herself. "I'm
glad you're here. I'm so fucking depressed."

Crystal gave her a long moist-eyed look, blew her nose and
brightened.

"Of course you're depressed, honey. Look at this shit!" She
pointed with disdain to a tray of grayish meat and instant mashed
potatoes, accompanied by a square of wobbly Jell-O, all untasted.
"Who wouldn't be depressed? Hospital food! Beats me how they
expect anyone to get well, eating that swill!"

Without further ado, she opened the huge plastic satchel that
was her trademark and began pulling out paper plates, plastic cartons, odd-shaped packets wrapped in aluminum foil and butcher's
paper.

"OK . . . there's pastrami on rye, corned beef on rye, this one's
Genoa salami and provolone on Italian . . . Kosher pickles, take your
pick, hon. . . . I got the garlic dills and the half sours. German potato
salad . . . you know, the kind with bacon in it. You like these big
fat Greek olives? Oh, yeah . . ." A small thermos emerged from the
bottom of the bag. "A wee drappie from the Scottish highlands. I
figure a place like this probably doesn't even have a liquor license."

"You crazy lady!" Vi shook her head in admiration and bit into a thick slab of pastrami. The crunch of peppercorns and caraway seeds, the tart flavor of deli mustard, made her remember that there was indeed a world beyond the hospital ward, a world of automobiles and desk diaries, of fun clothes and loving faces, and for the first time in days she had made contact with it. An earthy familiar world, as real as a pastrami on rye. Her world.

"My God, this is good!" She wolfed down two sandwiches, a couple of dills and half a container of potato salad, then leaned back replete.

"Well, at least your taste buds are functioning."

"Yeah . . ." Vi felt better. "But that's about all."

"So what happens next?" Crystal wanted to know. "Sherm says he hasn't been able to get in to see you. Your decision, I gather. What should I tell him? Jesus, the man's climbing the walls, he's so anxious . . ."

"And looking after Noonie OK, I hope."

"Yup." Crystal nodded. "He's been terrific with Noonie, no sweat. Told him you came down with a lousy bout of flu, is all." She began tidying up the remains of their picnic, brushing crumbs off the blankets before resettling herself into the visitor's chair.

"I'll take that Scotch now, if you don't mind," Vi said.

"Sure 'nuf." Crystal poured a generous measure into a pleated paper hospital cup and handed it to Vi. "Right." She waited till her friend had downed the drink, then asked, "Have you told Sherm what the diagnosis is?"

Vi shook her head, no.

"Are you going to?" Crystal pursued.

For an answer, Vi wadded the empty cup into a paper ball, then gave a long slow sigh.

"I don't know," she said at last. "I was up all last night thinking about it."

She suddenly took the ball of paper and flung it across the room with a vengeance. It hit the wall with a dull smack.

"Yesterday," she said, "I went to this class they have here, I'm supposed to learn how to walk with my canes. Kept falling on my duff, but that's not the point. I looked at the other people, Crystal . . . and Jesus, it broke my heart. They were on walkers, in wheelchairs . . . the next thing to helpless. Young . . . a lot of 'em, too! And that's limiting it just to the folks who were in good enough shape to actually make it to the center. What about the ones who couldn't? And there are plenty of them, you betcha. I mean the ones who right now are lying in their beds like a goddam sack of potatoes, dead from the waist down, totally dependent on other people. Not even able to go to the john on their own, for Chrissakes. That could be me in a couple of years," she burst out.

"You don't know that!" Crystal was shocked.

"There's no guarantee, but it's a live possibility. If I can use the word 'live' in that sense. Browning says I've had a really bad attack and there's no telling when the next one is coming. Though if I hear the word 'unpredictable' one more time, I think I'll scream. Thing is, Crystal, the fucking disease waited all these years for Round Two, it just may want to make up for lost time. At best," she threw out, "I'm going to be dependent on these goddam canes. Never run, never go ice-skating again with Noonie, never go disco dancing even. Jesus, that one hurts. We've had a lot of laughs in those places . . ."

"We sure have!" Crystal nodded.

"But the big crunch is . . . what's going to happen when that son of a bitch Winfield finds out? Aaah . . ." She placed a hand against her breast. "I feel like there's a ten-ton truck parked on top of me right now."

"Heartburn," Crystal said. "You shouldn't bolt your food."

"Heartache," Vi said, and averted her gaze for a long painful moment.

When she looked up, her eyes were bright and hard.

"I've decided not to tell Sherm," she said at last. "I want to get married . . . I need to have him behind me."

Crystal gave a soft low whistle.

"What'll you say? You'll have to give him some story or other. How else will you explain away the canes?"

"I'll tell him I tripped in the shoe store, pulled a muscle, tore a ligament . . . something like that, but it'll take a couple of months to heal, so why don't we go ahead and get married anyhow. I think Sherm will swallow it, provided you don't spill the beans. Who's going to tell him different? Browning? Unh . . . unh. Browning wouldn't have to give him the time of day. There's this . . . what d'you call it? . . . that hypocritic oath that doctors take. They can't talk about their patients out of school."

"And after you and Sherm are married, then what?"

"I'll play it by ear. Just act dumb until the next attack."

"That's very heavy," Crystal said. "Maybe if you told him the truth, he'd want to marry you anyway . . . ?"

Vi shook her head slowly. "That's what I kept turning over at three o'clock in the morning. It would be nice to believe that love really conquers and all that jazz, just like in the movies. But then I'd ask myself, what I would do in his place? Would I be willing to spend the rest of my life playing caretaker to a basket case? No way! Anyhow, I'm not going to take the chance. It's a lousy thing to do, but what choice do I have? Am I being a total shit, Crystal? On second thought, don't answer that."

"It's your life . . ." Crystal sighed. "And I guess you're just being practical. But you can't keep him on hold much longer. He's champing at the bit, he keeps asking me what's going on."

"Tomorrow," Vi breathed. "Browning tells me I should be out of here tomorrow. He says it's time to pick up the pieces of my life. Well . . ." She mustered an unhappy grin. "The pieces don't come any bigger than Sherm."

4

SETH OPENED THE FRENCH DOORS AND LOOKED OUT OVER THE WHITE coral sand and pristine curve of Sapphire Bay.

"Mmmm!" He grunted with satisfaction. "What a morning! What a day! What a life! Let's have breakfast on the terrace, shall we, darling? The Marriners can spare us for a few more hours."

Under the lacy coverlet, Annie stretched like a contented cat. "You say that every morning," she murmured. "Some houseguests we are. They must figure us for sex maniacs, lazing around in bed like this."

"You mean we're not?"

"That's beside the point." She laughed. "Listen, we can hardly spend an entire week in St. Thomas and go back to New York pale as paper. What'll people say?"

"They'll say we've been having a second honeymoon."

"How can we have a second when we never even had a first?" she asked.

"Well, I don't know what we've been doing these last few days, but I think we may have set a world's record."

With that he wrapped a towel around his waist and stepped out into the sunshine.

She watched him with undisguised satisfaction.

Maybe not a world record, but certainly a Petersen household record for nonstop lovemaking. What a week it had been.

Not since their first discovery of each other years ago in Boston had sex been so consuming, so rapturous. Perhaps it had to do with the seductiveness of the surroundings. Villa Narcissus, with its shaded gardens and sunlit balconies, its Oriental traceries and latticed walks, the lulling splash of its pools and fountains, had been designed for the pursuit of pleasure alone.

"My seraglio," Margot had said.

And Annie, now lying like an odalisque in the cool shadow of the bedroom, felt the justice of that word. From the moment she and Seth had stepped across the threshold they had fallen upon each other in an utter wash of sensuality.

"Oh, God," he had said, "I want you like I've never wanted you before. It must be something in the air."

But it was something that was not in the air, Annie recognized, that had worked its chemistry upon them. An absence, a magnificent lack.

"There are no clocks in the house!" She noticed only after several days. "Not a one, except in the kitchen for the cook."

For if Margot had managed to create a miniature palace of the senses, she also had contrived to banish time.

No clocks, no meetings, no urgent phone calls, no deadlines—nothing but an infinity of self. Who had the time for this kind of lovemaking back in New York, the leisure to explore every erotic possibility? It was a career as engrossing, as exhausting as music. Or chemistry. Or whichever other foolish ways upon which lovers wasted their time.

On the balcony, Seth was leaning over the railing.

"Henry," he called down to where the Marriners' houseboy was cutting roses. "Would you bring us up some coffee . . . ?"

"Yes sir!" The music of the islands was in the young man's voice.

". . . and some fresh mangoes?"

"Sir . . . You be wanting something more?"

"A couple of croissants with jam." Seth turned and looked back into the bedroom, all smiles.

"Come on out, Annie. Come look at the sea."

She fumbled for a robe and joined him.

"You don't need to button up." He slipped a hand around her neck. "No one to see us between here and Tortola. Just the sea, the sky and my beautiful Annie. How come we never went to the Caribbean before, I wonder?"

"Because we were always too broke," came the reply.

"A most perceptive answer. God, this is paradise."

They stood for a while, bodies touching lightly, absorbing the beauty of the tropical morning. A heron broke through the azure sky and skimmed the water, leaving a silver streak in his wake.

"Blizzard in New York," Annie remarked. "Someone mentioned it in the restaurant last night."

"Zat so?" Seth grinned. "Makes the view even better. Nothing quite so great as soaking up the sun when you know everyone else is freezing their ass off."

"You rat!" She giggled. "Where's your compassion for the frozen masses?"

"Same place yours is, love. You know the yuppie credo: It's not enough to know that you've won. You have to know that other people have lost. You're right, we should go to work on those tans today."

Henry arrived, wheeling in breakfast on a serving cart.

While the Petersens watched, he set the table with a flamboyant pride. The coffee in its silver urn just there, the croissants piled high in a porcelain basket, tiny pots of jam, golden curls of butter, yellow Tiffany dishes full of sunshine, napkins folded into crisp rosettes, fresh carnations and hibiscus in a Lalique vase. Table set, Henry stood back to observe the effect of his handiwork, nodded, smiled, then was gone with the slap slap slap of bare feet upon tile.

Seth sat down and unfolded his napkin.

"In my next incarnation," he said, "I'm going to follow Gerald's example and marry a millionairess."

"You going to follow Gerald's example in this incarnation and learn how to fly?"

They had flown to St. Thomas in Gerald's Learjet and at one point he had allowed Seth to take the controls. Seth had found the experience stimulating.

"Yes, maybe I will," he mused, "if I can ever find the time. Would that worry you, darling, if I took up aviation?"

"I don't think so," Annie said. "Although I see Margot gets jumpy when Gerald flies."

"She fusses too much. Gerald's only problem is overwork."

"Yours too," Annie replied. "Your first vacation in a year, and all you can squeeze is one measly week. We don't even get to stay over till New Year's."

"Breaks of the game." He raised his head to the sun. "Pour me some coffee, will you, darling?"

They sat and breakfasted in perfect harmony. Tomorrow this time, they'd be back in New York.

Seth helped himself to another croissant.

"You don't have to go back, you know, darling."

"You're reading my mind again. Of course I'll go back with you."

"What for? Margot's staying on for another week, she'd be delighted to have your company. Besides"—he shifted in his seat—"I've got such a frantic week coming, I'd probably never get a chance to see you. Starting two new projects. Then next week, there's this press conference, did I tell you? Some brainstorm by our PR gal, sort of an open house for reporters, or maybe it's Wall Street analysts. Anyhow, I've got my work cut out for me. But you stay on, darling. You've been working like a navvy all winter, what's the crime in stealing a few days for yourself?"

"But the movers . . . ? I have all that packing to do."

"You pay people to do that sort of thing, Annie. They'll do it right down to the last bobby pin. So why should you rush back to the lousy weather? Besides"—he smiled—"it would please me to think of you down here all tanned and beautiful."

She laughed. "What about that yuppie credo of yours? Doesn't it work in reverse? Isn't the worst part of slushing about in over-shoes and snow tires the knowledge that other people will be loung-ing around in the sun?"

"You're not other people, love," he said fondly. "You're us."

Margot was delighted when Annie announced she would stay. "And I'll make sure Gerald looks after Seth."

"Oh, Seth doesn't need any looking after," Annie said.

"You mean," Margot whispered conspiratorially, "after all those long late morning sessions of yours, you're sending him back to New York too exhausted to indulge in hanky-panky?" And when Annie turned crimson, Margot squealed. "I really hit it. You've worn the poor man out. Well, that's one recipe for keeping a hus-band out of mischief. Rather a good one, I daresay. They are such helpless creatures."

Annie hardly knew whether to laugh or protest. It was Margot's view that all men were weak and vulnerable vessels, all women were predators, and that in any relation between the sexes, infidelity was the unremarkable norm. Perhaps this was so in Margot's circle of the rich and self-indulgent. They had nothing but time on their hands. But in the real world . . . ?

Seth a weak and vulnerable vessel indeed! Annie tried to picture him with a blond showgirl on either arm. Too ludicrous for words. "I trust Seth," Annie said. "He's a domestic animal at heart."

"Of course he is." Margot nodded politely. "I was only teasing."

And the matter was dropped.

The next week sped by. Her last night on the island, she stood naked before the bedroom mirror, admiring her tan. Seth would be delighted. She smiled. She'd never looked better, more glowing.

And as she packed the last of her beachwear into the suitcase, it was all she could do to keep from singing.

She was going back to a new year, a new apartment, a new life.

Maybe this time next year, she'd be pregnant. Perhaps she already was. Not that Annie believed in prophecies, but she wasn't so quick to jeer at them either, not when they told her what she wanted to hear.

That very afternoon, she and Margot had gone to visit a Haitian obeah woman who lived in a hut outside the village.

It was a lark—nothing more—although Margot claimed the woman was famous for the accuracy of her visions.

"Don't you dare tell Seth." Annie giggled. "He just hates what he calls 'rank superstition.' "

"I won't . . . as long as you don't tell Gerald."

Annie entered first.

The room where the ancient crone held court reeked of sweat and incense and dried blood and musty herbs.

"No crystal ball?" Annie teased, but her joke remained unacknowledged. For a tiresome quarter hour, the old woman rattled on in what Annie presumed to be Creole, arranging and rearranging a heap of chicken bones.

At last, she looked up from her labors, fixed Annie with great luminous black eyes and intoned, "You who are two will be three."

"Is that all . . . ? Does that mean . . . ?" Annie suppressed a tremor. "Can you be more specific?" Even *Cosmo* did better than that.

The woman repeated the phrase, but as she spoke, she placed a hand on Annie's belly. Despite herself, Annie thrilled. Only one meaning could be deduced.

"Good fortune?" Margot queried when Annie came out.

"The best. Now it's your turn."

"Watch the steps, hon," Sherm cautioned. "They're icy."

"I'm careful . . . I'm careful."

Breath held tight against imminent disaster, Vi managed to negotiate the front stairs, all two of them, without mishap and reeled into the living room in a clatter of canes.

"Damned if I can get the hang of these mothers," she cursed as Sherm lumbered into the kitchen to make coffee.

Then the bedroom door swung open and out popped Noonie, like a jack-in-the-box on a tightly coiled spring.

"You're back!" he screamed. Next thing she knew he was on top of her with a single running leap.

"Wow, kiddo. You nearly knocked me off my pins. How come you're not in school this morning, honey?"

"Sherm said . . ."

But whatever Sherm had said was now beyond Noonie's power to relate, for with a heaving sob he had thrown his arms around his mother, clinging like a shipwreck victim to a life raft. Through the thickness of his heavy cotton sweatshirt, she could feel his skinny body shuddering, like a cornered animal. It had needed this to remind her how frightening her absence must have been to him. Why, he was almost as scared as she was.

"Hey, Noonie." She hugged him back till her arms ached, then waited for his trembling to subside. "Stand back and let me take a look at you. Have you grown? Or are you still the same runty kid?"

"Aw, c'mon, Mom." He made an effort to recoup his macho image. "It's only been a week."

"Yeah . . . a week too long. What've you been doing with yourself? How's school? Tell me . . ."

As he brought her up to date with hot doings at JFK Grammar, Vi managed a quick stocktaking. The boy looked well—not merely glad that she was back in circulation, but well tended, even clean behind the ears for a change.

The apartment, too, was spotless, rather more so than when she'd left it.

In the kitchen, Sherm waited for the reunion to run its course before emerging with coffee and cookies on a tray.

"OK, kid. Give your mother a chance to catch her breath. You can have two chocolate chip cookies, no more, and then you better beat it to school."

"Aw, Sherm . . ."

"Nope, you're not using this as an excuse to play hooky. Your mother will write you a note and then off you go."

Noonie dawdled over his milk, nibbled the cookies in prolonged slow motion, till Sherm, aware of his anxiety, finally clapped a hand on his shoulder. "C'mon, Noonie, easy does it. Your Mom will be here when you get home."

Still, he seemed reluctant to leave.

"You gonna drive me to school, Sherm?"

"What's the matter, you can't walk? OK, Noonie-O. Get your coat and I'll run you over." He winked at Vi. "Back in five, sweetheart."

Vi watched her men go with a mixture of gratitude and guilt.

Having someone play father was the boy's idea of heaven. Too bad it required a major fraud to pull it off.

Sherm had, as anticipated, taken Vi's explanation at face value when she presented it last night.

"Ligament, huh? You really must have done a job on it. God, you women are so vain. Well, that's the last time you wear three-inch heels, tootsie. You're lucky you didn't break something."

With no conscious sense of irony, she promised him she would stick to sensible shoes in the future.

"The thing is, I might be hobbling on these sticks for quite a while yet . . . Maybe even right down the aisle."

"Yeah . . . well . . ." Sherm sighed and accepted the presumed inconvenience. "At least it's only temporary . . ."

Vi made no reply. She had lied quite enough for one evening.

But now, waiting for Sherm to come back from school, she was assailed with doubts. He didn't deserve this of her. Maybe Crystal was right, maybe he would be willing to marry her, disability and all.

She tried to visualize their life a few months hence.

Suppose she suffered another attack in the near future? A more devastating round? Then he would know that she had lied to him.

And even if she was lucky, one of the favored few to enjoy the "optimum scenario," as the doctor had termed it—even should she be blessed with a long and uneventful remission, a good deal of damage had already been done.

She couldn't fob him off with that story indefinitely. She was never going to walk normally again. Sooner or later, Sherm would insist on seeing a doctor with her, on finding out why her "ligament" refused to heal.

Either way, the truth would out within a month or so. Only by then, of course, she and Sherm would be safely married. She would make it up to him as best she could.

Still! Some track record that would be! Vi made a moue of distaste. She had secured her first husband through outright blackmail, her second by way of a despicable fraud. Even if Sherm could live with her on those conditions, she didn't know if she could live with herself.

Except she wasn't doing it out of selfish motives; she was doing it for Noonie. And that, as Crystal would say, made it kosher. Whatever else this swindle might be, it was one smart move. You had to be a realist in this world.

The front door slammed. Sherm had let himself in.

"Still sitting here?" He smiled. "How about I heat up your coffee?"

That dear man.

"No thanks, I'm fine."

"Then how about a little mood music? I could do with some."

He went to the stereo and rooted around for something to his taste.

" 'Can't get no satisfaction.' " He sang along with Mick Jagger, then executed a few swivel-hipped turns across the floor for her delectation, like a bird in a mating display. For a big man, he moved with sinuous grace.

"Oldies but goodies." His fingers snapped to the beat. "They don't write 'em like that anymore."

A lifetime of habit tugged at her toes, urged her to get up and dance.

"Come sit, Sherm." She patted the cushion. "And fill me in on what's been happening in the office."

"Sure, kid." He waltzed over to the sofa and nestled in, then gave her a rundown on the status quo. Which deals had gone through, which had soured. They'd arranged for her to do desk work for the next few weeks "until you're on your feet again."

Then he talked about their wedding plans. The house. The closing date was set for the thirtieth. They still had furniture shopping to do. "As soon as you're up and about."

Then he talked about the time he'd pulled his back out, skiing. And when he broke his collarbone in high school.

"Jesus, I drove everybody crazy, so I know how it feels to be cooped up."

His mood was cheerful, but behind all the well-meaning chatter, she kept tuning in on a single underlying pattern, phrased in half a dozen different ways. "As soon as things are back to normal" ran the thread of his thoughts. Sherm was waiting for the day.

Vi waited for him to wind down.

"Listen," she said, "I want to thank you for helping out with everything. Noonie, the whole schmeer. Even the apartment looks great. What did you do, have a cleaning woman in?"

"A couple of times. I didn't think you'd want to come home to a shambles. Christ, I missed you, babe." He snuggled close and nibbled on her neck. "I had the maid put clean sheets on the bed, all fresh as a daisy . . ." Even sitting next to him, she could feel his body heat. At his touch, she felt a swell of apprehension.

"It's been nearly a week, sweetie." His voice was soft, his eyes warm and adoring. "That's a long time without a little loving. I'll be gentle as a lamb, I promise. That is . . . if you're in the mood."

"Maybe a little later." She couldn't bring herself to face him. Sex was the furthest thing from her mind. She was indescribably weary, a hundred years old.

"If you don't mind, Sherm, I'd like to take a nap. Anyhow, you should be getting back to the office."

"Whatever you say, love." He rose to give her a helping hand, but she was afraid he might take the measure of her weakness.

"Hand me my canes, will you, Sherm?"

Sitting down on the sofa had been a tactical mistake. It was too low, too soft, virtually impossible to get sufficient leverage. She was conscious of Sherm watching her with a puzzled air.

"You need a hand?"

"I'm fine," she raged, trying to align them with the floor. "Just fine."

"Gee, honey . . ." Sherm watched her struggle to her feet. "You sure are a menace with those sticks. Good thing it's only temporary."

A second later she was flat on the floor, canes flying across the room like missiles.

"That fucking kid!" She wept tears of frustration. "Why the hell doesn't he put his fucking skateboard away?"

"Are you hurt?" Sherm was down there beside her.

"Only in my pride." She wiped her eyes on the back of her hand.

"C'mon," he soothed. "I'll help you into bed."

"I can't . . ." she began.

"Of course you can. Give yourself a couple of weeks. Now just put your arms around my neck."

But she was shaking her head with a grief that went far beyond physical pain.

"I can't, Sherm." She looked into those dark trusting eyes. "I can't do this to you. I can't cheat you this way . . . you deserve so much better."

"I don't know what you're talking about." His face was a question mark.

But five minutes later he did.

"Give me time," he said. "Time to think it over, learn to live with it. Give me twenty-four hours."

The next day he was back on the stroke of noon, formally dressed with a dark suit, white shirt and a striped tie. The night had aged him, his cheeks sagged with fatigue.

"You look like you're going to a funeral." Vi tried to keep it light. "Mine, by any chance?"

He pulled up a chair and sat opposite her at the little table where they had breakfasted so many intimate mornings.

"There's nothing in the world," he began, "that I want more than to marry you."

Unaccountably her heart leaped. She had not expected this. Afraid to breathe, afraid to break the silence.

"That is . . ." he clarified. "I wanted to want to marry you. I wanted to feel good and noble and faithful, to look at myself in the mirror each morning knowing I'd done a fine and honorable thing. That's one part of me. But another part of me, Vi . . . the deepest part of me . . . won't let it happen."

His voice broke and he turned away from her. When she saw his face again, the eyes were brimming unashamedly.

"I'm a young man, Vi. Only thirty. I'm healthy and full of life. I want a wife to do things with, to share laughs, vacations . . . to run a home. Yes, a proper home. And I want children. Is that so unreasonable? Not just Noonie, but kids of my own. I love you, Vi. You're a terrific lady, but I'm a vigorous man, healthy . . . in my prime. You know, the two of us . . . our relationship . . . it was always based on doing things together. We went places, we skied, we sailed, we disco'd." He paused. The words stuck in his craw. "We . . . we had such great sex, you and I."

"Is that all I was?" Her bitterness broke through. "A piece of ass? A good fuck?"

"Oh Vi," he pleaded. "Don't make it harder than it is. You know how much I care for you—you're someone very special—but sex is like the sun to me. I love it . . . I need it. It's what makes me a man, and I don't want to live without it."

"Well, neither do I, Sherm," she cried out. "You think I don't have feelings? Desires?"

She never should have refused him yesterday afternoon. It had been a grievous error, had sent him down this road. Instead, she should have taken him to her bed, loved him with all the skills at her command, granted him the favors he liked best.

She should have waited until she was in his arms, his juices hot inside her, before ever confiding her plight. Dear Sherm! He could never refuse her anything, least of all in bed. The man was a soft touch, bless him. Looking at him seated across the table, wretched and shamefaced, she could see he was suffering. He hated what he was doing almost as much as she did.

Perhaps it was not yet too late.

"We could go to bed now, Shermie," she murmured, her voice full of remembered pleasures. "This very minute, if you'd like to. I would. You know, I may not be able to run the four-minute mile, but I'm still capable of making love."

"*You* may be"—he wiped his eyes—"but I don't think *I* am. I doubt if I could get it up, Vi, considering the circumstances. Ever-Ready Sherm, you used to call me, just like the flashlight battery. Turns on at a touch."

"And lasts and lasts and lasts."

She reached over and touched his lips with gentle fingers, worked a soft passage into his mouth. It was a prelude to a sweet familiar joy.

"Would you like me to go down on you?" she whispered.

For a moment he trembled, then took her hand and placed it on the table.

"It's no good, Vi. They say sex is all in the head. I guess maybe it is, because I can't get what's in my head out. Last night, I called up a neurologist friend of mine. I wanted to know the worst—and the best. He told me it's a degenerative disease."

Vi reached for the feeble pun, but didn't have the heart. She said nothing.

"The doctor told me—and I guess you know all this—you'll probably wind up in a wheelchair, helpless . . . incontinent." He was weeping openly now. "God forgive me, Vi, I can't . . . I can't rid myself of that image. It would be in bed with us every time, hanging over us like a sword . . ."

"Please . . . !" She made a superhuman effort to keep control. How extraordinary that it should be she who was comforting him! The weak offering solace to the strong. "Please, Sherm, no more. I understand. I'd probably do the same thing in your place. It's all right, baby. It's all right."

He blew his nose, then went into the bathroom for an extended visit. She could hear the water running in the sink. When he emerged, eyes red-rimmed but dry, he brought with him an emotional distance.

"I talked to them at Orson Realty," he said. "They appreciate you won't be able to work actively with prospects at this point. They're willing to offer you a desk job, however. No commission, though. Just straight salary . . ."

The impression was unmistakable: he dreaded her coming back. Her very presence would be a perpetual accusation.

"I've got some sick leave coming," she said. "I'll take that first and then I'll see . . . Maybe I'll look around for something else, something nearer home."

"What I thought, Vi"—he made an effort to disguise his relief— "is, you might want to get yourself some computer skills. It's the coming thing, babe, BASIC . . . FORTRAN, the language of the future. Then you could maybe run a business right from your living room. Do some free-lance bookkeeping, word processing, this Lotus Symphony stuff . . . who knows what you could parlay it into. You're a bright lady. I'd like to help you set it up, Vi. What I propose, if it's OK with you, is I'll put some money in your bank account. Let's say five thousand. Enough anyhow to buy yourself an IBM, learn the lingo . . ."

Five thousand. It was five times the "good-bye" money Ross Winfield had offered her years ago. She had refused Ross's bribe. Had, in fact, derived a perverse pleasure in turning it down. But Ross had owed her. Sherm didn't.

"Thank you." She smiled. She was conscious of doing him a favor, letting him buy an easier conscience with the money. "That's very generous, very gentlemanly, and I'll be delighted to take it."

"Good." He exhaled heavily, a man reprieved from death. "And suppose I have my cleaning woman come around a couple of times a week? I'm sure you could use the extra help, and I'll pick up the tab."

"You don't have to, Sherm."

"That's all right, Vi. I want to."

She refused to cry where it showed. What was the point of sending the man on a guilt trip? He felt bad enough already. So they sat a few minutes longer in sticky silence. Everything that could be said had been said. And those things that remained unspoken would take forever.

"Well . . ." He got to his feet with a heavy scrape of the chair. "I guess I'll be shoving off. Anything I can get you before I go?"

No, she shook her head.

He was halfway out the door when she called after him softly. "How about a kiss good-bye?"

He walked over to where she sat and kissed her solemnly on the forehead. "Good-bye, Vi. And all the luck in the world."

Then the door shut behind him.

She sat for a long time with the memory of his lips on her brow. Then she picked up her canes and made her way out onto the porch.

The street was empty, except for a neighbor a few houses away, shaking dust out of an ancient rug. Sherm's car was gone. He was gone. In her heart, Vi knew it was forever.

It was a brilliant day, cold but sharp with sunshine. In the clear air, colors dazzled. Fresh snow glittered in the branches, pristine as a bridal veil. A few high clouds trailed their whiteness across the sky.

Vi leaned against the railing gazing into the hard blue ether.

"You up there!" She raised a cane and thrashed it against the sky. "You son-of-a-bitch God," she screamed. "You go to hell, do you hear me? Go to hell!"

The woman down the street put down her rug for a moment and surveyed her with mild curiosity.

But Vi's eyes were fixed on the cold angry heaven.

"Why me, you motherfucker! Why me?!"

5

THE MOVE TO PARK AVENUE TOOK PLACE THE DAY AFTER ANNIE'S return. "At last." Seth looked about him in satisfaction. "At last we're living like proper human beings."

"Better." Annie grinned. "Like princes."

Five spacious rooms with high ceilings and handsome wainscoting, even a little maid's room that could serve as a den for Seth—all this in addition to a view over New York's most elegant avenue. "Who could ask for anything more?" Annie sang.

Her first week back was spent in a flurry of decorating: painters, paperhangers, carpet fitters, furniture deliveries. "What do you think?" Annie held up some swatches of Laura Ashley wallpaper for her husband's delectation. "The yellow or the rose pattern?"

"You choose," came the answer. "I'm busy."

So the yellow it was, tiny daffodils to brighten their bedroom with an eternal promise of spring. She also chose a Biedermeyer desk as a housewarming gift to her husband, a charming incentive for him to work at home every now and then. Back went the upright piano to Steinway's, replaced now by an ebony grand.

"And not a moment too soon," Ari said, for Annie's career looked nearly ready to take wings. She was devouring new music at a voracious rate, not just the staples of the repertoire but some of the more interesting minor roles. Practical, that, for Madame had begun talking about auditions for the Met and City Center.

"Of course, the principal roles are booked two years in advance, but I'd like to see you get launched in some supporting parts."

"Utility infielder." Annie laughed, remembering Seth's long-ago remark, while Madame returned a puzzled stare.

"Next autumn," said the tiny coach. "By next autumn I believe you will be ready."

"What do you think, Seth?" She caught her husband on the run one morning.

"Terrific," Seth breathed and dashed off yet again to the lab. "We'll talk about it later . . . I'm busy."

Busy busy busy. Who wasn't? It was the pitch and tempo of New York. One of these days, Annie promised herself, she and Seth must really take time off, spend a relaxing evening on their own. Just the two of them. Talk. They had a lot of catching up to do. But meanwhile, life was too busy.

A few weeks after the move to Park Avenue, Runaway Max fell to his death.

The news, delivered by the doorman, greeted Annie on her return from a voice lesson.

"SPCA's already been here and gone. They had to scrape him off the sidewalk. Damned thing just came zooming out of the sky like a dive bomber . . . lucky he didn't kill someone. Don't know whose cat it was, Mrs. Petersen, but we think it may have been yours."

"Nooo . . . !"

Annie tore past him into the lobby, punched the button furiously for the elevator. There had to be some mistake, she told herself as the elevator inched its way up. Not her Emperor Maximilian. He was too smart, too canny to do a dumb thing like that. Someone else's cat. Had to be.

She opened the door and began the familiar barrage of lip-smacking rat-a-tat-tats that usually fetched him from his nefarious haunts.

"Pssss ts . . . ts . . . ts . . . ts . . . Come on, Max . . . come to mama."

Within, there reigned the distinctive silence of an empty apartment, but Annie refused to let it seep into her consciousness. Instead, she began ransacking the closets, the cupboards, the high shelves, the space beneath the kitchen sink, even the empty packing cases in the spare room. "Ts . . . ts . . . ts . . . come on, Max . . . tssss." Anything but accept the inevitable. Max was sly, he was, with his crafty games, his elusive feline version of hide and seek. She even looked inside the clothes dryer out of desperation.

For how could her Max have gotten out of the apartment? It was wintertime. The windows were shut, the door to the terrace firmly locked.

Only in the little corner den a window had been propped open a few inches to dispel the odor of fresh paint. As Annie froze in an icy sweat of realization, a pigeon, nestled on the ledge, took flight.

Poor Max, the truth honed in on her. Poor gallant, crazy, wily, reckless Runaway Max. Following his instincts, birding to the end. This time, however, there had been no warm, grubby alley waiting a few inches beneath his feet, but a drop of sixteen stories.

Had he sensed what was happening on his long descent? Had he known fear? Panic? Did he suffer after hitting the ground? Unbidden, his soft remembered mewling filled the silence. She could not bear the thought of Max in pain.

Devastated, Annie fell into the nearest chair and reached for the phone. As never before, she needed the comfort of Seth's sympathy.

"I'm sorry," said the voice-of-the-week at the other end of the line. "Dr. Petersen is in a meeting."

"It's important," Annie cried. Was it, really? Yes, dammit, it was. "Would you call him out, please?"

A minute later, Seth was on the phone, sounding rushed and anxious.

"Annie . . . you OK? What's the matter?" and when she told him, he followed her recitation with, "Was anybody hurt in the fall?"

"No . . . at least not according to the doorman. Max . . ." She wept. "Max was the only victim."

"Thank God!" Seth breathed a sigh of relief. "He could've killed somebody, and Jesus . . . we might have had a lawsuit on our hands. I'm sorry, baby." His voice softened suddenly. "I know you feel lousy about it, but these things happen. Look . . . I'm in the middle of a big meeting right now, can't stay on the phone. Why don't you get out of the apartment for a couple of hours? Have tea with a friend? Better yet, go buy yourself something. I'll be home as soon as I can. Six, six thirty, no later than seven at any rate. OK, sweetheart?"

It was nearer eight when he finally appeared, bearing a gorgeous bouquet of hot-house tulips.

"Harbingers of spring. I thought we could both use some cheering up. Let me just put 'em in water."

Tulips disposed of, he settled in beside her on the sofa. "Stretch out, love. Put your feet up, head in my lap." Comforting hands stroked her hair, soothed her forehead. "Poor darling . . . you've had quite a day."

At his touch, she burst into tears.

"Easy now, love," Seth consoled her. "It was only a cat. A pretty cantankerous one at that."

"You don't feel the same way about animals," she grieved. "You never did."

"Don't be mean, Annie. He was my cat too, you know. But let's face it—Max was not the world's greatest pet. Always was a little bit goofy, if you ask me. And shed? My God! Every place we've lived in has been one giant hairball. You've complained about it plenty yourself. I know you're feeling miserable, darling, and it's a sad way for Max to go, but as I said—it's only a cat. We can get another one tomorrow, if you like. Next time, though, let's be practical and get one with short hair."

"I don't want another cat." She was weeping again. "I want Max, dammit. Faults and all, I loved him."

Seth waited for her tears to subside, then fixed them both hefty drinks.

"You don't want a cat at all," he divined. His face was grave, meditative. "You want a baby."

She wiped her eyes, and took a deep gulp of bourbon.

"You're so smart, aren't you?" She almost managed a smile. "You always tell me what I think before I think it."

But he was right, of course. Max had, at best, been a substitute. Hairy, cantankerous. Not even particularly lovable compared to most other pets. She had let herself get overattached.

"Let me look into some of these fertility clinics, Annie. Gerald would know who're the best people to see, maybe the time has come to start investigating, get some testing done . . ."

"Oh, I don't know." Annie sighed. "I really don't know."

They had discussed it so many times before, all the various tactics and remedies for childlessness. Realistically, there were ample choices: fertility pills, artificial insemination, test-tube pregnancies, even adoption as a last-ditch possibility. Yet each time Annie managed to fob the questions off into some semidistant future. Age thirty-two would be a deadline, maybe. Thirty-three. Thirty-five at the outermost. Seth had never understood her reluctance to avail herself of sophisticated measures.

"That's why these techniques were developed," he urged her, "to supplement where nature falls short. Babies are babies, Annie. They don't make a distinction as to how they were conceived."

Theoretically she agreed. Rationally she seconded the motion. Emotionally she balked.

At heart Annie remained an unreconstructed romantic. To her mind, children should arise spontaneously from the act of love, not through the medium of an impersonal lab assistant adept in state-of-the-art gadgetry. The wonders of high-tech science were all well and good, but they were as nothing compared to the wonders of love.

Instinctively she twined her arms about her husband.

He looked so grave and stricken himself, she realized. Max's death must have shocked him just as deeply, only Seth—typical male—had managed to hold it in.

"Let's go to bed, Seth. Let's comfort each other."

He nodded and headed into the bedroom without a word.

"Best remedy in the world, if you ask me."

As always, she felt better after love. Not happy, given the events of the day. Merely better.

"Uh huh." Seth rolled off her with a grunt and settled under the covers, staring moodily at the wall. "God, I'm tired . . ."

Yes, she concluded, in his way Seth too was grieving over Max.

"You know," she said, "I couldn't help thinking . . ."

"Yes?"

"Well, Max's plunging out the window like that—it's a very inauspicious start. Like a premonition, in a way. I mean, here we've just moved into this fantastic apartment . . . and now this!"

She shivered, then pulled the blanket up around her.

Seth turned to face her.

"He was a low-rise cat in a high-rise building, Annie. I'm sure it's happened a thousand times."

"But so soon . . . even before we had a chance to settle in. Almost as if we weren't meant to be here. I know you'll say I'm irrational but—"

"Oh, for God's sake, Annie." Seth gave her a piercing look. "If you're thinking what I think you're thinking, you're being more than irrational. You are talking rank superstition, stuff and nonsense. Put that idea out of your mind, once and for all."

"You're right." She snuggled up to him, reassuring herself in this uncertain world with the familiar curves of his body, the concrete warmth of his skin. "You are absolutely right, as usual."

Life wasn't opera with its curses and forebodings. Max was just a cat chasing one bird too many.

She burrowed deeper into Seth's warmth and shut her eyes.

Hours later Annie woke from a troubled sleep to reach for him, but he was not in bed.

"Seth . . ." She fumbled for the light. "Seth . . . I had the most awful dream."

On his pillow lay a note:

Had to go back to the lab for a couple of hours catch-up. Don't wait up for me.

It was dawn before he came home.

Later, looking back on that terrible day, she knew that she was right.

Max's death had been an omen.

❀

In her dreams, she was always sailing. Beating hard to windward, heeling sharply, her muscles tensed, heart pounding, throat dry with excitement, bare feet only inches above the roiling water. All it would take was a faint slackening of the hands, a momentary failure of nerve to wash her overboard.

But—and that was the beauty of it—she was in control. Every step of the way in full control, meeting the challenge.

It wasn't enough to cruise blithely over the smooth surface of a kiddie's pond; the true joy was in taking on the sea in all its contrariness. To go one on one against the pull of the current, to feel the shift of wind on her cheek, on her ears. And then, to outsmart every element, to win through against all the forces of nature.

To prevail! Therein lay the glory of sailing. One person, frail and imperfect, one small craft pitched in a limitless sea: beating the odds together.

The wind came up again, smartly now, whipping her face, sending a spray of spume needle-sharp against her skin. She tightened her grip. On the far horizon, warm harbors beckoned, enchanted islands offered the sweet rewards due the homecoming sailor.

For at the end of the day, after the long, hard struggle, there would be laughter waiting for her, warmth and love.

That was the dream.

Every morning she woke to the reality, in a sweat of rage, hands clenched. Teeth clenched too, dug in so hard against each other her jaw ached.

"Gee, I could hear your choppers grinding in your sleep," Noonie volunteered one morning.

"You shouldn't snoop outside people's bedroom doors," she snapped back.

Mornings were hateful.

Each dawn brought with it a cold blast of unsparing truths, the reality of another dozen waking hours to be got through, and Vi would pull herself out of bed even wearier than she had fallen into it the night before.

"You are not making the effort," Sally Atkins would scold.

Vi's physiotherapist, a sweet black girl, managed to combine a beaming smile and a no-nonsense air. For all her ready sympathy, Sally stubbornly refused to countenance self-pity in any of its myriad forms. She felt that Vi was slacking off.

"No more alibis. By now, you should be an expert with the canes."

"So what are you going to do?" Vi replied. "Give me an F for failure? Listen, honey, I've flunked out of better schools than this."

But Sally was right. Vi was not making the effort. Nor did she intend to make the effort—that would be an admission of disease—even though everyone she knew had counseled acceptance.

"God moves in mysterious ways." Her landlady nodded knowingly. "It's not for us to question."

Was it Vi's imagination or had there been a certain satisfaction behind Mrs. Rojak's sympathetic cluck? It's a judgment, the superior tone seemed to imply. But a judgment for what? For using a little embroidery on some of her real estate deals? Or ignoring parking tickets? Who didn't? Or was her plight a dire retribution for all those free-wheeling nights full of casual sex and easy laughs, all those well-earned hangovers?

But Vi couldn't buy that.

Had she contracted clap or herpes or even AIDS, she might have understood. Might, conceivably, have even accepted her lot. At least there would have been some connection between what she'd done and what was being done to her. And even then, the punishment would hardly have fitted the crime, because there was no crime. She had given occasional pleasure to herself and a goodly number of gentlemen. She hadn't lied or cheated or betrayed.

No, she had done nothing to warrant this unmerited assault upon her body, and she was damned if she was going to bow her head as though she had and meet her fate in quiet acceptance. She was not going to endure it, and that was that.

The first couple of weeks after she came home from the hospital, she had been inundated with company: friends bringing everything from Parcheesi boards to hot-house flowers, neighbors with great lashings of chicken soup.

"What have you told Noonie?" well-wishers asked.

"I haven't told him anything," she retorted, "and if you as much as breathe a word, I'll never speak to you again."

For she could not confide the nature of her illness to Noonie without the accompanying diagnosis. No cure. That was part of the package, the part that she denied. Denied vehemently, time and time again, to anyone who cared to listen.

Eventually her visiting list dwindled down to one. Misery may love company, but the feeling wasn't mutual. Others found the very sight of her depressing. Why not? She depressed herself.

In the end, only Crystal continued to turn up regularly, which

Vi found ironic. To think that her most loyal friend should prove to be not someone she'd shared her bed or work with, but a fellow swinger from her singles-bar days.

"I'm going to beat this thing," she promised Crystal.

"Of course you are, hon."

At least there was one person who didn't counsel acceptance.

It was simply a question of mind over matter.

The more she thought about it, the more obsessed she became with Browning's remark that the real struggle would be inside her mind.

She would think herself well, will her recalcitrant body back to strength and good health.

Why not? Wasn't her life, until this happened, a case history of the American dream made good? Hadn't she pulled herself out of the gutter, risen from poverty, bastardy, to become—for Chrissakes—a licensed real estate broker, a person with standing in the community? She hadn't broken the pattern by passive acceptance. She had fought back every step of the way, always offering resistance, refusing to be the patsy of fate.

"I'm gonna do it," she told herself. "I'm going to get rid of these canes and walk on my own two feet no matter what the witch doctors say."

It was merely a question of concentration and willpower, like when she gave up cigarettes a couple of years ago. She had read an article in the Sunday supplement about secondhand smoking and decided to quit for Noonie's sake. A miracle feat it had been, going from two and a half packs a day to zilch, but she had done it with no outside help. No hypnotists, no fancy support groups. Her own determination had done the trick. Granted, MS was a tougher opponent, but what had worked once could work again, provided she poured herself into it, with no holds barred.

For weeks, Vi immersed herself in the literature of hope. There were reams of books lying around, she discovered, popular manuals that addressed themselves to every problem known to man, spiritual *and* physical.

There was Ron Hubbard. Gurdjieff. Carlos Castaneda. She tore through their publications like a prospector searching for gold, coming up empty-handed each time. She enjoyed an even briefer fling with the Indian swamis, before dismissing them out of hand. Not only was the diet disgusting, but the idea of astral projection turned her off. Suppose it worked and she found herself holed up in some cruddy town in Nepal drinking lamb piss? Better off dead. Reincarnation, on the other hand, seemed quite attractive, provided you were willing to write this lifetime off as a total loss. Maybe she'd come back in another lifetime as Shirley MacLaine. *All singing all dancing*. But who could wait that long!

Her problem was—as the nuns back at Saint Agnes had observed long ago—Vi Hagerty had no talent for the mystic. She returned the swamis to the library and searched the shelves for more pragmatic advice. It was there in abundance.

Own Your Own Life, one book promised. *Smart Cookies Don't Crumble*, said another. She loved and learned with Leo Buscaglia, was OK along with Eric Berne. Success was but a matter of Will, said Gordon Liddy. (Although look where he wound up.)

After a month of desultory probing she discovered Norman Vincent Peale and Dale Carnegie. Oldies but goodies, as Sherm might have said. Their messages pierced her to the core.

You can do it! they proclaimed. You can lick the world. Think upbeat. Think confident. Think positive. The positive winner wins the race. Even on canes? she asked herself. But there would be no canes if she thought positively enough. *You can do it*. She would positively will them away.

She would will herself well!

Her pet fantasy (after sailing the Caribbean) was dreaming up appropriate fates for "the constant companions," her bitter term for the two rubber-tipped canes that accompanied her everywhere.

She would have them chopped up and made into toothpicks. Dip them in bronze, like baby shoes, and send them to Dr. Browning with her compliments. Firewood was, of course, a possibility, but she didn't have a fireplace. Nonetheless the idea of their being consumed in flames was delightful.

In her favorite reverie, however, she would have the canes sharpened into murderous stakes and drive them straight into the heart of that vampire Ross Winfield.

If he had a heart!—which she doubted.

For Ross was continuing his own contest of the will with a determination that showed no signs of abating.

For months now, she and Dom Tarantino had played the stalling game. Letters had been exchanged, questions asked, clarifications sought on a dozen lawyerly points, whys and wherefores spun out ad infinitum. Thus far, Ross had not pushed his hand.

"But," Dom explained, "he's not going to be put off much longer. He wants to see the boy and he has declared his intention to work out something solid with you."

"Stall him again," Vi instructed. "And for God's sake, don't let him tumble to the fact that anything's wrong."

Who knows? Another couple of weeks and maybe that Norman Vincent Peale stuff would pay off.

But Ross was to make his next move before Positive Thinking had a chance to exert its maximum power. The call came one frosty February morning while she was doing her nails.

"Hello, Vi," came the greeting from the other end of the wire, and her heart skipped a beat. Even after all these years, his voice was instantly recognizable—that combination of silk and cold steel.

She swallowed and wished she'd never given up smoking.

"Are you there?"

"I'm here." The nail polish clattered to the floor, stained the white rug to the color of blood. "How are you, Ross?"

"I tried to reach you at Orson Realty"—he sounded friendly, but puzzled—"and I was told you don't work there anymore. Are you out of a job, Vi? In some kind of financial trouble?"

Her answer had been prepared weeks ago.

"Well, Ross, I've decided to go into business on my own, do a little free-lancing. What the hell! Why should I let the agency hog all the commissions?"

"Uh huh." There was a pause while he mulled this over. "And is business good? You making a lot of sales?"

"No complaints." She struggled to keep the tremor out of her voice. "Only wish the Fed would lower interest rates, but on the whole I'm doing pretty good."

"Glad to hear it. I'm calling," he said softly, "because I don't seem to be getting anywhere with your lawyer, this Tarantino fellow, and I thought it might be more useful if you and I sat down and talked like civilized people."

"I'm awfully busy . . ."

"I'm busy too!"—there was more steel than silk in the voice now—"and I'm getting damn tired of being given the runaround. Either we work out something amicably, you and I, or I'll get myself a court order tomorrow. You can't keep me from seeing the boy, you know. I'd just like to do it without causing unnecessary ructions. So what'll it be, Vi . . . friend or foe? Take your pick."

She ran her tongue around dry lips.

"OK," Vi breathed. "I'll see you."

"Right. Now when are you going to be in Manhattan next?" he pursued.

"I don't get into Manhattan at all these days. Hardly ever." She pulled out the war plan concocted with Crystal for just this eventuality. "So if we're going to get together it'll have to be out here. Sorry about that. Suppose I take you to lunch?"

He picked a day. She picked another. Finally on the third try, there could be no more weaseling out. She didn't want him to get any testier than he was already.

"Agreed then," he confirmed. "Next Friday. Lunch. I'll come by your apartment and pick you up."

"No no," she said, "I'm out with clients all morning. What say we meet at . . . there's a nice little road house near Bloomfield, the Purple Parrot." She gave him directions to Crystal's place.

"Right. At twelve thirty sharp."

"Sharp!" She hung up the phone. Like a stake into a vampire's heart.

"Your voice!" Ari folded his arms across the keyboard and contemplated her with a quizzical expression.

"What about it?"

"It's changing. You sound different."

"How different?" She gave him a sharp look.

"Harsher, darker . . ." He raised his hands to stave off an invisible blow. "But interesting!"

She studied him with a noncommittal expression.

"My, my, Ari . . . what big ears you have."

Ari was not alone in discerning a change in Annie's singing. Madame Natasha too had recognized it some days before.

From the start, the two women had wrangled amiably about

certain musical matters. There was a fourth dimension, Madame claimed, an uncharted area beyond the limits of printed text. Yet at those limits, Annie shied and turned away.

"Emotion!" the little Russian would exhort. "Dazzle me with emotion. It's all there inside you—I know it! But you're too cautious, too private a person. Forget being a lady. Reach down and bring everything out—your passion, your ardor. Your frustrations, too. Now!" She would rap the piano smartly with her knuckles. "Forget about beautiful singing and make me laugh, make me cry. I command you to send chills down my spine."

Excellent advice, Annie admitted, but enormously hard to follow. Like many sensitive people, she was hobbled by the fear of making a fool of herself, of overstepping the boundaries of taste and decency.

The breakthrough, when it came, was neither conscious nor deliberate. She had been singing Verdi for Madame—"Pace pace mio dio"—an aria she had sung many times, when suddenly the floodgates of feeling opened. Without warning, the music poured forth in a wash of raw emotion, a rush of adrenaline, while Madame watched from her station at the piano.

Annie finished the aria drunk with the knowledge that she had sung her soul out.

"Yesss . . ." Madame Natasha drawled hesitantly after the last vibration had died. "Yesss . . . although one perhaps doesn't want to go quite so far." But there was unabashed respect in her voice. "And now, Annie, if you'll please put that down without breaking it. It's a very precious item."

Put what down? With a shock, Annie discovered she was clutching a Lalique paperweight with all the force at her command. Grip it any tighter, and she would be holding a handful of blood and shards.

Red-faced, she returned the object to its perch on the mantel, her fingers still throbbing from the tension. "I don't know what to say. I must have picked it up without realizing it. I have no idea what came over me."

"Perhaps Verdi came over you," Madame answered thoughtfully. "The torment of Leonora . . . the force of destiny. Yes . . . you certainly seem to be moving closer to the emotional depths of the music. Now"—she drew a deep breath—"we must get down to specifics . . ."

The next half hour, characteristically, she spent in a pulling apart and putting together of each line in the music, with the precision of a watchmaker. But at the lesson's close, she put her hand on Annie's shoulder.

"Don't forget what happened today," she said. "What you did. How you felt. It was important."

Annie nodded. Despite the paucity of praise, Annie could tell Madame Natasha was delighted by this newfound passion. As delighted as Annie herself was alarmed.

In fact, Annie knew very well what had come over her.

Jealousy. Simple old-fashioned sexual jealousy. And it was eating her alive.

But a few months earlier, how Annie had sneered at the ravings of Tosca. Histrionics, Annie had termed it. Behavior hardly worthy of a shop girl, let alone a great artist. Jealousy, as infantile as it was unwarranted.

Let Tosca storm across the stage in melodramatic postures. Let her deduce betrayal from a blue-eyed model in a painting. That was theater. In real life, such response would be preposterous.

Or so Annie had thought. But now, to give Tosca her due, at least that woman had some shred of evidence on which to build her fantasies. A girl in a painting may not be much, but it was something.

Whereas Annie had nothing she might point to. Not a smear of lipstick, not a stray earring, not a single scrap of paper—nothing at all to confirm her suspicions beyond a gut feeling, a profound unease. Yet it sufficed to convince her that after nearly ten happy years of marriage, her husband was having an affair.

Her first vague doubts were stirred the night after Max's death, when she had woken to find Seth gone.

In itself a midnight trip to the lab was not so unusual. When the creative juices were running, he often worked round the clock. But to her knowledge there was nothing exceptional on the front burner at Medi-Tekk these days, no volume of work at a critical juncture. Had there been, he would have mentioned it.

That night, she had sat up well into the small hours, puzzling over his disappearance. They had made love a few hours earlier, exhausting love as she recalled. Yet even in his passion, it now struck her, there had been a dark anguished quality. And afterwards, his mood had been so bleak.

She had ascribed it to Max's death, but at heart she knew better. For all his wonderful qualities, Seth was not a sentimentalist about animals. His work precluded that. The trouble, she divined, lay elsewhere. Why couldn't he sleep? Even odder, why had he chosen to go out on this particular night, even as Annie was grieving over Runaway Max? She had counted upon him for comfort, just as he always counted on her. Yet he had stolen out of the house like a sneak thief the moment she had nodded off.

The following night, she had gone to the theater with friends, Seth having begged off, and returned around midnight to find him in the den, huddled over the desk ostensibly transcribing notes.

At her entrance, he shoved a piece of paper into his notebook, then snapped it shut. Did she imagine it? Or was there something furtive in the gesture?

"How was the show? Lily Tomlin as funny as they say she is?" As he spoke, he slipped the papers into his briefcase.

"Funnier." Annie narrowed her eyes. No question but that Seth looked edgy. "Too bad you couldn't have come. You could use a little relaxation. What did you do all evening, by the way?"

"Lab," he grunted. "Doing a little catch-up."

The second time in two days, she noticed, he'd used that term.

"I should think you'd be all caught up by now," she explored discreetly. The time had come to discover what was troubling him so. "I mean what with your mice doing so well . . ."

"New projects," was the laconic reply.

"Oh? I thought you'd decided to ease off a bit."

Unaccountably he bristled. "You know, Annie, I've got a lot more things going on besides the one experiment. Jesus, what do you think I do up there . . . play backgammon? We've got a dozen new projects starting up. Big ones. You want a list of 'em, Annie, I'll draw you up a list . . ."

"Well, you needn't get so huffy about it." She felt thrown on the defensive. "Anyhow, did you have dinner at the lab?"

From his startled expression, she knew this was the first he'd thought of food all evening.

"Yuh, I ate."

She didn't believe a word of it.

"What did you have, exactly?"

"I had . . . um . . . um, a ham and cheese sandwich."

"Uh huh!"

"On rye," he added, as if this concrete detail would provide collaboration. "With mustard and lettuce."

"Would you like me to put something in the microwave? Beef stew? Lobster newburg? I'll see what's in the freezer . . ."

"No no . . . I'm fine."

But clearly he wasn't fine. He radiated tension, like a rubber band stretched to the uttermost. Instinct told her it must be a problem at the lab. If not a technical one, then some personal clash that had set him brooding. Another run-in, perhaps, with the execrable Leavitt. Or, conceivably, some difficulty with Gerald. That, surely, would explain a great deal. If so, he would feel better getting it off his chest.

She came to where he sat and framed his face with her hands.

"Do you want to talk about it, darling?" Annie's voice beckoned with warmth and love.

"Talk about what?" He raised his eyes to hers, unwavering.

"About whatever it is that's bothering you," she answered gently. "I'm not the enemy, you know. Whatever the trouble is, you can confide in me."

He held her gaze for a long silent moment. Then took her hands from his face and let them drop.

"There is no trouble, Annie. Just a little tired, that's all. Now, why don't you turn in? I'll be along in a bit."

She kissed him good night and went to bed. Ten minutes later she could hear him in the bathroom, vomiting. It was the sound of a man retching on an empty stomach. He then fell into bed exhausted.

The incident frightened her.

What had he been writing when she had come in? Something, clearly, not for her eyes. If he were in some sort of trouble, then surely she ought to know. Most likely it was nothing, some technical problem or other, but she wouldn't be able to sleep until she had satisfied herself.

She watched him lying by her side, dead to the world. All she had to do, she told herself, was slip into the den, open his notebook and find the paper.

All! her New England conscience shouted back. *Did you say All?!* That was a gross invasion of privacy, almost on a par with opening other people's mail. *For shame. What do you expect to find? Secret assignations? Forged checks? Embezzled funds?* Rubbish.

Drugs, then. According to the popular press, everyone and his grandmother was into cocaine. Yet she couldn't picture her husband in that situation. Maintaining control was too important to him.

For all she knew, Seth might have been engaged in nothing more sinister than planning some surprise for Annie, one of his fabulous treats, like the gold bracelet or dear old Runaway Max or the airline tickets he'd come up with now and then to be placed under her coffee cup in the morning.

And wouldn't she feel the fool for poking her nose in. True, her birthday had long since come and gone, their anniversary was still some months ahead . . .

For half the night she weighed the pros and cons. Just before dawn, curiosity triumphed over scruples. Hating herself every silent inch of the way, she slid out of bed and went into the den on bare feet.

His briefcase lay where he had left it, on the floor alongside the desk.

Bluebeard's wife, she cursed herself even as she stooped to pick it up.

To her astonishment the briefcase was locked. Not one, but both combinations had been turned.

To secure it in the office was one thing, given the dog-eat-dog nature of the place. But to lock up his papers at home? Against her? It was as though he had known that she would come prowling.

"Hands up!" she half expected to hear him thunder. "You're under arrest."

Heart pounding, she replaced the briefcase, taking great care to position it exactly, then crept back to bed in a wash of dread and guilt.

Half a dozen times over breakfast next morning, she was tempted to raise the matter, to ask him outright what he had locked in his briefcase. But what could she say? *I got up in the middle of the night to spy on you.* How could she humiliate herself in that manner?

Instead, they breakfasted in silence. She picked at her food while Seth retreated behind the wall of the *New York Times.* Finally he folded the paper and got his coat.

"I may be working late tonight, honey." The inward eyes. The perfunctory kiss. "I'll give you a ring about dinner."

She watched his departing back with mixed feelings, then sat down over coffee to think her discoveries through.

By the third cup of coffee, she had arrived at certain conclusions, ugly but inescapable.

Seth had changed.

Reviewing the last couple of weeks, she realized with a sense of shock that this broodiness of his had begun upon her return from St. Thomas.

She had come back tanned, happy, in a rush to get back to her music. Yet even then, at the edge of her consciousness, she was aware that Seth seemed unusually tense.

Preoccupation with work, Annie had diagnosed, plus the natural anticlimax that comes with vacation's end.

Mentally, she pushed the matter to one side; she had enough on her own plate not to dwell upon what she took to be a passing mood.

Now thinking back on it, she remembered one tiny incident. Not even an incident, really. Nothing more than a harmless remark. Yet in retrospect it took on new meaning.

Her first night home, she had stripped to show off her tan and Seth had placed a hand on her thigh. "You look terrific that dark," he'd said. "Very sexy."

Dark. She was dark as an Indian. Dark as the voluptuous Chandra with her ripe breasts and smoldering eyes, with her musky scent and sexuality.

Yes, something had happened while Annie and Margot were relaxing in the Caribbean sun. Her husband had gone to bed with Chandra.

She tried to push the image from her mind.

Seth wasn't like that, she knew him too well.

If a man is going to stray, Annie firmly believed, he will stray. If not, he won't. It was hardly a question of opportunity.

God knows there had been plenty of casual adultery among their

186

circle in Galveston. For that matter, there were always sweet young things about had he been so inclined. Seth wasn't.

Not my husband! How many times had she crowed inwardly, when her girl friends confided in her. Other women's husbands had affairs, God knows. They slept with secretaries, with colleagues, with waitresses, with their wives' best friends. But not Seth.

Whatever else his excesses may have been, he had never given her the slightest cause for suspicion. He'd passed the proverbial seven-year-itch with nary a spasm, and reflecting on their delirious time together in St. Thomas, she felt she could vouch for the intervening years. Nor was being on his own for one week in New York sufficient to launch him down the primrose path.

And yet, her gut feeling could not be denied.

It had to be Chandra. Where would Seth have time for anyone else? Remembering her one brief meeting with the girl, Annie bridled. The sensual way Chandra had brushed against Seth, the air of intimacy and exclusion she projected: there had been deliberation in those gestures. Clearly the young woman had set out to seduce Seth, to claim him for her own. The more Annie thought about it, the more sense it made.

Chandra was an alien on whom time was running out. Perhaps she nursed a dream that Seth might get a divorce and marry her. Then she could stay in America forever. Who knows? Chandra might even—Annie shivered at the prospect—yes, even try to get pregnant by Seth. It was the oldest game in the world. And what irony if that woman should succeed where she herself (the obeah woman not-withstanding) had miserably failed.

Oh, there were motives enough. But even without them, Seth was an attractive man, the kind a young girl might well lose her head over. And, Annie forced herself to remember, he was a man—not a god.

She pictured the scenario as it must have happened. Seth, sexually keyed up after their intense week in the Caribbean, returning to New York to spend lonely nights in the lab. With Annie gone, what else had he to do? And Chandra too would have seen her chance and seized it. Would have stayed late one evening, sleek and perfumed to place his hand on the opulent surge of her breast. His long white fingers caressing that smooth dark skin. "I like you dark," he would murmur as he touched her nipples. "Very sexy."

Then his lips followed the path his fingers had traced, sucking, nibbling . . .

No! Annie stood up with a rattle of coffee cups. Wasn't it enough to acknowledge the possibility that her husband was unfaithful? Did she have to torment herself like this? Make a pornographic movie out of every caress?

Very well. For the sake of argument, suppose she accepted the fact that Seth had gone to bed with Chandra. Once only, while Annie was away. A slip, as brief as it was meaningless. Even though it hurt like hell, conceivably Annie might live with it. Swallow her pride and try to put it behind her.

But what if it was more than a momentary weakness? What if Seth was in the midst of a full-blown affair? Indeed, what else could account for his crazy moods, his erratic hours? In which case, every word, every gesture since her return from St. Thomas had been a deliberate lie. *Working late at the lab. Working early at the lab . . .*

Even now as she rinsed out the coffee cups, they might be touching . . . kissing . . . lying on the narrow sofa in Seth's office. Door locked. Bodies locked. *My wife suspects something*, Seth might this very moment be whispering in her ear. And Chandra would giggle.

Annie clanged the dishwasher shut.

Whatever was going on—an affair of the flesh or of the heart— one thing was clear. The arrangement was giving Seth more misery than pleasure. She had never known him so woebegone, so tautly strung. Clearly, the man was riddled with guilt, and that, if nothing else, provided her with meager consolation.

She observed him without comment the next few days and found her insight confirmed. Seth was wretchedly unhappy. Unresponsive to her touch, her love. Rejecting her in a hundred subtle ways. Yet for all the hurt and devastation she was enduring, for all her fear that she might lose him, Annie—unlike Tosca—was incapable of wild scenes and accusations.

Perhaps, she thought, Seth is waiting for me to rescue him from Chandra's clutches, to bring him back into the fold.

If Chandra offered certain seductions, so did Annie. She determined to win him back in bed, for Annie too had wiles, charms. Perhaps these past months she had been too busy, too involved with the demands of her own growing career and he had felt neglected. If so, she would make it up to him with a thousand kisses. And only then, when he was nestled safely in her arms, when that dreadful girl was farthest from his thoughts, would she dare show the depth of her anger, her hurt. Only then would she permit herself to hear his confession.

"Let's have dinner at home tonight," she cornered him one morning, "just the two of us," wringing from him a reluctant promise.

That afternoon she went to Bergdorf's and blew a month's household money on lingerie, as Margot had often urged her to do. What doesn't show, according to Margot, was every bit as vital as what did. Even if no one else knew you had it on.

And so Annie treated herself to French panties the color of wild honey. Next, a matching negligee of gossamer silk and a lacy wisp of a gown so provocative, it should have been declared illegal, the whole ensemble held in place by nothing more substantial than spaghetti straps and hope.

She spent the balance of the afternoon getting the works at Georgette Klinger's: facial, nails, hair, massage. "Don't rub the tan off," she told the masseuse. *My husband likes dark skin. Very sexy.*

When he came home that night, she was waiting for him, soft and tender in honeyed silk, perfumed at every touch point of her body.

"My, my, don't you look lovely," he greeted her. "Is that a new outfit you've got on?"

She swirled around like a model, the chiffon parting to reveal a flash of thigh.

"Do you like it, darling?"

"Very nice"—his voice was matter-of-fact—"although it doesn't seem awfully practical for cooking dinner."

"I thought we might have drinks first, unless you want to shower before we start . . ."

"I'd prefer a drink. I'm kind of bushed."

He plopped down on the sofa with a weary air.

"I made margaritas, Seth. Shades of the good old days in Texas. Remember when we used to down 'em out on the patio?"

She went into the kitchen and fetched the tray.

"Just like old times," she toasted.

He licked the salt off the rim of the glass, then sipped his drink steadily, making desultory conversation all the while. The recent Mideast hijacking. The new Alvin Ailey ballet. The problem with this year's Green Bay Packers. It was a curiously impersonal performance, polite but distant, the kind of manufactured small talk that might precede a business lunch with a stranger. Medi-Tekk gossip was conspicuous in its absence. Seth limited his range to "safe topics."

At last, he put down his glass.

"What's for dinner, Annie? I'm kind of hungry."

She looked at him chagrined. *Me. I'm for dinner.*

"I thought"—she put down her drink and slithered her arms about him—"I thought . . . we might make love first." The spaghetti straps slipped from her shoulder. She felt the rough tweed of his jacket against her skin. "It's been so long, Seth . . . a week. Since the night Max died. You're hardly ever home anymore."

Despite all her good intentions, her voice began to tremble.

"I'm sorry, darling." He gave her a kiss and a squeeze, then began wriggling out of her grasp. "I don't know that I feel up to it right this second. I've had a tiring day. Would you mind terribly if I had another drink, maybe had a bite of dinner . . .?"

"What's the matter with you?" she burst out, tears and anger contending. " 'It's too hot, it's too cold, I have a headache . . .' Every night it's something else. I thought it was the woman who was supposed to make those excuses."

"I'm not a machine, Annie," he snapped, then made a conscious effort to control his irritability. "I know what you're thinking . . . we had a lot of fun, a lot of marvelous sex down in the Virgin Islands, and we did. It was terrific. But you know, that kind of thing goes in cycles. I expect it has to do with hormonal variability. Whatever, I just don't feel up to it tonight. Believe me, darling, it has nothing to do with you."

"Then what does it have to do with?" She was moving very close to the edge now.

"Annie." He stood up. A blind had gone down over his features, blank and final. His eyes grew cool. The words, when they came, were spaced and dangerous. "Don't hound me. Just accept what I tell you. It has nothing to do with you. Do you understand that? Nothing. Now, if you'll excuse me, I'm going into the kitchen and make myself a sandwich."

From that night on, an unseen barrier divided them.

They lived together, talked together, on occasion even slept together, but their old intimacy had become a thing of the past. Undoubtedly, the involvement with Chandra was continuing, perhaps even had deepened, yet there was nothing Annie could do.

She still lacked proof, the "smoking gun," but even if she had proof in abundance, it would hardly have mattered. She was afraid to confront her husband. Who knew what Seth might do, pushed to the wall? Given time, she felt, his passion might run its course. Yet with every passing day, he moved away from her.

Sometimes she had the notion he didn't see her, didn't hear her. The classic pattern of the absentminded professor. Except that foolish stereotype had no place in their household. More than most men, Seth had an uncanny knack for keeping all the elements of his life in sharp focus, like a juggler with half a dozen balls in the air.

Only, for the first time in their years together, Annie had ceased to be one of the elements.

She found herself living on a heightened emotional pitch. The anguish she could not speak became internalized, working its way through her system like water in a subterranean spring, hidden from the world, bottled up under pressure until one day it suddenly burst forth without warning. It was in her voice, now. In her art.

※

In an area hardly notable for the excellence of its restaurants, the Purple Parrot managed to keep a low profile.

The menu was eclectic: a little Italian, a little pseudo-French, but mostly mainstream American. Ask what the *soupe du jour* was and the waitress would tell you "the soup of the day."

Nonetheless, for Vi's purposes it was superb. The place was convenient. The comfortable window booths afforded privacy. Moreover, she had the connivance of a strong ally.

The day of her lunch with Ross, she arrived a half hour early.

"Here—" She handed her canes to Crystal. "Put 'em somewhere out of sight until he's gone."

"Right!" Crystal stashed them in the kitchen, then returned to check last-minute details.

"Looking good." She hummed her approval. "Very businesslike. Is that what they call power clothes?"

"My one serious suit." Vi laughed nervously, then smoothed down the jacket. "I used to wear it to impress heavy clients. Do I look successful to you, Crys? The big-shot real estate exec, wheelin' . . . dealin' . . . spielin'?"

"You look fine . . . fine, honey. Don't worry—everything's going to be OK. How about a drink to calm you down? A wee drop o' the highlands?"

Vi shook her head vehemently. "Nope, I need to stay stone cold sober for that mother. Maybe a cup of coffee instead. Black."

For the next twenty minutes, she watched the road anxiously. A tight-assed Porsche, sleek as a silver bullet, pulled up and parked in front of a fireplug.

That arrogant son of a bitch.

And there he was, sweeping through the door as though he owned the joint. And handsome! My God! Her heart stopped. Handsomer than ever, with the high color and gloss of animal health setting off sparks against the elegant dark pinstripe of his suit. A camel's-hair coat was slung over his shoulders, film-star fashion. Yes, she thought, Ross looked like a million, which was probably what he was worth.

He surveyed the restaurant with a look of faint distaste, before discovering her in the booth.

"Well hello, Vi!"

The smile on his lips didn't extend to his eyes. The voice was warm by designation. For a moment Ross hesitated, as though deciding whether the occasion called for a kiss. Instead, he pulled off a pair of pigskin gloves and shook her hand vigorously. Their flesh touched, for the first time in a decade.

"How splendid to see you after all these years. You're looking very well, Vi."

"You too, Ross."

Better than well. He radiated vigor and sex and success.

"No complaints, Vi. Life's been treating me well."

"So I see." She glanced through the window at his Porsche. "By the way, Ross, you're parked illegally."

"Am I now?" He laughed, then signaled for the waitress. "Well, if I couldn't fix a little traffic ticket, I'd be some lousy lawyer, wouldn't I?"

He smiled. She read his message. *I can fix a ticket. I can fix you. I can fix anything.*

"Right. How about a drink, Vi? What'll you have?"

"No booze. I've got a big closing coming up this afternoon, so I'll settle for another coffee."

"As you wish." He cocked a finger at the waitress. "Coffee for the lady and I'll have a Tanqueray gin extra dry on the rocks with a dash of Perrier, no twist. And would you bring me the wine list, please?"

The waitress looked at him as though he were a visitor from another planet.

"Red or white?" she asked.

Ross rolled his eyes in Vi's direction, as though they were sharing a private joke.

"Well, that settles the finer points." He laughed. "Your house red and a couple of menus."

"Sooo . . ." he exhaled, engaging Vi in eye-to-eye combat.

"So . . ." she replied.

So are you still fucking secretaries? she wanted to ask. *Still burning up the sheets in midtown hotels?*

"So how are things at Slater Blaney these days?"

"Excellent . . . excellent. I'm a full partner, you know."

"Yes . . . you wrote me . . ."

The waitress brought the menu.

Ross scanned it with raised eyebrows.

"You are a regular here, I gather, Vi. What would you recommend?"

"I'm having the meat loaf. It's usually pretty good."

"Meat loaf." He smiled. "OK, make that two. My God"—he turned to Vi with a mock-winsome expression—"I haven't had meat loaf since I was a kid."

"In Queens."

"Huh?"

"Since you were a kid in Queens," she reminded him, then instantly regretted the lapse. Honey, not vinegar, was how she'd planned to play it.

He studied her for a moment, then stabbed her with an icy smile.

"Well, I'm not in Queens anymore, Vi. I'm in fifteen rooms and four acres out in Oyster Bay. With stables. My wife likes to keep horses. I married Tom Porterfield's daughter. You remember him, don't you? Big heavyset man, head of litigation?"

"That was a long time ago," Vi said.

"And you . . . you never remarried, I gather. Pity. You really ought to be living a little better after all these years . . ."

"What's that supposed to mean?"

"I drove by your apartment on the way here. That's a fairly run-down neighborhood, by my lights. Not a very desirable environment for raising an impressionable boy."

"It's a perfectly respectable neighborhood." She tried to keep the panic out of her voice as the waitress brought their platters and a bottle of California red. "Besides, I'm thinking of buying a house one of these days, what with business so brisk."

Her statement went unacknowledged.

"I'll open that." Ross took the bottle, inspected the label, then uncorked it with a sommelier's skill. "Nothing wrong with a good California burgundy . . ."

"None for me, thanks." Vi placed her hand over her wineglass. Ross leaned back thoughtfully.

"No booze . . . no wine. Interesting. Are you AA by any chance, Vi? You used to have a little drinking problem, as I recall."

Beneath the table, a muscle in her leg began to twitch. Did he notice? No, thank God. He was too busy playing his own nasty game.

"I am not an alcoholic," she enunciated. "And I resent your imprecation . . ."

"Implication, Vi. Imprecation means curse."

Well, imprecate you, buddy.

". . . but if it'll make you feel better"—she sighed—"then pour me some wine, and we can toast the good old bad old days. You know, Ross, you haven't changed at all."

"Oh yes!" He filled her glass, then pinioned her with his stare. "I've changed. I don't stampede so easily anymore. I'm a lot smarter, a lot tougher than I was back then. So let's cut the formalities and get down to business. You have my son. You have shut me out of his life . . ."

"I!" She was outraged. "I shut you out! You would never even admit he was yours, for God's sake. Never even asked if it was a boy or a girl."

"How could I?" Ross answered in a quietly reasonable tone of voice. "Where could I ask? You walked out on me before he was born. I didn't know which hospital you were at, never heard a word from you until you served me with divorce papers. And even then, that was through lawyers. Now, even though I have remarried well and happily, my wife and I have not been blessed with children. Is it fair, your honor, that I be deprived of the love and companionship of my only child? . . . this boy who was taken from me even before birth?"

She stared at him aghast. "So that's your line, is it? You don't care what you do to the truth, do you?"

"That's what happened, Vi." He gave her an unflappable smile, then addressed the absent judge. "My memory is absolute on that score. And only now, after many years of searching was I fortunate enough to locate the lad. Young James . . . Jim." He nodded. "Yes, I think he should be called Jim. Noonie doesn't sound very dignified. Who'd you name him after, by the way?"

Vi had named him after the obstetrician, for lack of any other man in her life at the time, but she was damned if she owed Ross even that slim an explanation.

"Mmmm." Ross took a tentative bite of his lunch. "You were right. The meat loaf is very good. More wine?"

She sat and watched him polish off the meat loaf, two helpings of peach pie and a pot of coffee while he limned out Noonie's future for her benefit.

"A good prep school, that's what the boy needs. There are a number of excellent day schools in my area. I think the best arrangement would be to have the boy live with us during the week, and you could either visit or have him weekends, and maybe a month in summer, if he would like it. Although summers are marvelous where we are. We have a beautiful pool, horses, just about everything a kid that age could want. Yes, I imagine the court will find that an equitable arrangement. Unless, of course, you have some counterproposal . . ."

Vi sipped her coffee nervously.

"Why can't you leave him be, Ross?" she pleaded. "He's not a rich man's kid, he wasn't raised to be one . . ."

"All the more reason. Why should you try to deny him this opportunity?" Ross replied.

Beneath the table, her leg started twitching again in a familiar manifestation. Ross couldn't see the spasm; nonetheless he must have detected some movement, for he asked, "Do you have to go to the ladies' room, Vi? That's OK. I'll wait."

"Nope," she answered. "I'm fine."

Fine! She was in agony. Worse than the rack in a medieval torture chamber.

For at the mere mention of the ladies' room, her bladder had responded with a frightening urgency. She had to go. Desperately. And right this second.

Ever since she'd come down with this wretched ailment, control had been a problem. As a rule, she stationed herself near the john when she went out, ready for any emergency. But today distance wasn't the problem. Ross was. For how could she get up without the canes, make even the simplest of moves without giving the game away?

Never, never should she have drunk all that coffee, had the wine, the two glasses of water. She must have downed a gallon of liquid in all. Sheer nervousness it had been, unthinking stupidity, and now she could almost feel her kidneys floating.

If she didn't get to the john in one minute flat she would ... would what? The answer was painfully clear.

For a wild moment, she considered the consequence of just piddling where she sat. Could she do it, meanwhile keeping up a busy chatter, and expressionless face? Was there a chance that it might escape notice?

Impossible. Easier to rob Fort Knox in broad daylight dressed as Dracula, because once she let go there would be no halting the flood. In her mind's eye, she could see the urine flowing in an ever-increasing stream, out from under the table, trickling across the floor. A tile floor, worse luck. If it were carpeted, she might have chanced it. But tile! Even if he didn't see anything, he would hear the downpour. Like goddam Niagara Falls, only louder.

No. Mustn't. Control control control.

If ever positive thinking was called for, if ever willpower would save her from disaster, this was the moment. *Norman Vincent Peale,* she beseeched, *where are you now that I need you?*

Or even astral projection! Yes, wouldn't it be terrific if one of those swamis came along and transported her to the ladies' room with a snap of the finger? Now you see her, now you don't.

Beneath the table she clenched her fists, digging her nails into the palms of her hands. Concentrate on the one pain, she reasoned, and forget the other. Trouble was, it didn't work. If anything, it only intensified her need.

For a moment, she was tempted to blow the whole deception. Tell Ross the truth and throw herself upon his mercy. She'd give anything—her savings, her soul, anything!—just for the privilege of taking a leak. The only thing she wouldn't give was Noonie, and as for Ross's mercy? She crossed her legs tight.

". . . so you see I'm really talking equity, Vi. Fifty-fifty, so to speak, although he'd be living mostly with me. Look at it another way, though, and actually you'd be coming out ahead, because I'd be taking up practically all the financial burden . . ."

"Got a cigarette, Ross?" If she couldn't pee, the least she could do was smoke.

Ross frowned. "That's a nasty habit, Vi. Not the kind of example you'd want to set a prepubescent child, either."

"Forget it." She recrossed her legs for the tenth time. The restaurant had emptied out, lunchtime was over. They'd been sitting there for nearly two hours.

"So what do you say?" Ross asked.

"About what?"

God! If she ever had to do this again, she'd bring a relief tube. No way she was going to make it much longer.

"About settling out of court on these terms?"

"What terms?" she stalled.

"Goddam!" Ross's patience was running out. "We just seem to be going around in circles. I had hoped we could settle everything amicably. However . . . my lawyers will be in touch with your lawyers."

Her lawyers. Little Dom Tarantino in his flyblown office. She already owed the man five hundred bucks. OK. Lawyers it would be, legions of them, if he would only go now and let her scramble to the ladies' room.

Ross checked his Rolex. "Two thirty. That's as much of my time as I can piss away on this nowhere conversation. The bill please." He signaled to Crystal, who was waiting in the wings. For a moment, Vi could almost have kissed him. Going at last. She willed him to his feet, but instead he dug out his wallet and extracted a sheaf of credit cards. Oh lord! It would take forever!

"Don't let me hold you up, Ross." She gritted her teeth. Maybe thirty more seconds and he'd be gone. "My treat. I said I'd take you to lunch."

At last . . . at last! he got up to go.

"Can I drop you somewhere, Vi?"

She shook her head. "I've got my car outside."

"OK"—he slipped his coat off the hook—"if that's the way you want to play it."

And then he was gone.

The moment the door shut, Vi let out a holler.

"Crystal, quick! My sticks. If I don't make it to the john . . ."

Crystal popped out of the kitchen as though on springs.

"Help!" Vi breathed. "I don't know if I'm going to make it."

"You'll make it . . ." Crystal fell in with her sense of urgency. "Just easy now . . . watch your step."

Vi was halfway across the restaurant, when the front door swung open.

"I forgot . . ." Ross began, then stopped short to absorb the scene before him.

And as Vi stood on her uncertain canes, she could contain herself no longer. Body and brain panicked in unison.

"God help me," she cried, as a warm torrent ran down her legs and formed a dark streaming rivulet across the tiles.

Ross looked from the canes to the floor then back to the canes.

"I'll be damned!" Then stepping carefully to avoid the puddles on the floor walked to the booth where they had sat. On the bench lay his pigskin gloves.

At last his eyes met hers, and when he spoke, there was a note of triumph in his voice.

"I'll be damned." He pulled on his gloves with meticulous care, while she watched in horror. "So that's what you've been hiding. Why, Vi . . . you're a cripple."

❦

In February, Mark Wilkins came through New York from Texas, and Annie welcomed his visit with a sense of high expectation.

The past month had been agony, intensified by the fact that she could share her suspicions with no one.

Had Seth changed? Some days she was certain; on others, riddled

198

by doubt. In a court of law, she didn't have sufficient cause to charge him with a speeding ticket, let alone adultery. No mysterious dinners on his credit cards, no telltale signs on his linen.

When he was making an intermittent effort to be nice, she scolded herself for succumbing to hysteria. New York took a toll on people, it must be remembered. The crime, the tension, the competition, the pressures of establishing themselves anew: of course he was edgy.

What was needed, Annie felt, was the corroboration of someone who knew Seth when. A friend from what he now called the bad old days.

And who better than Mark?

"We'll take him to dinner at Le Cirque," Seth suggested. "Bet the poor bastard doesn't eat like that down in Galveston."

So Le Cirque it was, with *foie gras* and Dover sole and *medaillons de veau sauté*.

"Sure beats my old lady's chili," Mark volunteered cheerfully. He cast a respectful eye on the elaborate sconces, the rich carpeting, the wine cooling in an ice bucket, the Broadway star sitting at the next table. "You guys do pretty well for yourselves."

Annie waited for an opportunity to catch Mark alone. As soon as Seth went to the men's room, she tackled him in an urgent whisper.

"How does he look to you, Mark?"

"Looks fine. Why, is something wrong?"

"Just asking." She fidgeted. "I wondered if you noticed anything different about him compared to the old days."

"Yup," Mark answered. "He didn't used to wear Gucci shoes."

"I meant . . . does he strike you as tense, Mark? Nervous?"

"A bit, I suppose, but who wouldn't be, in the spotlight like that? After all, Seth's become the proverbial name to conjure with. What are you driving at, Annie?"

"Something's eating him," she blurted out. "I wondered if by any chance he confided in you."

Mark gave a noncommittal shrug.

"Maybe he's running into a few snags at the lab."

"No," Annie said. "He would have told me if he were. Everything he touches seems to come up roses . . . very much the fair-haired boy. It has to be something else."

"Or," Mark added, "he might be resentful about Marriner . . . the way the old man co-opted his work. Conceivably, Seth could be looking at a Nobel Prize in another few years. He may resent the idea of going halvesies on it."

"Seth's a realist." Annie sighed. "He knows you don't get ahead without getting along. At least he's not being cheated out of his discovery—which can happen too, as you well know. All told, Gerald's done a great deal for him . . ."

"And vice versa," Mark added.

"Granted," she agreed, "but that's not what's troubling him. I thought perhaps he might have said something to you in confidence. A chance remark. Men sometimes tell each other things." She dared hint no more broadly than that.

"He didn't." Mark's sense of male solidarity had been threatened. "And if he had I certainly wouldn't say."

And that—most unsatisfactorily—was that.

For the next few weeks their marriage staggered on uneventfully. The locked briefcase remained a constant. The locked eyes, as well. The psyche firmly bolted against all possible intrusion. Increasingly Seth went his way, Annie went hers, but her misery sat heavy inside her, a great undigested lump until she knew she had to confide in someone she trusted or explode.

She would talk to Margot. Wise, worldly Margot, who—it appeared—was right about men's failings after all. The two women had become close that last week in St. Thomas. Most important, Annie could count on her discretion. Perhaps even profit by her advice.

☀

" '. . . the lavender eyes and luminous porcelain skin that made Margot Trent the most gracious actress of her generation.' Who wrote this crap?" Ward Daniels flung the galleys down across Claire Pulham's desk.

"You did, sweetheart," his managing editor chirped sweetly. "See? It's got your name on it."

"Lavender eyes! Porcelain skin! How about saying she pisses Chanel Number Five? That ought to complete the image. As I recall my final draft, I described Mrs. Gerald Marriner as a sixty-one-year-old former movie star. I may even have called her attractive, which was damned charitable of me, all things considered, since she was peripheral to the burden of the story. A little background color, that's all. But never, Claire, never in my drunkest hour have I been guilty of such ass-sucking knee-bending boot-licking . . ."

"Stomach-turning?"

"Thank you, stomach-turning fawning fatuous flatulent fulsome prose."

"Are you done fulminating?" she asked.

"No. I am not done. Take a look at the photograph, will you? Jesus, you must have had every retoucher in town working over-time on this one. Bet they wore out their little airbrushes deleting every teeny wrinkle. Come on, Claire, we're talking sixty-year-old broad . . ."

". . . with a porcelain skin."

"You did it!" He shot Claire a look of pure venom. "You took my perfectly respectable, thoroughly researched, brilliantly written arti-cle and turned it into this pile of shit."

"I vass only obeyink orders," she mocked. "From on high they came, baby. The highest of the high. Fact is, that little bit of rewrite you so object to was done by none other than our Lord and master . . . should I face the East before divulging his name?"

"Strone Fucking Guthrie!"

"Yes, Lord Guthrie, Earl of Swill, as you so charmingly put it. Paying homage to an ancient flame."

"Christ!" Ward slumped into a chair. "She must have been some bit of nookie in her day. Listen, Claire, do me one big favor. Take my name off the piece. Give the story some other by-line. Edgar Guest, say, or Barbara Cartland . . ."

"No can do, honey. The issue's already gone to bed. It'll be out on the streets before you know it."

"I'm going back to the front," Ward groaned.

"What front?"

"Any front. Wherever they've got a shooting war on."

"The world's at peace."

"Worse luck. Frankly, I'd rather be sniped at by gun-toting Arabs than have my stories butchered like this. I feel like a whore, you know that? I've felt like that ever since I was given this goddam assignment. And the funny thing is, I can't shake the notion that there really *is* a story there."

" 'The Wonder Workers of Medi-Tekk.' You've written it, Ward."

"No no. Something deeper. Juicier. That place gave me really bad vibes." He rubbed his hands with gusto. "Like . . . remember that piece I did on Pentagon procurement? Or the one on industrial espionage in the Silicon Valley? That sort of story. I've got a nose for the genuine stuff, and believe me, Medi-Tekk stinks along with the best of 'em. That's what's intrigued me about the setup. All the backbiting, the politicking, the competition, the big bucks, everybody scrambling to be first at the feedbag. Pure pressure cooker!"

"You make 'em sound like a bunch of Wall Street gunslingers."

"But they are!" Ward crowed. "That's what makes it so interesting. You think these guys give a rat's ass about the suffering masses? Forget it. That's strictly incidental. Because we're talking corporate types here, with corporate motivation—money, prestige, winning for the sake of winning. And therein lies the irony. That out of this . . . this sleazy venal struggle comes something of genuine benefit to mankind. Like a rose growing out of a compost heap. In fact, I used that image in my article."

"Yes you did."

"And you deleted it."

"Yes I did."

"Oh fuck it," he groaned, his rage largely spent. "I wrote it as I saw it, and this is my reward."

"It was a good story," Claire consoled, "before Guthrie got his mitts on it."

Ward sighed. "If I had any balls left, I'd quit this lousy rag."

"And do what? Write a book? Isn't that what all you journalists are supposed to have stashed away in the bottom drawer of your desk?"

"Why not a book? How does the *Life of Strone Guthrie* hit you . . . subtitled from *Porno King to Press Lord, the Unexpurgated Version*. You know how he got his start, don't you? Scandal mongering for some shitty little paper that used to feature these incredible stories. 'Ingrid Bergman Loves Lassie—the bestial truth about Hollywood's oddest couple' Or 'Soho Hooker Raped by Archbishop. " 'E put the fear o' God in me, 'e did." ' I've heard tell that in Guthrie's news-gathering days he managed to plant a microphone under the mattress of King Farouk's suite at the Claridge—"

"Oh, Ward," his editor cut him short. "You really are such a misanthrope. So sour about life . . . so jaundiced. Comes of living alone, I suspect. What you need, my friend, is the love of a good woman."

"Sweetie." In spite of himself, Ward laughed. Last night's Gennie had given him a head-to-toe workout. "I've had the love of a thousand good women."

"I know you'll think I'm behaving like a fishwife . . ." Annie began, then stopped short, hindered by a latent sense of betrayal.

"I can't imagine your ever behaving like a fishwife," Margot comforted, although in fact the behavior of fishwives was a total mystery to her. "I can only gather that Seth has gone and done something beastly."

"You know, then!" Annie clutched at the remark. Was Seth's adultery already so notorious as to provide the Marriners' dinner table with small talk?

"Good lord," Margot protested. "I don't know anything at all. Except, my dear, I do know *you*, and what else in creation could cause you such distress? Only men. And since it's you, Annie, only Seth. I see it, I feel it. You positively radiate misery, poor lamb. Do you want to tell me about it? Of course you do, darling. That's why you're here, isn't it?"

Here was Margot's "little sitting room," a charming corner that seemed the perfect site for confidences. And Margot the ideal recipient, as she sat on a flowered chintz sofa, feet tucked under like a comfortable Cheshire cat.

Annie took the plunge.

"I think Seth is having an affair."

"*Think?*" Margot raised an elegant eyebrow. "You're not certain then?"

"Gut certain," Annie said. "All my instincts say he is." With that, she embarked on a day-by-day recital of recent events, while Margot asked the odd cogent question.

"Has he ever slept at the lab before, Annie?"

"Well, yes."

"Any out-of-the-ordinary expenses?"

"Actually, no."

Indeed, in the telling, her string of damning events rapidly diminished. By the time she finished, she supposed Margot would find the evidence pretty slim and had already geared herself for a polite rebuff ("tempest in a teapot, darling"), followed by the assurance that all was well, except for Annie's overheated imagination.

She was therefore stunned when Margot nodded a heavy-lidded concurrence.

"Well, that's what it sounds like, lovey. An old-fashioned case of hanky-panky. I must say I'm shocked that he hasn't been more discreet. Quite shitty of Seth, really. I mean, his lab assistant! He ought to know better than that!" Margot frowned over the tackiness of such a liaison. "Have you confronted him, Annie?"

"God no!" came the answer. "I haven't said a word. In fact, I feel like a coward, clamming up this way, but I don't want to make things worse."

"Quite right." Margot was emphatic. "The most sensible thing you can say is nothing. Look . . . if you accuse him of having an affair there are two possibilities. One, he denies it—in which case you won't believe him, so you add one more complaint to the list. Or—worse luck—he admits it. Well, that's not going to make you feel any better, is it? And the last thing you want, darling, is to get his back to the wall. Corner Seth, and he may feel honor-bound to defend the girl. All you'll have done is throw the two of them even closer together. Listen to me, Annie. I know it's hard to keep it all bottled in, but your best move is doing nothing. At heart, Seth's crazy about you. Anyone with half a pair of eyes can see it. So take it in your stride and wait until the affair burns itself out."

"I can't." Annie burst into tears. "It's eating me alive. If Seth cheated once, he'll cheat again, and my bet is next time will be even easier. And I can't help thinking, it's partly my fault . . ."

"Your fault?" Margot's eyebrows rose.

"If we had children . . ." She wept. "If I'd been able to get pregnant, given him something more to come home to . . ."

"Rubbish," Margot broke in. "Don't blame yourself for Seth's misbehavior. Don't blame him too much, either. He's a man, darling . . . a very attractive man in a city populated by the world's most predatory women. Worse yet, now that he's on his way to becoming a huge success, he's going to find temptations galore. Power's the most potent aphrodisiac. Every woman alive becomes a groupie once she's within touching distance of a celebrity. Maybe they think if you sleep with them, some of the magic rubs off. I'm afraid you'll just have to learn to live with success."

"By success you mean infidelity, don't you? And I should resign myself to the fact that Seth screws around?"

Margot nodded. "Yes, if you want to stay married. And as far as children go, think, Annie! Think how much worse the situation would be if you were pregnant and couldn't trust him. At least this way it's just the two of you. My advice to you, pet, is to take the oldest remedy there is. Sauce for the goose, as they say. After all, he's not the only charming man in New York and you're a stunning woman. Give Seth a taste of his own medicine."

Annie dried her eyes and almost managed a smile. "Hardly my style, Margot. I'm a one-man-at-a-time woman, I guess. Anyhow, I don't see how my committing adultery is going to fix up our marriage. That only happens in Noel Coward comedies."

"Adultery!" Margot clucked. "Such a heavyweight word for such a minor infraction. Mind you," she cautioned, "I'm not saying you should go to bed with the first good-looking man who comes along, although on the other hand I'm not saying you shouldn't. Especially if the first man who comes along is Robert Redford."

Despite herself, Annie laughed.

"There!" Margot seized upon it. "See? Even the idea of a midwinter dalliance lifts the spirits, doesn't it? Tell you what. I'll keep my eyes open for some suitably 'significant other' and leave the rest to you. You needn't indulge in anything stronger than tea at the Plaza with perhaps a kiss or two behind the potted palms. It's wonderful for the ego, and conceivably a little romance might also have the virtue of making Seth jealous. As for this wretched Chandra, I'll have Gerald fire her."

"No!" Annie cried. "Absolutely not. I don't want Seth to think I'm interfering in his affairs . . ."

"They're your affairs too, Annie. Don't worry. I'll see it's handled discreetly. Seth won't know and she'll be out of your hair."

But Annie shook her head. "It's no good. He's the one who'll have to end it. Otherwise . . ."

"Otherwise?"

"Otherwise, I don't think I can live with him."

"Oh dear dear dear," Margot soothed. "Such talk. Now finish

your drink and follow me. I have something very special I want to show you. Guaranteed to chase the blahs away."

Moodily, Annie trailed her hostess through the vast apartments into the luxurious dressing room that held the heart and soul of Margot's wardrobe.

"Have a pew, darling."

Annie sat down at an Empire vanity table and faced her image in the mirror. Bleak, she decided. As bleak as the February day.

"Ah, here we are." From a dresser drawer, Margot had retrieved a black leather jewel box as deep as it was wide. "I was saving it for a special occasion, but since you seem so down in the dumps, we'll make today the day. Go ahead, Annie. Open it."

The hinged lid swung back upon a fitted interior lined with crimson velvet. A tiara nestled in its depths—but such a tiara as might grace a queenly head. The filigree was delicate as silver lace, the *pavé* stones had been sculpted into icy crenellations, each topped by a tear-shaped gem so faceted as to capture the light and send it back a hundredfold.

"Superb!" Annie gasped. "What an extraordinary piece."

"They're not real diamonds, of course," Margot commented. "If they were, it would be worth a dozen kings' ransoms. Nonetheless . . . it *is* gorgeous, if I say so myself."

"Exquisite." Annie cradled the glittering arc in her hands. "And look at how it catches the light. Is it stage jewelry, by any chance? Something from a play?"

"Clever girl," Margot applauded. "Actually it's something from an opera. From *Tosca*, to be precise. I remembered your telling me about this fabulous soprano who made such a sensation years ago . . ."

"Maria Jeritza?"

"That's right, Jeritza. Well, this belonged to her. She had it made in Vienna in 1915, wore it the first time she sang *Tosca* at the Metropolitan back in 1921. I looked up pictures of her in the opera books. She was a great beauty, you know, as well as a remarkable singer. Oh, but she must have looked magnificent on stage with that tiara and gowned in red velvet, I would think. Yes, red velvet would be the perfect accompaniment. Now don't ask me how I've come by this treasure. We scoured for weeks, my secretary and I, used all kinds of devious ways and means, but"—she crowed—"here it is. Now, if you'll just sit still for a moment . . ."

She reached into a china bowl filled with hairpins and with deft fingers began pinning Annie's long dark mane high on her head. "Yes, this definitely calls for an upswept style. I think the tiara should encircle the hair, don't you?"

"But . . ." Annie spluttered.

"No buts," Margot mumbled through a mouthful of pins. "And don't tell me I shouldn't have done it. Of course I should have, and your first big role, I want you to wear it. Wear it and think of me. There now!" She placed the tiara like a crown around her handiwork, then stood back to admire the results. "What's your verdict, darling? Isn't it wonderful?"

Wonderful.

Too moved for speech, Annie gazed into the mirror and the vision of Tosca gazed back, her face borrowing light and radiance from the gleam of the tiara.

Vissi d'arte. I lived for art. Tosca's aria rose to her lips.

She shut her eyes for some minutes, singing the music in her mind. Blinked them open. And with that second vision, the present fell away and she saw herself—someday, someday soon, perhaps—another Jeritza, another Callas—standing tall and resplendent while the sound of cheers and bravos filled a vast dark theater.

Then she blinked herself back to the present with a sigh.

"Is it too heavy?" Margot asked, but Annie, bemused, could only shake her head slowly. It was heavy, but not with measurable weight, only with the richness of tradition, with the magic of the past.

"We should put it away now." Margot knelt by her side and began working the tiara free of stray tendrils.

Then she halted, her head on a level with Annie, and studied the mirror image with a quizzical expression.

"Two faces in the mirror," she said, "yours and mine."

And as Annie looked at her puzzled, a solitary tear made its way down Margot's cheek. She brushed it away and got up to replace the tiara in its velvet shelter.

"Ah, how I envy you, Annie."

"Me?" Annie spun around. "You envy me? Why, Margot, how could that be?"

"I envy you your talent. Your future. Yes, Annie, I envy you your youth as well. God, how I hate growing old!"

"But, Margot . . ." Annie felt her throat grow thick. "How could you possibly envy anybody? You have so much . . . !"

"So much what? So much wealth?"

"So much beauty," Annie said.

"Beauty." Margot briskly began moving about, putting things away, a silk scarf there, a hairbrush here, as though the mere handling of artifacts would throw a scrim over her fears. "That's all I've ever had, and now even that is slipping away. There was a time, Annie, when I could walk into a room and feel every man's heart stop at the sight of me. It was like an electrical charge. Women, too." She smiled at the memory. "They used to be so afraid of me, afraid of comparisons, afraid I was going to take their lovers and husbands and eat them up whole. But now . . ."—she slammed a closet door shut—"I walk into a room and everyone says, 'Oh, Margot, don't you look marvelous!' as if I were Mount Rushmore. A bloody national monument, that's what I've become, a walking testimonial to the art of the plastic surgeon. Even my face isn't my own anymore, and that's all I had, all I ever was.

"I come from a fairly distinguished family," she continued. "My father was the world's greatest authority on Sir Francis Drake. My mother read Jane Austen and wrote monographs. Both my brothers have had notable academic careers. So smart, so terribly clever all the Trents were. Except for me. The only talents I ever could call my own, Annie, were a face and a bosom. Well, the bosom is mostly silicone, and the face is going fast, and what will I be left with. Children? No, I decided against them when I was your age. Do terrible things to the figure, I told myself. What's more, they were a positive encumbrance in my real career, which was really nothing more than the pursuit of men. I'm sure you think that very vain and foolish of me, Annie. What kind of life's work is seduction? But it was all I was really ever good at, so I did it. The pursuit was fun, I must admit. The sex"—she drew a breath—"the truth is, I suspect it's a vastly overrated commodity. Going to bed with romantic figures is almost always a disappointment, sad to say."

At that moment, Annie pitied her—a woman, she surmised, who had never experienced sexual fulfillment, the vast quantity of lovers notwithstanding. With a warm glow, her own thoughts turned to Seth, of pleasures they had shared, the happinesses exchanged. Had Margot never known that sweetness? Apparently not.

"So here I am." Margot spread her palms out, empty-handed. "Three marriages, four face lifts and God-knows-how-many lovers later, and what do I have left?"

"You have Gerald," Annie said softly.

A shadow passed across Margot's face.

"Yes, I have Gerald."

She stopped as though to catch hold of herself, then changed her mood with the deliberation of a viewer switching television channels.

"What on earth am I going on about? Here I was, so determined to cheer you up, and will you listen to me? Indecent exposure, nothing less. Ignore all previous messages, Annie. I think what we both have here is a case of midwinter blues and I've got just the prescription. Music. Dancing. Let's have ourselves a costume ball."

"A what?" The shift of mood had caught Annie by surprise.

"A costume ball. You know, that article about our men is appearing in *Worldnews* two weeks from now, and I think we should celebrate with a gala party. Everybody dresses up in tons of finery, mountains of jewels. Love it. In fact, let's make it in honor of Seth. Yes, definitely Seth will be the guest of honor. Don't think I'm unaware of how much Gerald owes him . . . how much we both do. Without him, there wouldn't have been a story. Well, this is how I'd like to express my thanks."

The nakedness of Margot's acknowledgment embarrassed Annie. "It's not necessary," she murmured.

"No, not necessary, nonetheless I want to do it. But don't tell Seth it's for him. I'd like that part of it to be a surprise. Make me a list of his special friends, although not—I think—the execrable Chandra, and I'll handle invitations. And, of course, I'll add some super people of my own. Now what'll be the theme?" She pursed her lips. "Saints and sinners? It's been done. Great men of science? That would be apt but boring boring boring. All the women would come dressed as Marie Curie. I know." She clapped her hands. "Golden days of Hollywood. Everyone will come dressed as their favorite movie role. What do you think, Annie? Sound like fun."

"Sounds terrific." Annie giggled. "I shall come as Rin Tin Tin."

"You'll do no such thing, lovey. You will come as somebody very glitzy, very glamorous. I expect to have all kinds of important people here for you to meet. Besides, it'll make Seth appreciate what he's got. Now"—she stood up, the earlier mood thoroughly dispelled—"let's go make up a guest list."

※

"It was super."

Super. A new word in his vocabulary, Vi noticed while Noonie gushed out details of his weekend with the Winfields.

"Ross . . . I mean Dad took us ice-skating at Rockefeller Center yesterday, and then we went downtown to his office. He's on the eightieth floor. You know what? You can see the Statue of Liberty out of his window? Well, Dad says . . ."

With mounting alarm, Vi listened as Noonie fleshed out what had clearly been the high time of his ten-year-old life.

". . . fixing the horses' hair, only they don't call it that, Mom, they call it currying. Did you know that? Curried horse." He giggled. "Dad says it sounds like something you'd order in an Indian restaurant. And there's this one horse, she's a beauty, a roan . . . her name's Thunderbird. Well, Dad says . . ."

Dad says this. Dad says that. Ross could be very seductive when he chose and didn't she know it.

Dad says, up yours, Vi. I'm going to take this child away.

"He wants more than visiting rights," her lawyer spelled it out. "And now he feels he's got a winner on his hands. You are, in his words, 'unable to cope with the physical needs of a growing boy.' "

"He can't do that," Vi burst out. "Even hookers get to keep their children. They can't dump on me just because"—God, how she hated the word—"because I'm handicapped. I've raised Noonie from the day he was born, supported him. Doesn't that count for something?"

"It counts for a lot, Vi, and the courts will take that into consideration. The point is, now that Noonie's getting older, more independent, he may very well have the last word in the matter . . ."

"You mean if the choice were up to him—me or Ross?"

"That's right."

"In that case, I'm home free."

But now, hearing Noonie's bedazzled account of life among the Long Island horsey set, she began to tremble for the future.

". . . so what do you say, Mom? Is it OK? Can I go?"

"Go where, honey?"

"Skiing. Weren't you listening? Dad and Debbie are going skiing over Easter. It's out west . . . place called Absent . . . Accent . . . ?"

"Aspen." Vi glowered. "Shit, Noonie, that's way the hell out in Colorado. He's only supposed to see you on weekends."

"I know." Noonie looked grave. "That's why he asked me to ask you. He says, is it all right if he has me for the whole vacation?"

"No, it damn well is not all right!" Vi snapped. "That wasn't the arrangement. Where does he get the nerve . . . !"

"Please," he begged. "Just this once. I've never been on a plane. Dad says we'll fly first class and I can have the window seat . . ."

"The answer is no!" Vi shouted. "N-O. As in no way, no never, no go. You're spending Easter here with me and that's final."

Noonie burst into tears and fled.

For what seemed like an eternity, she sat outside his bedroom door, listening to him sniffle and moan as though the end of the world had arrived. You're being a shit, she told herself, a selfish shit. What kid in his right mind wouldn't want to go skiing? Only why did it have to be with Ross!

At that moment, she would have given her soul for the privilege of saying, "I'll take you skiing, Noonie." Instead, she swallowed her hurt and opened the door. Noonie was lying prostrate on the bed, clutching his favorite Star Wars spaceship to his breast.

"Noonie?" She placed her canes on the bed and sat down beside him. Even his hair was damp with tears. "Noonie honey, talk to me."

No answer but a tremor of the shoulders.

"All right, babe, if it means so much to you . . ."

"Oh, Mom!" There was no need to complete the sentence for he flung his arms around her in unabashed joy.

"OK, OK." She wiped his streaming eyes. "This one time, I'll make an exception." Then curiosity got the better of her. "What's . . . what's your father's new wife like? Is she nice?"

"Debbie? She's super," Noonie babbled happily. "She's all big and warm and smiley. Kinda pretty."

"Terrific," Vi said.

Noonie must have heard an alarm go off, because he didn't respond straight off. "Oh, Mom"—he twined his arms around her, and gave her a kiss—"not as pretty as you."

Late into the night his kiss troubled Vi. Was it heartfelt or deliberate? Already, she believed, Noonie was picking up Ross's style, learning how to lie, to manipulate. Already he was being swept away into a life that promised more glamour than anything Vi could offer.

"This fucking disease," she told Crystal a few days later. "It's poisoning my life. Last Sunday, while he was whooping it up in Oyster Bay, I went to church for the first time in maybe ten years. The big one over on Hardesty Road. Six priests, no waiting . . ."

"You actually went to confession?"

"You kidding?" Vi laughed. "I'd still be there! No. I just wanted—oh, I don't know—some comfort, some guidance. So I tell the father my story, and he says I should make a pilgrimage to Lourdes. Jesus, I blew my stack. 'Is that all the help you can give me? I should go to Lourdes and pray for a fuckin' miracle?' And you know what he said? That blasphemy was a sin. Oh, shit, Crys, from the day I came down with this thing, everything in life has gone wrong. But I'm not ready to throw the sponge in. I can't believe"—she clenched her fists till the knuckles bleached white—"I can't believe with all the miracles of science, there isn't a cure out there somewhere!"

Two days later Crystal phoned her in a state of high excitement.

"I'm coming right over with a copy of this month's *Worldnews*. Now, I don't want to get your hopes up too high, hon . . ."

"What are you talking about?" Vi's blood began pulsing.

"Well, there are these two doctors in New York. Research guys. And it looks like they've found that cure!"

※

As anticipated, Seth was not enthusiastic about the prospect of a costume ball. Indeed, in his present dour mood, he had no enthusiasm for anything except—Annie presumed—his sordid little romance.

"I'll feel like an asshole getting dressed up in some dumb costume."

"Oh, come on, Seth," she wheedled. For a moment she considered telling him the gala was on his behalf, but Margot had sworn her to secrecy. "You can't not go."

"Why not?"

"Because . . . well, think of Gerald. How do you turn down an invitation to the boss's biggest party of the year?"

"With the greatest of ease," Seth answered.

"Then think of me," Annie pleaded. "I'm really looking forward to it. Please, Seth . . ."

"OK," he conceded. "For your sake. But I warn you, I don't have the time to waste chasing around for a costume."

"I'll take care of everything. Just tell me who you want to be and I'll whip it up, one way or another." She thought back to their student days, when they'd watched old serials at the Brattle in Cambridge. "How about coming as Flash Gordon?"

"No, not Flash. I'm not appearing in public wearing tights." Seth mulled the problem over for a moment. "Well, I'm too tall for a Munchkin and too flat-chested for Marilyn Monroe . . ."

"Seriously . . ."

"Seriously . . ." He gave a eureka snap of the fingers. "Just the thing! I'll come as Frankenstein. Yes . . . I think that would be most apropos." A curiously wry smile flitted at the corners of his mouth.

"Which Frankenstein? Do you mean the mad doctor or the monster?"

"Oh, the monster." He laughed. "Definitely the monster. I think all it takes is some floppy pajamas."

"And a helluva makeup job. OK, Seth." She was delighted to see him smile for a change. "Just leave the details to me."

The next day, she made the rounds of the theatrical costumers, scored easily, then called up Lainie Carpenter to get the name of a top makeup artist.

For her own role, Annie wavered between bride of Frankenstein (which would be both funny and suitable if not glamorous) and Katharine Hepburn in almost anything. Then mindful of Margot's injunction that she look her best, she settled on Hepburn as Woman of the Year—smart, sexy and sophisticated all in one. A hunt through New York's antique clothing stores yielded a slim forties gown of black silk crepe with shoulders a yard wide, high necked, bare backed, a dress that slithered rather than walked, demanding to be topped off with tons of costume jewelry. The total effect was stunning.

* * *

"What do you think, Seth?" She modeled the outfit for him a half hour before they were due to leave for the ball.

"I think they might just pass a law against you, Annie. Inciting to riot."

She inspected herself, pleased with the results: the highlighted cheekbones, the hair sleeked into a glossy page boy. Oh, they knew something about glamour in those days, she acknowledged.

As for Seth, he submitted apprehensively to the ministrations of a tiny Viennese lady who was slapping on makeup with gusto. First the chalk-white base, then the heavy-lidded eyes, then a penciled line of surgical stitches across the forehead, matching the Boris Karloff photo on the dressing table.

"This is taking forever, Annie. We're going to be way late."

"Relax," she answered. "The limo isn't coming till nine."

"Limo!" Seth exclaimed. "We're just going a few blocks away."

"But we're going in style, just like movie stars. I rented us a Rolls for the night."

He laughed, and Annie felt that was a good start to the evening.

They arrived late by design, the last of the guests. At the door the butler, that impeccable personage whose upturned nose had once sniffed at Annie's coat, announced them with a stentorian flourish.

"Dr. and Mrs. Seth Petersen."

"My God," Seth whispered. "It's a mob scene."

Margot had thrown all the ground floor rooms open, great French doors leading one into another to create a vast ballroom. The rugs and usual furniture had given way to parqueted floors and banquet tables. The rooms thronged with guests dressed in a dazzling array of sequins and spangles. Bogarts and Marx Brothers mingled happily with Mae Wests and Garbos and Scarlett O'Haras. Margot was resplendent in her green Lucrezia Borgia velvet, neck and arms hung thick with the famous Allegorio jewels, while Gerald made a portly Valentino sheikh.

For a moment, the crowd fell silent as the band, hitherto silent, struck up the buoyant hit from *A Chorus Line.*

One . . . fabulous sensation.

"What's going on?" Seth turned to see who had entered behind them, half expecting at least the president of the United States.

Then the applause began, hesitant at first, swelling as they made their way across the ballroom.

"I don't think our costumes are that great." Seth knit his brows.

"It's not your costume they're applauding"—Annie slipped her arm through his—"it's you. This is all for you."

But before this information could be absorbed, Margot had rushed forward to greet them, planting an exuberant kiss on Seth's cheek.

"Congratulations, our own darling Frankenstein." She raised her champagne glass and her voice. "To Medi-Tekk's . . . to medicine's Man of the Year"—the toast rang out—"and his lovely Woman of the Year."

Annie turned to Seth, heart in mouth. Was he pleased by all this fuss? Embarrassed? Dear God, make him be pleased.

For a minute, he struggled with a swarm of conflicting emotions, then suddenly his eyes cleared and he let out a triumphant whoop.

"Annie! You planned it all along!" In full view of the crowd, he kissed her roundly. "Bless you, darling. I never expected this!"

And suddenly, he was surrounded by a sea of admirers, all eager to kiss the cheek, press the flesh.

That's my husband, she thought and trembled. Proud? The word hardly did justice to her feelings. For all his faults and evasions, for all the torment of recent weeks, he was a glorious man, a born winner. Was there a woman alive who wouldn't be happy to trade places with her tonight?

The buffet was spectacular: Maine lobsters, Scottish salmon, Beluga caviar, French ortolans. The guest list, even more so.

You couldn't take two steps without encountering a famous face. The Buckleys were there, the Kissingers, the Mailers, the Hovings. A cowboy-hatted Baryshnikov was seen tangoing with a Minnie Mouse who proved on closer inspection to be Navratilova. "Hey!"— Seth nudged her—"That's that gal who makes the blue jeans," and Annie turned to smile at Gloria Vanderbilt.

There was Lord Guthrie with a sport-jacketed Ward Daniels in tow.

"I've come as my favorite character," Ward explained his civilian garb. "Myself. How's life on Park Avenue treating you, Annie?"

"Not bad." She grinned and took a flute of champagne from a passing waiter in movie usher's uniform.

"The Cinderella girl." He laughed morosely. "From Diet Pepsi to Dom Perignon. You can tell me all about it one of these days."

"You bet."

Throughout the evening, Annie floated on a sea of champagne and happiness. In the crush of the crowd she and Seth would slip apart to come together as if by chance in an elaborate ballet of ever-changing partners—"Darling, I'd like you to meet . . ."—only to separate again and form a new milieu.

Early on, she had lost track of the gallantries, the toasts, the stream of proffered invitations. She only knew it was the night of their lives.

"Margot tells me you sing even more exquisitely than you look," a lightly accented voice addressed her. Annie found herself looking into a pair of humorous eyes set in a darkly handsome face. Close-cropped hair was topped with the rakish headgear of a French Legionnaire.

"You're . . ." The name floated beyond her grasp on a wave of bubbly.

"Beau Geste, at your service." The dashing figure bowed from the waist with a continental flourish.

A conductor. That was it. A conductor, taking a bow.

"You're . . ." The head cleared, recognition came and with it a thrill of delight. "You're Polonius von Brüning!" She clapped her hands.

"Polo to my friends," he returned, "of whom I hope you will soon become one."

He was slighter than she had pictured, the podium apparently adding inches to his stature, but even away from the dais he exuded power and authority with every muscle of his well-knit being. To be expected, Annie thought, in a man who routinely imposes his will on a hundred or so musicians.

"I didn't recognize you without your baton."

He slapped the ornate dress saber on his side. "Actually this is my weapon of choice." Then, lowering his head conspiratorially, he added, "I'm told it's essential to be fully armed at all times when visiting New York City. Muggers, you know."

He had spoken in such a somber tone that for a moment, she thought he was serious. But the black eyes were full of mischief, teasing, testing, trying to decide: Was Annie someone to have fun with—or someone to make fun of?

The champagne had loosened her tongue and her inhibitions. She contemplated the saber, smiling blandly. "I thought perhaps you used it instead of a baton. So handy for putting down uprisings in the orchestra. Although you lose a lot of concertmasters that way."

"Also useful, dear lady, for cutting temperamental sopranos down to size . . ."

"*Touché.*" She winced. "You do realize, Polo—if I may call you that—"

"I insist . . ."

"That your saber makes you the only maestro in the world who not only conducts *The Barber of Seville* but manages to throw in a few haircuts and a shave simultaneously."

"Enough, enough." Polo von Brüning laughed and patted her shoulder pads. "I never fight with women who are built like football players."

"That's my forties look. You like it?"

"I like the look, I like the person. And I was intrigued by what Margot said about you."

"Which is . . . ?"

". . . that you're the new Callas or Maria Jeritza, I forget which."

"Oh lord!" Annie rolled her eyes in disavowal. "Margot must be drunker than I am."

"Of course, as you know our dear hostess is totally tone deaf." Polo had managed to turn the effusiveness of Margot's praise inside out. "Listen to that ghastly orchestra she's hired. I'm sure I'd much rather hear you. Will you sing?"

Annie looked at him alarmed. She was drunk, but not that drunk.

"Absolutely not. I wouldn't sing under these conditions . . ."

"No no no." Polo waved an impatient hand. "I don't mean that kind of singing. We're not working tonight, we're playing. So let's commandeer the bandstand and make music. Gershwin . . . Duke Ellington . . . What do you Americans call them . . . oldies but goodies?" He was pulling her by the hand through the already thinning crowd of partygoers over to where the band had just finished its set. "You do sing jazz, of course. All Americans do. It's ordained in your Constitution."

He seated himself at the piano, stripped off his jacket and began noodling an intro with the limber-fingered ease of the born musician. She recognized an old Fats Waller tune.

"*Pourquoi pas?*" He grinned. "Why not?"

Pourquoi pas indeed?

Without further ado, Annie hoisted herself atop the piano, long legs crossed and dangling, then gave him an imperious nod.

" 'No one to talk to . . . all by myself . . .' "

The booze and secondhand smoke had made her voice throaty, provocative. No mike wanted or needed. A handful of listeners gathered round as she and Polo wended their way through Duke and Cole Porter and vintage Bessie Smith.

Nearby, she saw Seth surrounded by a cluster of women. He had removed his makeup and now looked not at all monstrous. Simply a remarkably attractive man in a crumpled black suit, up to his ears in perfumed admiration. The price of fame. He caught her eye and winked.

Margot was right. Flirting was good for whatever ails marriages. Annie leaned across the piano to Polo, propping herself up on one elbow, and lit into a bluesy version of "My Funny Valentine," low and sexy. Polo had the good taste to flirt back shamelessly until the orchestra returned.

"That was fun." Annie glowed as Polo helped her down. "Where'd you learn to play jazz like that?"

"At Le Jazz Hot Club in Breslau. Where else? And now, *gnädige frau*"—he lifted her hand to his lips and kissed it—"I must take my leave. I'm scheduled on a flight to Chicago this morning. I have a ten o'clock rehearsal there. No Fats Waller, I'm afraid. Only Mahler."

"Shall we meet again?" She was half teasing, half serious.

"It is written," came the reply. "And the next time you shall really sing for me."

They exchanged amused smiles, two game players who had passed a pleasant hour as Seth waltzed over to claim his wife.

"Ought I to be jealous?" he asked in a good-natured voice.

Polo tipped his kepi, then heaved a mock sigh. "Regrettably, no."

It was nearly dawn when the party broke up and the Petersens took their leave.

Seth dismissed the Rolls waiting patiently at the curb. "We'll walk if you don't mind, darling."

She didn't mind at all.

A fine mist was falling, mild with the promise of early spring, and as they made their way through the quiet streets, populated here and there by a scattering of early risers on their way to mundane jobs, he put his arm around Annie and drew her close. There was intimacy in that gesture, warmth, a sense of we-two-against-the-multitudes. She rubbed her cheek against his black worsted jacket, to reassure herself of his presence.

"Happy, Seth?"

He murmured a long-forgotten endearment and brushed his lips against her cheek. "I ache for you."

She turned her head to kiss him back. His face was wet from the mist, pleasantly rough with the start of tomorrow's beard.

An elderly jogger, muffled up against the chill, beamed at them. Lovers, his smile said. Beautiful creatures from another world.

As the jogger passed, Annie was conscious of how they looked, what they were, of the thousand silken threads that held them together. She was powerfully aware too of Seth's yearning and of her own. When they reached home, they would make love, and all the night's excitements—its joy, its sensuality—would be expressed in the mingling of their bodies.

This night past, she sensed, had put the seal on his wanderings, ended his indecision. He was hers once again, a little sadder, a little more tarnished. No longer the flawless white knight.

Nonetheless hers, God be thanked.

With a pang, she realized how close they had come to losing each other. She shivered.

"Are you cold, darling?" Seth asked. "Should we take a cab?"

"I was." She turned to him in the lamplight. "I was colder than I've ever been in my life, but now I'm fine."

※

Every afternoon at five, Gerald Marriner played squash for a half hour at the Beekman Athletic Club across the river from Medi-Tekk. It was part of the new "fitness" regimen imposed on him by his doctor, Egon Reiner, and if the program had no other merits, at least it served as an occasion for Gerald to demonstrate camaraderie with his staff.

To be invited to play at Beekman ("invited to lose," according to the more cynical staffers) was an opportunity not to be missed, a chance to go one-on-one not only in the confines of the squash court, but in the relaxing postlude of sauna and showers. In the easy intimacy of the locker rooms, Gerald would unwind, be accessible, and it was then that a thrusting young scientist might seize the chance to tout a pet project, ask for a raise, gather those reassurances that were hard come by in the frantic milieu of the lab. "The Beekman Club" Gene Leavitt quipped, "is the one place where you can catch the great man with his pants down."

The Wednesday following the Marriners' costume ball, Seth asked if he might join Gerald for the afternoon workout. For twenty-five minutes on the squash court, Seth held back, let the older man gain a seeming advantage, then closed in quickly the last few minutes of play to smash his way to a clean victory.

"Hey, fella," Gerald panted. "Don't you know the rules? You're supposed to let me win. All my other opponents do."

"You wouldn't want me to blow my game for tactical reasons, would you?" Seth teased. "I'm a competitive guy."

"Who isn't?" Gerald returned, and both men laughed. "Let's go sweat."

For two months now, Seth had dreaded this moment, spent long agonizing hours debating its necessity and finally come to the conclusion that Gerald's confidence was vital. Last Saturday night had decided him. It wasn't the ideal solution, but Seth was savvy enough to know he didn't live in an ideal world.

Duly, he sweated away his claustrophobic half hour in the sauna, making small talk with Gerald, while two men on the opposite bench discussed an impending corporate merger with gusto.

"Sweet deal," one of them repeated. "You're talking one sweet deal," while the other rubbed his hands with satisfaction.

Wall Streeters, Seth thought, wheeling, dealing and probably stealing their way through millions, cheerfully screwing little ole Aunt Minnie in Dubuque with her half a dozen measly shares tucked away in the safe deposit box. That was the name of the game, he supposed, and who was he to quibble? At last, the men left and he was alone with Gerald.

"Well, I've sweated enough for one day." Gerald proposed to follow suit. "How about you?"

"Gerald?" Seth was suddenly very aware of being naked, vulnerable. "There's something I wanted to bring up with you . . ."

"Sure thing." Gerald recognized his cue and leaned back awaiting confidences. "Whatever's on your mind, Seth, feel free."

Seth wiped the sweat off his face with the back of his hand.

He launched a trial balloon. "I've been having a few problems at the lab."

"Problems?" Gerald swung to full attention. "What kind of problems, Seth? Technical . . . personnel . . .?" He sat very still and waited.

"In a sense, both," Seth answered quietly, then tried another exploratory line. "There could be . . . a discrepancy"—yes, that was the word—"a discrepancy arising between certain of my lab results and the printed data." He waited for Gerald to absorb the import of his statement before going on, waited for the invitation to proceed.

Despite the heat of the sauna, Gerald had turned frighteningly pale. For a moment, he said nothing, then he got up off the bench.

"If you'll excuse me, Seth"—his voice was shaking—"I'm going to take my shower," and without a further word he left the sauna and headed for the stalls.

For what seemed like an eternity, Seth sat on a narrow wooden bench in the shower room, the silence broken only by the sound of water running furiously. Briefly Seth considered going into the stall. Perhaps something had happened to Gerald. The man had looked like death a few minutes earlier. But then the water stopped, and in a moment, Gerald stepped out calm and smiling, a white towel wrapped around his waist.

"Well, fella!" He flung a damp avuncular arm around Seth's bare shoulder. "We don't want any negative thinking around here, do we? Of course not. Now, I didn't even hear what you said back there in the sauna. Seth, my boy . . . whatever data you've got, I'm sure they're good enough." He paused, and his voice took on a firmer edge. "And if they're not quite good enough as is, then you'd better see that they are. After all, my name's going on those papers, too."

He sat down beside Seth on the narrow bench, and the intimate smile made a comeback. "You know, I wouldn't want the next director of research at Medi-Trekk to be worried over what I'm sure are a few minor inconsistencies. Happens to the best of us."

Seth felt numb, dizzy. Yet not altogether surprised.

"Of course," Gerald continued, "there are no guarantees in this business, but I'm getting on, plan to retire in another year or two, and the problem of my replacement has already been raised at board level. Of course it's too early to make a firm promise, but . . ."

The conditional hung in the air.

In the ensuing silence, their eyes met and locked. Gerald nodded slightly. Seth was the first to look away.

"I'll want to make some changes in my immediate staff," he murmured. "A new secretary, another couple of techies. And my assistant . . . Chandra. She hasn't worked out quite as well as I had hoped . . ."

"My boy," Gerald cut him short. "You have carte blanche. Make whatever changes you require. And don't look so down in the dumps about it, Seth. All junior personnel are expendable. They'll find other jobs. And now"—he got up and headed for his locker—"I'd better get on home before Margot sends out the troops."

Gerald dressed, returned to find Seth sitting where he had left him. "Is everything OK, Seth?" There was concern in his voice.

Seth raised a thumb in an unequivocal gesture. "Everything's fine, Gerald. Just fine."

❦

A bang. A crash. The sound of furniture toppling. World War III had arrived, followed by Dotty Handler's outraged voice saying, "You can't go in there without . . ." Then the door to Ward Daniels' office flew open to admit—

"Hi, I'm Vi Hagerty."

Ward rubbed his eyes in disbelief. How could an itty-bitty five-foot woman raise such hell? The answer lay in a pair of rubber-tipped canes which she wielded with an ineptitude that inspired awe.

Across the room she lurched, sideswiping a pile of stacked galleys, missing an open filing cabinet. She was heading toward his desk, where God knows what chaos she could wreak. In the nick of time Ward flung a protective hand over his typewriter as the woman stumbled into the visitor's chair. Behind her, Ward's secretary was jumping up and down like a turkey the week before Thanksgiving.

"I'm sorry," Dotty wailed. "She just barreled her way in . . ."

"OK, OK," Ward soothed her ruffled feathers. "I'll handle it."

His first instinct was to call Security and have them give the little broad the old heave-ho, except how do you bounce a cripple? He gave his secretary the high sign. Five minutes, his outspread fingers signaled. Dotty knew the routine. She'd call in five minutes to say he was wanted in a meeting.

"Now, what can I do for you, Ms. Hagerstrom?"

"Hagerty . . . as in Kiss Me, I'm Irish."

Ward leaned back and folded his arms. "Is that supposed to be a funny remark?"

Her reply was to sit quietly for a moment wringing her hands, a fragile figure in a bright green suit with fancy beading.

"I don't have all day." Ward drummed on the desk top. "So get on with it please." In fact, he had a good idea as to why she was here.

"It's your article," she said, "about those two guys who found a cure for MS? 'The Wonder Workers'? Well . . . I want you to put me in touch with them. I've decided, I'm going to be the first person they cure."

Ward stifled a laugh. "Just like that!"

"Why not?" She was pretty when she smiled. "There has to be a first time for everything, right? There was a first man on the moon, a first test-tube baby, a first woman president . . ." She was warming to her subject.

"Wait a minute!" Ward held up a hand. "Have I missed something? A woman president? Did Ron hand the Oval Room over to Nancy while I was shaving this morning? Enlighten me."

"I mean in England. They have a woman president there . . ."

"Mrs. Thatcher is prime minister," Ward corrected.

"Same thing. I'm mean if you're going to pick hairs . . ."

"Split hairs, not pick. You pick nits." What the hell was he doing in this crazy conversation?

"Well, anyhow, she's a woman, and she's the first. See? That's my point. Someone always has to be first. So why not me with this cure?"

The buzzer on his desk sounded.

"Mr. Daniels, you have a ten o'clock meeting in the boardroom."

"Ah." He rose to go. "Well, thanks for stopping by. I'm glad you enjoyed my article and now my girl will show you out."

"But you haven't heard what I want!" Her blue eyes were bright with anguish.

"I've heard exactly what you want. You want to contact these two scientists. Well, I'm afraid I can't help you there, Miss Hagerty. I suggest you write directly to Medi-Tekk. Now, if you'll excuse me . . ."

"Oh, but I have!" She clutched his arm. "I wrote them. Phoned them. I was there all day yesterday, just sitting on the curb, but they wouldn't let me past the gate. The place is a goddam fortress. And these doctors—Marriner, Petersen. I can't get to speak to them. I try to reach 'em at the lab because they're not in the phone book, but every time I call they're either out of town or in meetings or they're on another wire . . ."

"Yes . . . well . . ." He didn't want to get physical, but she refused to budge, her long red nails still embedded in his sleeve. "You've done your best. That's all anyone can do. Now I really have to go . . ."

"I'll wait." She released her grip.

"You can't wait!" Silently he cursed. The damn woman was driving him out of his own office, and he had no place in particular to go. "This meeting could take all morning . . ."

"That's OK, I've got nothing but time."

"And then I have a lunch date . . ."

Her eyes narrowed suspiciously. "Enjoy." She gave a thin-lipped smile. "I'll be here when you get back."

"Have it your way, sweetheart."

He'd go down to Moriarty's and toss back a few with the boys from UPI. She'd get discouraged in an hour or two and piss off. In the meanwhile, he was taking no chances. Without a word, he locked his Rolodex phone list into a desk drawer and pocketed the key.

It was two thirty before he returned, with a few Scotches and a pound of Moriarty's finest sirloin inside him. She was sitting exactly where he'd left her, only her face was paler now, more drawn.

"Look here," he barked. "I don't know what precisely it is you want out of me . . ."

"An introduction. All I want is to talk to them. Just give me their addresses is all I ask. Their phone numbers. Anything. If they won't see me, well, maybe their wives . . ."

"That's out of the question," he snapped. "I'm a journalist, not a go-between . . ."

"I'll pay you," she said. "I've got five thousand dollars in the bank. Just name your price . . ."

"Jesus God!" Ward threw up his hands. "You actually trying to bribe me? Listen, kid, I've turned down better offers than yours. As far as I'm concerned, this conversation is at an end. If you want, I'll call you a taxi. If not, you can sit here till doomsday."

With that, he turned his back on her, and began thrashing out a think piece for the May issue. "Taking Aim at the Gun Lobby," it was entitled—a topic dear to his heart—although this little lady here threatened to make him revise his views about deadly weapons.

For an hour he pecked furiously, but the prose refused to sing. Out of the corner of his eye he would glimpse the bright green of her suit, feel the heaviness of her presence. It stifled him.

"You want some coffee?" he asked when the wagon came around.

"No thanks."

Her sit-in had already lasted five hours, during which she'd had nothing to eat or drink, unless you counted the occasional stick of chewing gum. She was afraid to leave her station, Ward surmised, for even a glass of water, a trip to the john, in case he seized upon the occasion to lock her out. Such determination.

He fetched himself coffee and came back to his desk with a sense of being victimized. The woman was exploiting him, turning her misery into a tactical advantage. With a sigh, he swiveled to face her.

"That's not how it's done, you know. There are channels, systems, procedures. And if and when they get around to doing clinical tests, there's no guarantee the treatment will work. Believe me, there are plenty of people in the same boat, all equally deserving of sympathy."

"I'm not asking for your sympathy, buddy. All I'm asking for is a couple of lousy addresses. Is that so much?"

"Look, Miss Hagerty . . ."

"Vi . . ."

To call her Vi was to give her an opening, proof that she was getting to him. Damn her! Didn't she know when she was licked?

"Look, Vi. You've got the wrong customer. I'm an observer,

that's all. If you were my friend . . . hell, if you were my wife even, I wouldn't act any differently. You see, I'm a journalist, a mere purveyor of fact. It's against my principles to get involved."

Vi Hagerty frowned for a moment, absorbing this information.

Then "Well, fuck you, Mr. High-and-Mighty Journalist," she yelled. "If that's how you'd treat your friends, you sure as shit don't need enemies." Her words came out in a staccato burst, the blue eyes throwing off angry sparks. "Listen, Daniels, if it was just for me, do you think I would sit here taking your shit, making an ass of myself hour after hour? You think I have no pride? No feelings? This . . ." She opened her bag, pulled out an accordion strip of snapshots, flung them across his desk. "This . . . is what I'm here for . . ."

They were pictures of a skinny kid with glasses, playing stick ball, making faces, doing all the sappy things kids do. One photo in particular caught Ward's eye: the boy and a woman in cut-down blue jeans waving gaily from the deck of a small ketch. Healthy, carefree faces. Pretty woman. Lovely legs. Barefoot. Hair blowing in the wind. He pushed the string of photos back to her.

"Your son, I gather."

It was all the opening she needed for the story to emerge, and as she charted the details, Ward found himself getting suckered into her plight against his will. Against his better judgment, as well. She had pinned her hopes on such a crazy solution.

Patiently he heard her out, then offered his own brand of advice.

"Be a realist, Vi," he urged. "Accept what's happened. Otherwise you'll just make things harder."

"Listen," she came back, "if I were a realist, I'd have thrown in the sponge a long time ago. All I have left is hope!"

She leaned back in the chair, energy spent, and he intuited that in a few more minutes she would go. At least with Ward Daniels on this particular afternoon, Vi Hagerty had thrown in the sponge.

"Forget about the Marriners," Ward said softly. He had a swift image of Margot's aloof, spotless beauty. "They don't live in the real world. Besides, you'd never get past the butler. Now, I don't know if this is going to do you any good at all . . ." He unlocked his desk and pulled out the Rolodex, riffling through until he found what he wanted. Then he scribbled a name and address on a memo pad. "OK. This is the Petersens' home address. If you think it's worth it, give it a try, although I have my doubts. The husband's a pretty cool customer, you might do better going after the wife. Her name's Annie and"—he should be strung up for what he was doing—"and she's got soul."

"Oh, wow!" Vi ferreted the paper away in her bag, then reached for her canes. "I don't know how to thank you . . . I really don't."

She leaned over the desk to peck his cheek, missed a foothold and staggered, sent his coffee cup crashing halfway across the room.

"Oh shit, I'm sorry." She began dabbing the hot liquid off his draft of the gun lobby story as Dotty Handler flew in to the rescue.

"It's OK, Dot. Ms. Hagerty was just leaving. Look, Vi, do the world a favor—" He sighed and pointed to her canes. "Will you learn how to use these fucking things? And give me a ring one of these days, let me know how you make out."

"Betcha!" She beamed and left without wreaking further damage.

"Some nerve!" Dotty Handler clucked as she mopped coffee off his desk. "That woman has some nerve."

"Yup." Ward Daniels watched the retreating figure with grudging admiration. "She sure as hell does!"

❈

It was over. As Margot predicted, the errant sheep had come back to the fold.

"Now"— her friend beamed—"now aren't you glad you followed my advice and kept the peace?"

Annie was and wasn't. The months of self-imposed silence had taken a toll. And though—thank God!—their marriage had survived, she was haunted by a sense of unfinished business.

If only Seth would be honest with her. If only, now that it was done with, he would discuss what had happened and why. They'd probably wind up in a shouting match, but that was all right. At least he'd have got rid of his guilt, she'd have worked off her anger. For how could you truly forgive, she asked herself, if you couldn't forget? And how could she forget, until the air was cleared?

Yet Seth seemed determined to bury the past, and she was reluctant to force him. Instead, the Petersens picked up the strands of their lives—the rounds of dinner parties, concerts, theaters, the lazy sexy Sunday mornings in bed with the *Times* and with each other— with the pretense that there had been no Chandra, no betrayal.

If anything, Seth was busier, fuller of plans than ever.

He came home one night with a dozen travel brochures. "OK, pick your spot. We're going to take that trip to Europe I promised you a zillion years ago. This very summer. And we'll do it in style. First class all the way, babe. Why not? Financially we're on a roll."

They spent mouth-watering hours mapping their dream trip, balancing the châteaus of the Loire against the antiquities of Greece, the craggy pleasures of Scottish castles against the glitter of the Salzburg Festival. He was taking pains to do everything right. Her reward, she concluded, for having behaved like a lady these past months.

And though he never admitted to anything remotely resembling infidelity, he managed to let her know it was finished. That, at least, was her interpretation when, shortly after Margot's ball, he took her for a wildly expensive dinner at La Caravelle. Somewhere between the roast duck and the dessert, Seth casually mentioned that he had hired a new assistant. "Seems like a nice guy . . ."

"Oh!" Annie swallowed hard to keep her voice level. "What happened to . . . um, Chandra?"

"Immigration cracked down on her," Seth stated. "They didn't extend her visa. She's going back to Pakistan end of this week."

But that answer was no answer at all. Had the affair been broken off because of red tape, rather than through Seth's initiative? If so, Chandra was the first, but probably not the last.

"I thought," Annie picked her words cautiously, "that you were going to plead for her at the hearing . . . get her a green card."

"I decided against recommending her," he said flatly. "She wasn't working out all that well. Now"—he buried his nose in the menu—"enough of boring office gossip. More important, what would you like for dessert? Gerald says the Bavarian Cream here is terrific."

Annie was of two minds about Chandra's dismissal. Naturally, she was delighted the girl was gone. Yet she was shocked at the unfeeling way Seth had maneuvered the break. Such calculation! as though his lover were nothing but an unsatisfactory employee. He must have testified against her in a closed hearing, jeopardized her name. In which case, Chandra never knew what hit her. Not that Annie felt sorry for that home wrecker, but still—what a way for a love affair to end!

"Seth's like a new man," Margot observed. Sadder but wiser, was Annie's reply. But she recognized he was a new man indeed. A harder man. Tougher. Not tough with her necessarily, Annie conceded, but in his approach to the world at large. Like iron that had been fed into a crucible and forged into steel, Seth emerged subtly changed. In the process, a certain tenderness, a vulnerability, had been lost.

Soon after, Annie opened their American Express bill to find the evidence she had once sought for in vain. The smoking gun, indeed. There could be no other explanation for an $850 item from Tiffany's, purchased the same day as their dinner at La Caravelle.

What had he bought the girl as a good-bye gift? A watch? A ring? The invoice didn't specify.

Then it struck her. A gold bracelet! Yes, a wide gold bracelet suitably inscribed. To Chandra from Seth. Or had he chosen a more private imagery? A chemical equivalent to *Le Spectre de la Rose?* The thought made her wince.

She stuffed the bill back in the envelope and resealed it. Let Seth pay the damn thing himself. She didn't want him to know she had seen it. Maybe Margot was right, some things were best left unspoken.

She had been singing that morning, the Easter music from the *Messiah* at a Good Friday concert in St. Bartholomew's. Now she walked the dozen blocks up Park Avenue to her apartment in a buoyant mood.

"Hello, Sandor." She gave the doorman a breezy salute as she turned into her building.

"Oh, Mrs. Petersen—" He followed her into the lobby. "Your sister arrived right after you left."

Annie swiveled in surprise. Linda in New York? Although she had mentioned something about coming east this spring, bringing the kids. "I hope it's all right," the doorman said, "but I let her into the apartment. I thought she'd be more comfortable . . . ."

Annie rode up in the elevator wondering what had brought Linda in on such short notice. And unannounced. A problem with Len? Hard to figure her brother-in-law for a swinger. But then, she'd never figured Seth for one either . . .

"Linda?" She turned the key in the lock. "Linda? I'm home." Then she stopped. "Who the hell . . .!"

For the woman on the sofa—small, blond—was a total stranger.

"Please . . ." said the intruder.

"Oh, God!" Annie spotted the canes. Her hand flew to her head in instant comprehension. Oh, God, this was everything they'd moved from Horatio Street to get away from, the reason why they'd got an unlisted phone, the penalty they paid for Seth's success.

"Please," the woman said. "Please don't call the cops!"

Annie heaved a sigh. "I'm not going to call the police, but you'll have to go. This is an intolerable intrusion."

She swept into the room with a no-nonsense stride, as if to make a territorial claim. But the woman remained motionless, except for an anguished clasping and reclasping of her hands.

Oh, shit. Annie was at a total loss. Should she ring downstairs and tell the superintendent to show her out? She didn't have the heart. The poor soul! She looked to be at wit's end, pale beneath the make-up, eyes filled with the terror of a cornered animal. Annie knew the look from the labs.

"Mrs. Petersen, my name is Vi Hagerty and believe me, I wouldn'a come here if I wasn't absolutely desperate . . ." The voice, with its Brooklynese inflection, spoke of mean streets and hard times.

"I'd like to know who gave you our home address?" Annie broke in.

"I . . ." More wringing of the hands. It was to keep them from trembling, Annie divined. She had tiny bones, delicate as a bird's, fragile, frangible . . . "I don't want to get anyone in trouble."

"You've already gotten our doorman in trouble," Annie said mildly. "He shouldn't have let you in. And how did you know I have a sister?"

"I was guessing. I woulda tried anything, Mrs. Petersen . . ."

Annie folded her arms, shook her head.

"In fact, it beats me how you passed for her. You don't look the least bit like either of us. No family resemblance at all."

As soon as the words were spoken Annie became painfully aware of how she must indeed appear to her uninvited guest. Aware of her height and presence, of the elegance of her black concert dress, of the diamond earrings that had been Seth's Christmas present. Aware of the high-ceilinged room with its French windows and Japanese prints, of the overflowing bookcases, of the Steinway grand gleaming blackly in the far corner with its message of culture, wealth and privilege. Aware of the spring in her step as she had entered, of the cheeks glowing from the brisk walk up the avenue.

Yes, aware, above all, of her own—*rude health.*

A funny expression that was, as though health were a matter of manners. But now, standing here, tall and blooming, she could visualize her own well-being as an assault, an act of aggression. At the least, it showed a lack of consideration for her guest. Rude crude health.

How lucky she must look to an outsider—one of the favored few, a woman to whom bad things never happened. In a way it was true. What tragedies had ever befallen Annie? That her cat had died? Or her husband had had a brief affair? Her unwelcome visitor was forcing Annie into a larger perspective.

She wavered between sitting down and granting the woman five minutes or—what the hell, it was lunchtime. According to Sandor, she must have been waiting here for hours.

"Would you like some coffee, Miss Hagerty? Or is it Mrs.?"

"Vi," came the answer in a happy gasp. Oh, the relief in those eyes, the joy of being spared a swift unceremonious departure. "Everyone calls me Vi. Thank you, Mrs. Petersen, I'd love a cup of coffee."

"And . . . a sandwich or something? I must have a can of tuna fish somewhere . . ." She found herself apologizing. "I rarely eat at home."

"Anything, Mrs. Petersen. Anything at all."

The formality bothered Annie. There were enough inequities between them without adding that of nomenclature.

"It's Annie," she said. "Now if you'll excuse me for a few minutes, I'll make us some lunch." She headed for the kitchen, playing for time in which to frame a few tactful words of refusal, but Vi traipsed after her, canes clattering.

"I thought maybe you could use some help, Mrs.. . . Annie."

"Nope!" Annie buried her face in the depths of the cupboard, as much to compose herself as to explore the possibilities for lunch. "Thanks anyhow. You just sit down, Vi, and make yourself comfortable."

Yes, there was tuna, enough things for a salad. And a can of that terrific pâté she'd been saving for a special occasion. With French bread and a nice piece of *chèvre*, that should make a delicious lunch.

After all, the least she could do was offer the woman a decent meal.

Annie adjusted her apron, put on the coffee and began assembling the salad.

As she worked, she managed a stream of small talk. "I'm not usually this dressed up so early in the day"—perhaps an explanation was in order—"I'm a singer, you see . . ." and even as she rambled on she could feel Vi Hagerty's bright blue eyes fixed upon her.

"You don't have children, do you?" Vi asked suddenly.

Cold fingers clutched Annie's heart.

"What makes you say that?"

Vi looked about. "Oh, anyone can see it. All your things are so nice and tidy, no scuff marks on the linoleum. Me, I'm always washing dirty fingerprints off the wall."

"No." Annie fixed her eyes on the mixing bowl. No dammit, we don't have children, so will you please not remind me? Please steer clear of my personal life?

But Vi barreled on.

"I do. He's ten years old." The dam suddenly broke. "He's all I've got and I'm going to lose custody. Please . . . don't turn your back . . . you're the only person in God's world who can help me. You and Dr. Petersen . . . you're the only ones . . ."

"Stop!" Annie whirled around, foolishly clutching the salad bowl. "It's not like you think. My husband isn't even a medical doctor. He works with animals . . . with laboratory mice. I'd like to help but there's nothing I can do. Maybe some financial assistance . . . ?"

"Fuck money!" Vi burst out. "Everybody wants to buy me off. Put a few bucks in my hand and maybe I'll have the decency to crawl back under the woodwork. Well, money means less than nothing. I don't want a goddam handout. I want to be cured. I want to walk into that courtroom on my own two legs . . ."

She honked into a tissue, then wiped her eyes, penitent. "I didn't mean to curse, but I can't sit back and let this happen. I guess it's hard for you to picture, what with your not having kids of your own, but all I ask is—put yourself in my place."

Was it possible? By what leap of the imagination could Annie picture herself inside the nightmare of those frightened eyes? Picture her body inside that damaged frame? But one thing she could picture. She could picture a woman with a child.

Annie put the food down, then settled into a kitchen chair. "Go ahead, Vi. I'm listening . . ."

Go figure.

Vi did her best to rein in her exuberance while her hostess was in the bedroom, getting into what she called "civilian clothes."

Go figure that someone as rich and slick as Annie Petersen would turn out to be so sympathetic! Thank God Vi had stuck it out, not panicked, which had been her first reaction on seeing the spread. Suppose they accused her of stealing? It made her nervous—all the books, records, the cases full of music, that enormous piano. No place like home, for sure. And with all those goodies lying about, the woman opens her refrigerator and there's nothing in it but a piece of goat cheese that stunk to high heaven. Some weird household!

Vi sighed and sipped her cold coffee. Even in her real estate days, rich people had been a total mystery. And yet . . .

And yet she and Annie had understood each other in a way that had nothing to do with style or money or background. Woman to woman. It was that simple. Or that complicated, maybe. And when Annie had asked about Noonie—what he looked like, how he was doing at school—Vi had picked up the note of longing in her voice. The woman ached to have children, was Vi's guess; you could almost feel sorry for her. All that dough and an empty house.

Annie emerged from the bedroom in a sweater and slacks. Her eyes were red-rimmed.

"I can promise nothing, you understand."

Vi's heart skipped a beat. "Only you should talk to your husband. Or let me speak to him . . ."

"No no," Annie interjected. "I'll handle it myself. He's bound to be sympathetic, but the testing is most likely out of his hands. I believe they contract the trials to independent hospitals, and then, of course, I don't know what the criteria are. Whether they're looking for advanced cases, early cases, which form of the disease they plan to treat. And besides," she added, "they won't even begin clinical trials until they've finished with the test animals. They have to satisfy themselves that there are no serious side effects. At the earliest,

Phase One testing won't be scheduled till next autumn and Seth feels even that's premature . . ."

"I can stall 'em in court." Vi crossed her fingers under the table. "With a little luck, we can hold out for another few months . . ."

"And then"—Annie sighed—"comes the great big But. There's just no way of knowing if the treatment is actually going to work. It may not be effective with people . . ."

"It will be," Vi burst in. "It's gotta be. I can feel it in my bones. Besides," she added ruefully, "what have I got to lose?"

Unexpectedly, Annie crossed over to where Vi sat and encircled her in a spontaneous hug.

"I'll do my best, Vi. I've got good vibes too. I'll start working on my husband tonight."

Vi returned the embrace.

"Ward Daniels was right about you . . ." She pushed back the lump in her throat. "He said you had soul."

"Soul indeed." Annie gave an embarrassed laugh and disentangled herself. "Well, at least now I know who the culprit is. That so-called hard-boiled reporter! I bet he was a pushover. Anyhow, my car's downstairs. So if you get your things together, I'll run you home."

※

"No!"

Annie had expected a refusal her first go-round. She'd never before requested such a favor of Seth.

She had waited to catch him in a mellow mood and now, over a midnight brandy in the living room, she pleaded Vi's case.

Seth heard her out, then put down his snifter and massaged the bridge of his nose wearily.

"I'm surprised at you, Annie, letting a perfect stranger pull a number on you like that. You start by getting suckered in with the first sob story that comes in off the street, and end up running a mission. Annie, love, your intentions do you credit, but you're just too soft-hearted for your own good . . . The answer is no."

"Why not, Seth?"

He sighed. "OK, you want me to lay it out, one two three? One. I have no direct involvement with setting up clinical trials, nor do I intend to. That's Gerald's department . . ."

"You can speak to Gerald."

"Two. When the trials are set up, they'll probably use the double-blind method. Half the patients get the treatment, the other half get a placebo, and not even the administering doctors know which is which. Your pal may wind up right where she started."

"A fifty percent chance is better than none at all . . ."

"Three—" He leaned forward, chin in hand, to examine her with a puzzled air. "Three. I don't interfere in your career decisions and I don't expect you to interfere in mine. It's a simple question of autonomy . . ."

"That's not quite true, Seth. You interfered—and I'm awfully glad you did—when you set up my audition with Madame Natasha."

"I smoothed the path, that's all . . . facilitated something you were bound to do anyhow. I've always supported your ambitions as I presume you do mine. I back you when I can. But never"—the idea must have hit a nerve, for his voice began to rise—"never once have I presumed to tell you that you should sing this passage louder or put a little more oomph in your Mozart or whatever. Never! And you know why, Annie? Because I'm not competent. I'm a rank amateur when it comes to music. Sure, I've learned a little of the lingo over the years—by osmosis, as it were—just as you've picked up some of mine. But I would never dream of making a professional judgment about singing. All I ask is the same courtesy in return. Hands off! Because if I know fucking little about the finer points of bel canto, Annie, believe me, you know a helluva lot less about science!"

"Why are you so angry?" Annie was shocked. "You act as if I'm threatening you. I asked you a favor, you said no. I ask you a reason, and you go off on this diatribe. I always thought we had a fifty-fifty marriage, that we shared things—including professional problems—and you jump on me for a simple request . . ."

"I don't like to see my wife being taken advantage of . . ."

"Your wife!" Unaccountably, the phrase stung. "Well, I'm my own person too, capable of making judgments. All I ask is that you explore this as a possibility. I made a commitment to Vi Hagerty . . ."

"You had no right to."

"Maybe not, but it's done. I feel for the woman. I think life gave her a raw deal . . ."

"What did she do, drag out her winsome lad for inspection, the better to wring your withers, my dear?"

"I never even saw him. He was skiing with his father in Aspen."

"Jesus!" Seth snorted. "Kid really has it rough, doesn't he? Did it ever occur to you the boy might be better off with his father? You're probably causing more harm than good. Believe me, I can see how it all came about, and I'm sure your sentiments are admirable. It's Good Friday, you'd come back from church full of noble music . . . lofty thoughts . . . Let's face it, love. You were ripe for the plucking."

"Funny," Annie said. "I forgot about its being Good Friday . . ."

Seth saw his opening and seized it. "Well, I bet your Hagerty woman didn't. Her timing couldn't have been better. After all, a person would have to be made of stone to turn down a request like that on the very day that Christ died. You want to do something humanitarian? We'll make a donation to a charity. What do you say I give five thousand dollars to the MS Society . . ."

But Annie was lost in her own train of thought.

"Good Friday," she murmured. "Vi was sitting right where you are only a dozen hours ago and you know what . . .? This afternoon, for the first time in my life, I had a glimpse into the abyss."

"Annie!" Seth turned pale. "What a thing to say!"

"You and I, Seth, we skim across the surface of things, worrying about our careers and whether to buy a new Volvo and which French châteaus we're going to visit, while just below us there's a whole other world, seething, roiling, dreadful beyond our comprehension. Because even when our life was in what we used to call the pits, when we were living on canned spaghetti in Oak Ridge—even then, we had it made! We were healthy, we were happy, we had each other, terrific futures. What has either of us ever known of real hardship? We've been fortune's darlings, doing just what we want to do. You have your lab, I have my music. We can both congratulate ourselves on making positive contributions to society. And we do all these commendable uplifting things among people who are just as smart and clean and healthy and successful as we are. But that doesn't mean the abyss isn't there, inches below our feet. This afternoon, I looked at Vi sitting on this sofa—powerless, desperate!—and you know what I felt? There but for the grace of God . . ." She stopped to wipe her eyes on the cocktail napkin. "Fitting sentiment for Good Friday, don't you think?"

Seth listened, visibly moved, then poured another brandy.

"Why should you feel guilty about leading the good life, Annie?" he said softly. "You're not taking anything away from anyone. There's no point in wallowing in other people's misery, darling. It doesn't lighten their load. You only succeed in making yourself unhappy too. And I want you to be happy . . ."

"Do you?" She looked up sharply. "I thought about a lot of things this afternoon, myself as well as Vi Hagerty. I thought about what in my life had caused me the most pain, the deepest hurt. And it was you. Not some outsider, but you, Seth!"

He started to say something, then lowered his eyes. It was as close to an admission of guilt as he could manage.

"You owe me, Seth," she added. "Think about it."

With that she left the room.

A little later, he came in munching on a Mars bar to where she sat reading in bed.

"Want a bite, Annie?"

She shook her head no.

"Good book?"

She nodded yes without meeting his eyes. There was really nothing more to say, and she chose not to let him off the hook with casual conversation.

He sprawled out beside her fully clothed, chewed the candy, stared at the ceiling, at last delivering himself of a heartfelt sigh.

"If I do this favor, Annie"—he picked his words carefully—"and believe me, it is a favor, can we get back on the old footing?"

"Why, Seth!" She put down her book, surprised. "Are you offering me a deal?"

"Guess so. I want to go on record that it's against all my principles, having you interfere like this. But shit, Annie! I hate the thought of our being adversaries. It makes me feel like the world is coming to an end. OK, I'll do what you ask . . . I'll speak to Gerald in the morning."

He got up and started peeling off his clothes, tossing them in the general direction of the laundry basket, muttering all the while—*under protest . . . no big deal . . . last I want to hear about it . . . What the hell were we arguing about, anyway . . .*

Then he stripped off his shorts, turned and held them up above his head with a silly grin.

"Truce?" He waved the white flag.

"Truce." She giggled. "Now will you come to bed?"

Seth switched off the light and dived happily under the covers.

"The nice thing about getting mad"—he laughed softly—"is making up. Can we kiss and make up now?"

She slid into his arms, suddenly hungry for his mouth. He tasted of chocolate.

"Delicious," she murmured.

Seth's response was to draw himself up above her waiting body. Then with the flat of his palms, the tip of his tongue, he began to explore all the textures of her flesh as though he had never known it before. As though she were some beautiful newcomer who had found her way into his bed and his heart. It was a voyage of rediscovery, an affirmation of their love.

She shut her eyes beneath the soft barrage of his caresses, as feathery hands and curious tongue defined anew the curve of her lips, the tautness of her nipples, the sweet-salt path between her breasts, the secret skin of her inner thighs, the shy hollows at the base of her spine. Beneath his touch, she lay trembling, never knowing where the next soft stroke would alight.

He lay his head across her belly, nibbled gently on her pubic hair while the flat of his thumb nestled against her. She answered with a rush of lubricity. "Devour me," she murmured, then spreading her knees wide, welcomed the warmth of his head between her legs, the sinuous tongue snaking inside her, seeking the spots that pleasured her most.

"Like new." He rose, lips gleaming, and now when he kissed her, his mouth tasted not of chocolate but of herself. Yes, like new. She coiled her legs about him, feeling his strong firm buttocks against the soles of her feet.

For all the years together, all the love made and kisses exchanged, all the thousands of intimacies—tonight they were like first-time lovers.

Against the flat of her stomach, Seth pressed against her, aroused and insistent. His ache matched her own. She slipped her hand down to the firm column of flesh and drew him, hot and thrusting, toward her moistness. He entered in a swift, grateful surge and began the rhythmic dance of love.

"Mine," she cried, then gripped his buttocks to lead him, languidly at first, teasing and tantalizing, then ever farther and stronger into the depths of her body until she no longer knew where he ended and she began. Their flesh, their breath, their very lives were once more one and inseparable.

"Mine!" he shouted in the moment of climax, and their bodies exploded together.

They lay for a long time in each other's arms, exchanging endearments and sweet inanities.

"Seth"—her last thought surfaced before sleep caught them out—"don't ever go so far away from me again."

She woke the next morning, lazily content, to find Seth already dressed for work.

"Don't get up, lovey." He beamed down on her with the satisfaction of a cat in cream. She knew the feeling.

He brushed her cheek, patted her rump and left. Annie had half-dozed off before she remembered.

"Vi!" She jumped out of bed and was on the phone to New Jersey two minutes later.

"Vi!" She could hardly keep her voice from bubbling over. "Guess what . . . you're on! My husband says he'll take care of everything."

There was a joyous squeal at the other end.

The two women babbled happily for a few minutes more, and by the time she hung up, Annie was feeling very pleased with herself.

Well, she had cause. True, it had taken a bit of emotional blackmail to bring Seth to come around, but it was worth it. Her bet was that Vi would be back on her feet before the year was out. And in large part thanks to Annie's intervention. Fabulous! But ironic, too, in its way.

Because if Seth hadn't had that affair with Chandra, if he hadn't been riddled with guilt and eager for atonement, he never would have gone along with her request.

Go figure—she marveled—that out of all that emotional turmoil, something really wonderful would emerge!

PART
THREE

I

Show me a man who lives near the Jersey Turnpike and I'll show you some poor polluted son of a bitch.

Ward Daniels opened the sun roof of his Datsun and happily breathed in the warm June air. Full of sulphur and smoke and lovely toxic waste. A symphony of smell, a chemical cocktail. Even the names of the towns reeked with an unforgettable pungency. Perth Amboy. Rahway. Metuchen. Secaucus. Dickens himself couldn't have done better. What a stink! What a story! "The Politics of Poison."

Only this one he would write as he saw fit. *Worldnews* owed him that much after all the shit he'd taken on the Medi-Tekk assignment.

As he drove north, the fumes dissipated, smoke stacks gave way to budding trees, industrial towns dribbled into suburbia and just as Ward was about to head back into Manhattan, he saw the Bloomfield exit. What's-her-name lived here. No . . . not Gennie, it was Vi something. Vi Hagerty, the gal who damn near got him canned a few months ago.

On impulse, he turned off the highway.

The last he'd heard from her had been Easter weekend, when she'd rung up incoherent with joy.

"Well, I'll be dipped," had been his immediate reaction, following which he tucked the whole business away in the back of his mind, where it might have stayed if not for one nasty episode. But now, three months later, he wondered about the sequel. And the woman too. Ballsy little broad, she was.

A mile off the highway he pulled into an Exxon station, looked in the phone book and found the listing. She answered on the first ring, bubbling, delighted to hear from him.

"I'm in a phone booth," Ward broke in. "What say I pick up Chinese and bring it over?"

She directed him to the nearest Ptomaine Palace, asked for barbecued spare ribs and food enough for three. Noonie was home.

The neighborhood was pleasant, if unprepossessing, not so different from where he grew up outside of Richmond. The kids here still played stickball. As for Vi, she looked wonderful. The eyes were full of sparkle, and she handled her canes—he was pleased to see—with considerable skill. Was it hope that had prompted these changes, or had she finally come to grips with reality?

Ward busied himself unpacking a dozen steaming cartons. "It all looked so terrible, I figured maybe there was safety in numbers."

"Hey, Noonie," Vi hollered out the window, and one of the stickball players from the pavement detached himself from the game to come in.

"Noonie, hon, this is Mr. Daniels I told you about. Hands off the wallpaper . . ."

The grimy paw left the wall leaving a smudge behind, to be thrust firmly into Ward's own.

"Hi." Noonie pumped vigorously. "My mom says you're the world's greatest reporter. Like Clark Kent, only better."

"Your mother is a woman of rare perception. Now, why don't you wash up and set the table so we can eat this swill before it gets cold and gelatinous?"

"Gelatinous . . ." Noonie laughed. "What an awesome word." He left the room, rolling it about on his tongue with gusto. "Dja-like-a gelatinous? Manhattanous Gelatinous . . ." Ward could hear him giggling in the next room.

There goes a boy destined to make his mark on the English language, he thought. Like his mother. "So, Vi, what's new at the front? You still planning"—he disliked the term "guinea pig"—"to be the, um, test pilot on this project?"

"Yup." She grinned. "Looks to be this fall sometime. They have to wait until they've run a certain number of mice through their hoops and then yours truly gets her turn. Not a moment too soon.

We managed to stall off the court hearing for another few months.
I pleaded that there were exterminating circumstances."

"And your ex was willing to go along with the delay?"

She acknowledged his surprise.

"I couldn't believe it either at first. But you know what I
figure? He thinks he's gonna buy Noonie off with a summer lolly-
gagging around the swimming pool, riding horses, romancing the
pants off the kid, because legally Ross is on pretty shaky ground, at
least as far as custody goes. And you know what else I think?"—she
lowered her voice—"I think he's betting on my having another attack
between now and then. He's hoping I'll turn up in a wheelchair, dead
from the waist down. Son of a bitch. I can just picture his face when
I waltz in there doing high kicks like a goddam Rockette."

Dangerous dreams, dangerous dreams.

"I've been working out," she added. "Getting in shape. Here . . .
feel the muscle." She flexed her arm. "And as soon as I'm well, I
want to start my own business. Real estate consultant. I got a computer, learning all sorts of cute stuff. And after hours? Don't ask.
I'm going to have myself a ball."

Her optimism unnerved Ward, but before he could comment,
Noonie announced the imminence of dinner.

They ate in the kitchen, out of the cartons. The food, to Ward's
surprise, was excellent.

"You never get this in China." He speared a morsel of steak. "In
fact, you rarely see real meat at all. They serve you stuff like duck-
foot webbing, pig snouts, strange and unmentionable giblets . . ."

Noonie was watching him openmouthed.

"You been to China?"

"Yup. Went from Beijing right to the Afghan border."

"I've never known anyone who went to China."

"Lot of things you don't know, kiddo."

Noonie pondered this, feeling his manhood was being impugned.
But curiosity got the better of him.

"What's it like in China?"

"Outside of the fact that you can't get a decent steak . . ." Ward
launched into his favorite Chinese anecdotes, laundering some, em-
broidering others. The boy had his mother's blue eyes and with each
story they widened in awe. A born audience. Ward couldn't resist.

"So there I was. Fell right off the riverboat smack into the Yangtze.

Now, you might think that's no worse than falling into the Hudson, but you'd be wrong. Do you know what the antipodes are, son?"

"Antipodes," Noonie echoed with delight. Clearly another great word to be set alongside *gelatinous*. "No, I don't."

"Well," Ward amplified, "the earth is round, as you know, and the antipodes are the part of the world that's directly opposite where you are. Now, if you fell into the Hudson, your body's buoyancy would float you up to the surface. But in the Yangtze, what with China being our antipodes, it works the other way around . . ."

The blue eyes clouded in doubt. With a child's wariness of being teased, he was struggling to absorb this fact when Vi spoiled the game by laughing aloud.

"I knew you were kidding," Noonie jumped in. "So there! You don't know everything. I bet you don't even know how to play casino."

"Of course I do," came the answer, "only who would want to play that pansy game? Now, I bet you don't know the first thing about poker. Vi, get the cards . . ."

He spent an easy hour explaining the principles of five-card stud and it was after ten when he got up to leave.

Vi walked him to the door.

"Thanks for coming, Ward. It was a great evening—for both me and Noonie."

Not great, perhaps, but relaxing. He had enjoyed the change of pace.

"I'm working on a story downstate this month. If I get a chance I'll drop by again."

"Any time, Ward." She had dimples when she smiled. "I'm practically always home."

He drove back to New York in a thoughtful mood. Had he erred, putting her in touch with Annie Petersen? Vi's belief in this "cure" bordered on the delusional. She refused to admit the possibility of failure, of less than 100 percent results. If the trials proved a dud, it would break her heart. Better that she had never hoped at all. Not for the first time, Ward questioned his own involvement.

Yet that Noonie was one terrific kid, worth fighting for, and who knows? Maybe the treatment would work miracles. Maybe she could hang on to the kid after all. He sure as hell hoped so.

Yes, Ward would have made the same choice again, despite the consequences. For what he hadn't told Vi—why make her feel guilty?—was that Seth Petersen had lodged a formal complaint to *Worldnews.*

"The man is really pissed off," Claire Pulham had said when she showed him the letter. "He would like your scalp on a platter, and I can't say as I blame him. Read."

. . . unethical behavior, invasion of privacy, betrayal of trust, total disregard of confidentiality . . .

"Yeah yeah yeah." Ward handed the paper back. "So . . . are you going to fire me?"

"I ought to." She sighed, then made a show of dropping the letter into the wastebasket. "Just don't ever let this happen again. Next time . . ."

"There won't be a next time, Claire. Keep your hair on."

And that had been that.

Petersen's behavior had puzzled him at the time, puzzled Ward still, as he waited in the line of traffic at the Lincoln Tunnel. Not the angry letter demanding he be fired (although it struck Ward as an overreaction), but that in spite of his legitimate outrage, Petersen had nonetheless complied with Vi's request. Why? He could just as easily have said no, especially since the two of them had never met. The man was under no obligation. Why set this precedent?

It must have been the wife's doing, Ward concluded. Annie Petersen had put pressure on her husband, be it through tears or just plain nagging, and the man had knuckled under. To please his wife, for Chrissakes. Amazing!

Personally he liked Annie. Maybe he'd call her for lunch next week, give her the word on Vi Hagerty's progress. She'd be interested. Yeah—Annie was OK, although of course he wasn't married to her. To anyone, thank God.

The traffic jam was breaking up, and as Ward entered the tunnel he pulled the sun roof shut against the carbon monoxide fumes.

Amazing—shook his head in wonderment—that a tough cookie like Seth Petersen would let a woman sink her hooks into him like that.

❈

Everything—but everything—had been lined up for the autumn. Auditions with the Met, with City Center, the possibility of a contract with New York's leading concert management. She and the indefatigable Ari had grubbed for days in the archives of the Lincoln Center Library, come up with enough little-known works to assemble a program entitled Famous Composers—Forgotten Music, then mailed out flyers to every university and college in the northeast. More than a dozen had responded favorably. Off the wall, said Lainie Carpenter. Off the beaten track, Annie laughed. "Awfully interesting," said the precious young man from Eclectic Records who thought there might well be an album in it.

"We're looking at a mini-concert tour," she told Seth as she totted up the growing commitments. *And* the figures. "Funny thing is, with all these concerts, by the time I've paid Ari and met our travel expenses, we do just a little better than break even. And I'll need some new clothes for the tour . . ."

"Money," Seth assured her, "is the least of our problems." He even offered to finance a New York debut recital. Why not! His Medi-Tekk stock was breaking through the ceiling, and now there was talk of a merger with one of America's largest pharmaceutical companies. "If it comes off, we'll be paper millionaires. And if it doesn't, we'll simply be very well heeled. So go ahead, buy yourself some fancy duds. Knock 'em dead, sweetheart." His immediate contribution was a leather-bound five-year diary, "just the item for long-term planning." Annie made the initial entries with gusto.

The only shadow in her life, now that Seth was on good behavior, was her continued inability to get pregnant.

In the months since St. Thomas, she had come to place a childlike trust in the words of that old obeah woman. You who are two will be three. There had been a ring of prophecy in the phrase, Annie felt. Which only went to prove to what lengths people would go— even smart people—in order to believe what they wished to believe. Of course the year was only half over. In the fall, if nothing happened, she would take Seth's advice and consult a specialist.

In the meantime here she was in Paris on a warm July evening with her problems a million miles away. And she was going to enjoy.

"The trip of a lifetime," Seth promised. First, this week in Paris, where he was attending a seminar at the Institut Pasteur ("It'll make part of our trip tax deductible"); another week in the château country, hitting every three-star restaurant en route; then a few days in the south of France. After which Seth, unable to spare more time, would head home while Annie proceeded to Salzburg for the festival.

Did she trust him to be alone in New York after what they'd been through? Last winter, one week in St. Thomas had sufficed for mischief to rear its ugly head. What would he do with two or three?

But though the memory rankled, she refused to live her life in a stew of suspicion. It would destroy everything: their marriage, their dreams of family, even her career. For how could she possibly go on tour if she had to worry about Seth's fidelity every night?

"And are you enjoying Paris, Mrs. Petersen?" the young Frenchman sitting next to her inquired politely.

"Wonderful"—she gave her good-wife smile—"city of dreams."

Especially, she thought, now that the seminar was over and she would have her husband to herself. The final session had taken place that afternoon, and Seth had invited a handful of the younger scientists to be their guests for cocktails at the Plaza Athenée. Just a couple of boring hours to be got through and then their own vacation could properly begin. "I hope you don't mind, darling," he'd apologized beforehand. "But I want to give the kids a bit of a treat. The Plaza's so elegant and you know what a pittance researchers live on . . ."

Didn't she just! This reversal of roles amused her. "Kids." For years, Seth had been the kid, the bright young junior, living in the penumbra of such giants as Tarky and Marriner. And now he was the mentor, dispensing advice and sympathy, while keeping a recruiter's eye open for talent. The man-of-science, man-of-business all in one. Seth was gearing himself for the eventual directorship of Medi-Tekk, and wouldn't that be nice. Chauffeured limos to work!

She sipped her wine and let her mind wander to their forthcoming drive through the Loire. Ward Daniels said they mustn't miss Chenonceaux.

Only a week ago she'd had a bibulous lunch with him in the Oak Room. Somewhere around the third glass of bourbon, he mentioned having spent an evening with Vi Hagerty and son.

Annie was surprised.

"I had no idea you kept in touch, Ward. You know, I sometimes suspect you of being a closet pussycat."

"Don't get mushy," he warned. "It was just an impulse. But let me tell you, that woman is walking on air—metaphorically speaking, of course. One happy lady. Amazing what hope can do."

"What a nice thing to hear!" Annie could feel her spirits lift.

"Can't help wondering, though, if she's heading for a fall. She's got such blind faith in your husband's discovery."

"Well, I'll tell you something." Annie succumbed to a surge of wifely pride. "So have I."

When she got back to the States, she ought to give Vi a ring, see how she was making out. Anyhow, she'd send her a postcard from Paris. Ward too. Maybe postcards tonight, then tomorrow they really must go to the Louvre . . .

"How dare you!"

Seth's voice cut through her reverie like an electric knife.

"How dare you, Evans! What the hell are you trying to imply?"

She looked up to see her husband's eyes blazing with rage. The object of his wrath was a diffident soft-spoken Welshman.

"I meant no disrespect, Dr. Petersen." Beneath boyish freckles, the young man had turned pale. Nonetheless, he seemed determined to have his say. "I assure you, none at all. I merely wondered where our team had gone wrong. We've been losing mice by the thousands in similar experiments. Not one survivor. Perhaps you'd do us the favor of forwarding your raw data . . ."

"My what . . . !" Seth's voice rose to a scream.

Annie watched him, startled. Never had she seen him so angry, so close to losing control. His knuckles were white, clenched like a prizefighter's. He was ready to hit the man, she realized with shock. But Evans wouldn't give up.

"I'd like to see your raw data. Your original notebooks . . . photographs. It really would be an enormous help . . ."

"An absolutely outrageous request!" Seth cut him short. "I find that both uncalled for and demeaning."

The entire party had fallen silent, mystified by this extraordinary outburst, and Seth, now sharply aware of a dozen puzzled eyes upon him, made a visible effort to regain his calm.

"Sorry. Didn't mean to sound off like that . . . young Colin, is it?" He patted the man's arm briefly. "I'm afraid I'm a bit testy these days, working too hard the last few months. Of course you understand we can't permit that data to leave our lab, but I assure you, all the pertinent material will be published. As to your specific problems, I'd like to point out that my work calls for some very specialized technology. We're uniquely equipped. Perhaps one of these days, those Tories you've got running things will loosen up funds.

Then you people over in Cardiff will probably wind up showing *us* how!"

He managed a smile, but the damage had been done. For though Evans accepted the apology without demur, the incident cast a pall over everyone. Within twenty minutes, Seth's guests had taken their leave with limp apologies, uncomfortable at the prevailing mood.

As soon as they were gone, Seth called for the bill. "Whew. That cost a bundle! I think I'll let Medi-Tekk pick up the tab on this one. What the hell . . . it was work, not play. Now shall we go try this *choucroute* place on Boul Mich that Rene LeGros says is so terrific?"

Annie, who had said nothing for the past half hour, looked at her husband as though he were a total stranger.

"I don't believe what I saw and heard."

"I'm sorry." Seth shrugged. "I shouldn't have blown my top. But when some snotty kid a year out of Cambridge starts telling me how to run my lab . . . Oh, fuck it. Let's forget the whole business. As of right this second, I'm officially on vacation."

But Annie couldn't forget it. She'd glimpsed a Seth she never dreamed existed. She had seen him angry before, seen him resentful and suspicious of outsiders. But never on this scale.

Was this the Seth Petersen his colleagues knew and feared, full of repressed fury, dark instincts? The other Seth, the one who had already betrayed her with Chandra, a man both cold and secretive?

The thought lodged inside her, heavy and undigested as they sat over heaping platters in a left bank café.

"Try the *saucisse vaudoise*." Seth put a piece of sausage on her plate. "It's delicious."

But her stomach was too knotted to admit food.

"How can you eat like that," she muttered, "after the way you behaved this afternoon? I sure as hell can't."

"I said, forget it, Annie. I have. I refuse to let one stupid incident spoil our evening."

"It's already spoiled mine." A note of hysteria crept into her voice. His response was to become defensive.

"Are you going to make a scene, Annie?"

She drew a deep breath. "Yes . . . I think I am." His behavior had reopened a wound and all the festering poison that had been stored within her during that time of betrayal now welled up. Overflowed.

The injustice of it all. That Seth should have been able to walk away from his dingy affair scot-free, while Annie had been forced to swallow her wrath day after day. No longer! She had a reckoning due her. The time had come for her to call Seth to account.

"Yes," she repeated. "I'm going to make a scene."

Their eyes met. Flashed.

"Well, for Chrissakes," he whispered, "not here." The restaurant was packed. Already the elderly English couple at the next table bore an expectant look.

"Waiting for the fireworks?" Seth jibed at them. "Sorry to disappoint." He threw down a fistful of franc notes and they went back to the hotel in silence.

"OK." He settled down in an easy chair, arms crossed, while Annie paced. "Get it off your chest, whatever's bothering you."

Annie looked about her. The room was so handsome, so opulent. The chambermaid had turned the blankets back, placed chocolates in golden foil on their pillows, put fresh fruit in the bowl. This was a place to make love, not do battle.

She began without hesitation. "All the time you were sleeping with Chandra—"

"Hold it right there," he interrupted. "I never slept with Chandra."

She looked at him with open skepticism. "Come on, Seth, don't play the innocent. What kind of fool do you take me for? I could tell when it started, it was during that week I stayed down in St. Thomas and I know exactly when it ended . . ."

"I swear to God, Annie, this is all your imagination. There was never anything but lab work between Chandra and me!"

His insistence unnerved her. If he could deny that, he could deny anything. Seth had never been short on nerve.

Of course it was Chandra. The pieces all fit. And she wasn't going to be lied to again.

"Well, Seth, you can swear all you like about not sleeping with Chandra, but you sure as hell weren't sleeping with me. What am I to make of a man who spends every waking hour at the lab, comes home—when he comes home at all—with his ass dragging down to there, eyes all fucked out. Weeks went by, you couldn't even stand to touch me. You deceived me, Seth. It hurt then. It hurts now. I don't know when it'll stop, but as long as you go on trying to fob me off with lies, it's going to keep on hurting. How can I live with you if I don't trust you?"

"Annie! I beg you, be reasonable!"

"I'm sick and tired of being reasonable. All these months of keeping my mouth shut, no scenes . . . no accusations. Well, I've had it up to here, Seth. I swear to God, you're not the man I married. I looked at you this afternoon lacerating that poor Welshman for no reason at all and I didn't recognize you. What a shit you were! Well, I may still love you, Seth, but I don't think I like you anymore. Jesus, I couldn't believe my eyes this afternoon. Someone gets in your way and you dump on him. You looked ready to kill. Is that what happened with Chandra? She got in your way? I bet she did. That's why you called it quits so suddenly. You got her pregnant, didn't you? So you simply dumped her . . . shipped her off to Pakistan. Is she having a baby, or did she settle for a gold bracelet as a souvenir?"

"No!" he shouted. And again "No!" this time so loudly the crystal prisms of the chandelier vibrated. He suddenly slumped down in his chair and buried his head in his hands, radiating misery.

She stared at his crumpled figure, frightened by the sense of havoc that had been unleashed in the room.

"Then what, Seth?" she cried, white-lipped. "What the hell is going on? How can I live with you if I can't trust you from one day to the next?"

His head bobbed in mute acknowledgment. Then he sat up and faced her, eyes feverishly bright.

"I wanted to spare you this, Annie"—the voice was scarcely audible. "As I told you at the time, it had nothing to do with you, but you didn't trust me. You persisted in this"—he sighed—"this delusion of yours about Chandra Patel. And I allowed it. In fact, I didn't have much choice. In a way, your misinterpretation took the heat off. It kept you from asking questions. Well, Annie, you were right on a couple of points. You were right about when the trouble started and when it ended, although in another way it will never end. But you were dead wrong about the cause." He gave a short sardonic laugh. "Christ, I wish it were as simple as a roll in the hay. But you see, it wasn't Chandra at all, at least not directly."

"Then what, Seth?" Was this another ruse? Nothing he said made any sense.

"It was the mice, Annie."

She felt a chill of premonition.

"You see . . . something went wrong with the mice."

❈

It happened the week she had stayed on in St. Thomas. Did she remember his telling her about a press party?

The event had been arranged by Liz Bonner, who headed up Medi-Tekk's public relations department, and it had seemed a good idea at the time. With a corporate merger in the air, the lab was in search of favorable press. Thus far, Strone Guthrie's publications had enjoyed a near monopoly on news from Medi-Tekk. Now it seemed wise to open the doors wider, inviting journalists from general magazines, newspapers, even the networks. With luck, they might get a segment on the six o'clock news.

"Stuff these guys with jumbo shrimp and Jack Daniel's," Liz told Seth, "plus a little of your personal charm, and we'll have the kind of coverage that money can't buy."

Privately, Seth had written the afternoon off as an enjoyable waste of time, the gathering being more social than informational. Anything the reporters wished to know they could find in the brightly packaged press kit with its dozen handouts.

So Seth mingled happily, eating canapés, making small talk with newsmen.

"Oh shit!" He'd dropped some hot sauce on his jacket. "That's what comes of wearing a three-piece suit."

The reporter from *Newsday* duly laughed. "You should've stuck to your lab coat."

As if on cue, Liz Bonner came up, followed by a young man with a couple of cameras hanging from his neck.

"Actually," she said, "Dr. Petersen is one of our more colorful scientists. His usual professional attire is jeans and a baseball cap. What's your team, Seth . . . the Mets?"

"The Boston Red Sox." Seth grinned. "From my Harvard days."

"That would make a cute picture, wouldn't it, Wendell?" She turned to the photographer. "Drs. Marriner and Petersen working together informally at the scene of their discovery . . ."

"And the mice," Wendell added. "How about your posing with those famous mice?"

"Well, I don't know." Seth didn't want an army of reporters traipsing amongst the cages with whiskey glasses and lit cigarettes.

Liz drew him aside and began whispering in his ear.

"Listen, this guy's from AP. The photo could go out over the wire services. Do us all a world of good. You in your baseball cap . . . just the warm, friendly touch we need. You know what people think about hi-tech science. How about showing 'em we're human beings too?"

"The place is a lab, Liz, not a zoo. And those are very valuable animals."

"Well, suppose we limit it. Just you and Dr. Marriner, Wendell, and oh . . . say, one reporter? Would that be OK?"

"If you clear it with Gerald."

"I already have. He thinks it's a good idea."

"OK." Seth shrugged. "Give me five minutes to change and I'll meet you downstairs."

"Don't forget your baseball cap."

"Right."

"Or the mice."

"I'll even get 'em to smile for your photographer fellow."

"How do you do that?"

"I ask 'em to say 'Cheese.' " Seth laughed and went in search of his clothes.

He hadn't spent much time in the basement since his return from St. Thomas, too busy catching up on paperwork. Nor had there been any compelling reason. The mice were being maintained on a low dosage of medication; the daily figures he got indicated all was well. So he walked into the animal lab—duly clad in jeans, white jacket and baseball cap—with no premonition of what awaited.

The room was empty when he entered. He walked down the aisles to the far corner to where the cage housing Lot 31 sat on the shelves, but even before he reached them, his heart stopped.

There had to be some mistake. Someone must have rearranged the cages, got them all out of order. He stared in disbelief, then swooped down to check the lettering on the cage. No, his eyes weren't deceiving him. There it was, the familiar raised plastic letters slid into the tab. Lot 31B, followed by his initials. Everything exactly where it should be, neat and proper.

Except the mice.

These weren't the spry, resilient creatures he had paraded so flamboyantly in the conference room but a few months earlier.

Something terrible had happened since he last saw them. He reached into the cage and picked one up. In his hands, the creature twitched uncontrollably, fighting for air.

"It was awful, Annie. Awful. In my life, I'd never seen anything like it. Goddam thing was in spasms, head to tail. Pain must have been excruciating. For a moment, I thought the eyes were going to pop right out of their sockets. My God"—even now, the memory made him tremble—"it was like a vision of hell!"

In horror, Seth dropped the animal back. His mind reeled.

Had some plague, some epidemic of monstrous virulence, swept through the lab? But no. All was well in the neighboring cages. Only this cage—the one containing his most important subjects—had been singled out for catastrophe. Not all of these mice, either, but too many. Five of his prize specimens were thrashing about in agonized death throes. It could only be a matter of hours.

"And I didn't have a clue what had gone wrong. Kidney failure, respiratory failure, some kind of crazy side effect . . . ? Jesus, I'm not an animal pathologist! All I knew was that the whole fucking experiment could be going down the drain. And then . . ."

And then the phone began to ring nonstop. He stood there helpless, paralyzed. Already precious minutes had ticked away. Gerald and the media people would be down any second, yet all Seth could think of was disaster. The project discredited, his career ruined, his name become a laughingstock. Never in his life had he felt so helpless, so utterly impotent.

And still the phone kept ringing. With a Herculean effort, he broke free of his trance and picked it up.

"Seth, my boy? Are you ready for us?" Gerald sang out, cheerful and confident.

The receiver slid out of his hands. He was running sweat.

"You there?" Gerald inquired into the silence. "Is everything all right? Would you like a hand with the mice?"

In a voice that came from a great distance, Seth heard himself answer.

"Couldn't find a decent pair of Levi's, Gerald. Just give me another few minutes."

"OK." Gerald laughed. "Don't want to photograph you bare-assed. Five minutes, then ready or not, here we come."

Five minutes! He could barely control his panic.

Then it came to him.

"Annie, believe me. What followed was a split-second decision. Not even conscious. My instincts took over. It was like . . . like I was operating in a dream."

The moment he hung up the phone, he removed the sick mice. He would make a substitution. But how? Clearly he couldn't use healthy subjects. A routine hematological check test would reveal the imposture right away.

Then it struck him. There were the follow-ups.

Every original experiment, no matter how successful, had to be replicated. Thus at set intervals, Seth would repeat the procedure exactly with a new batch of mice. There were five follow-up sets already in the lab. It was painstaking work to keep track of their respective reactions, the kind of job that made him restless, but necessary to ensure the validity of results.

Even in his panic, one part of his mind was working lucidly.

He moved the cage into a corner of the room, where the television eye could not follow. Then he fetched the second set of treated mice, removed five of their number and slipped them into the first cage. Working swiftly and silently he repeated the procedure—mice from the third batch into the second cage, from the fourth batch into the third—till at last he came to the last of the follow-ups. The sixth batch. They had begun treatment only a few days before.

Yes, he could do it! Tomorrow, he would "discover" that the mice in that final set were defective (a regrettable but not unusual occurrence) and he would throw them out and start afresh. Which would leave him five complete sets of treated mice, all of which had been injected with the antibodies, each a living testimonial to the efficacy of the test.

Who could tell? Gerald? A photographer standing a few feet away? To the naked eye all the mice looked the same. He would figure out the corroborating details tomorrow, but right now, the door to the lab was opening and in stepped Gerald with his retinue.

"I see you found them all right."

"What?" Seth whipped around.

"Your jeans and baseball cap. I see you found them."

The party advanced toward him all smiles and bustle. The photographer held a light meter up to his face.

"Say 'Cheese,' Seth." Liz Bonner grinned.

"No!" Annie was thunderstruck. "You wouldn't do a thing like that. I don't believe it . . ." The whole story was too incredible.

"What the hell else could I do, Annie? Push had come to shove."

"But Seth!" The reality hit her. "You've committed fraud!"

"Do you think I'm bragging about it? It goes against my grain, against all my professional ethics. Thou Shalt Not Fake Data. The first commandment of science. But you've got to consider the pressure I've been under right from the day I arrived there. Perform. Produce. Beat everyone else to the finish line. That kind of stress does something to a man. It's not like music, Annie, where the big decision is whether to sing Mozart a little slower one day, a little faster the next. What's the worst that can happen? You miss a note? You have a memory lapse? Big deal. Audiences expect the occasional goof, probably lap it up. But I'm not allowed that kind of luxury. I had to make an on-the-spot judgment and run with it. Anyhow, what's done is done . . ."

* * *

Yet even as he was covering his tracks, faking data, adjusting numbers on the substituted mice, he kept searching for an honest way out. If only he could discover what had gone wrong with the experiment, there might be an escape hatch. But there were no clues. Nothing to go on. Not even the mice themselves. For in a panic at being caught red-handed, he had thrust the dying specimens into the waste disposal system. They were destroyed beyond recall. Of all the decisions made that day, it was the one he regretted most.

For weeks he practically lived in the lab, those weeks Annie believed he was having an affair. But his only affair was a desperate search for the truth.

Was it something in the feed? In the medication? Some genetic defect in the mice themselves? He spent hundred of hours going over the charts, checking out every possibility, including the most farfetched. Was it a practical joke? Too outrageous. Then the idea began to take root: his mice had been the victims of sabotage.

In a grotesque way it made sense. Any colleague might have done it, poisoned the animals in a fit of mischief or self-serving ambition. Seth wasn't universally beloved. His chief suspect was Gene Leavitt. But he dare not make such a charge without proof.

He'd interrogated the technicians, the security staff, the fellow who cleaned the cages. His inquiries were beginning to raise eyebrows. He questioned Chandra, of course, but only to a point, for he sensed that she was growing suspicious. Given her familiarity with the experiment, how could she miss his drift? He believed that she might have already tumbled to the substitution.

Her silence was more eloquent than speech, for she had taken to moping about the labs, troubled and unhappy. At any moment she might blow it all sky-high. He took care to handle her with kid gloves.

At last, he ran out of leads. Foul play was the only answer that made sense. But what to do? For even had he found proof of Leavitt's malfeasance, how could he expose the man without exposing the cover-up? Too much time had passed.

Thus Seth was trapped, caged as neatly as one of his mice. Yet he still wasn't sure he'd go through with it. Even as he falsified reports, he struggled with guilt. Some days he wavered, tempted to make a clean breast of everything, take the blame, the bruises. But should he sacrifice his happiness, Annie's too, for the principles of scientific truth? He lived in an agony of indecision.

Then came the night of Margot's ball.

"I walked through that door, Annie, and it was the most glorious experience of my life. 'It's for you,' you said. And all eyes turned, everybody praising . . . admiring. It was so sweet . . . so sweet, knowing I was it. Seth Petersen, Hero. I loved it. And in a flash, I knew what I was going to do. Hell, Annie, a man would have to be crazy to choose failure over success. This is what I wanted, what I'd dreamed of ever since I was a kid. Could you expect me to throw it away because some son of a bitch in the lab had fucked around with my mice? No way. Anyhow, there wasn't a thing Leavitt could do without putting his own neck in a noose. And the beauty of it was"— an unmistakable pride informed his voice—"that I could pull the whole thing off. It was a helluva gamble, took a helluva lot of smarts, but I could do it. And I *did*, Annie. I've pulled it off."

๛

The man might have been a total stranger.

She sat down on the bed dazed, unable to fit the pieces together and come up with someone who was recognizably her husband.

If she had seen remorse, she might have wept with him. If she had seen guilt, she would have consoled, taken on the burden for her own. How could her heart not go out to the man she loved in this wretched predicament? But before her was a triumphant stranger, someone who had fought a dark battle and won, a victor collecting his spoils.

Of course he was sorry the whole business had come about. It had been a nightmare. But instead of repentance, there was pride in his having brazened it through. All by himself.

"Then all the experiments are tainted," she said.

"Technically, yes."

"And all our success, all our good fortune is built on mislabeled mice and faked data."

"You're putting too severe a construction on it, Annie. I personally am convinced the treatment is effective. OK, not 100 percent, but nothing is ever 100 percent. I'm just not going to martyr myself to make a moral point."

She could see that. Understand it. Perhaps even agree with it. But what troubled her now was a different matter.

"Why didn't you tell me?" she said at last.

"I'm telling you now."

"No. Not tonight. Tonight you were forced into it . . . I gave you no choice. Why didn't you tell me the truth as soon as it happened? We could have gone through it together, made the choices. Hell, Seth, I had a right to know. I'm your wife!"

"I didn't want to worry you, darling. It's not a pretty story. Besides, do you recall one night last summer I came home bitching about the lab, and you and I got into a shouting match? Well, you indicated way back then that you didn't want me bringing all the grief from Medi-Tekk home with me."

"No." Annie shook her head slowly. "Not good enough. You have treated me as though I were an outsider, a competitor. But my future was involved too, so don't palm me off with that kind of answer. What were you afraid of?"

"I wasn't afraid. But it was something I had to decide for myself, Annie," came the muted reply. "I didn't want you putting pressure on."

"Pressure!" A vein in her neck began to throb. "When have I ever pressured you? When have I ever gone against your interests? What are we . . . two separate people? But rather than confide in me, you let me stew all that time. You saw I was climbing the walls with anxiety. You saw it and you said nothing. Were you afraid"—she stared at him—"what? that I would blow the whistle on you? Go to Gerald? Something crazy like that?"

"Yes, if you must know. I was worried in case you let something slip, intentionally or otherwise. You can—now, Annie don't take this as a criticism—but you can get fairly high and mighty at times."

"You didn't trust me!" The revelation stunned. "You didn't believe I would stick it through with you."

"Oh, come on, Annie." He shuffled uncomfortably. "Be reasonable. I shouldn't have told you as much as I did . . ."

"Why?" she picked up. "Is there more to tell?"

He got up wearily, brushed his lips against her cheek.

"I don't want to argue, sweetheart. It's been a grueling day and I'd like to hit the sack. If you want, we can thrash out the loose ends tomorrow, although I'd much rather we put the whole business behind us. Sleep on it too, Annie. It won't look so bad in the morning. I promise."

Ten minutes later, he was dead to the world, but for Annie sleep was impossible.

Too many questions remained unanswered. Seth had been glib, even convincing, yet when it came to hard questions he had out-maneuvered her by going to sleep.

Not that she condemned him for what had happened that day. Anybody might have done the same in those circumstances, with so much riding on the outcome. Money. Fame. Honors. Success.

If the story ever got out, though, there would be hell to pay. The scientific community would have Seth's scalp, let alone his job. And the repercussions wouldn't stop there. The validity of the whole program would be impugned. They'd have to start again from scratch, postpone the clinical tests until next year. How rotten for all those people who'd pinned their hopes on the cure.

For Vi Hagerty.

Annie had been so pleased with the role she played in Vi's life. She felt a deep involvement in her welfare. What a tragedy for Vi if everything ground to a halt. And all because of Leavitt's misconduct.

If indeed it was Leavitt! That part stuck in her craw. Granted, he was a cutthroat competitor, but to commit such a crime, the man would have to be the scum of the earth. Seth chose to believe he was, but the fact remained that Leavitt provided him with a convenient scapegoat. He could stop looking for other explanations.

But what if there was something fundamentally wrong with FG-75? With the whole experiment? She recalled the scene with Colin Evans. Clearly, the young Welshman had hit a raw nerve. Seth, too, must have his suspicions.

Too many questions.

She pulled a chair up beside the bed, nibbled chocolates, gnawed her nails, and contemplated Seth's sleeping body.

No moans, no stirrings of an uneasy conscience, just the steady rise and fall of his breathing. Yet he must have gone through hell.

Put it behind you, he had advised Annie. Just as he had on the night of Margot's ball. But she could not. Too many questions . . .

"Seth . . ." She shook him gently. "Seth, I don't want to go to sleep with so much unresolved."

"For God's sake," he murmured through a haze, "take a Valium."

"It's not that I can't sleep. It's that I don't want to . . . not until we've sorted this out."

She shook him again. He woke up, rubbed his eyes irritably, checked his watch. Two o'clock.

"It's waited all these months. It can wait until morning."

"Is it possible,"—she wanted to know, "that there's some flaw in the treatment, that it might have nothing to do with Leavitt?"

He grew instantly wary.

"I told you I've satisfied myself."

"That's not what I asked, Seth. I asked if it were possible . . ."

He got out of bed and poured himself a cognac.

"Anything's possible, Annie. It's possible the mice got together and formed a suicide club."

She ignored his sarcasm. He had said what she feared most.

"And you knew that possibility existed when you arranged to have Vi Hagerty's name placed on the list . . . the possibility that the experiment is unsafe."

"Wait. A. Minute." Seth was livid. "I did you a favor with the Hagerty woman. You argued . . . you pleaded, so don't throw it back in my face. And there's absolutely no proof the experiment is unsafe!"

"You destroyed all the proof, Seth. And what about Gerald? Isn't he entitled to know what's going on?"

Seth gave a curt laugh.

"He knows exactly as much as he wants to know, which is damn little. Believe me, Annie, if I thought there was real risk involved, I'd call a halt to the Phase One trials. What kind of man do you think I am?"

"I don't know." She peered at him. "I don't know how your mind works anymore. And then there's Chandra . . ."

"Ye gods, Annie," he yelled. "You still harping on that? How many times do I have to tell you, there was nothing between us. Nothing!"

"Then why did you get her deported?"

"Are you deaf? Didn't you hear anything I said? The woman was a threat, a potential time bomb. I couldn't have her hanging around."

"But she'd done nothing," Annie protested. "An innocent girl. She never harmed you in any way. Except you were so eager to cover your ass, you didn't give a damn what happened to her. You used her, then threw her away as though she were garbage . . ."

"You're dramatizing, Annie. In fact, I wrote her an excellent letter of recommendation. I believe she's got a job already in Lahore. She'll be happier in Pakistan in the long run, is my bet. Anyhow, the Third World needs good scientists more than we do."

"I see. You spared your conscience with a fulsome letter, and what else did you give her? Let me guess. A gold bracelet suitably inscribed."

"A watch, as it happened." Seth narrowed his eyes. "A very nice, quite expensive Movado. She was pleased as punch. Maybe it wasn't the ideal solution, but let's face it—the girl was expendable."

Expendable. There are two kinds of people in this world: us and them. Chandra was one of "them."

"Nasty!" she said. "A nasty thing to do and say."

"I don't get you, Annie. First you're pissed off because you think I'm sleeping with Chandra. Now you're twice as mad because you found out I wasn't. I feel I handled the whole thing very well. Jesus, whose side are you on?"

Whose side indeed! She didn't know. All she knew was that Seth had been devious as hell, keeping his life hidden from her for many months. Devious and hard. He had "handled" Chandra. "Handled" Annie too, for that matter. Had treated her not as an equal partner or a beloved confidante, but as an outsider, unworthy of being entrusted with his secrets. That knowledge cut through her, leaving open wounds.

"I shouldn't have to take a loyalty test," she said finally. "I've always been on your side. But what about you? Where was your loyalty, I ask? Your trust? You took the seminal decision of your life and never bothered to inform me, let alone consult. And all the time you were hanging on to your secrets, I was in agony, absolute agony. You must have seen it . . . known what I was going through . . ."

"Annie, I can't be responsible for your suspicions."

"But you used it . . ." Her gorge rose. "It was convenient. It kept me from asking the wrong questions. You let me suffer, Seth"—the realization hit her—"when all you had to do was tell the truth."

They wrangled through the night, bitterly, with no softening of attitudes till at last Seth slammed his fist on the night table. "Enough," he shouted. "As far as I'm concerned, the subject's closed. And if you think you're going to turn the next two weeks into a nonstop inquisition, then fuck it. Fuck the whole vacation. I only took this trip to please you. I'm telling you, Annie, we either drop the matter once and for all or . . ."

"Or what, Seth!"

"Or I'm taking the next plane back to New York. I don't need this shit, Annie. I've got enough troubles as is."

"You do that!" she screamed. "You go back to your precious mice. But don't expect me to follow suit. I've waited a lifetime for this trip, Seth, and I'm not going to be cheated out of it."

"Just as you please," he said grimly. "It will give you time to cool off."

In the morning they sorted out the passports, the traveler's checks, repacked the bags.

"Will you be following the same itinerary?" Seth asked.

"I don't know," she said. "I'll keep you informed."

He caught the 11 A.M. Concorde to JFK, and ordered himself a pair of double Scotches.

"Back in time for breakfast," said his seatmate.

Back in time to spend the day at Medi-Tekk. Just as well. He'd been apprehensive about staying away from the lab so long. Who could say what mischief was going on behind his back?

Never should have told Annie, he cursed himself. That fucking Gene Leavitt was wrecking not only his research but his marriage. Well, Seth would get the goods on him yet, exonerate himself at least in Annie's eyes.

By the time he got off the plane three and a half hours later, he was thoroughly drunk.

2

HE'D WRAPPED UP THE POLLUTION STORY AND IT WAS A BEAUT, so there was no longer any excuse for making side trips to Bloomfield.

Except that Ward had fallen into the habit. Once or twice a week he'd pop in for an hour, play some cards with the kid, or just sit around with Vi.

Having a woman as a friend was a novelty for him. Experience had long ago taught him women were a predatory race, seeking commitments in the mildest of statements or—worse yet!—putting the squeeze on for a wedding ring.

Funny, he reflected, but as a teenager he'd had a tough time making out, couldn't even score with those dumbo baton twirlers back in high school. And they put out for everybody!

But get your nose in the limelight and the whole world wants a piece of you. Even ax murderers were swamped with proposals of marriage. Such were the rewards of fame.

From the day Ward won that first Pulitzer, the broads had declared open season on him, drawing a bead on his heart, his hand and his wallet. It damn near took the pleasure out of sex.

Once he'd found himself sitting next to a movie idol on a plane. Hank the Hunk, the star was known as, having made his career playing tough guys. Although there were whispers that the man was gay, Ward was nonetheless curious how a professional heartbreaker coped with armies of panting females.

"Why do you think I spread the rumor I'm a faggot?" came the answer.

Ward howled with laughter, then the star went on to say something that stuck in his mind for years. "When you're famous, every day is Sadie Hawkins Day."

By now, Ward had a long list of snappy retorts for seemingly sympathetic women who wanted to know "why a wonderful guy like you isn't married." His replies ranged from the cutesy to the insulting, but they all bore the same message: *hands off*. Which didn't stop them one whit.

During the last few years, he had found the easiest solution was to avoid the company of "nice" women entirely, preferring to limit female companionship to one-night stands. If some of the girls were just a cut above hookers, no matter. At least they knew better than to have false expectations.

Thus—with the exception of his editor, Claire Pulham, who was fat, fifty and had a live-in arrangement with a scrawny fashion model half her age—Ward knew remarkably few women on a chatty basis.

Accordingly he came to value the odd hour he spent at Vi's. The boy was nice, even worshipful, which Ward found immensely flattering, but most of all his hostess managed to make him laugh.

Vi's use of language floored him, yet there was something shrewd about even her most egregious abuses.

"It's not a 'plastic saint,' Vi," he corrected her once. "The expression is 'plaster saint.' "

"When was the last time you were in a religious supply shop?" she asked. "They're all made of plastic these days."

Go argue with that. Yes, she was good company, but the best part of it was that Vi wanted nothing from him, having already attained her goal that day he gave her the Petersens' number. He could relax in her company.

For a while he toyed around with the idea of using her as a basis for a human interest story, a follow-up on the Medi-Tekk piece, but her character vanished when he put it down on paper. "You're ineffable," he told her. "Well, eff you, buddy," she shot back.

And of course she had no romantic designs on him. How could she, in her situation? Yet in a way, Ward felt slightly miffed by her absence of interest in his private life. She inquired about his work, his travels, his meetings with the famous, but never once did she ask if he were married, let alone ask why he wasn't. Didn't she specu-

267

late? Didn't she care? A dozen times he'd been ready with a fancy comeback, but she never put forward the appropriate question.

In fact it was Ward himself who raised the matter one hot July night over beer and pepperoni pizza.

"Haven't you ever wondered how come I never got married?"

She looked at him genuinely puzzled.

"Why should you get married?" she asked. "Why should anyone, unless they have to?"

"You are so right, Vi." He attacked the pizza with renewed gusto. "There speaks an intelligent woman."

She no longer dwelled on her disability, convinced that the magic "cure" was but a few months off. As for Ward, a born gloom spreader, he had already voiced his reservations on that matter. She refused to be disillusioned. Well, that was her business and who could say? Maybe it would work out as planned. Maybe there really was a Santa Claus. He would have let the matter drop, except for his concern about Noonie.

"What have you told him is the matter?"

"I told him it was just temporary, that I'll be right as rain before he knows it."

"Don't you think," Ward proposed cautiously, "that maybe you should tell him what's wrong?"

"No, I don't!" she snapped. "And if you do, I'll never speak to you again, Ward Daniels."

"OK! OK!" He raised his hands in a truce sign. "I'll butt out."

"Because if there's one thing I hate it's a Nasty Parker."

"A Nosey Parker."

"Same thing."

Annie flung open the French window. From the Avenue Montaigne came a muted fugue of taxi horns and laughter. Everyone in the world was having fun tonight except her.

For the last two days, confused and lonely, she had kept to her room wondering whether to stick it out or take a plane home. Minute to minute her reactions wavered. Concern for her husband, trapped in a no-win dilemma. Relief that he had never slept with Chandra. Frustration in having misjudged the situation so thoroughly. And ultimately anger. A sense of having been betrayed nonetheless.

Seth had lied to her consistently, let her suffer a thousand jealous pangs rather than trust to her discretion.

As for the mishap in the lab, surely his conclusions were correct, and Gene Leavitt the author of his miseries. The alternatives were unthinkable.

But assuming he'd done nothing morally wrong, then all the more reason for confiding in Annie. He must have weighed the risks and decided against it.

What a bastard he could be! This past week she had glimpsed the dark side of Seth in action. The tough guy. The fast-tracker willing to sacrifice anything or anybody in the heat to get ahead. A far cry from the Seth she knew and loved.

She recalled years ago running into a woman he had fired for incompetence. Embarrassed, Annie had apologized for the turn of events. "I know my husband can be very demanding." The woman had snorted, then replied, "At least I'm not married to him, thank God!"

Go explain that there were two Seths: the public persona—ambitious, driving, sometimes driven—and the wonderful private person whom Annie knew to be full of warmth and love. The best of Seth had always been reserved for their marriage. She flattered herself in having been the intimate exception to all his rules.

And what was her reward? To be lied to, manipulated, deliberately misled. The more she thought about it, the angrier she became. So much for his trust! So much for his loyalty. So much for her going back to New York in sackcloth and ashes!

Crazy! Here she was in Paris, for Chrissakes. A childhood dream come true. Antonia Sayre Petersen had finally made it, and in style!

At her feet the most beautiful of cities, in her bag an inch-thick stack of credit cards and traveler's checks. And the most use she could make of this delicious conjunction was to sit in her hotel room and brood!

Yet there was something daunting about being on her own in the world's most romantic city. She knew no one here, and she couldn't help wondering if Seth's stomping off was yet another manipulative ploy. A way of bringing her around. For what kind of vacation could Annie have on her own? Without him, the champagne of the journey would be flat. What good were three-star meals and grand scenery, if you had no one to share them with? The more she thought about it, the more certain she became: Seth gambled on Annie's following him home, remorseful and compliant.

"Well, that's what you think, Mr. Seth Petersen," she murmured to nobody in particular. "I'm staying and I'm going to have myself the time of my life."

Tonight, for instance. Weeks ago, they had made a reservation for dinner at Lasserre, which Seth said would be the high point of their week in Paris. She checked her notebook. Nine o'clock. That gave her an hour.

She reached into the closet and plucked out the green silk jersey dress she had bought for just such a gala occasion. Sleek and glamorous, accentuating the emerald of her eyes. Yes, she would wear the silk, adorn herself with diamond earrings, silver sandals, a great lashing of St. Laurent's Opium. Then she would sally forth a woman of the world. Who is that extraordinary creature—heads would turn—so chic, so mysterious? Why is she dining alone?

Very well, she would enjoy the whole charade, pull it off as securely as though Seth were by her side. She would prove to herself that she was not merely an unaccompanied woman. She was an independent woman as well.

An hour later she found herself seated under the stars as the ornately painted ceiling pulled back to reveal the open sky. Every detail that met her eye was exquisite: the crystal decanters, the glorious floral arrangements, the china, the silver, even the tiny elevator that had taken her up as though she were a precious gem in a jewel box. The maître d' expressed his condolences that *M. le Docteur* could not join her, the waiter recommended the *pâté d'anguilles* (was that eel? she wondered, her operatic French not filling this particular bill), *et puis le bisque de homard, et puis le caneton à l'orange*. Or perhaps Madame would prefer *les quenelles de brochet?*

Yes yes yes. She ordered with abandon as the sommelier arrived with the wine list. It ran about the size of the Manhattan phone directory and Annie looked at it nonplussed. If only Seth were here, the fugitive thought floated past. He was so knowledgeable about wines. The sommelier recommended a vintage Haut-Brion.

Yes, thank you, she breathed, relieved the decision was taken out of her hands. Yes, a bottle of the 1973. Her earlier confidence threatened to abandon her. A woman of the world who couldn't choose a wine? Moreover, could she manage a bottle all by herself? At these prices, could she afford it?

Why not? *Pourquois pas?* It was going on Seth's American Express card anyhow and if he groused—well, it was a helluva lot cheaper than watches at Tiffany.

The wine arrived. The waiter opened the bottle, poured some into her glass. Annie sniffed just as Seth would have done, rolled a bit on her tongue, made the appropriate noises, nodded. He poured the wine into a crystal decanter and left.

So she sat there, a lone woman in an elegant dress in one of the world's most beautiful restaurants, sipping wine, looking (she hoped) enviably glamorous. Then it struck her. There would probably be a half hour wait between courses. What on earth would she do with herself in the interim? Where would she look? What would she do with her hands? No wonder people took up smoking.

With painful self-awareness, she realized she was the sole unaccompanied diner in the room. Far from envying her, the other diners probably pitied her. If they thought about her at all. Most likely, only the waiters commiserated. And there was a minimum of two more hours to be got through. She couldn't bolt her food. It would be an indecency with cuisine of this order. Alternately, she couldn't simply sit there like a piece of furniture.

In New York, she wouldn't have hesitated to pull out a book. When she lunched at the Carnegie Deli, her normal procedure was to bury her nose in a score or a paperback while waiting for her sandwich to be served. In fact, she usually managed to eat and read simultaneously, but at this gourmet mecca such behavior was out of the question.

If only Seth were here! But if he were, they'd be bickering.

Is this, she wondered, what it's like for performers who spend their lives on the road? Except for actual concert dates with the green-room festivities, did touring artists often wind up eating alone, silently, in the finest restaurants around the world? It was a disturbing thought.

The waiter brought the *pâté d'anguilles*. She savored it thoughtfully. Exquisite. But she must eat slowly, make it last, for a century more would elapse until the second course.

Nibble nibble. Sip sip. The wine waiter materialized silently to refill her glass the moment it passed the halfway mark.

At the next table, a middle-aged woman dripping pearls clinked glasses with her companion and murmured sweet nothings. Across the room, a large and fashionable party were sharing laughs. What came next? Oh yes, the lobster bisque. She glanced at her watch. Only nine thirty. Ye gods! The meal would be interminable.

She counted the petals in the flower arrangement, then began on the hatchings in the damask, hoping she looked suitably happy and engrossed.

A friendly hand tapped her shoulder.

Seth! Her heart stopped. He had come back, fully penitent.

"I didn't recognize you without your shoulder pads."

Annie swung her head up astonished to look into the smiling face of Polo von Brüning.

"We were speculating why such a pretty woman should be dining alone"—he indicated the large party at the far end of the room—"decided you were a femme fatale, and then I remembered you from Margot's ball. May I sit down for a minute?"

May you! Annie was ready to award him the Legion of Honor for saving her life. *You see?* she almost gloated to the waiter. *I'm not a loner at all. I'm the kind of person who just "happens" to run into celebrities like Polo von Brüning every day.* Perhaps he would ask her to join their party.

"A mercy you're here." He took the chair next to her. "I'm with the most boring group of people, you can't imagine. French socialites, pillars of the Paris Opéra!" He made a face. "Deathly dull, but necessary, I'm afraid. Sometimes I feel more like a fund raiser than a musician. And what brings you here, Annie?"

He pronounced her name with a long *a*, giving it a mittel-European inflection. All very exotic, a part of her new femme fatale persona. The confidence that had fled her earlier began to return.

She was on vacation, she told him, her husband having regrettably been called back to New York on business, and at the moment her plans were still vague. "And you, Polo? Will you be in Paris for a while?"

He shook his head. "I'm off tomorrow. I have a little place in the south of France where I hide from the world a few weeks every summer. With not a patron of the arts in sight." He nodded in the direction of his table. "Nor any temperamental opera stars, either. Total isolation."

"Ah, pity," Annie said. "The last time we met, you said you'd like to hear me sing. I was hoping I might audition for you some day soon. At your convenience, of course."

He leaned forward, chin on fist, contemplating her.

"How much have you had to drink this evening?"

She couldn't believe her ears. Did he see her request as nothing more than a drunken proposal?

"I'm perfectly sober," she protested.

"I never doubted it, *ma chère*. But as you know, alcohol is bad for the vocal cords. If I'm to hear you, it should be at your best, you understand."

"I've had one glass of wine." Her heart began a rapid tattoo. "My voice is fresh and rested."

"Very good." He smiled and motioned to the waiter. "Bring Madame some Perrier water please, she wishes no more wine. And now, I'm afraid I must get back to my table and spend another hour in purgatory. Meanwhile, enjoy your dinner, Annie. I'll return about ten thirty and take coffee with you. Then if you choose, you may sing to me tonight. I have a studio on the Quai Voltaire."

The room was classic in its simplicity. A few chairs, a long white sofa, a marble table bearing a white Brancusi bird. By the windows, a pair of ebony grands nestled, yin and yang, with the gleam of ivory keys at either end.

"Do sit down, Annie." He took off his jacket, tugged at his tie. "Make yourself at home. If you wish to warm up, vocalize, please do. I'll only be a few minutes."

He vanished into another room to return in rehearsal clothes: black jersey turtleneck, black running pants, slim and sensual as a cat. Cat's eyes, too, above aristocratic cheekbones. A very beautiful man.

"Ah," Polo said, "now I'm comfortable. And you?"

"Perfectly, thank you."

"No you're not." He came over to where she sat and placed a hand on her bare arm. "You're very tense. I can feel it with a touch."

"I suppose I am," she admitted. "I hadn't counted on auditioning for anyone when I left my hotel tonight, maestro. Least of all you."

"Just relax," he said and slipped around behind her chair. "Shut your eyes. Let your mind go white. If you'll allow me . . ."

He placed his hands on the back of her neck. They were cool and dry. Then with a soft rotary motion, he began massaging her with gentle thumbs: the base of her ears, the back of her neck, the hollows that nestled above the collarbone.

"I'm not making love to you," he answered her unspoken question. "Or at any rate not yet. I'm preparing you to sing."

She shut her eyes. And even as he caressed her, she could feel the tension leaving her body, the muscles of her throat relaxing until her whole being ached only to sing.

"I'm ready now," she whispered.

With a flash of white teeth, he went over to the piano.

"Excellent," he said. "Now, what will you sing?"

"What music do you have?" she asked. Whatever the repertoire, he would need the piano accompaniments. But instead, Polo tapped his head. "I have all the music you need, right in here."

And so she sang. She was Leonora and Tosca and Eurydice that night. There was nothing she couldn't do, no power not at her command. Suddenly every emotion was hers to explore, from the sensual to the sublime. To say she was inspired hardly explained the phenomenon. There was a chemistry, a magic between them. Before long, it had ceased to be an audition and became instead a coupling as profound and intimate as sex.

Gradually she and Polo moved beyond the realm of opera and roamed the repertoire with the unfettered joy of freebooters. Three centuries of music were there for the taking. They developed a kind of verbal shorthand where half a dozen words sufficed as the transition.

"Rachmaninoff Vocalise," he would say. She might follow with "Bach Cantata 104."

"Berlioz," he announced. *"Songs of a Summer Night."*

"Which one?"

"Oh . . . 'Spectre.' "

So she sang "Spectre de la Rose" as she had once sung it for Seth. As the phrases floated languidly out over the Seine, she felt a momentary pang of betrayal. For before this night was out, Annie knew that she and Polo would become lovers. How else could such a night end.

At last he closed the lid of the piano, turned off the lights and came to where she stood.

"It's almost dawn, Annie." He took her hand and led her to the window. "Come see the river."

Across the cobbled quai, the Seine curved its path through the heart of Paris, silent and mysterious. The only sound she heard was the singing of blood in her ears.

Wordlessly, her body yearning, she turned and opened her mouth to his and with a kiss wiped out time past. For in this magical room there was no space for memories, only for the arts of music and love. With fine smooth fingers, he slid the dress from her shoulders. It fell to the floor in a whoosh of silk. She undressed quickly, in a wash of sensuality, conscious of his eyes, of the morning breeze that played against her naked spine.

"If you knew how beautiful you are." He smiled. Then with motions swift and lithe as a cat's, he stripped before her.

He had the body of an athlete: lithe, muscled, slim-hipped. Not tall—but graceful as he drew her to him in a seamless flow. They touched at every point: mouth to mouth, nipple to nipple, thigh to thigh.

"Think," he murmured, "of a faint and lovely waltz." Then, in the silence of the studio, mouths linked, bodies matching, they began to dance.

She shut her eyes, surrendering herself to the excitement of exploring unfamiliar flesh. So long . . . so very long since she had known another man's touch. Tentatively she ran her tongue across Polo's teeth. Even the taste of his mouth was different. Erotic. Every texture was as fresh as first-time love.

Now his fingertips were discovering her breasts, her thighs, the dark moistness between her legs. A lazy thumb caressed her to the gradually quickening rhythm of her heartbeat.

275

"Keep me from fainting," she murmured; then placing her hands on the smooth flesh of his buttocks, drew him taut against her.

And still they danced, caressing, arousing, eyes half closed, bodies liquid and welcoming. Then moving slowly to unheard music, he entered her, insinuating himself into the depths of her body.

He drew her down on the long white sofa and covered her throat with kisses. "Andante, my darling. Slowly slowly. We have hours yet ahead."

The noonday sun found them still intertwined, head-to-toe, toe-to-head. Yin and yang. Annie smiled, satiated. Like the pianos.

That afternoon, they left for the south of France.

❦

From the time he'd poured himself off the plane at JFK, Seth hadn't known a minute's peace of mind.

Annie's onslaught had left him thunderstruck. He had anticipated shock and dismay on her part. Admittedly, he had committed a gross breach of ethics. Nonetheless, once the initial jolt was over, he had every right to expect her sympathy. After all, he was, ultimately, not the perpetrator but the victim of wrongdoing. Didn't Annie understand? Didn't she see how wretched he felt? How put upon he was?

And then, she had gone on to voice doubts about Leavitt's culpability. As though Seth would willfully put lives at risk! That she could even *ask* such a question made him writhe.

A pity society had done away with medieval torture chambers, for Seth would cheerfully have stretched Gene Leavitt on the rack in order that Annie might hear his confession. "Now . . ." he kept saying to her in his fantasy, "now are you satisfied?"

Yet although one half of him regretted having confided in her, the other half heaved a sigh of relief. The months of watching his tongue had exacted a toll on his nervous system. He was used to being open with Annie, accustomed to her unquestioning approval. Given time, he assumed she would gain perspective and become, not just reasonable, but supportive. What had surprised him beyond measure was her reaction to Chandra's dismissal.

How vehemently his wife had flown to the girl's defense, once the question of adultery was laid to rest. One might think the two women had been the dearest of friends. Annie and Chandra! Surely the world's oddest couple. Except possibly for Annie and Viola Hagerty.

Seth's father maintained there was a conspiracy of women, against which men were powerless. "Get two of 'em in a room," Wally Petersen liked to say, half-joshing, "and you're up against a goddam union."

But not his Annie. She had never belonged to the female Mafia, never relied on a backup team of women friends and relations to get her way. Until recently, she and Seth had worked out their problems privately. In this situation, as in all others, her first loyalty—indeed her only loyalty—must be to him.

Already he missed her. Two weeks on his own in the sweltering city were enough to confirm that Seth was not born for bachelorhood. He missed her face over the breakfast table, her familiar body in bed at night. But most of all he missed the small talk that he suspected made up nine-tenths of all married conversation.

Had Annie phoned, had she sent him one proper letter in the spirit of compromise, he would have been on the next plane to Europe. But her only communication had been two brief notes: the first telling him she had left Paris for the south of France; the second, bearing a Nice postmark, announcing she was taking time to "think things through."

Think *what* things through, for Chrissakes? Exasperated, Seth had thrown the letter in the wastebasket, then spent the next three hours, Guide Michelin in hand, phoning every major hotel in the Nice area. She was registered at none. Or at least, not under her own name.

Her prolonged absence was ceasing to be a mere embarrassment; it was turning into a cause for anxiety. What had got into the woman?

"Where's Annie?" Gerald had asked when Seth had explained his own sudden reappearance by claiming the pressure of work. And he had come up with some lame excuse about her wanting to toot about Europe on her own. But in Gerald's eyes he had seen a flicker of fear. Ever since that day in the sauna, Gerald had treated him with kid gloves: wanting to know no more about the "discrepancies," yet simultaneously seeking assurance that all was under control.

"Don't worry." Seth begged the question. "Everything's fine."

Gerald's answer was a faint nervous smile.

But where indeed was Annie? Why didn't she keep in touch? With each passing day, Seth's mood grew darker.

Thus he was in the vilest of tempers when, late one afternoon, coming back from the men's room, he discovered his office door ajar. Had he left it like that? His heart thudded. For locked away in that room were his private notebooks, his raw data, the nuts and bolts of his deception. Material that would be damning to the tutored eye.

Silently he crept up to the threshold only to have his worst fears confirmed. There behind the desk, brassy as a bluejay, Gene Leavitt was bent over, reaching into an open drawer.

"You!"

Six months of accumulated stress surged through Seth like an electrical charge, tensing every muscle in his body. "You lying, thieving son of a bitch!"

Leavitt looked up, startled.

"What the fuck . . . !"

Then Seth sprang. With a burst of animal power, he bounded across the room in a single leap. The impact knocked Leavitt off his feet. His head hit the floor with a crack.

"You scumbag!" Seth flung himself atop the man, and he began pounding, pummeling, fists out of control. "I ought to kill you . . ."

Beneath the rain of blows, Leavitt opened his mouth to cry out. Nothing emerged but a strangled grunt. Then, with a body-wrenching jerk, he slid out of Seth's grasp. For a minute more, the two men grappled, rolling over and over against the cold vinyl tile. Seth had height. Leavitt had breadth. They both had the strength of their rage. At last, in a final swell of fury, Seth managed to push his opponent's head to the floor. Then Seth was on top of him, pinioning the man's shoulders with his knees. His thumb began to press against Leavitt's windpipe, his fingertips turned bloodless and white.

". . . ought to kill you . . . kill you . . ."

And then Seth saw it. Saw not just terror in Leavitt's eyes—but astonishment! Utter confusion. Seth's heart stopped.

"My God!" he cried out. The man had no inkling of what lay behind this savage assault. He was innocent!

But before Seth could relinquish his grip, there came the sound of running feet, startled voices. Hands clutched at him—men's hands, women's—pulling him off, prying his tensed fingers loose.

"Christ, Petersen," Norm Salter hollered. "Let go! You're killing the man."

Seth fell back, stunned, while a badly shaken Leavitt was helped into a chair. A half dozen people clustered round him.

"You all right, Gene?" somebody asked.

"Yeah." He rubbed his neck tenderly. His voice was hoarse from the ordeal. "Nothing broken. I'll be OK. Jesus . . . the man's a fucking maniac. I come in to borrow a lousy razor and the son of a bitch goes berserk . . ."

Razor. Seth's mind cleared in a shot. Yes, the little Remington electric Annie had given him last year. He always kept it in the bottom drawer of his desk. It was no secret.

"I'm sorry." Seth stumbled to his feet, numb with shock and horror. He had almost killed the man. Might have, had their struggle not been heard in the corridors. "God, I'm so sorry . . . I don't know what . . . I thought . . . I thought it was an intruder."

Every eye was on him—quizzical, troubled. The stunned silence that followed recalled that hideous scene at the Plaza Athenée with Colin Evans. Only worse.

"Gene, please . . . it was a terrible mistake. I can't tell you how sorry I am." Seth rose, put out his hand. "Let's shake and forget it ever happened."

With deliberation, Leavitt dusted off his coat and gave his neck a final twist. Then he got up to look Seth in the face. This time the dark brown eyes showed neither fear nor hesitation. They glowed with one emotion only: raw hatred.

Without a word, he turned and stalked out of the room.

"You're lucky Gene's not pressing criminal charges," Gerald said. "I had to do a lot of fast talking. As it is, everybody in the building knows you two were going at it hammer and tongs. Although nobody, including me, knows why."

"It sounds worse than it was, Gerald." Seth was gulping down a double Scotch in Marriner's office a half hour after the fiasco. Never had a man needed a drink so much. "I promise it won't happen again."

"But why?" Gerald wanted to know.

"Let's say"—Seth thought of Leavitt's stricken eyes—"we had a basic misunderstanding."

That night, Seth couldn't sleep. To think that he—a man whose mission it was to cure pain and suffering—had nearly murdered someone in hot blood. For the first time in his life, he had totally lost control of himself. And all for nothing.

That was the worst of it. For nothing. For Leavitt's ignorance. Leavitt's innocence! Damn the man.

That fact lodged deepest in Seth's troubled mind. For if Gene Leavitt hadn't sabotaged his experiment, hadn't willfully destroyed his mice, then what had?

He lay alone and tormented in the darkened bedroom, his body aching from the events of the day.

Where was Annie now, he wondered? What would he tell her when she returned?

Worse yet, what would he do about the upcoming clinical tests? Had he come too far to turn back?

※

Infatuated? Yes. Intoxicated? Decidedly.

In love?

On balance, Annie thought not, that is, when she thought about the matter at all, which was rarely. Indeed, why think? Why spoil the cloudless days with remorse and anxiety when life could be reduced to the four essential pleasures?

"Sex. Food. Sleep. And music," she announced with a sense of awed discovery.

She was lying on the roof terrace, contentedly naked, when this revelation came to her. In the dazzling light of the Provençal sun, every sensation seemed heightened, intensified. The piercing black-green of cypresses against the hillside, the texture of the matting against the silk of her skin, the languid hum of distant bees. When the wind shifted, the air was pungent with the scent of wild thyme.

Polo laughed at her definition.

"You have one item too many, Annie." He propped himself up on one elbow and watched her fondly. "Sleep is a total waste of time, *ma chère*. And on reflection, I'm not so certain about food."

"Disagree!" Annie took a pomegranate from a majolica bowl and bit into its flesh. It tasted tart and sweet, like Polo. A burst of ruby juice ran down her neck, trailed a path across her breast.

Polo leaned over and licked it off with a lazy tongue.

"Well"—he kissed her nipple—"possibly food." Then he rolled over on his back, stretching his glorious body to accommodate the sun's blessing. "But only as an accompaniment. Otherwise, I agree. Making love and making music." He rested a brown hand on the tangle of her pubic hair. "What else in the world really matters?"

Dreamily, she wondered if Polo rated these two essentials in a particular order. She suspected not. Here in this whitewashed villa hidden in the hills above Vence, the boundaries became blurred. The past two weeks washed over her in a warm billow of sensuality.

"I could live here forever," Annie mused.

From the moment she came here, she determined to put all thoughts of Seth behind her. To free herself, if only for a while, from the darkness of their last day together. Here in Polo's villa, all was light, clean. She felt herself bewitched, as though she had left the charted world.

The house was charming, a mix of warm and cool. Everything in it was good to the touch. The half dozen rooms were scrubbed clean, simply furnished with rush-bottom chairs, oaken furniture, the crude bright pottery of the Mediterranean. White wooden shutters sheltered the lovemaker from the heat of the afternoon. There were no paintings on the whitewashed walls, few books or magazines. Had it not been for the piano and piles of music in the studio, one might have mistaken the villa for the household of a well-to-do peasant.

"Is this your home, Polo?" she had asked.

"Yes." He laughed. "For three weeks in the summer."

"But where do you live?"

"Live?" The question struck him as odd. "Switzerland for tax purposes, France for fun, New York and London for professional reasons. I'm on tour eleven months of the year, darling."

"But where are you from?"

Amused, he gave her his lineage. The son of a German diplomat and a French-Hungarian mother, he had been born in London, raised in Paris, educated in Switzerland and Vienna.

In fact, she soon discovered, Polo was equally at home everywhere and nowhere, a man as devoid of nationality as he was of personal ties.

True, he had a wife, a Frenchwoman of consummate chic and substantial fortune, whom he saw on half a dozen occasions throughout the year.

"Zoë enjoys being married to a celebrity," he explained.

"And you?"

But the answer was obvious. Polo liked the protection that the married state afforded. He had no reason to alter his status.

"You understand," he told her the first time they made love, "we are friends and colleagues, nothing more."

"Do you make love to all your colleagues?"

"Only when they're as beautiful as you, *ma chère.*"

"Yes." She licked his taste off her lips. "I understand."

One was endowed with only so much emotional capital, he explained, making the distinction between that and sexual vigor. Given that basic endowment, one might expend it in art or fritter it away in a morass of sentimental relationships. Let romantics choose otherwise, Polo preferred to channel his deepest feelings into music. He rarely read, had little interest in politics or sport or social questions. His life was structured so as to avoid any obstacles or commitments that might stand between himself and the podium.

Thus in his way—and he was the most sexually adept, most physical man she had ever known—Polo was as ascetic as a monk. Superbly disciplined, he rose at dawn each day to exercise as rigorously as an athlete in training for the Olympics. "Conducting takes physical strength," he said. "I want always to be at my peak."

The result of these labors was a body of almost classic beauty: taut, well muscled, supple and strong. She never tired of watching him, never wearied of his lovemaking, even though she sometimes suspected he might have been equally content with someone else.

He showed remarkably little curiosity about her background or the state of her marriage, accepting her husband's absence without comment. He was more interested in Annie's future than her past.

"There are only three types of musicians," Polo would say. "Bad. Good. And world class. Annie, you're good. But you could be world class. All it needs is total dedication. Now, let's begin again . . . from bar thirty." He would sing out a cue in his pleasantly nasal voice and Annie would pick up the musical line.

Every morning they made love, then worked together until lunchtime, ate and made love again. After which Polo would send Annie away for two hours while he studied scores for the forth-coming season.

Some days she slept those hours away. But most often, she would walk down the narrow winding path into town.

The town was charming, with an old quarter full of stone houses and jewel-box squares, little shops with treasures tucked away in their cool depths. Above all, the outdoor markets fascinated her, piled high with the produce of Provence. Green-globed artichokes with spiky tops, shiny phallus-shaped courgettes with the yellow blossoms of morning still upon them, bulbous tomatoes so soft and vulnerable they bled at the touch, great purple aubergines, glossy as satin. There was an erotic quality to almost everything on display. The food of love, she came to think of it.

Then, her string reticule filled with luscious produce, she would stroll over to a café on the Place du Frane and drink iced Pernod, momentarily at peace with the world.

Never had life been so physical, so uncluttered. New York was far away in time and space. As for Seth and his dark secrets, she pushed them from her mind. They were shadows across the sun. Polo was right. Life was simpler, better without emotional compli-cations.

She would finish her Pernod, exchange *au 'voirs* with the *patron* and return to Polo's aerie on the hillside, hungry once more for music and sex.

"I'm terribly fond of you, Annie," Polo would say. She presumed he was fond of his other lovers. Not that it mattered. He was a cheerfully amoral man and she was fond of him too. Fond of the dream they were living. Dreaming it would never end.

"Wake up, Annie." Polo patted her gently. "You'll get burnt and I don't want to send you back to New York looking like an over-cooked lamb chop."

"Back!" She opened her eyes, then shielded them from the late afternoon sun. But of course. How time had slid by. "Then you're really off to London tomorrow?"

"Must, *ma chère*. I'm conducting at Glyndebourne on Saturday. *Manon Lescaut*. Come into the studio and let's go over the first act, shall we? By the way, do you know you smile in your sleep?"

"Do I?" She was delighted. "And yes, I'd love to do some Puccini. Just let me just throw something on . . ."

"To sing Manon?" Polo laughed and led her by hand into the music room. "Surely you don't need clothes for that. In fact, considering the nature of her profession, the dear girl was probably never more herself than when in the nude."

So Annie sang to him, naked and unself-conscious, the warmth of the Provençal sun still on her body.

At one point he stopped playing, folded his hands and listened to her unaccompanied voice.

"I love . . ." he paused.

"Yes?" She turned to him astonished.

"I love your breasts and your thighs and your sweet lovely cunt." He smiled up at her affectionately. "But most of all, I love to hear you sing. Someday, Annie, someday we will have to perform together."

He left the next day for England. An elderly couple came from the village to close up the house "For another year?" Annie asked. "*Oui, madame.*"

She spent a long thoughtful night at the Hotel Negresco in Nice, adjusting herself once more to city sounds. The interlude had been a dream. A necessary one, a time of healing. Yet the real world couldn't be put aside much longer.

For the first time in weeks, she permitted herself to think about Seth. Had she been too hard on him, too unforgiving? Had her affair with Polo been essentially a way of hitting back, of repaying Seth for having made her suffer so?

Whatever the answer, she wouldn't find it here. In the morning, she boarded the flight to New York.

3

SAILING.

Only this time it wasn't a dream. This time it was her hand on the tiller while Ward grappled with the boom. For a man of the world, he wasn't much in the sporting department and if it hadn't been for Vi calling the shots, they'd probably be drinking up the Atlantic by now. But it had been the best afternoon of the year. Sheer bliss.

"Watch that jib," she hollered as a gust of wind swung the sail around, "or you're gonna wind up with a skull fraction."

"Don't get smart, Vi! Anyhow, I think it's time we headed in. I'm getting blisters the size of golf balls."

"OK, OK." She giggled. "Just follow my instructions."

She issued a stream of commands, interspersed with the occasional shriek of alarm, and through a mixture of luck and ingenuity managed to guide Ward back into Greenwich harbor.

"Whew!" The poor bastard was mopping his brow, a man who was glad to see land. "Can we put on the auxiliary motor now? Come in under power? I think I read somewhere that most accidents happen at the takeoff and landing points."

"That's planes, honey." Vi laughed, starting up the motor. "Boy, are you some lousy sailor."

"Careful is all. I don't want any harm to come to this tub. It belongs to my boss, after all."

He watched as Vi maneuvered the boat into the mooring, tied a granny knot with practiced ease and tossed it deftly around the nearest stanchion.

"OK, Ward. You can breathe easy. We're all tied up and home free, barring hurricanes."

Ward's response was to clamber down into the cabin and return with a bottle of Wild Turkey. Then he sprawled into a deck chair next to hers.

"I don't know about you, but I could use a drink." He poured a jigger of bourbon into a plastic cup, handed it to her, then poured a double for himself. "Too bad the kid wasn't here. He would've enjoyed himself."

"He sure would!" Vi agreed. "Noonie would have gotten a chance to see the real Ward Daniels in action."

"Was I that bad?"

"Worse." She laughed. "Jesus, you should've seen yourself up there. One look is all it would take to set Noonie straight. You know, he thinks you're the greatest thing since sliced bread."

"A young man of rare wit and perception."

"Yeah." Vi nodded. "But don't get carried away. He says pretty much the same about his old man. Mr. Ratfink Ross took him to Yellowstone, camping . . . did I tell you? I had a postcard this morning. Picture of a big fuckin' grizzly bear. What a crock he is! Ross, I mean, not the bear. For a guy whose favorite position is lying flat on someone else's back, he's gotta show Noonie that he's the world's A Number One outdoorsman. It's like he makes a point of doing all the things with Noonie that I can't handle anymore. Christ! The two of 'em'll be climbing Everest next."

Ward looked at her with a brooding expression.

"It's not a Tarzan contest, Vi. Give the boy credit for some judgment, some loyalty. Ten years of caring don't just go out the window."

"He's a kid." Vi shook her head. "What do kids know? They measure everything in units of fun. Like Ross measures everything in units of money. Well, fun or money, I don't have an awful lot going for me these days."

"Do us both a favor, Vi," Ward said softly. "Stop bad-mouthing yourself. I've gone and borrowed this scow just to please you, the least you can do is relax and enjoy it."

"That's what they say about rape, isn't it? But you're right, Ward. I bitch too much. Anyhow, she's not a scow. She's a thirty-foot sloop with racing sails and very yar."

Ward celebrated this news by pouring them both another round of drinks, while Vi explored the picnic hamper.

"Mmm . . . starved."

She bit into a ham sandwich, then washed it down with a mouthful of bourbon. The booze tasted good, warming. Best part of a sailor's day, she thought, like the nineteenth hole was to golfers. The sun was low on the horizon, the waters of the Sound shifted from gray-blue to a shimmering rose.

"What's she like, your boss?"

"Claire? She's a hundred and eighty pounds of killer tomato, but otherwise OK."

"Do you sleep with her?"

Ward nearly choked on his drink. "Jesus, what a question! I'd sooner crawl into the sack with Godzilla, but as it happens Claire's tastes run more to Valkyrie types than to yours truly. Thank God!" he added. "What made you ask?"

"Just wondering." She took another swig. "What's a Valkyrie? Some kind of German wolfhound?"

Ward burst out laughing. "Valkyrie is another way of saying 'big broad.' "

"Oh. You mean your boss is a dyke. I've never done that," she added pensively. "Gone to bed with a woman, I mean. There's a gal over at the rehab center thinks I should try it. According to her, that's all that's out there for people like us. Other women in pretty much the same lousy shape. But I don't know. The idea turns me off. I guess I've always liked men." She turned away from him into the gathering dusk, swallowed the lump in her throat, then poured herself a fresh cup of bourbon. The whiskey made her feel better. And if she was a wee bit drunk, what the hell? She hadn't tied one on since last Christmas.

"Actually I don't suppose I'm the person to quibble." Vi managed a laugh. "I've slept with just about everything else. Jesus, I've had more one-night stands than Ritz has crackers."

"Who hasn't," Ward muttered.

The liquor had soothed her pain, loosened her tongue. She felt a need to talk.

"Ever been to a singles bar, Ward? I used to go to this joint down on Route 22 . . ."

And she was off and running, recalling the good guys, the goofy guys, the marathon runners, the sixty-second dropouts, the klutzes, the kinks, the men with half-forgotten names and well-remembered idiosyncrasies.

"And then there was Sherm . . ."

The dusk had settled into night now, and she could barely make out Ward's figure a few feet away, but she knew he was listening intensely. Even with her eyes shut, she could feel his presence, his acute awareness. Had she shocked him with her tales of promiscuity?

No, not Ward. Her bet was that he could match her man for man. Or woman for woman as the case might be.

If so, he made no comment, merely poured out the last of the bourbon. My, my, but they'd gone through a lot of booze that evening. Tasted good. Felt better. Finish it off and she might be able to obliterate the past. Better yet, obliterate the future.

"I was kinda sorry when Sherm left," she said. "I liked him a lot. A sweet, sweet man. He was the last of 'em, of course." She sighed, and downed the remaining bourbon. "We used to sleep snuggled up like spoons in a silver drawer. You couldn't have slipped an angel's hair between us. I guess that's what I miss most. Not the disco scene so much . . . not even the sex, although I miss that like crazy. Just . . . oh, I don't know. A man's touch, grabbing a cuddle in the middle of the night . . ."

Her voice began to tremble. "I'm only thirty, young really . . . and it's possible that I'll never sleep with a man again. Never wake up to a warm loving body in my bed."

"Don't, Vi . . . Don't dwell on it."

She looked out over the lights on the shore. Pretty frame houses. Happy couples, drinking, having dinner.

"It's true, though," Vi whispered. "What man in his right mind would want to have sex with a sack of cornmeal? Because that's what I'll be, Ward, sooner or later, if this cure stuff doesn't work. Oh, God!" She fought to hold back the tears. "I can't bear to think about it."

In the darkness, he found her face with his hands, with his lips.

"You're so wrong, Vi. You're so special. What man in his right mind wouldn't want you?" His voice was very solemn.

"Thanks," she breathed. "But you don't have to say that."

"No, I don't have to." He placed his arms around her in an all-encompassing embrace. "I want to. I want to make love to you

288

tonight. Your cheeks taste of salt, Vi. Don't cry. Please don't cry."

"It's not tears, Ward. It's the sea." She laid her cheek against his hand. "The spray of the sea. I never cry."

For a long while they clung together, rocking gently with the tidal rhythm of the boat. With his lips he brushed her throat, her cheeks, her eyelids, kissed the salt away. She shut her eyes, opened her mouth to his, dizzy with expectation. Just once more to know the warm feel of flesh on flesh, to lose herself in a lover's arms, enjoy the rough male perfume of sweat and sex.

He would leave in the morning, she was sure, most likely with a gasp of relief, but the morning was forever away. Tonight, all she hungered for was closeness. Closeness and love. Every fiber of her being ached for his touch.

"You're trembling," he said.

"It's getting cold. Let's go to bed, Ward."

"Yes, let's." In the dark his voice was disembodied. He might have been any man, every man. She ran her hand across his unshaven cheek. Ah, but it was Ward. Unflappable, wonderful Ward. Nothing shocked him, she remembered his saying. Even so, it hurt her to ask. So unromantic. So essential.

"I'll need my canes, Ward, to get into the cabin."

"No you won't, Vi. Put your hands around my neck."

He slid a firm muscled arm beneath her knees, then carried her, a piece of precious cargo, down the steep steps into the tiny cabin. "Why, Vi . . ." He laughed. "You're as light as a bird."

Somewhere in the back of her mind she resolved to remember every detail of their lovemaking, each tiny caress, in case this was the last passionate sex she would ever have. But of that long white night she could only recall fleeting moments.

Tender. He had been so unbelievably tender with her. The supple hands beneath her buttocks, the seamless entry into her body's depths, the soft words she could barely distinguish.

Long after that night, she would recall his face in the stark light of the hurricane lamp, inches above her own, intense and impassioned, delving into her eyes. It was a vivid image. She would remember, too, although she could never think why, his washing her face, combing out her hair as she lay drowsing upon the lemon-striped sheets in that narrow bunk, lost to everything but the bliss of his touch.

❧

Jesus F. Christ!

Ward wedged his eyes open to find himself in a rock-hard bed with a world-class hangover, an aching back and Vi Hagerty burrowed against his chest.

Jesus Fucking Christ. How had he let this happen!

Warily, he disengaged an arm from under Vi's head and hoisted himself up to evaluate the latest turn of events.

Had she suckered him into this situation, he wondered, or had he done it all by himself? A fifty-fifty proposition, he decided. Never should he have let her go on about the good old days. That kind of talk always led to a roll in the hay, especially in tandem with so much booze. The wisest step would be to write off the whole night as a drunken aberration.

Except that he had known exactly what he was doing. He had felt—*what?* Ward paused to analyze his feelings. *Sorry for her?* Perhaps, but he had never before gone to bed with a woman on compassionate grounds, otherwise he would have slept with half the female population of South East Asia. When it came to good works, Ward preferred to make a contribution to the Red Cross.

Yet last night, he admitted, the sexual overtures had been his, not hers, which was all the more astonishing. In some unorthodox fashion, the woman had gotten to him, breached his defenses and tapped some deep well of tenderness within him he hardly knew existed. It was not an emotion he felt comfortable with, and he grew momentarily resentful. She had made him lose his objectivity.

In retrospect, it struck him that Vi had always had the upper hand, from that first day when she had wrung the Petersens' address from him. He had acted against his own best interests then and had done so once again last night.

Now, he looked down at her naked body, curled up against him, frail and delicate as a bird. A lovely body. He hoped those fuckers at Medi-Tekk knew what they were doing. If she had been his wife—God forbid!—he wouldn't have let her play the guinea pig. Vi, too, must have some doubts, he gleaned from the conversation last night, or she wouldn't have spoken of a world without men.

"I never cry" was her fondest boast. Yet beneath the brash talk and the bold red fingernails there was a vulnerability painful to behold.

She never cried indeed—except in her sleep. In the middle of the night, Ward had woken to hear her groaning, gnashing her teeth. He turned on the light to find her face streaked with tears, her mouth contorted in pain. Fast asleep.

What fears, what terrors must inform her dreams, he could only surmise. At last he could bear it no longer.

"Shhh, baby." He had fetched a washcloth, gently stroked the tears away, smoothed her hair, cradled her in his arms until the dreams passed. "Shh, baby, it's going to be all right," he had crooned.

But it wasn't. Moreover, he had probably compounded the poor thing's troubles by raising her hopes. For all he knew, she might interpret last night as a commitment. If so, that notion would have to be dispensed with pronto. For no way was he going to get in any deeper with her. A man would have to be a Grade-A fool, let alone masochist, to get involved under these circumstances.

A lifetime's instinct of self-preservation rose up within him. Fight or flight, his adrenaline commanded.

Flight was better.

Alaska! Perfect place to cool things off. Only last week Claire had suggested his doing a piece on the conflict between the Eskimos and the Save-the-Whale movement. He had turned it down, but right now the idea seemed to have merit. Alaska it would be, a most legitimate excuse. Save the whales? Hell! He was saving Ward Daniels' ass.

As for Vi, he'd try to let her down gently. Certainly he wasn't going to cut and run first thing this morning. No, they'd spend a day sailing, then over a nice lobster dinner, he'd tell her about his new assignment.

Of course (he would assure her), of course (he resolved), he would keep in touch with her from time to time. Maybe even buy her the occasional drink.

After all—Ward Daniels told himself—he wasn't a total shit.

※

Annie's return drew a mixed reaction from Seth. Clearly, he was desperately glad to have her home. He had met her at the airport with flowers and a bear hug, eyes shining with relief.

"Good . . . so good to have you back."

Yet he was curiously reluctant to press for explanations. Where? When? How? Who? He didn't want to know.

"Did you ever get to Salzburg?" he asked at one point.

"No. I stayed in France."

To which Seth had nodded. "I see."

But what it was he saw, Annie couldn't fathom.

Seth, so observant of the physical world, could hardly have missed the telltale signs—the unbroken tan, the tiny bruises. But if he suspected infidelity (and he must have. What else could account for her silence?), he feared having his suspicions confirmed.

On the plane over, Annie had agonized. Should she make a clean breast of it? With every passing mile, the answer grew clearer. From the first bracing sip of Scotch and water, she felt herself moving away from the cloudless days of Provence and from Polo. To her surprise, she didn't feel guilty. Polo had given her warmth and laughter and uncomplicated affection. He had restored her wounded ego. In a way, Annie's affair canceled out Seth's infractions. He had had his secrets; now she had hers.

Should it come to a showdown, she would tell him the truth. She hated lying to Seth or to anyone. But if the incident could be glossed over, that surely would be best all around.

Why wound Seth needlessly? Why put him through the same emotional wringer she herself had endured? She'd had her revenge. And marvelous as those weeks in Vence had been, she recognized them for what they were. There had been no emotional commitment, no grounds for the destruction of a ten-year-old marriage.

For all his faults, Seth was the only man she loved, the only husband she could envision. True, a certain innocence had gone out of their union. That blind trust she once had was gone forever. But they were still thoroughly married, they would stay married. And God willing, they would have children.

For the first time in years she was relieved when she got her period (Now, *that* would have been a nightmare, carrying Polo's baby. Lord only knows what she would have done.)

She decided to wait another month before going to the fertility clinic. If the two Petersens ever were to become three—she couldn't put the obeah woman's prophecy out of her mind—God forbid Seth should have any doubts as to the child's paternity.

Yes—she concluded—Seth knew she'd been unfaithful and forgave her. Or at least chose to turn a blind eye. But now that it was over what mattered most was that their marriage had survived.

Yet what amazed her was how quickly she had slid from grace. And enjoyed it. If nothing else, her own lapse made her more tolerant about Seth's. Given the right prize, even that nice, reputable Annie Petersen was capable of succumbing to temptation.

In time, she came to agree with Margot's assessment: sexual infidelity was not a major crime, provided one was considerate and discreet. Sometimes in the midst of the city clamor she would think back to those days on the hillside and smile. That beautiful man. Every woman alive deserved one week with Polo von Brüning, and lucky Annie—she had had nearly three!

Like those magnificent desserts at Lasserre—luscious confections of pralines and crème Chantilly—Polo was a treat one might indulge in on rare occasions, before returning to the meat-and-potatoes of normal life.

Within a week she had pushed the interlude behind her and settled down to her familiar routine.

New York was quiet in August. Margot was in the Hamptons, Madame Natasha in Maine. There was nothing much to do but work. And now, Seth informed her, he too would be going on the road.

In the spirit of the times, Medi-Tekk was expanding, setting up research facilities in California's Silicon Valley. "I'm going out there to look over the premises, do some talent-scouting, hiring. A lot of those West Coast scientists don't want to move east."

"So Muhammad is going to the mountain."

"Something like that. That means I'll be pretty much commuting over the next couple of months. Will you be OK?"

She studied his face intensely. A worry line had found a permanent home between his brows. "I'll be OK, Seth. What about you? How's everything"—she tilted her head in the direction of the river—"out there?"

His voice dropped. "Everything's OK, Annie. Under control."

That night, long after she had gone to bed, she heard him poking around in the kitchen. She went in to find Seth had made himself a cup of cocoa.

"Hot cocoa in August?" She was puzzled.

"Couldn't sleep. You want anything, Annie? A Coke . . . a glass of milk?"

She poured herself a Diet Pepsi and sat down across from him at the wooden table.

Seth stirred his cocoa thoughtfully. "There's something I ought to tell you before you get a garbled version from Margot's grapevine."

Without embellishment, he told her of his attack on Gene Leavitt. Annie listened dumbfounded, unable to equate the Seth she knew with this kind of physical aggression. A twinge of guilt assailed her. Perhaps, had she been here, instead of dallying with Polo in the south of France, none of this would have occurred.

"Anyhow," Seth concluded, "I think that's why Gerald is sending me out to the Coast. My guess is he wants me off the scene until things cool down."

Annie sat very still, taking his remarkable news all in.

"Was it worth it, at least?" she finally asked. "Did you wring a confession out of the man?"

"You don't understand." Seth spooned the scum off the top of his cocoa with a look of distaste. "Leavitt doesn't have a clue about the goddam mice. I'm convinced of it."

"Which means . . . ?" Annie sucked in her breath.

"Which means, I'm back to Square One as to cause." He pushed the cup away and rested his head in his hand. "I can't drink this swill. Christ, I don't know what to do next. I'm sick at heart, Annie."

"Oh, Seth!" She covered his hand with her own. Whatever he had done, she would go along with him. All she asked was that he be honest with her, that they fight their way out of this morass together.

"Could you . . . could you quietly find an excuse to scrap these experiments for technical reasons and start the whole business all over from scratch?"

"Impossible, Annie. It would throw everything back a year. Anyhow, I couldn't do it without compromising myself. There's been so fucking much publicity, thanks to your pal Margot. Plus Gerald is raring at the bit, as you well know."

"But Seth . . ." She gasped. "They surely wouldn't go ahead with the clinical trials until all the research is confirmed. There are safeguards, aren't there? Don't other scientists have to replicate your experiments?"

Unexpectedly, Seth laughed. "We're a private company, Annie. We're not asking for federal funds so we're not subject to the same type of scrutiny. As for other labs replicating our work, why should they bother? That's the beauty of the thing, my insurance, so to speak. There's no incentive. Ask yourself, why should some lab invest half a million dollars and God knows how many man-hours, just to prove Medi-Tekk was correct in the first place? You don't get any prizes for coming in second. Besides, we already hold the important patents. No, Annie. I doubt that another lab will waste good resources trying to replicate my work, and even if they tried and failed, it wouldn't matter. It's very tricky stuff. You'd need a lot of specially modified equipment plus what's known as the personal touch . . ."

"The golden hands of Seth Petersen," she mused.

"You could say."

"You know what I think, Seth?" Annie chewed her lip. "I think we could be in very deep shit. Maybe you should see a lawyer."

He shook his head no.

"I won't go to jail, if that's what's worrying you, Annie, if the past is any kind of precedent. Making the basic assumption that my work is valid, there's no reason I should ever be found out."

"And if you are?"

His eyes narrowed, his face grew hard.

"Then I'll have joined a particularly exclusive scientific tradition. Not the same noble tradition of Pasteur, Lister and company. More of a footnote to history you might say. The long-shot artists who gambled and lost. Console yourself, Annie. I'm not the first person to fake a little data, do a bit of touching up here and there, or put the best possible construction on a bit of dubious research. At best, you could call it a hopeful interpretation. I'm not saying fraud is endemic, but it happens, going all the way back to Paul Kammerer and his midwife toads. And Kammerer, you should remember, was considered the giant of his day. Or remember Summerlin at Sloan Kettering touching up his mice with a Magic Marker and passing them off for skin grafts? It was the scandal of the seventies, and funny thing was, research eventually proved him right. Then there was Spector over at Cornell a couple of years back, Darsee at Harvard Med. None of 'em went to jail, if that's any consolation. So it's not likely I'm going to wind up behind bars either. Behind a begging bowl, more likely. Because if this gets out, Annie, I'm ruined. I'll be a leper in a white coat. Count on it. Anyhow, if all goes well, no one will ever know, and I'll have been justified, don't you see?"

Annie sat there, feeling the breath knocked out of her. As long as there was a convenient culprit in Leavitt, she had spared herself the broader implications. No more!

"You're talking means to an end, Seth."

Seth avoided her eyes. "That's not the phrase I'd choose."

"But that's what it comes down to, isn't it?"

All Annie's misgivings assailed her afresh. She wanted to do what was best for Vi Hagerty. But what was best? To put her faith in the cure or take her chances in the custody case? Suddenly, Seth's description of the dying mice returned to haunt her. He had been so graphic. Excruciating spasms. Eyes popping out of their heads. She recalled his exact words and shuddered. A vision of hell.

"It's too risky, Seth. Can't you stop Gerald from going ahead with the Phase One trials, at least until you've tested more animals?"

"Out of the question. Gerald's gung-ho to go ahead."

"But I keep thinking about what you said, how terribly the mice had suffered. Suppose it was the treatment that was killing them. Suppose it has those side effects on people—"

"Annie," he interrupted, "you're being morbid. Of course there's risk. There's an element of risk in every clinical trial, in every drug on the market. People die from taking aspirin, as far as that goes, yet nobody questions the benefits of aspirin."

"There are risks and risks, Seth. A vision of hell is what you said."

"Don't throw my words back on me, Annie."

He rose and emptied the untouched cocoa into the sink, then rinsed his hands under the faucet in a ritually cleansing gesture.

"Believe me, Annie, I'm not happy about any of this. But if I started thinking of worst scenarios, I'd drive myself crazy. What do you want from me?" There was real anguish in his voice. "You want me to make a public confession? You know I can't do that!"

"Promise me one thing." Annie began grasping at straws.

"That depends . . .."

"On what?"

"On my ability to deliver."

He turned away and meticulously dried his hands on a paper towel.

Annie hesitated. She couldn't possibly ask Seth to strip himself naked before the whole scientific community. He was her husband, dammit, not some common thief. You didn't sacrifice the man you loved for a moral principle. The scandal would destroy his career, wreck their very lives. There had to be an alternative, a course of action that would minimize the damage, spare both the patients and Seth himself.

"Promise," she said, "that you'll go to Gerald, tell him everything. How you falsified data. Why the tests can't take place. Lay it on the line, and Gerald will have to go along. He doesn't want public exposure any more than you do. Then the two of you can concoct some excuse for calling off the trials, at least until you're certain that FG-75 is safe. You have to do it, Seth."

He swung around to face her, every muscle of his body tensed.

"Or else . . . ?"

"It's not a threat," she murmured. "It's an entreaty. I beg you, do this for me. And for yourself."

Slowly, slowly, he exhaled a long breath of air.

"Very well, Annie." He bowed his head in surrender. "I promise."

※

Noonie returned from Yellowstone cross as a grizzly.

"You want to tell me what's wrong, hon?" Vi inquired a couple of times, but all she got for her efforts was a surly "Nothin'." The third time she asked, he exploded.

"Jesus, Mom, will you stop treating me like a little baby?"

"Will you stop acting like a little snot?" she answered.

True to form, he slammed out of the room.

She hadn't a clue as to what had got into the boy, but whatever it was, it would take a crowbar to pry it loose. That was one stubborn kid, she conceded with a mixture of exasperation and pride. As for pride, she managed to swallow a little of her own and put in a call to Ross.

"Did anything happen when you were at Yellowstone?"

"Like what . . . ?"

"Oh, I don't know." Vi sighed. "I thought you two guys might have had a falling-out . . ."

"Wishful thinking, sweetheart. Maybe he's just unhappy to be back home. I'll see you in court, ninth of November."

I'll see you in hell.

She ended this totally unsatisfactory conversation by hanging up. Damned if she could figure whether the boy was pissed off with her or his father. For the dozenth time she wished Ward were around. He could usually get Noonie to open up.

But right now Ward was freezing his ass off up in Alaska. That is, presuming he actually went to Alaska! For all she knew, he might have gone underground in New York City, hiding out behind a false mustache and beard. Christ, the man had been scared shitless that last day together. What did he think? That she was going to make a scene, put the screws on him? How little he knew her.

In fact she'd gone out of her way to let him off the hook.

"Listen, Ward. I want you to know it was a one-night stand, OK? You don't owe me beans."

"You really mean that, Vi? I don't want you thinking I'm some kind of super-swine."

"Forget it, hon. We're big boys and girls. What the hell . . . you made me feel great last night. Sexy . . . desirable. It was fantastic, what I remember of it anyhow. Jesus, I had a lot to drink."

"Yeah . . . we both did."

"Anyhow, thanks for the dance."

She'd pecked his cheek and that had been that.

Maybe Ward would phone when he got back from wherever, more likely not. Too bad. She would really enjoy a repeat performance. Hell yes, she could've used a couple of weeks of that stuff. Maybe even a lifetime's worth.

"Where's Ward?" Noonie asked his first day back.

"He had to go to Alaska on business. I'm not sure when he's coming back."

Noonie never asked about him again.

"Something's bugging the kid," Vi confided to Crystal.

"Probably just doesn't want to go back to school after all that vacation."

"Yeah . . . probably."

4

ALTHOUGH HER AFFAIR WITH POLO SEEMED TO HAVE RUN ITS
course, Annie's admiration for him remained untarnished. His
words haunted her for a long time after they parted.

You can be world class, he had foreseen, a judgment so momen-
tous that even a month later, she trembled in recalling it.

Polo hadn't said it to flatter. She knew him better than that. Despite his cheerful amorality in most matters, he was unswervingly
honest when it came to music. All he had done was voice his belief.

World class. The idea was almost frightening. It was the ultimate
goal of the artist. The highest accolade.

There were countless superb musicians, artists of the finest caliber
enjoying major careers who never achieved world-class stature.
Thus one might be the mainstay of the San Francisco Opera, the
concertmaster of the Boston Symphony, the best damn pianist in
Amsterdam, and still be virtually unknown a couple of hundred
miles away.

World class was when people who knew almost nothing else about
music knew who you were.

Polo himself was world class. As were Pavarotti, Sutherland, Stern,
Domingo, Pollini, von Karajan, Richter, Bernstein, Arrau. Performers equally welcome in Rome and Tokyo, London and Caracas,
the invited guests of every major orchestra, every opera company
worth its salt. They were names that resounded beyond the usual
world of music lovers to touch the hearts of the general public. Say
"Horowitz" and wham! an instant army of people with camp chairs
lined up waiting for tickets. Was Pavarotti appearing? You needn't

bother to specify which opera. The house had been sold out two years in advance.

World class. Maybe there were a hundred musicians in all who had achieved membership in this most exalted, most exclusive of clubs. And there was Polo telling Annie that it was time to apply.

"All it takes is total dedication."

Dedication, plus a few lucky breaks.

Madame herself had intimated as much, albeit in more cautious terms.

"You have the talent, Annie, and you have the voice. The question is, do you have the will?"

Damned if she knew.

Seth began commuting to California, coming home weekends and then off again Monday mornings. It was rigorous, but he seemed to be enjoying the change of pace. Perhaps they both needed a little relief from each other.

"Is everything going to be all right?" she asked him. "That business with Gerald?"

"Don't worry," he assured her. "It's taken care of."

Annie breathed a sigh of relief.

After Labor Day, Margot returned from the Hamptons and invited her to lunch at the Four Seasons.

"Well," Margot clucked as she gave her friend an approving once-over. "You certainly caused us a great deal of worry this summer. Was he worth it?"

"Was *who* worth it?" Annie felt a flicker of anxiety. Had Polo boasted of his conquest to Margot? She couldn't believe it.

"That's for *you* to tell *me*, darling." Margot giggled. "But when a beautiful woman goes missing on the Riviera, and her husband comes home in a snit, what else can one think? I must say I was surprised, though. We thought you and Seth were getting along so beautifully these days. Of course, you don't have to tell me a thing if you'd rather not, lamb. Anyhow, I'm not one to be judgmental." Margot picked at her salmon with a puzzled air. "Although you sure took your time . . ."

"Took my time doing *what*, Margot? You're jumping to all kinds of conclusions."

"Took your time getting back at Seth for his having carried on so with that Indian girl last winter. Or was she Pakistani . . . ? I forget. No matter. Well, I always say, revenge is a dish best eaten cold under a beach umbrella in the south of France."

"But—" Annie spluttered. And stopped short.

But Seth had never carried on, she had started to say. Except how was Margot to know? Annie herself had only discovered the truth that night in Paris.

She studied her wineglass thoughtfully, reluctant to meet Margot's eyes. If Margot still believed that tale about Chandra, then she must have no notion of what had been going on at the lab. Gerald, clearly, confided in her even less than Seth had confided in Annie.

"I'm sorry, darling." Margot misinterpreted Annie's silence. "I didn't realize it still hurts after all this time. I'm an insensitive dolt."

For a split second, Annie deliberated. To say that there had been nothing between Seth and Chandra would call for an explanation. Better that Margot persist in thinking Seth a philanderer than that she, too, be dragged into the Medi-Tekk morass.

"If you don't mind, Margot, I'd rather not talk about it."

"Of course not." Margot patted her hand and switched to other topics. Southampton gossip. The forthcoming theater season. Her plans for renovating her house in Connecticut. Clothes. Parties. Trips.

Relaxed by the familiar turn of the conversation, Annie finished off her quenelles. The waiter came and cleared away.

"Do have something, darling." Margot paused in her chatter. "I'm told their chocolate cake is sublime."

Annie smiled, scanned the menu which seemed too much of many good things, was considering a simple lemon ice when Margot's voice floated across. ". . . so it looks like I won't get to England after all next month, what with the trials coming and naturally Gerald wants to be on the spot . . ."

"Trials? What trials?" The menu fell from Annie's hands.

"What trials! Really, darling, doesn't Seth tell you *anything?* I suppose not, now that he's out on the Coast so much, although he and Gerald keep in touch. I'm talking about *the* trials, darling, the Phase Ones our men are so keen about. They've been scheduled for October some time. They've already started cooking up the witches' brew. All terribly exciting. Why, Annie!" Margot peered around the room with a quizzical air. "You look as though you've seen a ghost!"

"No . . . nothing." Annie waved the waiter away with an impatient hand, then gulped down a glass of water. "Are you certain, Margot?" God, her throat was dry. She wet her lips and began again. "What I mean is . . . well, it was my understanding they were going to be postponed, that there'd been some sort of technical hitch, or whatever." She cast an imploring look at Margot, begging for confirmation, but her friend simply shrugged.

"Well, then you know more about it than I do, ducks. I don't follow Medi-Tekk business very closely, although I could have sworn Gerald said it would be October."

Annie suffered through coffee and the mandatory polite farewells before escaping to the nearest telephone. Two o'clock her time. That made it three hours earlier in California. Seth had gone to Los Angeles this trip, to scout out some new equipment for the lab. Staying at the Beverly Hilton? she tried to recall. Or was it the Beverly Hills? She fished out a change purse full of quarters. She'd try them both.

The Beverly Hills it was, but by the time the hotel operator rang his room, he had left for the day. No, Dr. Petersen had left no message concerning his whereabouts or his return. *Oh, shit!* Annie's heart started to pound against her rib cage. It could be hours yet.

"Have him call his wife," she instructed, "the moment he comes in. It's urgent. I'll be home the rest of the day."

She took a cab back to the apartment in a paroxysm of anxiety. What had gone wrong? What on earth did Gerald think he was doing? Only last week, Seth had told her not to worry, that he had handled everything. And now this bombshell from Margot!

There was the possibility that Margot had the facts wrong, but Annie doubted that. When it came to remembering details of dates and times and places, the woman was a walking calendar.

Don't panic. Annie geared herself for a longish wait. Seth often accused her of jumping to conclusions, and certainly her conclusion about Chandra had been wrong. Maybe this time too. Rather than condemn anyone unfairly, she would put the afternoon to use.

For the next hour, she worked listlessly on whatever music was lying on the piano, but her throat was tense with anxiety, her concentration virtually nil. Ironing, then, or boring housework. When it came to diffusing tension, nothing took the place of physical labor. And so Annie scrubbed the bathroom floor, cleaned the closets, polished all of Seth's shoes, then brewed a huge pot of coffee and sat down in the kitchen to await his call.

For the hundredth time, she told herself that there was probably a simple and harmless explanation. But the assurances refused to take root. For in this wretched business, nothing was simple. Almost from the start, there had been a pattern of lies and deceptions.

From a dark recess in her mind, an ugly thought began to surface. Could it be that Gerald was unaware of the risks he was taking? That he had no notion of anything wrong? If so, the conclusion was inescapable: Seth had never given him proper warning.

Impossible!

An unconscionable breach of trust.

Seth had pledged. In this very room, he had given Annie his solemn word that he would lay all the facts before Marriner. Across this very table but a few days earlier, he had sat and smiled and assured her all was well.

Whom can you believe if you can't believe your husband? Whom can you trust?

True, Seth had lied to her before when he deemed it prudent, but their relationship had since taken on a better, more forthright turn. The night he told her of his attack on Gene Leavitt, he made no secret of his distress, his misgivings. That same night, he had promised to stop the tests. Vividly, she remembered the moment: the bowed head, the resignation in his voice. Was it all an act, calculated to lull her into a false security? Had he manipulated her once again?

The half dozen cups of coffee had left her mouth tasting of acid, her stomach in knots. She rose and put on a fresh pot.

When the phone call did come through at nearly midnight, Annie jumped like a startled faun.

"Annie." Three thousand miles away, Seth's baritone came through, full of love and concern. "Darling, are you all right? I just now got your message."

She caught her breath. "Yes, I'm all right."

"You don't sound all right. You sound terribly upset. What's the problem?"

"The problem is . . ." Nothing for it but to plunge right in. "I had lunch with Margot today and she tells me Gerald is going ahead with the tests."

If she expected shock and dismay on the other end, she was sorely mistaken. There was total silence.

"Seth? Are you there? Did you hear me?"

"I heard you, Annie," came the cool reply. "Is that the emergency that couldn't wait?"

"But I don't understand. What the hell is going on, Seth? You said you'd speak to him, you said you'd get him to call a halt. Did you do it? Answer me. I have to know. I've been going crazy all day."

"Jesus Christ." His voice came through clenched teeth. "You call all the way from New York to subject me to the third degree. Boy, that is something! Since when do I have to account to you for my every movement? Listen, Annie, I'm getting goddam sick of being treated like a criminal. I'm sick of your questions, your emotional blackmail, all the things you seem to think I owe you. I take care of matters in my own way, thank you very much, so will you kindly butt the hell out of my business?"

"You *didn't* tell him!" Annie shrieked. "You son of a bitch, you never said a word to Gerald!"

But she was yelling into a dead line.

She listened to the dial tone for a few seconds more, then slammed the phone down.

She considered calling him back, then decided against it. For if that brief ugly conversation had settled nothing else, it proved that Seth had not spoken to Gerald.

Didn't he realize what he was doing? The risks he was running by going it alone? For if—God forbid—tragedy did occur, Seth would bear the sole responsibility. Suppose someone died. Suppose they all did. Suffered the tortures of the damned, and then died. How could Seth live with such guilt? His conscience would destroy him far more effectively than any public scandal. She had to do something to save Seth from himself. Now, before it was too late.

Gerald Marriner was her only hope. He was a discreet man. Powerful as well, and she could rely on him to avert an open scandal. And once he knew the facts, she'd do her utmost to plead for leniency.

304

"Seth's been under terrible pressure," she would say. Gerald would understand.

It was too late to phone him at home, but early the next morning, with only a few hours of sleep, Annie reached him at his office.

"I have to see you today, Gerald. It's urgent."

"I'm awfully busy, Annie." His voice was wary. "Can you tell me what it is over the phone?"

No, she couldn't, except to say it was a matter of vital importance to them all. How about tonight?

Tonight—Gerald said—Margot was having a small dinner party, but if Annie cared to come over around ten, they could have a brandy and coffee in the library.

"Just the two of us, Gerald. I don't want Margot involved."

※

That morning a postcard arrived from Alaska, addressed to Ms. Vi and Mr. J. Noonan Hagerty. The picture showed an Eskimo in full kit—fur parka and sealskin boots—standing next to a stuffed polar bear.

Reverse side depicts Aleut in charming summer costume (ran the message) *accompanied by blond girl friend. Be glad you're not here. Especially standing down wind. Back soon. Best.* Followed by an indecipherable scrawl that presumably was Ward Daniels' signature.

Vi propped the card up on Noonie's dresser and smiled. It was just the lift she needed that day. The past week had been rotten, a symphony of aches and pains and spasms. Doc Browning had termed it an "exacerbation" and discussed the merits of wearing braces. An exasperation, was how Vi thought of it, and fuck the braces. It wouldn't be long now. After six months of messing about, the guy who coordinated things up at Medi-Tekk had got in touch with Vi and set the date. Five weeks from tomorrow.

She would be one of twenty patients in a double blind experiment, only ten of whom would receive the actual drug. Neither patients nor doctors would know who got what until later, when the results could be evaluated. But Vi was sure she'd be treated with the real McCoy. After all, hadn't her luck held thus far?

In the meantime, there was plenty to be done, she was told. Medical workups, blood tests, tissue typing, plus a shitload of paperwork to go through. "We need your informed consent," the coordinator said and scheduled a meeting with the physician who would be giving her the treatment. It would take place at Gryce Hospital, located in the wilds of Brooklyn, which struck Vi as significant. She had been born in Brooklyn. Now she would be reborn there. What did they call that? Full circle . . . full cycle? Ward would know.

She wished he were here instead of chasing after whales. She needed somebody to be brave in front of, to pull her macho number for. Not that there was anything to worry about. Who said the Age of Miracles was past?

Los Angeles was a swamp, worse than Galveston. Seth trudged back to the hotel, his linen jacket wringing with sweat.

On balance, he considered it a successful trip. He'd spent the whole day at SOTA Spec-Tronics looking over the latest in high-tech lab equipment. Their stuff was fabulous, and Seth had felt like a kid in a candy store.

"We don't call ourselves State Of The Art for nothing," their salesman, Bob Bennett, had boasted. "And what we don't have, we can make up to your specs."

The two had spent the afternoon discussing prices and delivery dates, with Seth requiring occasional modifications. By day's end, he had bought over a million dollars' worth of goodies for Medi-Tekk.

"I'll have to get an OK from New York," he said, "but I don't anticipate any difficulties."

"A pleasure doing business with you." Bob Bennett beamed. "I'd very much enjoy taking you out to dinner this evening. I'll get us a reservation at Ma Maison, or any place you like. Just name it."

But Seth had opted out. All he wanted was to cool off, maybe relax over a drink or two, enjoy a little peace and quiet.

"A fucking swamp!" He collected his room key, then headed straight for the bathroom, strewing clothes as he went. He showered for twenty minutes, then, turning the air conditioner on high, sprawled naked atop the king-sized bed.

He probably should call Annie, but after that ridiculous conversation last night, he doubted that he'd be able to keep his temper.

He didn't understand her, *demanding* to know what was going on. What right had Annie to *demand* anything from him, after that number she pulled on him in Europe?

A man's wife comes home covered with bruises and bite marks and her only explanation is that she was relaxing in the south of France. She might at least have had the decency to wait till the black-and-blue marks faded. What was she trying to do to him? Get some kind of cheap revenge? She was breaking his heart, that's what. And he didn't have a clue as to who the man was, presuming it was only one. At any rate, it hadn't taken her long to find companionship. He couldn't bear to think of it.

And *then*! Annie starts preaching to *him* about honesty. Honesty, for Chrissakes. She'd taken ten years of absolute fidelity on his part, and flushed it away like a cigarette stub down a toilet.

It was enough to make a man weep.

He flicked the remote on the TV on, then flicked it off again. Nothing but trash. If he weren't so goddam depressed he'd go down and have something to eat. Instead, he stretched out on the bed and shut his eyes.

A few minutes later, there was a knock at the door.

"Yeah?"

"Delivery," a light voice sang out. Bellboy, he guessed. Or maybe bellgirl by the sound of it. Everything was so unisex these days. Even messengers.

"Yeah . . . just a second."

He slung a towel around his waist and went to open the door.

A woman stepped in the room. Dark blond hair, light blond mink. Huge tapestry handbag. Just the thing for hundred-degree weather.

"Hello." She smiled, revealing perfect white teeth, then let the bag and coat fall to the ground. Except for pale leather sandals and a fine gold chain around her neck, she was naked. The body was a *Playboy* centerfold come to life.

"I'm Honey," she announced.

Seth stood back and shook his head in awe. Standing before him was what he supposed must be a Grade A top-of-the-line Hollywood hooker, the kind that catered to movie producers.

"I'm afraid you've come to the wrong room."

God, she was astounding looking, all of a color. Tawny hair, tanned skin, even the eyes were flecked with the same honey golden hue. Contact lenses. Nonetheless the effect was electrifying. She was twenty-two, twenty-three, maybe.

For a moment she watched him watching her, and then took a step toward him.

"Oh no, this is the right room. Bob Bennett sent me as a way of expressing thanks from the people at SOTA Spec-Tronics."

Close up, he had never seen such skin. The texture of peach bloom. And extraordinary breasts, satiny and firm, the nipples so erect they seemed to be staring right at him. He tried to suppress a twinge of desire. She wore the same perfume as Annie.

"You still have the wrong room." He managed a polite smile. "That was very nice of Bob, but I'm a married man."

"Married men have fantasies too." She placed her hand on his arm. Her fingernails were golden as well. "I'm sure there are things you've always wanted to do that maybe your wife doesn't care for. Anything that doesn't leave marks. Let me give you some ideas . . ."

In her flat midwestern voice, she might have been a tour guide describing the wonders of Disneyland or the ice-cream girl at Howard Johnson's offering thirty-two flavors.

Seth felt his muscles tighten, felt himself grow hard.

Should he, shouldn't he? He'd never been with a whore before. As far as he knew, never even spoken to one. Contempt mixed with desire.

"Tell me . . ." He paused.

"The name's Honey." She smiled.

No, he couldn't call her that. He reserved all his endearments for his wife.

"Tell me, as a point of information." He nodded in the direction of those magnificent breasts. "Are those silicone implants?"

"Nope," she said. "The real McCoy."

She took his hand and very slowly rubbed his palm against her nipples. For a moment, he held his breath, then let his hand fall slack. "Everything is genuine and in perfect running order," she said. "I'll show you." Slowly she spun around like a model in a fashion show. The ass was as incredible as the breasts.

You have two choices, Seth told himself. He could have sex with this girl. Or he could get rid of her, then go into the bathroom and jack off like a teenager. Which would be a goddam dumb thing to do. Even as he considered, she had taken his hand and was tracing a

lazy line with it down the spine, between the buttocks. His fingertips made light contact with her rectum, slid across her labia. She
was lubricated front and back.

His heart was pounding, his penis starting to ache. Still he hesitated.

"I don't want to go home to my wife with a disease," he said.

"I have a letter from my doctor," she said. "Even a lab analysis.
I get tested every week. If you like, I'll show it to you."

"Such,"—Seth gave a mordant laugh—"are the lofty uses of a medical education. OK"—for they were still standing by the door. "Come
in, and don't bother with the fancy equipment. I think we can make
do with what we have."

He took off his towel and lay down on the bed, horny as hell.
Funny thing, though. He had no desire to be inside her. The idea of
delivering himself into a stranger's body was faintly distasteful. He
felt distanced even as she played with him, stroking his cock, felt
himself still very much the married man. At this point, he'd settle
for some simple relief.

He put his hands behind his head and shut his eyes.

"I want you to go down on me," he ordered.

She crouched atop him, head down, nipples rubbing rhythmically
across his chest as she took him into her mouth. She had a tongue
like a lizard, long and swift and as she brought him to orgasm, her
honey-colored pubic hair rubbed softly against his lips in invitation.
Did she want him to pleasure her too? Probably, but Seth had no
desire. He preferred being serviced, like a car in a garage. It was
more impersonal that way.

Nonetheless, she was very, very good. And so he told her when
she had finished.

"I think that's all," he said.

"I've been hired for the night," she replied. "You can have as
much as you want."

He turned to look at her with a faint curiosity.

"Tell me, what do you charge for a night's work?"

"I was a gift," she said. "Everything's been paid for in advance
by Mr. Bennett."

"I understand. Just put it down to my spirit of scientific inquiry.
What's your nightly rate?"

"Seven hundred and fifty."

"Hmmm." That was fifty dollars more than Annie's fee for a concert and Annie had to pay her accompanist out of that. Of course, the girl had to split her fees too, it was fair to assume.

"Thank you," he said. "I think that'll be all."

"Do you mind if I wash up before I go?"

She went to her bag and fetched a toothbrush, toothpaste, a bottle of Listerine, then headed into the bathroom. Clean she was.

The phone rang. Shit! What a time for Annie to call.

But it wasn't Annie at all. It was Gerald.

"She *what!*" he roared, unable to believe his ears.

The girl in the bathroom turned round to stare.

"Annie did *what?*" He was screaming. Stunned and unbelieving. "Told you *what?* . . . For Chrissakes, I ought to have her ass. Don't worry, Gerald. I'll fix it up somehow. Goddam!"

He slammed the phone down, body trembling, face black with rage. Goddam goddam goddam.

"You!" he called to the girl, his breath coming fast.

She turned round.

He beckoned her to him.

"Did you decide you wanted something else?" she said.

The blood was pounding in Seth's ears.

"On the floor," he said coldly.

She did as he asked.

He knelt behind her, his knees locking around her hips like an iron vise, then with hard hands spread her buttocks wide. She'd asked for it. Okay, she'd get it.

"You fucking bitch!"

Erect and powerful, he rammed his way deep inside her and began pumping with the grim relentlessness of a pile driver.

"You fucking bitch!" he cried, thrusting deeper. "How could you! How could you!"

He was weeping, shouting, no longer in control of himself.

"Bitch!" He came with a roar, then pulled away.

The girl stumbled to her feet and rubbed her bottom gingerly. "Jesus, mister. I won't be able to sit for a week."

But Seth, tears streaming down his face, scarcely knew she was there.

She got her coat and bag and left the room.

An hour later, Seth Petersen boarded the red-eye flight to New York.

※

She was working with Ari when she heard the front door slam, the thud of luggage being dropped.

"Seth?" She broke off singing.

"You go right on doing what you're doing," he said, tight-lipped and disappeared into the bedroom.

She turned to Ari. "If you don't mind, let's call it a day."

"Of course." He shut the lid of the piano. "Same time tomorrow?"

"I'll call you." She ushered him out.

Tomorrow! God knew what tomorrow would bring. One thing was certain: there would be a showdown today.

What else could have brought Seth back from the coast three days early? Gerald must have phoned him the minute she left the Marriners' house, burning up the wires with news of her treachery.

At their meeting last night, Gerald had made it abundantly clear that he was well informed, moreover that he had no intention of halting the tests. Throughout, he had remained suave, avuncular ("My dear girl, you're upsetting yourself over nothing"), smoothly reassuring ("well within the margins of statistical error").

The words were meant to calm. Instead they set off an alarm bell. Gerald and Seth, she concluded, had entered a gentleman's agreement. They had formed a conspiracy to defraud. Yet even as Annie recognized the truth, she hated herself for having informed on her husband. She felt shabby and cheap.

She heard him moving about in the bedroom, thought of going in and decided against it. Better to give him a chance to cool down.

He emerged a few minutes later, haggard but composed, wearing an old sweater and khakis.

"Let's go out for a walk, Annie. We have things to talk about."

They walked to Carl Schurz Park in total silence. Seth found a bench overlooking the river and motioned for her to sit. For a while she watched the scows, the occasional sailboat, the gulls scavenging for garbage. On the opposite shore, unseen yet making its presence felt, was Medi-Tekk.

Seth folded his hands, then began in a hushed voice.

"When Gerald called me last night, I had a whore in my room. I didn't arrange for her to come." He kept his eyes studiously lowered. "That's not the sort of thing I do. One of our suppliers sent her around as a gift. You know, like a bottle of booze at Christmas. She was very beautiful, very adept. I'd never been with a whore before. I found it a degrading experience. Hateful and degrading. I'm not like you, Annie. I don't really enjoy sex with strangers."

Annie reared back, stung.

"What happened in the south of France . . ." she tried to say.

"I don't want to know what happened in the south of France!" He turned to her, eyes brimming. "Spare me the gory details. In all our years, I've asked only two things of you. Your love and your loyalty. God knows, you've had mine! Anything within my power to give you, I gave. Voice lessons, clothes, a New York recital, whatever . . . if you wanted it, I'd do my damnedest. I love indulging you. It's one of the greatest pleasures of my life. The main reason I took the Medi-Tekk job was to make you happy. And this is how you reward me!" He blew his nose and stared moodily over the water. Annie could think of no reply.

"That night in Paris," Seth continued, "when I told you about the trouble at the lab, I expected some gesture from you. Some demonstration of your love and loyalty. I wanted you to tell me, 'No matter what you've done, Seth, I love you.' You didn't say that. Instead, you picked this crazy fight and two days later you're off God-knows-where screwing God-knows-who! Was it revenge, Annie? Revenge for what? What harm have I ever done you? And now this business with Gerald! What possessed you, Annie?"

"You promised me something." She began to cry. "You promised me you would put a stop to the tests."

"I never did, Annie. I promised you I'd speak to Gerald, and I kept my word. But you just went behind my back, anyhow."

"I had to!"

"For Chrissakes, Annie. How many times do I have to tell you—the business at the lab has nothing to do with you. Nothing!"

"It's evil!" she burst out. "I think what you and Gerald are doing is evil!"

Seth stared at her openmouthed, but at last Annie had found her voice.

"Yes, evil! It's not enough for you to say you've been a good and faithful husband. Although you weren't very faithful last night. Still, the world didn't fall apart, did it? But I want you to be more than just a good husband. I want you to be a good man, too. A good human being. You live your life in neat compartments, Seth. You always have. Tough guy in the office, softy at home, and never the twain shall meet. Only now the line between them is corroding, and what you do is spilling over into what you are.

"That night in Paris, when according to you I should have fallen into your arms, every inch the devoted wife, all I could think was 'This isn't the man I married. My Seth wouldn't do such a thing.' But then, my Seth wouldn't have assaulted a Gene Leavitt or gone to bed with a whore. My Seth wouldn't be playing God with people's lives. I can't believe you seriously plan to go ahead with this. I gather you've sidestepped a lot of guidelines already. I asked Gerald how such a thing could happen. I asked him, don't you need an OK from the Public Health Service? What about peer review, which Gerald seems to have bypassed quite nicely? Or the Helsinki Declaration? When I mentioned that, Gerald pulled his 'there there' number, as though I were a sweet but retarded child. I gather he thinks all the regulations are a pain in the ass. Not to worry, he told me. There are thousands of such experiments every year. No agency can monitor them all. He made what's going on sound like routine procedure. But you and I know it isn't. I've come to the conclusion that Gerald only cares about glory. But not you, Seth. I want you to be a finer man than he is, more courageous . . ."

"You want me to be a martyr, Annie. A martyr and an outcast. And what would we live on when I get my walking papers? I'll be a pariah, unemployable. Can you support us on your earnings?"

"I'm not saying this is going to be easy, but somehow we'd see it through. We've managed before . . ."

"Before," he broke in, "I was a young man on my way up—not out. We could always count on next year being a little better. From the start, both our lives have been predicated on my making good. Well, now I've made good, Annie. Don't ask me to turn back the clock."

"But what if someone dies, Seth? I keep coming back to that. What if the side effects are worse than the disease?"

"No one's going to die, Annie," he whispered.

"Can you guarantee that?"

"Oh, come on! Nothing in life is guaranteed safe. Not cigarettes, not aspirin, not even tampons, for Chrissakes. And they're on sale everywhere."

"So are automobiles," she shot back, "but you don't invite people for a ride if you think the brakes aren't working."

"Very well, Annie," Seth said slowly. "What if someone does die? I want to remind you, we're not talking about foisting an unsafe drug on the general public. It'll be another five years or so of testing before the drug is approved for sale. What's in question here is a handful of people, sick people, who have volunteered for a test procedure. As you may recall, they were beating our doors down for the opportunity. They asked to be guinea pigs. You may be sure every patient in these trials has given full consent."

"I thought the proper wording is 'informed consent,' " Annie said. "Were they informed about what happened to the mice in Batch One?"

"I don't know what hapened to the mice in Batch One. Neither do you. Get it through your head, Annie: if the only medical advances that existed were those that had been won without risk, we'd be back in the Dark Ages. There'd be no anesthesia, no antiseptics, no antibiotics, let alone fancy stuff like heart transplants and test-tube babies. Every advance contains an element of risk, every effective medication has a side effect. We could test out ten thousand mice, have 'em all respond perfectly, and there'd still be no assurance that the stuff would work on human beings."

"You're rationalizing," she shot back. "And you know it."

"I don't have to listen to this." He turned away from her, and fixed his eyes upon the river.

"One thing you're forgetting, Annie"—he finally broke the silence —"is the quality of these patients' lives, the kind of future they face. Under those circumstances, it's an acceptable risk. Be honest! Would you want to go on living with a disease like that? I sure as hell wouldn't!"

"I can't answer that," she said. "I don't know what I'd do. But you have no right to make that decision for other people, to say that they'd be better off dead. You're looking for excuses to go ahead and do as you please."

"I consider it acceptable risk," he repeated.

"Acceptable? With excruciating side effects you never even reported? You call that acceptable risk? Come off it, Seth. You keep telling yourself what you want to hear. These are people's lives, for God's sake, and you're going to have to live with the consequences. If you honestly believe it's so acceptable, then go tell them what the percentages are. Tell the doctors at Gryce Hospital, too. The authorities would never permit testing if they knew the crucial data were faked!"

"What the hell are you talking about!" Seth gripped her by the shoulders. He was ashen. "Do you have a clue what would happen if any of this leaked out? I'd be crucified."

"*You'd* be crucified," she shouted. Two benches away, an elderly gentleman with a dachshund turned to see what the fuss was all about.

Seth relaxed his grip. Annie lowered her voice. "All you can think of is yourself, your career. What about Vi Hagerty? What about the other people involved? They have rights too! Since Gerald won't act, I think you should go public. Explain everything, the stress you were under . . . the pressures. It's the only way."

"Are you crazy? Why don't you just ask me to commit hara-kiri in Grand Central Station? You say I've become a stranger. You don't know me anymore. Well, I don't know you, either, Annie. I never thought you'd betray me with other men, never thought you'd sneak behind my back to Gerald. I'm beginning to believe you capable of anything, any monstrosity. But if for one moment you entertain the notion of going to the authorities and blowing the whistle . . ."

They met each other's eyes, sudden enemies.

"If I do?"

"If you do"—his lips formed a narrow white line—"if you ever do such a destructive crazy thing, no one will believe you. What are your credentials? Where's your proof? You may be damn sure I've covered my tracks. No, Annie. You could never make a case. It'll be your word against not only mine, but against the word and reputation of one of America's most respected figures, for I assure you, Gerald Marriner is not going to sit back and let you wreck everything. He'll bring his weight and authority to bear. You'll sound like a crazy lady. A jealous bitch—hysterical, vindictive—pulling every dirty trick she can think of to get even with a husband who wants out. And I would! Oh baby, would I ever! How much treachery do you think I can bear? If you blow the whistle, we're through. There could never be anything between us again."

He broke off, shocked by the baldness of his ultimatum. Then he turned to her, desperate. "It's in your hands, Annie. Our marriage . . . everything. Promise"—his voice was anguished, beseeching —"promise me you won't do anything crazy like that."

She sat very still, then shook her head. "I can't promise, Seth."

"In that case"—he got up stiffly—"there's nothing further to be said. I'm going back to the apartment, pack a few things and take the five o'clock plane to the Coast."

He walked away without looking back.

For a while she sat there, too numb even to think.

A cool breeze whipped up off the river, ruffled her hair in an unwelcome hint of early autumn.

She looked at her watch. It was lunchtime. Too early to go home. Seth would be there, and she didn't want to see him again today. They both needed to cool off.

Instead she walked up through the park, turned into 86th Street, and killed a couple of hours at a Chevy Chase movie. It must have been a funny picture. All around her, people were laughing themselves hoarse. Five minutes after Annie emerged into the daylight, she couldn't even remember the movie's title. No matter. She resumed her stroll.

Bolton's, read the sign on the shop. "Designer clothes at discount prices." Annie went in, passed an hour trying on sportswear, finally settling on a little cotton knit sweater that matched her eyes.

Forty-five dollars. She hadn't even looked at the price until she handed the item to the cashier. A year ago that would have been a lot of money for a cotton sweater, grounds for serious deliberation. Since then, she'd been spoiled by carefree spending at Bergdorf's and Saks. But who could say? A year from now, forty-five dollars might once again seem a great deal of money.

"Cash or charge, miss?"

"Charge," Annie said. She opened her wallet, pulled out a half dozen of Seth's credit cards, selected one. Then, package in hand, she began walking the dozen blocks home. On Park and 83rd, a uniformed doorman stepped out on the pavement and blew his whistle. A cruising taxicab screeched to a halt. The doorman pocketed his tip. Annie watched, then moved on.

Blowing the whistle. That had been Seth's term. How extraordinary that he believed she might actually inform on her own husband. It had never occurred to her and was surely the most desperate recourse imaginable.

Instantly, she pushed the notion to the back of her mind. The implications were too ugly to consider. There was still time, thank God! Seth, or maybe Gerald, might yet have a change of heart.

And yet . . . what would happen if the walls came tumbling down? His career would be in ashes, he told her repeatedly. But what of her own? Could she make it without his help? Even if their marriage survived, what would they live on?

All the plans so carefully laid, the clothes, the coaching fees, the talk of a debut recital: none of it would have been possible without Seth's unstinting generosity. Careers in music were rarely launched on the cheap, and if Seth had invested heavily in Medi-Tekk stocks, he had invested at least an equal amount in Annie's future. *And this—* she recalled his words—*is my reward.* His single bout with a prostitute notwithstanding, Seth had been the best of husbands by any conventional measure. Loving, faithful, open-handed, supportive. He had made good on all his promises to her, always backed her to the hilt, promoted her welfare. Perhaps she was asking too much of him now, holding him to a standard of behavior that was unreasonably high. He was smarter than most men. She believed he should therefore be better than most men. Sadly, he wasn't.

With a heavy heart, she returned home.

Seth had already left. On the answering machine was the usual mixed grill of messages plus half a dozen calls from Margot, each on an increasing scale of urgency.

"Annie," the last entry played back, "I must see you. I'll be over there at teatime. Please be home."

Whenever Margot was upset, she became very English. Teatime, Annie presumed, would be just about now.

Her first impulse was to slip out of the building through the service entrance, having already endured a full day's supply of confrontation. But on second thought, she saw that Margot's visit could be a boon.

Where Annie had failed with Gerald Marriner, Margot might succeed, for if anyone could bring Gerald around it was his wife. In her soft, pliant way, she exerted enormous influence over her husband. And with her wealth, she could shield him from any economic consequences. After all, what was money to Gerald? And how much fame did any man need? Yes, Annie realized, once Margot's help was enlisted, she would be her staunchest ally.

With a lift of spirits, Annie put on the kettle, brought out the dark Indian tea that Margot loved, poked in the cupboard for biscuits. The water had hardly come to a boil when the doorman announced that her guest was on the way up.

Annie went to greet her at the door.

For the first time since they'd met, Margot Marriner showed all the ravages of her sixty-odd years. The face was a web of fine lines and deep shadows, the eyes faded to the color of old Delft. Without the multiform layers of makeup and the gay smile, she was virtually unrecognizable.

Shocked, Annie held out her hands in friendship, but Margot hurtled past her into the room.

"I'll get us some tea," Annie murmured, but before she could leave, Margot had burst into tears.

"What are you doing to Gerald, Annie!" she sobbed. "Are you trying to drive him into his grave?"

"Margot!" Annie spun around, horrified. "Please. You don't understand. The last thing in the world I want to do is hurt Gerald. Or hurt you either! Please!" She led Margot to the couch and sat beside her. "I'm just trying to do what's right."

Margot reached into her bag, took out a fine linen handkerchief and wiped her eyes. With a visible effort to regain control, she turned to Annie.

"I don't know what you said to him last night, but whatever it was must have been terrible. A half hour after you left, he was in a state of collapse, spent half the night under oxygen. Why are you doing this to us, Annie? What have we ever done to you?"

"Margot, listen." Annie explained urgently, "I'm trying to stop our husbands from doing something very dangerous, something we may all have cause to regret. The clinical trials that are scheduled for next month mustn't take place. It could be a disaster for all of us, the most awful tragedy. You have to talk Gerald out of it. Have him call a halt. You see, the research is tainted, no good . . ."

If she meant to shock Margot with this revelation, she had misjudged her, for her friend waved the words away with an impatient hand.

"Tainted! What's that to me, Annie? What the men do in the labs is their business, but when you come into my home and wreak devastation, that's my business. As for the tests, Gerald wants them and that's good enough for me. I know where my loyalties are. I don't understand you, Annie." The blue eyes fixed themselves on her face. "I don't understand how you can do this to your husband's career, to his happiness—let alone what you're doing to us!"

"Margot," Annie interrupted, "think of what could happen. Think of the people who are risking their lives. The side effects . . . my God! they could be horrible. People may die." She started crying. "Can't I make you understand?"

"Gerald is dying!" Margot burst out. "Don't you see . . . don't you care? My husband is dying! That's all that matters to me! You didn't know, of course. How could you? It's a deep, dark secret. Even I'm not supposed to have an inkling. He's got a heart like a ten-shilling watch. He could die at any moment, and all I can do is to see that he's spared unnecessary anguish. Don't do this to him, I beg of you. Annie, we've loved you and Seth like our children. You're very dear to me. You've become a part of my life this past year. I've always been good to you, haven't I?"

It was Annie's turn to fight back tears. Margot had been a true friend: thoughtful, generous—and not only with money. In her way, she was a gallant woman. In the face of her husband's death sentence, Annie realized, she had behaved with enviable grace and courage. "You've been wonderful to me, Margot. I'm grateful beyond words."

"I don't want your gratitude, Annie. I helped you because I wanted to. I still do. If there's anything I can give you, you need only say the word. I would rent the Met for you if you asked! Anything you want that's within my power. Anything . . . except *this*. Annie darling," Margot clutched her arm with feverish fingers, "I implore you . . . for all our sakes, let it be."

That was that!

She watched Margot leave with a sense of despair, for with her went Annie's last hope of reprieve, of containing the nightmare within what she had come to think of as her "family circle."

Gerald. Margot. Seth. The people she loved best. Yet in different ways, they all saw only what they chose to see.

Gerald had nothing more to lose, Annie realized. He was dying anyhow, and Margot's only concern was for him. As for Seth, he had found a convenient rationale and clung to it relentlessly. If MS victims couldn't be cured, then they were better off dead.

Was it possible? Annie didn't know. Vi Hagerty was the only one she'd ever met, and one couldn't judge a whole life on the basis of a single encounter months ago.

She had thought of Vi often. More than once, she had wanted to visit her, meet the boy, see how they were getting on. Yet the prospect was daunting. Vi was—Ward implied—inordinately grateful and Annie found that embarrassing. God forbid she should look like a smug Lady Bountiful, fishing for thanks.

Instead, she'd kept in touch mostly through Ward and his reports were always good. "Walking on air," he'd once told her, and Annie had almost burst her buttons. *I did that*, she would glow inwardly. *I made the difference*.

But now, everything had taken on a whole new complexion. The "favor" she had done Vi might turn out to be lethal. She had to know. Had to see for herself what life was like in the Hagerty household. Two days later, she drove out to Bloomfield.

"This time *I* make lunch," Vi had insisted, and she had gone all out in the effort.

The table was set with an elaborate spread: crusty rolls, lox, Bermuda onions, cherry tomatoes, cheeses, a wide assortment of salamis and sausages.

"Sit sit . . ." Vi ushered her guest into a chair while she put on coffee. How adept she had become, Annie marveled. How skilled in setting up the kitchen so that complex chores could be handled with an economy of movement. Helpless? The hell she was, no matter what Seth chose to think.

"OK." Vi finally sat down. "Dig in."

Annie looked at the buffet uneasily. Far too much food. "I don't know where to begin . . ." she said.

"Then I'll make you my special." Vi cut open a seeded roll and began assembling ingredients. A sliver of this, a slice of that, a little bit of everything else. Layer by layer the sandwich grew to astounding proportions. Vi worked swiftly and steadily, with deft fingers, wielding a knife with a skill that would have done credit to a surgeon.

They were in spasms—Seth's description of the mice suddenly blazed across Annie's mind. *Excruciating spasms.* No, Annie protested, not those clever, capable fingers, those firmly muscled arms.

She swallowed down a wave of nausea.

"Now, I top it off with a little Hungarian salami and there you are. I call it my international hero sandwich, something from seven different countries."

She handed Annie the plate.

"I don't think I could eat all that . . ." Oh God, was she going to be sick?

"Worried about cholesterol, huh? Forget it. Those health freaks will drive you bananas. Don't eat this . . . don't eat that. Takes all the pleasure out of food. Well, you only live once is what I say. Go ahead, Annie, taste it."

Gingerly, Annie took a bite. The combination was delicious, or would have been if her stomach hadn't been tied up in knots. If only she could expunge Seth's words from her memory . . .

"You're not eating, hon? Don't you like it?"

Annie forced down a few more swallows while Vi chatted on gaily. She spoke of her friend Crystal. Of the fun she was having with her computer. But mostly she talked about Noonie, with a fierce pride. How good he was in English, but fractions bothered him; he was a baseball nut, made planes out of balsa wood . . . a hundred trivial details from the state of his mind to the state of his bedroom.

"It's a swamp." Vi sighed. "Go find a pair of socks that match.

Believe me, Annie, living with a kid that age is like giving house room to a goddam tornado."

It was a boast, not a complaint.

"We want children, my husband and I," Annie astonished herself by saying. "We've wanted them for years."

Why was she saying this? She had never viewed Vi as a potential confidante, but now, under stress, her own worries poured out. The years of trying, the doctors advising this or that. The fellow she was seeing now had started her on fertility drugs, but she didn't know how effective they'd be.

"Oh, they'll work," Vi assured her. "I bet you they will. These scientists, boy! They know exactly what they're doing!"

"Do they?" The comment pulled Annie up short, and she didn't know what she might have said had not the front door shut with a bang!

"Hey, Ma!"—the heavy thump of a school bag being dropped. "Hey, Ma, I'm home!"

As though there could be any doubt.

He burst into the room with an Apache yell, then stopped, embarrassed to find a visitor there.

"Speak of the devil." Vi laughed. "Here he is." But at the sight of him, her eyes had lit up.

Eyes! What was it Seth had said about the eyes?

Annie, their eyes were popping out of their sockets.

She sucked in her breath, then looked again at Vi's face—the blue eyes bright with present joy, unaware of terrors that awaited. Yet she could picture . . .

"Noonie, this is Mrs. Petersen, that famous doctor's wife"

"Hi."

The boy came over, offering her a sticky hand.

Instead, Annie enveloped Noonie in a desperate hug. God, he was skinny—you could feel every rib through the T-shirt. Skinny, but substantial too. His damp body was firm and wiry. He smelled of chalk and sweat and Hershey bars and new sneakers. For a moment she breathed the scent in deeply, then released him.

"Hi, Noonie." There was a catch in her throat. "I've heard a lot about you."

He grinned, mumbled something, his eyes on the food platters.

What would he do if his mother died that way? Would he be

there to hear her screams? Or would he only know when it was too late?

He was picking at a roll.

"OK," Vi said. "Make yourself a sandwich and then will you go wash up? You smell like a basketball team."

He skimmed the table with the speed of a sea gull feeding off the ocean surface—a dill pickle, hunk of cheese, a macaroon—then disappeared into the bedroom.

Annie heard the groan of pipes, water running in the shower.

"Vi . . ." Her voice shook as she spoke. "Maybe you should wait with the tests. Let other people be the first, see how it works for them. I mean when you're doing so well . . ."

"Are you kidding!" Vi was thunderstruck. "I've been waiting six months for this day."

"It's just . . ." Where to begin? Where to end? If only Vi could read her mind. "It's just that . . . well, you never know. There could be serious risks involved."

Please Vi, back off. Hear me. Hear what I'm saying.

"What risks?" Vi was puzzled. "Look, the way I figure it, the stuff either works or it doesn't. And if it doesn't, I'm no worse than when I started, right?"

"But you can never be sure. I mean no medication is a hundred percent safe." Annie found herself pleading, echoing Seth but to different purpose. "People have had terrible side effects from taking aspirin, using tampons . . . and here we're dealing with an untried drug . . ."

A vision of hell. Seth said it was a vision of hell.

She herself had once had that vision. Had seen hell firsthand years ago, when she had opened a forbidden door to find the dogs in the pain-threshold tests. It was horrible . . . unforgettable. And those were just dogs, not human beings.

Please, Vi—listen to what lies behind my words.

But Vi was shaking her head vigorously. Whatever message Annie was trying to convey, she seemed equally intent upon rejecting.

"I'm an optimist, hon. A cockeyed optimist," she said. "I believe that the best is going to happen. Gee, Annie"—she furrowed her brow— "it sounds like I've got more faith in your husband than you do."

There was nothing more to be said. Even were Annie to blurt out the whole truth, Vi would not accept it. Like Seth himself, she didn't dare surrender the dream.

Nor could Annie bear to stay any longer. She was sick at heart. Sick to her stomach.

With a mumbled farewell and a good-luck kiss, she lurched back into the car, turned the corner, stopped. A second later, she was throwing up all over their brand-new Volvo.

🌑

All the time he was in Alaska, he had brooded about the wisdom of touching base with Vi Hagerty. Not that he needed an excuse one way or another. He was not a total shit, Ward Daniels continued to assure himself, but neither was he going to let this woman—or any other, for that matter—rack him up like a side of beef.

Accordingly, he had put off calling her until several days after his return, having devised a harmless outing, something guaranteed not to land the two of them in bed.

As always, she'd seemed happy to hear from him, but not—huge sigh of relief on Ward's part—as though she'd been waiting breathless by the phone.

"How was Alaska?"

"About as much fun as a root canal. The only ice I ever want to see again is at the bottom of a highball glass."

They'd chatted amiably for a while, then Ward had tendered his invitation. "I've got a box at Belmont for the Turf Classic. A chance to see some good thoroughbred racing on grass. This coming Saturday. What do you say?"

"If you don't mind, Ward, I'll take a rain check. I haven't been feeling all that great."

"I'm sorry to hear that, Vi. Is everything all right?"

"Just a little run down is all."

"What about Noonie?" Ward had asked on impulse. "Do you think he would enjoy a day at the track?"

"He usually sees his father on weekends, but hold on and I'll ask him . . ." A moment later, she was back on the wire. "Yes, Noonie would love to spend the day with you."

* * *

So here they were on a glorious September afternoon at Belmont Park with a cast of thousands, and Ward Daniels playing host to a ten-year-old kid.

"I bet you know all about horses." Noonie looked at him wide-eyed.

"Not enough to stay ahead of the game." Ward laughed. "But enough to know my way around. Come on, I'll show you the joint."

Noonie slid his hand into Ward's as they made a tour of the stables, the press room, the paddock where the horses could be viewed at close range.

"Hello, Angel." Ward waved, and a diminutive figure in racing silks came over to them. He had a wise old-young face.

"Hi, Ward. That your boy?"

"Nope. Friend of mine." Ward introduced Noonie.

"Well, kid," Ward said as the rider returned to his mount, "you've just shaken hands with one of the world's greatest jockeys."

"Honest?" Noonie was thrilled. "Gee, he's hardly any bigger than I am."

"He's big where it counts, here"—Ward tapped Noonie's forehead, then his chest—"and here. Now down to business." They went back to their seats and spent the next few minutes figuring out which horse to bet in the first. Then Ward invested ten dollars on Noonie's behalf.

"You have a rare and precious talent there, son," Ward remarked after the race. "To find a horse that can come in ninth in a race with only eight starters really takes some doing. Who do you like in the next event? I'm almost afraid to ask."

Noonie studied the racing form, brows furrowed.

"Do you ever wish you knew before, Ward?"

"Knew what?"

"Knew for absolute certain who was gonna win?"

Ward considered. "Nope. Definitely not. It would take all the fun out of betting. Like in poker—if you could look into everybody's hands, it would spoil everything. It wouldn't be a game anymore. Why?" For to his astonishment, Noonie's lip was quivering. "Is something wrong?"

"Nope." Noonie fell to studying his shoes.

"Don't hustle me, my friend." Ward placed a hand around

Noonie's shoulder. "Something's bugging you. The old newshound in me can smell trouble a mile away. You can tell me, Noonie. Come on . . . we're pals from way back. Is it something to do with your mom?"

Noonie snuffled, clenched his lips, then shook his head no.

"I have a new word for you, Noonie," Ward said softly, "a real doozie. You know, I'm a journalist. Which means you can tell me anything in confidence and it won't go any further, even if you robbed a bank. Because we journalists have something called"—he enunciated each syllable—"confidentiality. Can you say that, Noonie?"

"Confidentiality." Noonie repeated the word as though it were a magic charm.

"Well, what that means is that if you tell me something and ask me to keep it secret, I would never tell anybody. Never as long as I lived. It's like a solemn oath. You understand?"

Noonie nodded.

"Now, if I promise you confidentiality, would you tell me what's on your mind? It'll be strictly between us two."

"Posolutely absitively?" Noonie asked. He had *his* magic words, too.

"Scout's honor," Ward pledged.

So Noonie unburdened himself of his dark secret, then blew his nose into Ward's handkerchief, wiped his eyes and felt better.

They never did around get to picking a horse in the second race, but they lucked out with a long-shot winner in the third.

All in all, Ward reflected on the drive back to Jersey, it had turned out to be a satisfying day.

5

THEIR MARRIAGE HAD DEGENERATED INTO A NONSTOP WRANGLE.
"I want you to do the right thing, Seth," she kept nagging.
"I want you to let up on me, for Chrissakes."

His business in California was largely concluded; nonetheless he tended to make himself scarce these days.

"If you've started a campaign to drive me out of the house, Annie," he said at one point, "you're succeeding magnificently."

"The only thing I'm campaigning for is that you behave like a decent human being," she shot back.

He slammed into his den and spent the night on the couch. They didn't even exchange words the next morning.

Annie was at her wit's end. Indulge in public revelations, Seth had stated, and their marriage would be over. But with each passing day, that threat was losing its impact. Given the increasing level of anger and backbiting, the air of mutual mistrust, their union was already launched on a self-destruct course.

If only she had never learned Seth's secret! Then none of this would have ever come about. She and Seth would have remained friends, lovers, husband-and-wife, members of their own exclusive, very private corporation.

Briefly, she found herself envying the Mafia wives, those plump insular women who asked for and received no explanations as to their husbands' livelihoods; women who busied themselves raising children and cooking pasta and lighting candles to the Madonna while their beloved Giuseppes and Antonios (alias Joe the Knife and Tough Tony) ventured out into the world to deal dope, run brothels, extort money, fulfill "contracts"—that businesslike euphemism for murder.

How did such women greet their husbands upon their return from a hard day's labor? *Have a nice day at the office, dear? Anything new in the olive oil business?*

No, Annie surmised. In all likelihood, they didn't ask their men anything beyond the time of day. Were they clever, she wondered, or stupid? Clever, had to be the conclusion. They knew what they wanted out of life—home, husband and children—and knew the only way they could preserve it was by wrapping themselves in total ignorance. Not innocence, mind you. Ignorance. There was a profound difference.

Yet their ignorance altered nothing as far as the real world was concerned. The drugs continued to be marketed with new victims every day. The rackets thrived and took their toll. The contracts were duly executed in blood and bullets.

All that is needed for evil to flourish, ran the maxim, is for men of goodwill to do nothing.

Or perhaps for loving women to blind themselves against the truth.

She remembered seeing a film about the Holocaust, detailing the dark, hideous acts that had taken place in the camps. At the time, she had asked herself: where were the *wives* of the commandants?

That individual men were capable of great evil was a story old as Cain, yet Annie kept coming back to the same question. Where were the wives when all these horrors were being perpetrated? How could they live with men who were butchers, torturers, criminals? How could they feed themselves, clothe themselves on the proceeds of slavery and murder? How could they make love to them, bear their children? And yet, history confirmed, there were many devoted marriages in the ranks of top Nazis.

"She stood by her man," outsiders would say with grudging admiration when a miscreant came to judgment. Conjugal loyalty was considered a mark of character, a manifestation of courage. Certainly no one condemned these women for their actions or indeed their lack of action. On the contrary. They had passed the ultimate test of fidelity.

Thus Mafia wives continued cooking and caring for their husbands. The wives of atomic spies, ignorant up to the very moment of exposure, followed their husbands blindly into Russia. When Watergate was tearing the nation apart, Pat Nixon had managed a gallant smile through her tears, Mo Dean had radiated serenity. Every day, unremarked and unremarkable, thousands of women glossed over their husbands' dark secrets: the wives of IRA terrorists and corrupt officials, of malpracticing doctors and Wall Street embezzlers, of con men and child molesters. The list went on ad infinitum.

If these women didn't know what their men were up to, it was probably by choice. If they did, then they were silent partners to their husbands' crimes. Did that make them monsters of self-interest? Or martyrs to love and loyalty? At heart, were they any different from Annie herself? Who could say where love should end and duty begin?

Six months ago, Annie wouldn't have hesitated. She would have condemned these loving conspirators out of hand. One had, after all, standards to maintain, responsibilities to the world at large. She could never have conceived that Seth would join the ranks of the malefactors, that she herself might one day have to choose. The longer she dawdled and found excuses not to act, the greater her own complicity. It wasn't her secret, it was a secret that belonged to the victims.

Several times that week she drove out to Bloomfield, cruised the area where Vi Hagerty lived, driving round and round in an agony of indecision. Surely she ought to warn Vi of the hazards involved. At least let the woman make an informed decision on her fate.

But Vi Hagerty was just the tip of the iceberg, and Annie had no way of knowing who the other patients were. Yet it was imperative that they be warned.

She had given up on Seth and Gerald. They were too consumed by ambition, categoric in their desire to proceed. She had tried with Margot and failed. Conceivably, others at Medi-Tekk had an inkling of something amiss. But they would never come forth. Everyone wanted to be part of a winning team, to share in the prizes.

That left only Annie.

What could she do that wouldn't destroy Seth in the process? Even should she decide to blow the whistle, Seth and Gerald would repudiate her on the spot. Nothing would be gained but the destruction of her marriage.

No, Annie was not about to get up on a soapbox. But neither

could she sit back and let Vi Hagerty—hell, let any of the patients—put their lives on the line.

At last, after a week's agonized deliberation, she arrived at a feasible solution.

Ward Daniels was back in town. Smart, shrewd Ward with his nose for the truth. He, at least, would not write her off as a lunatic or a bitch. He knew important people, was able to operate in channels closed to her. And she could depend on him not to do anything rash—they were friends after all.

She would swear Ward to confidentiality but let Seth think that the game was up. Yes, if Ward leaned on him, the mere threat of exposure should suffice to bring the tests to a halt. Oh, the power of the press—even if unexercised! And if worse came to worst, if Gerald and Seth dug in their heels, then she would let Ward take the story public. He had stature. He would be believed. But of course, it mustn't come to that.

Heart pounding audibly, she reached him at *Worldnews*.

Could they have lunch tomorrow? she asked in an urgent voice.

No, not lunch. He had a prior engagement, but maybe they could get together for a drink later on.

"How about two thirty in the Palm Court at the Plaza?" he suggested.

Annie caught her breath. Done!

"I'll be there."

⚜

"Amazing country, America. Eh, laddie?"

Hands in pockets, Strone Guthrie observed the view from a long windowed wall of his penthouse in the U.N. Towers.

As if in response, three red-striped smokestacks across the river belched in unison. Ward Daniels could think of nothing to add. In any case, the question was rhetorical.

"I don't want to tell you how many millions of dollars this little aerie cost me"—the press peer turned to face his guest—"or you'd be asking me for a rise. I therefore find it instructive that in one of Manhattan's most expensive buildings, the view is largely slums, smokestacks and urban sprawl. Hardly different from my childhood in Glasgow. Whereas, you will notice, the occupants of those wretched little buildings down there can enjoy the glittering beauties of the Manhattan skyline. Democracy in action, one might say."

This ventured, the great man sat down and folded his hands over his stomach while a uniformed maid cleared the table.

The meal had been unspeakable. A thick brown soup followed by a murky brown stew, then a sodden brown bread pudding topped with a dollop of viscous yellow custard for contrast. Nursery food, Ward concluded, and indeed the little Napoleon of newsprint had stowed it away with the single-minded gusto of a child. Now, however, he switched to coffee, brandy and a thick cigar while Ward speculated for the dozenth time as to the purpose of this command performance.

"And are you aware, my boy, that this past year, the preferred reading of your fellow countrymen was the autobiography of Mr. Lee Iacocca. Followed"—he leaned forward, blowing a cloud of prime Havana into Ward's face—"by the autobiography of Mr. Chuck Yaeger. A car salesman and a pilot. Now, what do you make of that, laddie?"

"Everybody loves a success story, Lord Guthrie."

"Precisely!" Guthrie leaned back and rubbed his hands with satisfaction. "A success story. The universal dream. From rags to riches. From tyke to tycoon. From Grub Street to grandeur . . ."

From bad to worse, Ward groaned inwardly. The old bastard was going to write a book.

"We are going to write a book, Daniels."

"We?" Perhaps Ward had misheard.

"We. You and I. I'll supply the life, you supply the words. It will be a heartwarming tale of personal progress, an inspirational epic of triumph over adversity. Public relations, my friend, and never more necessary than now."

Guthrie hoped to build himself a television network over the next few years, but anticipated trouble in getting approval from the FCC.

"The Yanks don't fancy the idea of bloody foreigners taking over their airwaves. Especially this bloody foreigner. They persist in the notion I'm a sinister figure. However, we shall disabuse them of that misconception with this wonderful book you're going to write. From the depths of your typewriter, through the magic of your prose, my dear Daniels, your modest host will emerge as a veritable Mother Teresa."

With that he squashed his cigar into his coffee cup.

Ward was flabbergasted. His immediate reaction was to barf up the bread pudding and make a run for it. Caution prevailed, however, the prudence of a man with rent to pay.

"Of course, I'm very flattered, Lord Guthrie, but I'm a journalist, not a . . ." A *what*? The image that came to mind was *a laundress in a whorehouse*. "Not a ghostwriter," he blurted out.

"Of *course* you're a journalist, Daniels. Best damn journalist in the country. A respected crusader. A newsman whose truthfulness and credibility are beyond question. That's exactly why I've selected you for the task. Your name will be on this book, my boy" (*God forbid*. Ward shivered) "and on the royalty checks too, may I add. I would make them over to you outright. Aha! Now, that's a different story, isn't it? Do you have any idea, Daniels, what the royalties *are* on a million-copy best-seller?"

Ward had an excellent idea. Nothing less than the proverbial "fuck-you" money, a sum big enough, solid enough so that he could do as he chose for the rest of his life.

"You would take six months' paid leave from *Worldnews*," Guthrie continued, "devote yourself exclusively to the book. Live with me, work with me, eat with me" (*well, of course that was the downside*) "tell my story to the world so they may know me for the warm, lovable human being I am . . ."

A week earlier, Ward Daniels had turned forty-one. Curiously, he found that birthday, rather than the one preceding, to be the seminal juncture in his life.

Forty-one. More than halfway there. Other than a handful of awards, what did he have to show for his efforts? A bank account so slim the light shone through it when you held it sideways. Every dumb jock he'd gone to high school with was knee deep in the stuff, let alone wives and children. They'd spent the intervening years getting rich in real estate, in fried-chicken franchises, selling cars to other dumb jocks, while Ward had bounced around the Third World filing dispatches. Rolling stones may gather the occasional kudos, he observed, but they didn't gather that lovely green moss.

Maybe he would take Guthrie's offer. Sell his soul and buy a beach house in Tahiti with the proceeds. *Tuan*, the native girls would call him. Lithe and lovely creatures with amber skins. He could envision them now, fanning him with palm fronds, feeding him choice morsels as he lay in a hammock on his veranda. *Tuan Daniels*, the local wise man, beloved by all, a character right out of those Joseph Conrad novels that had fascinated him when he was a boy. A suitable fate, all things considered, for, like Conrad, he too would be writing pure fiction.

Already Guthrie was limning ways with which to deal with the more scabrous aspects of his life. Ward listened with half an ear.

"Well, laddie," the press lord finally got up, "what do you say?"

"I'd like a couple of weeks to think about it, sir."

Although he had virtually decided to do the sensible thing, he didn't want to admit, either to Guthrie or himself, that he could be so easily bought.

Guthrie gave an impatient shrug.

"Use your head. You won't get another opportunity like this as long as you live."

"I know that."

He made his farewells, then went down the elevator in a daze. It wasn't until he hit the street that he remembered his appointment with Annie Petersen.

Damn. Past three already. Didn't have a clue as to what the woman wanted. Still, an appointment was an appointment.

He whistled for a taxi.

The problem with this fucking town, Ward Daniels decided, was that you could never get a cab when you needed one.

But who would need taxis in Tahiti?

What on earth had induced Ward to specify the Palm Court? Hadn't she mentioned it was a confidential matter?

Maybe not. Annie had been in a state when she phoned him. Still was, the anxiety heightened by finding herself on display in one of New York's most visible meeting places. Immediately on arrival, she'd spotted people she knew, friends of Margot's laden down with packages. *Cut and run*, her instincts told her, *quick! before they see you.* Instead, she'd chosen a quiet corner table and lowered her eyes over a pot of tea, while a string trio offered Strauss waltzes.

Strictly speaking, it made no difference whether she unburdened herself to Ward here at the Plaza or in some dark alley or on prime-time television. The story remained the same. Annie Petersen was going public. Blowing the whistle.

Put that way, it sounded lurid. She could picture the headlines, duly distorted, on those magazines that you scanned while waiting in the supermarket checkout line: WIFE REVEALS SCIENTIST'S SECRET PLOT.

Better yet—MAD SCIENTIST. That was the cliché, wasn't it? Two words that usually appeared in tandem. Like *pious* and *Catholic*. *Crazy* and *Arab*. *Devoted* and *wife*.

Mad scientist, indeed. Seth was no madder than many another climb-the-ladder fuck-the-public executive pushed to achieve. He was a gambler, a high-stakes poker player going for broke. Obsessed, perhaps, but not classically mad. Seth was not Frankenstein—doctor or monster—despite his choice of costume for Margot's ball. Yet that must have been how he felt about himself, before he made the decision to tough it out.

Since then, he had grown so familiar with his act that it now seemed to him a commonplace. Yet nothing altered the facts. You either had done such a thing or you hadn't. And if you had, there was no way you could be "just a little bit guilty."

Any more than she herself could be "just a little bit pregnant." You were pregnant or you weren't. And now, after all these years of wanting and waiting, she believed she was.

Such timing! Such bitter, bitter irony. And Seth hadn't a clue. It was a measure of the distance between them that he was now unaware of her simplest biological rhythms. She was three weeks late, the first time ever. And sharp-eyed Seth, who never missed a significant detail, had missed this.

At any other time she would have been overjoyed, eager to share each moment, each tiny symptom with him. She would have gone straight off to the doctor to have the good news confirmed as soon as possible. Instead, she had trembled and said nothing.

For the first time in her life, she despaired. Their marriage was dying. This afternoon would likely bury the remains. When Seth was confronted with proof of Annie's betrayal, it would be over between them. He would leave her.

Then what? What kind of life would be waiting for her as a single mother? Impossible not to think of her own mother—that bitter, lonely woman struggling to raise her children single-handed. Of her childhood, growing up without a father.

The prospect was too painful to contemplate. She must push the matter from her mind. For how could she sit here prepared to wreck her husband's career, destroy his life, and all the while be carrying his child?

Annie had no illusions about the forthcoming interview with Ward Daniels. She was betraying Seth in a crueler, more final way than her dalliance with Polo last summer. Amazing that she had made it here at all, this afternoon. Even now she wasn't sure she could go through with it. She felt like a public executioner.

Ward Daniels was late. Almost three already. Perhaps he wouldn't show at all, and that would be the end of it. She shifted her eyes away from the lobby and glanced about the room.

The lunch crowd had thinned, leaving behind the occasional tourist and the odd party or two. At the next table, a young couple dawdled over cake and coffee, totally absorbed in each other. Suddenly, the girl giggled. Annie turned. She was fresh-faced and very pretty.

"Come on, Arlen," she cajoled. "Open up. You have to have a taste. It's divine."

She had filled a fork with a creamy scoop of chocolate cake and was reaching across the table to her young man. Arlen. Funny name. Sounded like "darlin'."

The man looked faintly embarrassed and radiantly happy, for the girl was offering more than cake. She was offering her love.

"Mmm." He swallowed a mouthful. "Delicious."

She ran a gentle finger over his chin to wipe away an errant crumb. He took her hand and kissed her fingertips.

Annie turned away, eyes filled with tears.

How many times had she and Seth exchanged these loving trifles, these sweetnesses, saving the best things in life for each other.

She had a swift vision of their roomy old kitchen in Texas. She had been baking *springerle*, those luscious Viennese cookies that Seth adored, when he had come home from a meeting all dressed up. His grant-grubbing uniform, he used to call that one good dark suit. It was reserved for important occasions, and he looked so terribly somber when he wore it.

"Here, taste!" She'd wiped her hands on her apron and offered him

335

a wooden spoonful of batter at arm's length. "But don't you dare come in. I'm confectioners' sugar all over."

Indeed the kitchen looked like the inside of a flour barrel.

And Seth had laughed, strode in anyway, taken Annie in his arms—apron and all—and given her a big, fat kiss.

"What'd you do that for?" she said.

"Because I felt like it."

Then the two of them had sat down and licked out the bowl.

Stupid memory!

With the last of the tea, she washed down the lump in her throat. It was quarter past three.

At the next table, Arlen had paid the bill and now the young couple were leaving, hand in hand, lost to everything but each other.

Daniels was probably not coming. Just as well. Annie called for the check. Then she scribbled a note and gave it to the headwaiter.

By the time Ward Daniels arrived, she was gone.

Sorry to have missed you, read the message. *It was nothing important after all.*

※

Seth came home to find her in the bedroom, packing.

"Annie!" For a split second, he froze in the doorway, shocked beyond words, then flew into the room with an anguished howl. "What are you doing!"

"I'm leaving, Seth." She sat down on the bed, sudden dead weight. "I did something today . . . I don't know if it was right or wrong. I had a date with Ward Daniels . . . to tell him everything . . ."

"Omigod!" Seth turned dead white.

"And I couldn't do it." She burst into tears. "I should have, I knew it was right, but I just couldn't. God help me, I couldn't bring myself to throw you to the wolves like that!"

It took Seth a moment to absorb this extraordinary news. A wave of relief flooded through him, followed by a surge of unbounded love.

"Oh, darling!" Seth crushed Annie to him, the words coming thick and fast. "Darling, darling Annie. Of course you couldn't! How can you ever forgive me for doubting you? I must have been out of my mind these past weeks, even to conceive that you'd turn on me. But in my heart, darling, I *knew* you would never do such an awful thing. We love each other too much for that . . ."

This was no outsider, his heart told him. This was Annie. His loyal, loving Annie, bless her! So emotional. So vulnerable. Always trying to do the right thing, by her lights. Annie felt things too deeply, that had always been her problem. But in the crunch, she came through.

As for her talk of leaving, despite the evidence of open suitcases and empty drawers, Seth refused to panic. Considering his behavior the past weeks, some such reaction was inevitable. Annie could be a bit quick on the emotional trigger, and most likely this was her way of retaliating for the hooker in L.A. That, Seth believed, must have been the final straw. Another man would have kept his mouth shut. Whoever said that honesty was the best policy had never been married to a sensitive woman. Seth conceded he had a lot to make up for.

Carefully, he lifted the suitcase off the bed. Within, Margot's diamantine tiara glittered in its box. Ah, Tosca! Seth was suddenly conscious of life imitating art. For Annie was a replica of her heroine: passionate, jealous, given to outbursts of temperament. Yet withal, profoundly loyal and loving.

He sat down and gently took her hands in his. Such sweet hands. *Dolci mani.* The poignant aria came to mind, that sublime moment when Mario Cavaradossi, heart overflowing with love and gratitude, takes the hands of the woman who has killed for him. Annie would know what was in Seth's heart and be moved.

"*O dolci mani* . . ." He smiled and brought her hands to his lips.

"Stop!" Annie broke from his grasp with an angry hiss. "Don't you touch me!"

He gaped at her in astonishment. Her eyes were blazing, her voice angry yet controlled.

"When Mario said that to Tosca"—she spat out the words—"her hands were covered with blood. As mine will be! As yours will be too! No, I couldn't turn you in, Seth. I didn't have the heart, or maybe the guts. But I can't go on living with you either, as though none of this had happened. It's hard enough to live with myself these days! Because when I kept faith with you, I betrayed innocent people, and that's unforgivable." She recoiled in a shudder of disgust.

"I loathe myself and I'd hate myself even more if I stayed on. Do you think I can live off your blood money? Go about my lessons, buy clothes, have fancy lunches on the proceeds of what you are doing? Never! I won't be bought, Seth. Even this apartment belongs to Medi-Tekk!"

She walked over to the window and looked out on the street below.

"I remember when Max died, and you said something about his being a low-rise cat in a high-rise building. Well, so are you, Seth. A low-rise cat! I had thought you were a bigger man, but I was wrong. You're living here under false pretenses, accepting honors that you have no right to claim. And I don't flatter myself that I'm any better. We're two cheap people who are doing terrible things. But this is where I get off. I couldn't spend another night in this place"—her voice dropped—"or another night with you as things stand. And if I have to go back to slinging hamburgers at a lunch counter, I'll do it, rather than be beholden to you. And now, if you'll do me the courtesy of getting out of my way, I'd like to finish packing."

At present, argument was useless, Seth perceived. It would only aggravate matters. Annie was sore as hell.

Quietly, he settled into a chair by her writing desk and watched as she packed with a grim determination. No books, no records, he observed. And just enough gear for two or three weeks away. By then, the experiments would already be underway. Once they were completed, her rebellion too would be at an end.

For whatever the outcome, Seth knew she'd be back. If his tests proved successful, she'd leap into his arms, penitent for every having doubted him. And if they weren't? Seth forced himself to consider the worst possible scenario. Even then, he could still count on Annie to stand by him. He gave her three weeks.

Their love aside, she was not a loner by nature. He couldn't picture her living without affection and intimacy, without the elaborate support system he had provided for her. What would she do in the cold world, alone? Unless . . .

Unless! A knife twisted in his innards. Unless she had a lover waiting somewhere. Three weeks wasn't much, but it was quite long enough for a romantic reunion in the south of France. Maybe Annie had already found her consolation.

The moment she left the room, he whipped open the drawer of the escritoire. Her passport was still there, thank God! Traveler's checks, too. She wasn't going very far, but even so, that was no guarantee. One needn't cross the Atlantic to find a trysting place.

A few minutes later she returned with an armful of opera scores and began wedging them into corners of the suitcase.

"I want to know, Annie"—his throat was so constricted he could barely speak—"if there's somebody else . . ."

"Is that what you think?" She turned around to scrutinize him with an expression more puzzled than angry. Then with arms folded, she met his eyes.

"Do you want to know what happened last summer? Is that it? All you had to do was ask and I would have told you. Well, your guess was right, Seth. I had an affair. A fling, it would be fairer to say. Someone I was fond of . . . we spent about three weeks together, and I haven't seen or heard from him since. Do you want to know who, Seth?"

Seth shook his head, no. Bad enough to picture his wife lying in another man's arms. No, he didn't care to put a name to that body.

"I didn't love him," she whispered. "I want you to understand that. He has nothing to do with my leaving. On long lonely nights, remember—I've never loved anyone but you."

She paused, eyes brimming with tears, and he sensed there was something else she wanted to tell him. Some secret, some unbearable intimacy.

Instead, she snapped the suitcase shut and rang for a cab.

"I'll be staying at Madame Natasha's until I find a place of my own. Good-bye, Seth."

He sat where she left him, in the little chair by the escritoire until the room grew pitch dark. Then he lay down on the bed, with a pounding headache.

At least, there was no one else. He believed her. Annie didn't lie. Now it was a question of strategy. What would be the best way to handle her?

He had a sense of déjà vu, and as he lay there the past came flooding back.

Of course! They had been through all this before, years ago in Boston, when Annie had refused his proposal. Then as now, she had some fancy notion of going it alone. They had said good-bye forever, as he recalled.

But Seth had waited, patiently, silently. Never showing his hand, never giving in to the dull ache of his loneliness. And it had paid off handsomely. Annie had come around.

She would do so again, if he played his cards right. No scenes, no recriminations, just the quiet passage of time. God knows they loved each other. He missed her already, even though these last few months had been hell on earth. In a lot of ways, he needed her.

But if Seth Peterson was certain of anything in this world, it was that her need for him was even greater.

Oh yes. She'd be back.

🌸

If Dom Tarantino's office had lost its flyblown frowsiness of late, if the magazines were now replaced on a weekly basis and the aspidistra had begun to show signs of life, the little lawyer had Vi Hagerty to thank. She was practically running the place.

"When are you going to join the twentieth century," she used to twit him, "and stop wasting your time on paperwork? All that stuff can be computerized. Letters, leases, wills, the everyday crap. You could save yourself a hunk in secretarial costs."

"Who understands computers?" He shrugged with Latin resignation.

"Me," she said. "Listen, bud. You need someone to send out bills. I bet you're as lousy at collecting from your other clients as you are with me. Let me do it for you to help pay my fees."

So he rented a computer and she began coming in. Within a month, she had a salaried job. For the first time in years, Dom found his books in order, his taxes promptly filed, even his plants watered regularly. For Vi, it was more a stopgap than a true career, but it paid the rent. Moreover, the stream of clients fascinated her with their tales of marriages on the rocks, vengeful landlords, feuding neighbors, petty crime.

But the case closest to her heart was her own.

Noonie's preference would be polled at the custody hearing next month, Dom assured her. It would probably be the deciding factor.

"Bring him in," Dom urged her, "and I'll coach him. Otherwise, how do you know what he'll say?"

"I don't." Vi gritted her teeth. "But I'm not going to pressure him. If all goes well and I get on my feet again, I think he'll come through for me. After all, Noonie and I go way back, and he's a good kid. But Jesus, he's growing into such a worry wart. Anyhow, another couple of weeks will tell the tale and I don't want anyone putting words in his mouth."

"You can be damn sure his father has no such scruples."

Vi shook her head thoughtfully.

"I wish I knew what was right," she said finally, for some of Annie Petersen's misgivings had rubbed off. "Maybe he'd be better off with his father. Especially if this cure shit doesn't work. Hell, why should I cripple his life as well as mine? Oh, God . . . I don't know." She sighed. "Maybe I'm being selfish in fighting it so hard."

※

"Where's Annie?" Margot asked, when Seth turned up at a dinner party unaccompanied and looking woebegone.

Across the room, Gerald caught her eye with a subtle, yet vehemently negative headshake. *Trouble in paradise*, she took that to mean. *Inquire no further.*

Without waiting for Seth's reply, she took his arm and steered him over to the most attractive woman in the room.

"Do me a favor, lamb, and be utterly charming to Diana. She just arrived from England and doesn't know a soul in New York."

Throughout dinner, Margot kept Seth in her sight lines. On the surface all was well. He ate, he drank (rather more than usual, she noted, but without visible effect), he flirted dutifully with the ravishing Diana; yet there was about him a remote, mechanical quality. He reminded Margot of the life-size automata in Disneyland—clever creations that fooled the eye, aping humanity to an astonishing T, yet powered only by wires and silicon chips. A triumph of technology.

At the far end of the table, Gerald too was watching Seth with the anxious eyes of a prison warden guarding an important prisoner. Twice during the meal, Margot saw her husband furtively swallow his blood-pressure pills. There were days when she wondered if he would even make it to the clinical trials.

"We're close to the grand finale," he had said only this morning, yet the stress was already taking its toll. The moment the experiments were complete, Margot swore, they would all escape. Enjoy a long, luxurious rest in St. Thomas. Annie, too, if she could be found.

While coffee was being served, Seth came over to her with a polite apology. If Margot didn't mind, he was leaving early. A bit under the weather, as he put it.

"Of course not, darling." She pecked him on the cheek, curious if he had arranged a rendezvous with Diana. But he left alone, in a dour mood, and Diana found instant consolation with another guest.

"What's the problem with the Petersens?" she asked Gerald as soon as the guests were gone. "I've been trying to reach Annie all week."

Gerald slumped into a chair, wearily massaging the bridge of his nose.

"She moved in with her music teacher."

"Really!" Margot was surprised and hurt. "She could have come here, stayed with me."

Gerald shifted uncomfortably in the chair.

"Your friend has a bug up her ass, to put it crudely," he said with an air of reluctance. "Somehow, Annie got this crazy notion we're up to some kind of mischief at the lab. I don't want to trouble you with the details, but the fact is, she's been putting the screws on Seth. Wants us to stop the trials . . ."

"And that's why she left him?" Margot was incredulous.

Gerald nodded. "Emotional blackmail. I must say, I'm very disappointed in her. We've always treated the Petersens handsomely. Why, you couldn't do enough for her, Margot! The problem is, if Annie starts sounding off in the wrong places, she could cause a good deal of embarrassment. Havoc, even."

"She wouldn't," Margot said quickly. "She'd never do anything to hurt Seth. Annie will stand fast and true."

"That's what he keeps saying, too. That she's reliable, there's no cause for alarm. Seth's the one I'm concerned about these days. He's coiled tighter than a watch spring. I practically had to drag him here tonight, but I didn't want him staying home alone, brooding. Forgive me, darling." He sighed. "I didn't mean to spread gloom. Let's talk about pleasanter things, shall we? That was a very good dinner party of yours, by the way."

"Wasn't it!" She smiled gratefully. "Fun people. And didn't Diana Ritchie look incredible!"

"Not half as lovely as you, darling."

"Mirror, mirror on the wall." She giggled.

"I mean it." He rose and took her face in his hands. "I was the luckiest man in the room tonight. The luckiest man in the world. Did I ever tell you, Margot, that I love you very, very much?"

"Not since this morning." She kissed him. "Now let's go to bed."

They made gentle love that night, and later as Margot lay beside him in the darkness, she brushed aside a silent stream of tears.

Mirror, mirror . . . These past years, he had come to be her mirror, shining back upon her with reflected light. She tried to imagine what her life would be after Gerald was gone. His love had illuminated her existence, and when he died, that image of herself—radiant and beautiful—would be extinguished forever. The darkness would descend. One could almost understand why aging couples made death pacts. Briefly, she cursed Annie for having caused Gerald such aggravation, then as promptly forgave her.

For Annie, she perceived, was as intricately bound to Seth as she herself was to Gerald. Margot never doubted her friend would stand by Seth to the end. She and Annie were, after all, sisters under the skin. Two women who accepted the one ineluctable truth.

Life held no meaning, no purpose, no prospect of joy, unless you shared it with the man you loved.

For days, Annie scarcely left the tiny back bedroom that Madame Natasha had cleared for her at the studio. She couldn't face the inevitable questions. Everyone would want to know what had happened. What could she say—that Seth was playing dice with human lives? She could hardly bear to think about their separation, let alone talk about it. Sometimes, she would hear the phone ringing in the next room and Madame's crisp statement that Annie was "unavailable." Phrased that way, it sounded as though she were a movie star being reclusive, rather than a fugitive from everyone she loved.

Thrice daily, the maid brought meals on a tray, and through the open door Annie often caught a snatch of vocalizing from the studio. Madame was giving lessons. The sound came from another world.

Each morning she woke dazed and disoriented, instinctively reaching for Seth. Then came the shock of consciousness. Of loss. For hours, she would lie there in the narrow bed, with tender breasts and tingling nipples, and fight despair. Pregnant she was, with or without a doctor's confirmation.

But if she knew her own body, she didn't know her own mind.

Almost everything in her life—but above all, wanting children—had been predicated on her marriage to Seth. She had hungered for not merely children, but family. Old-fashioned conventional happy family, like the ones in the TV commercials. Was that such a dream?

For admirable as so many single mothers were (Vi Hagerty came to mind), Annie didn't know if she was equal to the struggle. She had promised herself that her own children would have the best of everything. Love. Security. And a father they could look up to.

But who could look up to Seth, after what he'd done?

And then there was the question of money. Where would she live? What kind of job could she get? For she didn't kid herself about making a living out of music—not with a baby to support. A clerk in a record store was more like it. And so good-bye to all her dreams.

Maybe she should have an abortion. Say nothing to Seth and just go ahead with it. The freedom tempted her, the thought repelled her. There had been enough playing fast and loose with life already, and she might never become pregnant again. And it was Seth's child, too. In all fairness he should have some say in the matter.

Whatever decision she came to would have to be arrived at within the month, for time was running out.

The question wracked her without letup. In one sense, Seth had every right to know. Yet in another, Annie felt her obligation to him had ended. All debts were paid in full that moment when she walked out of the Palm Court with his secret still intact. She had saved his skin. Beyond that, their marriage vows had expired.

Sometimes she cried. Sometimes she slept. Mostly she wished that the world would go away and she might stay hidden in this little room forever.

Early on the fourth morning of her self-imprisonment, Madame Natasha burst into the room unannounced.

"Enough!" She threw open the heavy rep curtains and pulled back the blankets with a vigorous yank. Annie blinked in the light.

"Enough," Madame said. "Enough tears! Enough whining and pining. It's bad for the voice, don't you know? But anger, on the other hand . . ." Annie stared at her in horror. How insensitive could one be? But Madame babbled on. "Yes, anger. Now, that's a constructive emotion. Joan Sutherland sings like an angel when she's hopping mad. Wouldn't be surprised if she picks fights on purpose, just to produce that extra depth of tone. Whereas Nilsson usually manages to sound her best when she's under the weather. She likes the challenge, you know. For that matter, Marjorie Lawrence sang Isolde at the Met sitting in a wheelchair. So what's your excuse? Up . . . up."

With that, she dived into Annie's suitcase and began flinging garments on the bed: underwear, a pair of slacks, a cotton T-shirt. "Now, what have we here!" She riffled through the scores. "Good good good. We do some Mascagni this morning, eh? Be in the studio at eight o'clock sharp. You're scheduled for a lesson this morning, or did you forget?"

A half hour later the two women were hard at work, and had Madame accepted that sort of behavior, Annie would have smothered her in a grateful hug.

Thank you, she wanted to say, for restoring my sanity.

But instead, she offered a heated defense about her placement of head tones. All in all, it was a satisfying morning, and when they broke for lunch, Annie felt, for the first time in days, that she was ready to face the real world.

"Were there any calls for me while I was . . . umm, hiding out?"

"Ring ring ring," Madame grumbled. "You'd think I had nothing to do but answer the phone. Yes yes . . . there were calls."

She handed Annie a list. Margot repeatedly; Ari; Lainie; her mother (Oh, God—Annie winced—how was she going to talk her way out of this one?); her sister, Linda (at her mother's instigation, no doubt); half a dozen miscellaneous people. But nothing, she was quick to note, from Seth.

Which was just as well. She didn't want to see or speak to him.

"Do me a favor, Madame." She lifted her eyes from the lined yellow pad. "Let me be 'unavailable' for just a few days more. Then I promise to get out of your hair."

"As you wish, my dear, although you're welcome to stay as long as you like, on one condition."

"Which is?"

"You must work all the time you are here. You have a career to think about."

Annie smiled and cleared away the table.

"In that case, Madame, why are we sitting around here, wasting precious time?"

Madame never asked about the origins of Annie's quarrel with Seth, whether out of tact or a lack of curiosity. The latter, Annie decided, for in Madame's scale of values, experience and emotions existed for one purpose only: to be transmuted into music.

The true drama of life took place on the stage. Everything else— love, grief, rapture, death—was merely the raw material of art.

Even life's comic aspects existed to serve a function.

In the studio one morning she called a break and then rang for the maid.

"Bring us tea and cakes, Rose," came the imperial command.

A few minutes later the maid returned with a trolley full of pastries.

"Pie, Madame?" the girl asked.

"Yes, Rose."

At which point the maid picked up a slice of cream pie and lobbed it smack into Madame's face.

Annie gasped, caught her breath, burst out laughing.

"And there"—Madame Natasha was mopping the goo off her face—"you have the secret of all comedy. Human discomfiture. Now, my dear, shall we discuss the *opera buffa* of Rossini?"

Had Madame ever married, Annie wondered. The double-barreled name suggested a matrimonial fling, but the old woman, whose talk was otherwise larded with anecdotal memories, never mentioned a Monsieur Liadoff or Mr. Grey, as the case might be.

To pose a direct question seemed a breach of courtesy, for Madame had certainly respected Annie's own privacy. Yet she couldn't resist the urge to find out. Over lunch one day, she voiced her inquiry in a devious manner.

"Which is your family name, Madame? Is it Liadoff or Grey?"

"Grey was my father's name, and Liadoff my mother's. It is also the name of a thoroughly minor Russian composer, my uncle Anatol, as it happened. You never heard of him, did you?"

Annie shook her head no.

"Not surprising. You see, my uncle is chiefly remembered for a failure of sorts. He was commissioned to write a ballet score, was unable to meet the deadline, and as a result the job was turned over to another composer. The young man's name was Igor Stravinsky. The ballet was *The Firebird*. As you know, it made Stravinsky's reputation throughout the world. And my uncle went down in musical history as a footnote in a greater man's biography. Yet it's a name I'm proud to bear. You understand why, don't you, Annie?"

Clearly the tale was meant to be illustrative, but for a while Annie missed what Madame was trying to convey. When the perception came, she smiled. "You're saying, it's better to go down in the history of music even as a paltry footnote than not to figure in it at all."

"Only a handful can ever achieve what the world calls success, Annie," Madame said softly, "let alone true greatness. We must all make the effort, of course. To strive is our bounden duty. We owe it not only to ourselves and our teachers, but to music. Yet you could go to any conservatory, any international competition and hear superb young artists by the score. It's a lottery. A few will win. Most will not. After all, for every Stravinsky, there are a hundred Liadoffs, for every Horowitz, a thousand gifted pianists diligently practicing their scales. But that doesn't make them losers, Annie. I daresay, without them there would be no Horowitzes, because they create the environment in which the truly great artist can flourish."

"But nobody sets out to be a background figure," Annie protested.

"Your view is too narrow, my dear. These are dedicated musicians, honorable artists with a vital role to play. They bring great music to those who might never have known it. They raise the standards in provincial towns. They serve art in a hundred different capacities. After all, someone has to sing the lesser roles in operas, hold down the rank-and-file orchestral posts, or else there'd be no operas, no symphonies. Like me, many of them teach. But they are all of them part of a great tradition."

"I see." Annie nodded thoughtfully. Yet Madame's wisdom had

hit a discordant note. Art for art's sake, her coach was saying. All
other rewards pale by comparison. But if fame and broad acceptance mattered so very little, then she might as well have stayed in
Galveston. In which case she would still be happy. Still be living
with Seth.

She was pondering this when the phone rang in the next room.
Madame waddled off to answer it. Through the open door, Annie
could hear an astonished squeal, a sharp intake of breath, and then a
stream of rapid chatter.

"It's for you, Annie." Madame Natasha stood on the threshold,
brandishing the receiver. "It's important."

Annie waved a vehement no. "If it's my husband . . ." she began.

"It's not your husband. It's Polo von Brüning. And Annie"—she
burst into a smile—"he's offering you the chance of a lifetime."

❧

"Annie?"

Seth came home that night to be struck with an acute sense of her
presence. "Annie, are you here?"

He raced through the rooms, calling her name, but the only
answer was the hollow echo of his voice. Yet she had been there, he
was sure. A hint of her perfume lingered in the air, sweet and
evocative.

In the bedroom, he opened her closet door to seek confirmation,
uncovering a fresh patch of naked hangers.

Yes, Annie had come, ransacked her wardrobe and left.

He looked around the room for a note, a scribbled line or two.
Some word. Any word. That she was still angry with him. Or was
sorry to have missed him. Or simply that she had been here. The
message hardly mattered; all he asked for was a sign, some scant
acknowledgment that Annie was aware of his separate existence, that
he still figured in her life.

The top drawer of her escritoire protruded a fraction of an inch,
as if opened and hastily shut.

Fear clutched at his heart. Trembling, he pulled the drawer out
and emptied the contents on the bed.

Gone! He riffled through the clutter of bankbooks and receipts
and correspondence with increasing panic. Her passport was gone,
along with the supply of traveler's checks.

348

For the first time since she walked out the door, Seth was gripped with a sense of finality. The certain knowledge of a terrible, irrevocable loss.

"Don't go, Annie."

He buried his head in her pillow, desperate to summon up the warmth of her body, the softness of her touch. But the crisp linen had been washed and ironed clean of all memory.

"Don't go, Annie," he murmured once again into dead air.

Only the ticking of a clock broke the silence.

Too late, Seth—the sound mocked him. Too late.

"I was born for this."

Annie closed her score, opened the blind and peered out the window into the new dawn. Through breaks in the cloud cover, the English countryside played hide and seek, rolling and unfamiliar.

The red-eye special, Seth called these night-into-day flights and prided himself on his capacity to hit the ground running.

Well, so would she.

Less than twenty-four hours had passed since Polo's call.

"Catch the early evening flight," he instructed, "and I'll have a car waiting for you at Heathrow tomorrow morning."

"But ... but ..."

But essentially there were no buts, for as Madame had said, she had indeed been given the chance of a lifetime. And to think, Annie shook her head in wonder, that she owed this opportunity to the woman Polo insisted on calling "some damfool love-sick soprano."

The preceding winter, the sublime Irina Kaminskaya had defected to the West in a blaze of publicity. Then yesterday, she defected a second time, returning to the U.S.S.R.

"She missed her Russian lover. Can you imagine such idiocy?" Polo had laughed. But he was more outraged than amused, this unforeseen departure having taken place a scant week before she was scheduled to sing Tosca at the Royal Opera House in Covent Garden.

It was a benefit, Polo had said, a gala production separate from the regular series. He had assembled a magnificent cast.

"And you want me to substitute!" Annie's heart leapt.

"In truth, *ma chère*, you were one of four choices . . ."

"And the other three were unavailable, right?"

"You will be wonderful," Polo affirmed. "If I didn't believe so, I would cancel the performance. Now be on that seven o'clock flight. By the way, how do you want to be billed on the programme?"

Annie thought a moment, then told him.

Five hours later, Madame was seeing her off at Kennedy.

"I wish you'd come with me," Annie begged for the tenth time, but Madame said it was out of the question.

"However, my dear, on Thursday next at the appropriate hour, I shall light a candle for you at the Church of St. Nicholas."

"Well, don't forget the time difference." Annie smiled wanly, then admitted: "I'm very scared."

"Of course you're scared." Madame gave a vigorous nod. "It's permissible to be frightened. But use your fear, Annie. Make a note of how you feel, then use that emotion when you're Tosca, picking up the knife. And one more piece of advice. In the second act . . ."

"Yes?"

"Be sure to wear comfortable shoes."

"Oh, Madame!" Annie didn't know whether to laugh or cry. Instead, she squashed the woman in a hug. "You are impossible."

That was last night, but she wasn't scared now as the aircraft descended into Heathrow. Keyed up, yes, but confident too. The role was in her head and in her heart. In her bones.

From beneath her seat, she retrieved the leather case containing the Jeritza tiara—too precious a cargo to be consigned to other hands.

Twenty minutes later she had cleared customs and was looking about the terminal for her driver. Would Polo himself be meeting her at this ungodly hour? Then she spotted a young man carrying a cardboard sign.

ANTONIA SAYRE.

Why, that's me, she realized with a shock. A chauffeured Daimler drove her into London along with a stream of commuters.

At the Dorchester, there was a huge bouquet of red roses from Polo, accompanied by a message announcing a ten o'clock rehearsal. Everything felt so strange, so glamorous. It had taken a conscious effort to fight down so many years of habit and sign herself Antonia Sayre. After all this time, her old name sounded as exotic as a new one.

Mrs. Seth Petersen had ceased to exist.

⚜

"Just called to say hello." Ward Daniels scrupulously managed to muffle any anxious overtones. "How're you doing, Vi?"

"Just great," came the answer. "You know, I go into the clinic next Monday, would you believe!"

"Yeah, it's been a long haul."

"You telling me!" She gave a nervous laugh. "I started packing a suitcase this morning, put in all that sexy underwear I bought for old Sherm. I'm only going to be there a few days, all it is is a spinal injection. But what the hell . . . I figured I may as well wear all that Fredericks of Hollywood stuff and give the docs a cheap thrill. 'Cause God knows if any other guys are gonna' get to see me in my drawers."

"Oh, I don't know," he replied. Her original optimism had vanished, he noted with some surprise. Perhaps the long wait had worn her down. Now it was Ward, who had always cautioned her against crazy hopes, who found himself on the opposite side of the argument.

"My bet is, you'll be back at the singles bars in a couple of weeks, knocking 'em dead."

"Picking 'em up and laying 'em down." She laughed.

"Vi Hagerty . . . the Jersey Jezebel, the Bloomfield Beauty."

"Ouch!" She groaned. "What do you call that shit . . . illiteration?"

"Something like that," he said. "I've been subjected to bad influences lately."

"Who . . . your Mr. Guthrie?"

"Lord to you, toots."

"Yeah, it's gonna be real rough on you, making all that bread."

"I'll try not to suffer too much."

"Well, send me a postcard from Tahiti."

"I'll call you," he said. "Or you call me, just as soon as it's over. In the meanwhile, lots of love—"He stopped himself short. "Well, you know what I mean, lots of luck."

He hung up the phone.

He checked the clock. It was still early. Maybe he'd go down to Moriarty's, have a few drinks and find himself some cute little bimbo. He hadn't had his ashes hauled since his return from Alaska. Except he wasn't in the mood. Depressed, that's what.

351

Instead he pulled out his typewriter and began pecking away.

THE LIFE OF ST. STRONE FUCKING GUTHRIE
AS TOLD TO WARD DANIELS.

Born in a manger in the slums of Glasgow, this charming cherub was the son of a Scottish virgin of humble origins. At his birth, a star glowed brightly in the East, summoning the wise men. Ox and ass before him bowed.

Ward tore the sheet out of the typewriter, crumpled it and tossed it in the wastebasket.

There was only one ass that was doing the bowing, and his name was Ward Daniels.

PART
FOUR

I

"TOY TOY TOY."

Polo came to her dressing room fifteen minutes before curtain time to wish her good luck in traditional operatic fashion. Then he brushed her cheek with his lips.

"You look magnificent. Are you nervous? Don't be. Sing half as well as you did at yesterday's dress, and it will be a triumph."

With a final assurance of his total support from the orchestra pit, he left her to finish her preparations.

Behind her was the most strenuous week of her life. She had lost track of the hours involved. Music rehearsals. Stage rehearsals. Costume fittings. Publicity photos. The myriad physical details of a major opera production. In the fury of work, all the minor discomforts of early pregnancy now vanished, so intense was her concentration.

And then there were the bits of business, as Margot called them. How to get from here to there in the requisite number of bars. What to do with your hands. Your shawl. Your fan. In the second act did you sing "Vissi d'arte" lying flat on the floor (as Jeritza did)? or did you collapse onto a couch? or stand proudly at stage center?

"I'm going to sing it standing," she informed the director, Thorn Bradshaw, at the first rehearsal. "My Tosca isn't going to cringe before anybody."

Thorn, thank God, was English. One could communicate with him in terms other than musical, which was more than could be said

355

of her co-stars. Her lover, Mario, was the pride of the Vienna Staatsoper, while the villainous Scarpia was sung by a monosyllabic Dane.

"Crazy," she said to Polo. "Here we are, a Yank, a Dane and an Austrian doing Italian opera in London."

"And don't forget me," Polo added.

Annie laughed. "Whatever you are."

When she arrived in London, she had been both doubtful and curious about what her relation with Polo would be. In her mind, their affair belonged to a different segment of her life. Perhaps in his too, for the situation had yet to arise. He occasionally appeared with an exquisite English girl in tow. Yet the question of future love-making hung in the air, unresolved.

"We shall leave all other matters for after, eh?" Polo suggested, their first day together. "I want you to preserve all your energy and drive for the performance. So train like an athlete, and care for yourself like a hypochondriac. Above all, protect the voice." He spoke as though her voice weren't an integral part of Annie, but a separate and very valuable commodity temporarily entrusted to her care.

Accordingly, she exercised, vocalized, rehearsed, ate and went to bed early, while the glitter of London swirled around her. It was a city she and Seth had planned to visit together, but thus far all she had seen of it were the rehearsal rooms and her hotel.

She was living, it struck her, like a nun, eschewing all worldly pleasures for the present. In her leisure hours she rested, hardly daring to venture forth. God forbid she pick up a head cold in some crowded theater or shop. A mere sore throat could ruin her one big chance. One by one, a dozen remedies began collecting on the bathroom shelf, in a blend of superstition and insurance.

"Sing *mezza voce*," Polo had instructed at the first rehearsal. Half voice. Save the real power for the performance. And she had done so, husbanding her talents like a miser until yesterday at the dress rehearsal.

"I need this," she told Polo, and she had let loose in a glorious affirmation that the beauty and the strength were all there.

Now, through the dressing room door, she heard the orchestra sound the three bold opening notes.

* * *

[*Infidelities*]

TOSCA, *An opera in three acts by Giacomo Puccini*

A C T I: *The Church of Sant' Andrea della Valle in Rome. Angelotti, a political fugitive, is hiding from the police, when the artist Mario Cavaradossi enters the church. Cavaradossi is painting a fresco, depicting a blue-eyed worshiper, but puts down his brush to sing instead of his love for the beautiful Tosca. Angelotti emerges to beseech his help.*

"Your cue," Thorn Bradshaw murmured.
"Mario," Annie sang out from the wings. "Mario! Mario!"

At the sound of Tosca's voice, Angelotti conceals himself once more.

"Mario!" Annie sang out once more.
"There you go!" Thorn gave her a gentle push.
Annie stepped onto the stage, momentarily dazzled by the glare of the spotlight. From the pitchy darkness of the house, there came a buzz, a stir of curiosity from the audience. She could sense the craning of necks, the sharp refocusing of eyes.
Who was she, these unseen thousands wondered? Who was this obscure American soprano, suddenly plucked out of anonymity and thrust into the limelight?
But in that moment, Annie knew. She was Tosca. The spirit of the scene, the emotional fire of the music infused every atom of her being. She was Tosca, ragingly jealous, suspecting the man she adored beyond all reason of infidelity and lies.
She advanced across the stage to Mario, eyes blazing.
Whose voice had she heard? Tosca burst out. Whose face adorned the painting? Another woman!
Yes! Mario betraying her with an unknown beauty.
Seth! She relived the emotion. Seth and Chandra.
No matter that her jealousy was unfounded. Suddenly, the anger, the misery in her voice spoke of all that she had suffered.
"*Colei!*" Tosca's anguish poured out unfettered. "Confess."

Mario calms her fears, and the two reconcile in a melting love duet. As Tosca leaves, she looks forward to a night of love at their cottage in the country.

"Well done." Thorn grasped her hands while the makeup woman

357

dabbed on a fresh layer of powder and the dresser fussed with her shawl.

A few feet away, Bengt Arnold was adjusting a wig over his fair hair. Dressed in black from head to toe, the great Danish baritone suggested a truly sinister figure. He turned to give Annie a thumbs-up sign and Annie nodded back in breathless agreement. Yes, it was going marvelously, beyond her own expectations.

Mario tells Angelotti to hide in his cottage, then leaves. Scarpia, the Roman police chief, enters, seeking the fugitive. Finding evidence of Mario's complicity, he exults. He plots to destroy Mario and then possess Tosca, who has inflamed him. Tosca returns, seeking her lover.

This time Annie didn't have to be nudged.

Scarpia greets her, singing "Divina Tosca."

"Divina Tosca." Bengt stepped forward. At the touch of his hands, she recoiled, then cleansed herself by making the sign of the cross. For this black-suited figure repelled her. He was loathsome, reeking of the torture chamber.

Scarpia produces a fan left behind by Angelotti's sister and ignites Tosca's jealousy. As the church fills with worshipers, Scarpia kneels to pray, but cannot. "Ah Tosca," he sings, "you make me forget my god."

"Didn't I tell you?" Polo burst into her dressing room as she was changing for the second act. "Didn't I predict you'd be a great Tosca? A Tosca for the ages, *cara mia*. Already, the audience is going wild. Now let me look at you, *ma chère*. Turn around. Yes, magnificent!"

The costume was oppressively heavy, a sumptuous red-velvet gown, full-skirted with an embroidered train. Arms and throat glittered with jewelry. And encircling the dark luxuriousness of her high-piled hair, the Jeritza tiara radiated sparks of white light.

"Now," Polo breathed, "about the 'Vissi d'arte' "—for they had previously differed about the approach to Tosca's greatest aria— "take it as you feel it, *ma chère*, and I promise to follow. All I ask is that you be superb." He kissed her hand and returned to the pit.

[*Infidelities*]

* * *

A c t I I. *Scarpia's apartment in the Palazzo Farnese. Scarpia is dining alone. Through the window he hears Tosca singing in another part of the palace. Mario Cavaradossi is brought in. Scarpia demands to know the whereabouts of Angelotti, but Mario defies him. Tosca arrives as her lover is led away to be tortured. Tosca and Scarpia are alone. Suddenly, she hears Mario's scream.*

At the sound of the first scream, Annie reared back in horror.

Scarpia promises to stop the torture if Tosca will reveal Angelotti's hiding place.

What to do? Annie broke from Scarpia's grasp in horror. He was asking her to make an impossible choice—to decide who would live and who would die. There was no time . . . no time!

With a word she could spare her beloved Mario. Yet that same word would condemn Angelotti to death. Ah . . . the pitiful Angelotti. He was an innocent man. He had done her no harm. But if they caught him, they would torture him. Till his eyes bulged out of their sockets. Till he achieved the limits of pain. A vision of hell. And then he would die.

Vi!

The parallel was stunning. The image, inescapable. And as she sang, her inner agony burst through her voice. She couldn't do it! Couldn't make such a judgment! Yet each bar of the music pushed her closer to the brink of decision. God help her! Choose she must.

She advanced on Scarpia, fists clenched.

"*Assassino!*" she cursed him.

And then, with a strangled sob, Tosca—decent, honorable Tosca —destroyed an innocent life in the name of love.

Tosca betrays Angelotti and wins Mario's release. But before the lovers can depart, Mario once more taunts Scarpia. Now Mario himself is sentenced to death. Tosca begs for mercy. Scarpia says only she can save him.

"*Cuanto?*" Annie snarled. How much?

"*Cuanto?*" Scarpia smiled his urbane smile and poured some wine. "*Il prezzo!*"

The price is Tosca's submission to Scarpia that very night. Despairing, she cries out to heaven. "Vissi d'arte."

"*Vissi d'arte,*" Annie began with sheerest pianissimo, her voice pure and innocent as a child's. "*Vissi d'amore.*"

"I lived for art," Tosca's credo began. "I lived for love."

In her life she had injured no one. She had offered her music to the skies, given her jewels to the Madonna, her prayers to heaven.

"*Perchè, signor?*" she asked bewildered. *Why, oh Lord! Why me?*

Annie moved through the long demanding aria in a single unbroken crescendo, a relentless intensifying of volume and power, and now as she reached the music's climax, she drew herself up and called upon the deepest reserves of her voice.

"*Perchè*"—the music rolled out in a vibrant wave of sound to the farthest corner of the immense house—"*perchè me ne remuneri così?*"

And this . . . is how you reward me!

For several seconds, an awed hush obtained as she stood unmoving, lost to the world. Then the audience burst into rapturous applause. On the podium, Polo tapped his baton, wanting to maintain the dramatic impetus, but the ovation had brought the performance to a halt. With a smile, he laid down his baton and joined the applause.

Yet Annie hardly heard. For somewhere during that aria, she had crossed the line from art into life.

And this—Seth had said—is how you reward me.

But the words were hers now, the emotion wrung from the depth of her heart. Now she knew what must be done.

Across the stage, Scarpia was at his desk, writing the safe-conduct that would ensure their passage abroad. But first, he said, there must be a mock execution. As he gave orders, Annie prowled about the stage like a restless animal, while in the orchestra muted violins foretold disaster.

He must be destroyed. There was no other way out. He must be stopped, this beast, this murderer reeking of carnage and death.

In silence, she moved to the table where Scarpia's unfinished meal still lay. Reflexively, her fingers closed about the knife. She tightened her grip on the handle until her knuckles ached.

Scarpia was advancing, arms outstretched in a vile embrace.

"*Questo*"—with full force, Annie plunged the knife into his chest—
"*e il bacio di Tosca.*"

"This," she cried, "is the kiss of Tosca."

With a shout, he fell to the ground, pleading for mercy. But there
could be no mercy for his cruelty, no pity for his crime. Again and
again Annie stabbed him until her arm ached in the socket.

Bengt Arnold expelled a gasp of air. Stage knife or no, the ve-
hemence of her assault had knocked the wind out of him. From the
prompter's box came a long low *sssst*, while Polo looked up in alarm.
By tradition, Tosca was to have stabbed her attacker but once.

Annie stood over his twitching body and cursed.

"*Muori.*" Her voice trembled with hate. "*Muori.*"

Die. Die. Die.

*Scarpia is dead. Tosca washes her fingers, combs her hair, then
looks for the safe-conduct. It is in Scarpia's hands. She takes it,
then places a candle at his head, another by his left hand, and a
crucifix across his breast. "E avanti lui tremava tutta Roma"—
And before him, all Rome trembled. She gathers her cloak and
departs.*

Annie knew what was called for. The stage directions were ex-
plicit on this point. Singers had followed them for nearly a hundred
years. She herself had seen the ritual a dozen times.

Yet she could not, *could not* tear herself away from the body
at her feet. For it was Seth.

The discovery came with the force of revelation.

Always, she had believed Seth to be Mario, a creature of air and
lightness and love. A man worthy of her sacrifice, her love and fidelity. Only now did she know him for what he was.

Seth was the beast. Seth, the murderer, the man who cohabited
with evil. Seth was her Scarpia.

Excitement streaked through the house like an electrical current.
There was an awareness of tradition being flouted. The audience
waited, suspending breath and judgment.

"Candles," mouthed the prompter, "fetch the candles." But Annie
was deaf to instruction. She was rooted to the spot. Trancelike, she
traced her hand across her victim's chest, then slowly got up from
her crouch.

As the music moved inexorably to its close, she spread wide her palms, riveted by the sight of invisible blood. The supine body lay at her feet.

"*E avanti lui*," came the harsh whisper, "*tremava tutta Roma.*"

Then Annie bent over the man she had killed and spat in his face.

✳

Seth came home early that day, his stomach tied up in knots. An ulcer, perhaps. Or maybe too much takeout Mexican food. These past weeks he'd been dogged by minor ailments. Common sense told him his symptoms were psychosomatic, that there was nothing wrong other than grief and worry over Annie.

A few days earlier a plane had crashed in Jamaica. The moment he'd heard the bulletin, Seth had called the airlines in a dry-mouthed panic, on the off chance that Annie had been aboard that flight. She hadn't, of course, and afterwards he wondered what had possessed him. He had no particular reason to believe she had headed south at all. More likely Europe, knowing Annie. That was her idea of heaven on earth.

It was five o'clock in New York, late evening in London or Paris or wherever. Nearly bedtime three thousand miles away. Was Annie lying alone in the dark in a distant city full of strangers? For all Seth knew, she might have fallen off the edge of the earth. What if some misfortune happened to her! Who would know? Who would care?

The idea nauseated him. In all his thirty-four years, no one close to him had ever died. Although—he reluctantly admitted—he wasn't close to that many people. Logically, it was most unlikely that Annie had come to any grief. She was a vigorous, healthy woman, quite capable of looking after herself. But, he discovered, intellectual truths were different from emotional ones. That same night, he had phoned Madame Natasha, anxious for any news.

Madame was "not at liberty" to divulge Annie's whereabouts.

"But she's my wife, dammit!" Seth had hung up, disgusted and relieved. Had any disaster taken place, Madame would have told him. Nonetheless, after all the thousands of dollars he had poured into the woman's pockets, the least she might have done was give him a straight answer. But suppose she had, then what? What could he say to Annie beyond hello?

Don't despise me. Some conversational opener that would be!

He was capable of withstanding her wrath, her tears, even her infidelity; but her contempt was well nigh intolerable. Annie's words that final day had burrowed in his mind and refused to be dislodged. *A low-rise cat in a high-rise building.* The phrase stung.

If necessary, he could survive without her love, Seth told himself, but the loss of her respect was more than he could abide. A dozen times he had started letters to her—hurt, angry, reasonable, defensive. Without exception, they began, "I am not a low-rise anything." Even in print, the phrase rankled. Terrible, that the person who knew you best in the world should be the one who respected you least. In these unfinished missives, he didn't ask her return. All he asked was that those wounding words be unsaid.

Other women admired him, looked up to him. Indeed, no sooner had word got out concerning the breakdown of his marriage than Seth had found himself besieged. Every unattached woman at Medi-Tekk suddenly had an extra ticket to the theater or revealed herself to be a Red Sox fan, too. Even his secretary, that most sensible of persons, had invited him round for a home-cooked dinner.

"I'm divorced myself," Sharon said gently, "and I know you're going through a period of mourning right now. It's better not to be alone. I'm a pretty good cook and an excellent listener."

Seth had been taken aback. Was he wearing his loneliness on his sleeve? Briefly he wavered, the need to unburden himself contending with his pride. Pride won out. He thanked Sharon politely, stopped on the way home to rent a stack of cassettes, then watched old movies until dawn.

Tonight, *The Hound of the Baskervilles.* Seth loaded the VCR and had already sprawled out on the sofa anticipating a painless hour or two when the downstairs intercom buzzed.

"Ah shit!" He put the movie on PAUSE. The only company he wanted this evening was Basil Rathbone's.

"Who is it?" For a moment Seth thought he'd misheard.

Sandor repeated the name. It was unmistakable. Seth's instinct was to say a categoric no. But on second thought . . .

"You still there, Dr. Petersen?"

"Yeah, OK." Seth tucked in his shirttails. "Send the lady up."

❈

"*Ma chère.*" Polo swooped into the dressing room. "That was a marvelous—what do you call it?—bit of business, your spitting upon poor Bengt. Very effective, superb stagecraft, only why didn't you discuss it at the dress rehearsal? Our great Dane is furious with you for not having warned him. It was all he could do to play dead. Thank God for a fast curtain."

"I'm sorry," Annie said.

"About Bengt? Not to worry. He'll calm down. More important, the audience ate it up. The critics too, I shouldn't be surprised. Poor bastards are always grateful for any change from the tried and true. You may very well have carved yourself a niche in the annals of *Tosca*. All told, a dazzling second act, my dear, and you were a firebrand. Remind me never to get in your bad books. But what on earth possessed you to improvise like that? Did you have a memory lapse?"

Annie gave him a self-possessed and enigmatic smile.

"Polo," she said, "I have never been clearer-headed in my life."

A c t I I I : *The Castel Sant' Angelo. It is the hour before the dawn. As he awaits the firing squad, Mario bids farewell to the memory of his love. Tosca arrives, bearing the letter of safe-conduct.*

Annie stepped on stage to be greeted by a spontaneous ovation.

"It's for you," Polo mouthed, and her heart skipped a beat.

In older, gaudier days, opera stars bowed and waved and gave encores in mid-performance, at the cost of all dramatic coherence. No longer. Protocol demanded that she remain still and unsmiling, as though deaf to the thunderous applause and cries of "Brava!" until the cue to proceed could be given.

There, in that circle of light, time stopped.

For uncounted minutes that might have totaled an eternity, Annie stood bathed in the love of strangers. It was an astonishing experience, this sense of being adored and idolized by people she'd never met, couldn't see. To find herself the center of the universe, albeit for a single moment. Joy and gratitude and a faint sense of foreboding swept over her in turn. Was this how Seth had felt the night of Margot's ball, drunk with the heady wine of triumph?

[*Infidelities*]

At last, the applause dwindled and Polo raised his baton.

Learning of Scarpia's murder, Mario takes Tosca's hands and declares his love and gratitude. "O dolci mani." Tosca prepares him for the mock execution, explaining he must fall to the ground convincingly. The firing squad arrives and shoots. But to Tosca's horror, the bullets are real. Mario is dead. Only now does she realize the full measure of Scarpia's treachery. The soldiers come to arrest her. Tosca climbs the parapet, hurling a final challenge to her tormentor: "Avanti a dio"— Scarpia, we meet before God—then plunges to her death.

Avanti a dio. The music tore from her heart. Before God, there was a judgment yet to be made.

"In all, eighteen curtain calls!" Polo marveled.

"Nineteen." She grinned. "I was counting." Not a moment of that night would ever escape her. The curtain calls, the cheering, the flowers, the magnificent reception at an immense house in Belgrave Square belonging to one of England's wealthiest peers.

"Now," Polo had toasted her in Dom Perignon, "now you can drink and yell and dance and make love to your heart's content. You can even catch cold if you like, at least until you get ready for your next engagement."

And so she danced and drank and met hundreds of beautiful people until, at nearly three in the morning, Polo brought her back to the Dorchester.

"May I come up?" he asked. "If you're not too tired, the time has come to talk about the future."

Her first move was to kick off her shoes and wiggle her toes.

Then she curled up on the sofa to face Polo.

Already he was talking future repertoire, the reviews that they might expect a few hours hence, the merits of the various concert managements and wisdom of hiring a publicist.

"Polo," she broke in softly, "tonight was a fluke. A glorious, marvelous fluke. Don't think I'm not grateful to you, but we both

365

know that if Kaminskaya hadn't chucked it all for her Russian lover, she would have been at Covent Garden tonight. And I? I'd still be back in New York, practicing my scales."

"No, not a fluke." He shook his head. "Instead, think of it as a short cut. Because tonight, you made up for all those wasted years trailing after your husband in the provinces. Otherwise, you might have been here already. What matters is the future. I'm going on a guest tour of the Orient in a few weeks. Japan, China, Australia . . . It's not too late to change the programs, Annie. You're hot, now. There'll be a lot of interest in you. We could work up the great concert arias together, some Mahler song cycles . . ."

"I'm pregnant," she announced. "The hotel doctor confirmed it only yesterday. Don't look so alarmed, Polo. The baby's not yours."

For a moment he sat very still, considering this development.

"Your husband's then?"

Annie nodded.

"And do you still care for him?"

"I thought I did," she said slowly, "but now I hate what he's become. I realized that on stage tonight."

Polo got up and began pacing, and as he paced, his words fell into step. It was a litany.

"Callas, Tebaldi, Nilsson, Bumbry, Crespin, Price . . ." As Annie sat there, he listed the finest women singers of the century, then turned to her and paused, arms akimbo. "You know what they had in common, Annie, aside from great voices and international careers? They were all childless. Not an insignificant fact, you realize, and certainly not coincidence, either. For the most part, they were childless by design. Great careers have lives of their own, Annie. They can't brook those interruptions, can't allow the momentum to dissipate. Sacrifices have to be made, priorities must be set. I'm talking not merely of the demands on one's time that children entail, but the demands on one's heart. On one's energy. One's concentration. I grant you, women bear the heaviest burden in these situations, but even so, not exclusively. I myself have never had children. Given my way of life, my itinerary, what kind of father could I be? And from my own experience, the children of celebrities have a very rough time of it in the world. They know where they stand in the scheme of things. But think, while almost everyone you pass in the street can meet the requirements of parenthood, how many conduct a Mahler symphony or bring a Puccini heroine to burning life? To how many is it given to know the joy you must have felt tonight? One in a million? Not so many, perhaps. I ask you, what greater reward does life have to offer? Remember Tosca, dear Annie. Her credo . . . her belief. *Vissi d'arte.* I have lived for art."

"There's a second line to that aria, Polo. *Vissi d'amore.* She lived for love as well."

"And a lot of good it did her, *ma chère.* She would have fared better keeping her passion for her music." He folded her hand in his. "Whether or not you have your child is, of course, a decision only you can make, but it's my duty to acquaint you with the realities. You had a *succès fou,* tonight, Annie. A brilliant start, a glorious launch. But nothing more. Now is the time to exploit that success, fulfill the expectations you've raised. You should be singing wherever you have a chance. Be prepared to serve as every good opera company's last-minute substitute, at least until next year's plans can be drawn. After all, Kaminskaya's bookings will have to be filled. She and I were going to do Turandot next spring at La Scala. I want you to take her place, but you must start learning the role now. Take a few days off, if you need. Maybe even a week or two. But not six months or a year to have a baby. If you were established, that would be one thing. You could record, give concerts, theoretically even do opera, although I don't know how audiences would respond to a pregnant Turandot waddling across the stage. She *is* a virgin princess, after all."

Despite herself, Annie laughed. "There's a time-honored tradition of heavyweight sopranos, to put it kindly."

"What the audience liked about you, Annie, was that you broke with tradition. You gave them more than a voice. You gave them youth and beauty and drama. Those are among your biggest assets, *ma chère.* Capitalize on them now, for as you know, public memory is short. New sensations come along every day. Surely, you want to be recognized as something more than . . . what do you call it? a flash in the pan. The Tosca who spat on her Scarpia at Covent Garden and shocked everyone. Good as far as it goes, but it doesn't go far enough, for you can achieve so much more. You could be a diva . . . a goddess, for that is what diva means. You could sing all

367

the greatest roles in the finest opera houses all over the world. But if that is to be, then you must begin immediately. Another chance may never come. *Compris, ma chère?*"

"I understand," she said thoughtfully, "and I can't say what my choice will be. I just don't know, Polo. I've waited a long time for this pregnancy"—her voice thickened—"years and years. You're asking me to end it just like that. It's very hard, very cruel to have to choose . . . There's a life involved."

"I'm sorry, Annie," came his tender reply. "Truly sorry to force your hand, but it's not a decision you can put off for very long. I have to know about the Asian tour, about La Scala . . ."

"I realize, Polo. But before I make up my mind, before I even permit myself to think about it, there's something I have to do. It came to me while I was singing in the second act, and I can't tell you what it is except that it, too, involves life and death. I'm taking the first plane to New York this morning. My business won't take long . . . two, maybe three days at the most."

Polo rose and kissed her hand with continental formality.

"Bon voyage, my Tosca, and hurry back. I'll be waiting."

2

AT HEATHROW, SHE BOUGHT THE MORNING PAPERS AND TORE into the reviews. They ranged from good to rapturous. "At last," the *Guardian* fired its opening shot, "a Tosca we can fall in love with," then proceeded to misspell her name. Several of the reviewers had commented on the spitting episode, the *Telegraph* deeming it indicative of "American manners," while the *Times* described her "Vissi d'arte" as "shimmering and unforgettable." Polo was right about one thing. Without exception the reviewers commented on her looks and personality. "Not since Callas . . ." said the *Express*.

She tucked the papers into her flight bag, to be studied at greater length some other time, then she returned to the newsstand for half a dozen pads of lined paper.

All the way across the Atlantic, Annie honed her battle plan.

First, calls: To the *New York Times*. To Ward Daniels. To the director of the Gryce Hospital in Brooklyn. To the Center for Disease Control in Atlanta. To the Food and Drug Administration in Maryland. To the New York City Health Department. To Vi Hagerty.

That was for openers. One place or another, she was bound to connect. Then she wrote up a memo containing every detail she knew concerning the fraud, from the day of its inception on.

Next, Annie considered her backup strategy. Failing all other measures, she would turn up at the hospital gates Monday morning with a signboard and a loudspeaker. Stop the doctors physically if need be. So what if she made a spectacle of herself! All that mattered was getting the message across. Right to Life advocates had used similar techniques to considerable effect, and in a different way, Annie's cause also concerned the right to life.

As for that other life—the life she was carrying within her—she would postpone her decision a little longer before giving Polo his answer.

His arguments were compelling. Cash in now, he urged. The time will never be so ripe again. And the sound of cheering had been sweet.

Yet it would take another three or four years to consolidate her position in the opera world. If she chose, could she get pregnant again at thirty-five? And beyond that, could she do it at all—be both the loving mother and an international star?

Seth had tried to compartmentalize his life that way and failed miserably, the two halves of him constantly at odds.

Mario. Scarpia. Seth was both.

Right up to the end, she had kept on hoping his finest impulses would win out, but now the battle was over and Scarpia had triumphed. To this Seth she owed neither love nor loyalty.

With a shake of the head, she put all thoughts of him behind her. The day ahead would demand her utmost strength.

At one thirty the plane put down at Kennedy. The weather had turned raw and cold in the week she had been gone. Shivering, Annie scrambled into a taxi and gave Madame's address. It wasn't until the cab was clipping handily down the Grand Central Parkway that she realized one more chore left undone.

Gerald must be warned. In his condition, the shock of hearing such news secondhand might be lethal. It sufficed that she was wrecking his life. Damned if she would have his death on her conscience as well. Whatever Gerald's culpability, and Annie didn't minimize it, she would try to spare him this. She owed as much to Margot.

Long Island City, read the exit sign. Annie rapped on the plastic divider.

"Driver, take the next exit, please, and I'll direct you. I have to make a stop en route."

* * *

There it was, white and lowering, the source of all their miseries. Medi-Tekk.

A full year since she'd been here last.

"Sorry, lady." The driver blasted his horn, then folded his elbows over the steering wheel. "Can't get through. Looks like they're shooting a movie here."

A movie! Annie gasped. No, not a movie. These were television crews—ABC, NBC, the lot! Still photographers, too. In all, a veritable army of reporters had gathered on both sides of the Medi-Tekk gates.

"Wait here!" she shouted and flew out of the car. The first person she collared was a wiry-haired young woman wielding a Leica.

"What's going on? What's happening?" Annie implored.

"You work at Medi-Tekk?" The girl sniffed an inside story.

"No, but I know people who do! Please"—she pulled at the woman's sleeve, desperate. "I've got to know."

At nine o'clock this morning, Annie was told, Dr. Seth Petersen had telephoned the director of the Food and Drug Administration to notify the agency of his participation in a medical fraud and to demand the immediate cessation of all clinical tests. The story had gone out over the wire services shortly before noon and now the press, smelling hot news, had begun gathering.

"There he is!" Annie's informant suddenly shouted. "That's the guy." And the crowd suddenly broke ranks to swarm about the solitary figure descending the front steps.

It was Gerald, and now they were upon him like a pack of hounds in full cry. Annie tore past the gates. Across the courtyard, Albert, the Marriner chauffeur, was trying to maneuver the Rolls through the crowd and rescue his boss, but navigation was impossible.

"Gerald!" Annie tried to make herself heard above the din. "Gerald . . . where is he?"

There was no getting through. The director of Medi-Tekk was suddenly encircled, trapped by a battery of newsmen, a half dozen microphones thrust in his face.

"Statement!" The cry went up. "Do you have a statement to make?"

First Gerald shook his head, but there was no place to go, except back inside the building. He paused, visibly gearing himself to speak. "I regret to say that Dr. Petersen is an emotionally disturbed and unstable young man," came the trembling words. Gerald's lips were white as death. He looked close to collapse. "Properly, the man should be under psychiatric care. If Dr. Petersen did indeed falsify data, this is the first I or anyone at Medi-Tekk has heard of it. I have nothing to add. Let me pass."

"Why'd he do it?" the NBC man continued waving the mike.

"Was he under too much pressure to produce results?" the *Times* medical reporter wanted to know, but Gerald had finished his statement and now began elbowing his way through the crowd. At last, Annie saw a path through to him.

"Gerald!" She ran and grabbed his arm. "Are you all right? Where's Seth?"

At her touch, he shuddered. Then he fixed his eyes upon her, in a look of pain and total incomprehension.

"*You!*" he said. "You made him do it. Annie, you've destroyed us all."

Then Albert helped him into the Rolls and they were gone.

Where in God's name was Seth? At the hospital? On a plane somewhere? Seeking refuge in a darkened movie house?

"Park Avenue and Seventy-sixth." She jumped back into the cab. "And as fast as you can make it."

Home! In the eye of this storm, could he be hiding out at home?

The cab swung back onto the parkway. At a slight rise in the road, the skyline of Manhattan loomed before her in all its dangerous beauty. The shining city. The new Jerusalem. For one sweet moment it had been theirs.

As they drew in she could make out the high rises of the Upper East Side, sheer and spiky. Familiar buildings where she had visited friends and drunk cocktails and gone to parties.

Their penthouse days were over now. But in a different way, a far grander way, Seth had finally arrived at the top. He had soared. Risen above his fears, his failings, even his ambitions. The unexpectedness of his truth telling had left her breathless.

What courage it must have taken to pick up the phone and make that call. Seth had scaled the heights. A high-rise cat after all.

Suddenly, the image of Runaway Max transfixed her, plunging through the skies. God forgive her, she had taunted her husband with that epithet. She had a swift terrifying vision of Seth electing the same short path to oblivion. "You have destroyed us all," Gerald had said. Perhaps the ultimate victim of this tragedy, this continuing nightmare would be—not Vi, not Gerald. But Seth!

As the cab entered Park Avenue she opened the window and craned her neck out looking for police cars, ambulances, the apparatus of sudden death made visible, but nothing seemed out of the ordinary. Just the usual milling of traffic.

At her building, Sandor sprang to open the door.

"My husband . . ." Annie began shaking his shoulders. "Do you know where he is? Have you seen him?"

But all she could divine was that Seth had left the building shortly after ten. No, he didn't have any luggage, didn't call for a cab. He'd been wearing jeans and a sweater.

"Did he say anything?" Annie pleaded. "Where he was going? Anything at all?"

"He said it looked like rain."

And so it did.

Annie paid off the cabbie and took the elevator up, consoling herself that this comment on the weather hardly bespoke the suicidal man.

Inside the apartment things seemed more or less in order. The phone had been unplugged. Best left that way, she decided. The bedroom looked reasonably neat. On the kitchen table, the remains of a Chinese dinner had jelled in takeout cartons and there was a bouquet of roses on the sideboard. No card, though, which she found odd. Did Seth buy himself flowers, living alone?

With a peculiar sensation of being a guest in her own home, she made a cup of tea and settled down in the living room to wait for him.

"You made him do it," Gerald had said, and Annie tried to absorb his meaning. Had Seth gone public in a desperate attempt to win her back? If so, it was an astonishing proof of his need for her. Yet she didn't think their love had been the deciding factor. Seth wasn't a man to subject himself to emotional blackmail. He had done it because he knew it was right. Because at heart he was a fine and decent man. When it came down to the wire, Seth was Mario!

Relief poured through her, but she was too weary to sort out her emotions. The events of the past two days crowded each other in a jet-lagged jumble. Was it only last night she had stood center stage in Covent Garden? Incredible. She had been up thirty-six hours straight. Still, she wanted to be awake for Seth's return. Wanted to tell him how proud she was of him. Never prouder than at this moment.

Utterly exhausted, the fatigue of pregnancy catching up with her at last, she stumbled over to the television set. The VCR was already loaded. *The Hound of the Baskervilles*, starring Basil Rathbone and Nigel Bruce. Sounded good. Nothing like a thriller to keep the eyeballs propped open. Annie flicked the PLAY button, then stretched out on the sofa. A minute later she was dead to the world.

The room was dark when she woke up except for the flicker of the television set. Seth rose from the wing chair and turned it off.

"Hello, Annie."

"Seth!" She sucked in her breath. "Oh, my God! I was so afraid something might have happened to you."

"I'm OK." He switched on the table lamp. He looked weary, but curiously calm. Then nodding in the direction of the television set, he gave a brief laugh. "I've just heard myself described as 'an emotionally disturbed young man' on national television. I liked the 'young' part of it. Well, if nothing else, I've made one of Gerald Marriner's dreams come true. He finally got to appear on the seven o'clock news. Don't get up, Annie." He came and sat beside her on the sofa. "I don't dare ask what brings you back from wherever, and so I won't. Not right now. If you don't mind, darling, I don't think I can handle any more revelations today. I'm very tired. Tireder than I've ever been in my life. Otherwise OK. And you, Annie? Are you all right?"

"Oh, darling . . ." she said. "I was so worried about you. All kinds of crazy anxieties. Where did you go, Seth? What did you do all afternoon? Can you tell me?"

"No secret. I went to the Met. The museum, that is, not the opera. I spent the day in what must be the quietest, loneliest spot in New York—the Oriental rug galleries. Beautiful stuff, very restful. Medallions. Hunting scenes. Prayer rugs. Such elegant patterns, as intricate as anything you'd see under a microscope. Then I discovered I was woefully ignorant about Orientals. Didn't know an Ispahan from a

Tabriz. So when the museum closed, I went to Barnes and Noble and bought a book. It's on the piano. Then I had a tuna salad at Leo's and then I came home and watched the news. How I Spent My Day by Seth Petersen." It was a flat recitation, monotonal, uninflected, the voice of a man near the end of his physical and mental reserves.

"Just one more thing, Seth. Everything else can wait till tomorrow, but first, I'd like to know—did you make that call this morning because of me?"

"Funny question. Why? What difference does it make?"

"It makes a difference."

"Well, I guess you want me to say I did it all to satisfy you, but I'll be honest. Today is my day to be honest. I did it partly for you," he murmured. "Partly for me. But mostly, I suppose"—he managed a weak smile—"for those poor bastards who were going to be checking in to Gryce Hospital in a couple of days. I'd been moving toward that decision for quite a while. And now, Annie, I'm terribly tired. Can we not talk any more tonight? Let's leave all explanations, recriminations or whatever until tomorrow. Come to bed, Annie. Just lie beside me, darling." His voice broke. "I need the warmth of a human body."

She reached her hand to his face and touched the tears.

"So do I, my Mario."

"Mario?" He looked at her confused. "Who do you think I am?"

But Annie already knew.

That night, they slept in each other's arms, close, clinging, two survivors of a terrible shipwreck.

"Oh, babe." Ward phoned the moment he learned the news. "I grieve for you. I could hardly believe the story when it came over the wire service."

Except he could. From the moment he first set foot inside Medi-Tekk, he'd smelled *rat rat rat*, only on this one occasion he would have preferred that his instincts had steered him wrong.

Barring that, he should have gone along with his gut feeling then and there. Investigated. Asked the tough questions. Maybe the whole tragedy could have been averted if he hadn't danced to Strone Guthrie's tune. Too late now. All he could offer were a few trite words.

"How are you feeling, Vi? You think you'll be all right?"

375

"How can I be all right, Ward?" She was audibly weeping, without the excuse of sea spray on her face. It was a terrible sound, delivered from some private hell.

"Hold on a minute, will you?" she managed to blubber. He waited, pacing the apartment, the long telephone cord tangling around his legs like an anaconda. What the hell was keeping her? JERSEY WOMAN JUMPS TO DEATH. Or SWALLOWS POISON more likely. Jumping took a certain amount of mobility.

Will you stop the hell writing headlines? Ward disciplined himself. She was not a suicidal type. Although on top of everything else she must be furious with him. Look at it one way, and this entire mess could conceivably be laid at his door. After all, if not for Ward, she would never have connected with the sons of bitches at Medi-Tekk. Never have raised her hopes so wildly, so falsely. Yes, she had every reason to be pissed off. Hell, he felt sick about the whole wretched business. Then suddenly there was a noise on the line.

"You there?" he hollered.

"Of course I'm here." Vi sounded almost composed. "You don't have to yell." She must have gone to blow her nose or beat her fists or maybe pour herself a stiff drink, but whatever her choice of therapy, it had worked, for she immediately set about saving face. "Sorry 'bout that poor connection we had. This is better, huh? Look, Ward, I don't want to talk about it right now. Change the subject, huh? What's with you these days? Anything up?"

"Well, did I tell you, I'm leaving for London next week? Then Glasgow a couple of days, then off to Australia. You know, Guthrie commutes between continents the way normals do between the kitchen and the john. Got a pencil, Vi? I have a nice word for Noonie. Peripatetic." Ward spelled it out. "He can add it to his collection. It means you move around a lot from place to place. Well, that's me for the next few months. Wherever Guthrie goes, I tag along for the ride. I'll be flying back and forth . . ."

". . . like a yo-yo."

He winced. The image was too close for comfort.

"Beside the point. Anyhow, I want to see you before I go, say good-bye. Anything I can do for you, toots?"

The line went quiet again. Gone for another drink, he wondered?

"I've a favor to ask," she finally said. "This Sunday, well . . . I was supposed to check into Gryce Hospital. Now that's off, I'll have the day free. I was wondering . . . Do you think you could rent a sailboat and take me out for a couple of hours? I don't know"—she cleared her throat—"if I'll get another chance to do that number."

It was Ward's turn to clear his throat. "Consider it done, Vi. I'll be around first thing Sunday morning."

He hung up the phone.

Yo-yo, indeed. How about *flunky? Stooge? Whore?*

Ward could find a lot harsher words to define his function in the Strone Guthrie entourage. But Vi, bless her, had seen straight through his blather.

And what a prize yo-yo Ward Daniels had been!

"So . . ." Seth finished his eggs and poured himself another cup of coffee. "I guess I owe you an explanation."

Annie folded her hands with an expectant air.

Twelve hours' sleep had refreshed her, put her back on her feet. Brought her life into focus. Seth wasn't the only one with secrets to be shared.

The weeks after Annie left had been, for him, a time of painful self-scrutiny.

He began by going way back, even to the days before he met Annie, to the moment when he dropped out of med school.

At the time, he had pacified his father with a surface explanation. "The greatest good for the most numbers, is what I recall having said." But the real reason, he could only now admit, was his fear of the patients. The first time he accompanied a teaching doctor through the cancer wards at Mass General had been a nightmare. Successive visits only confirmed that sense of panic.

He dreaded their pain, their needs, walked the wards in constant terror that a desperate hand might reach out to him, a dying voice beg for something that Seth could not grant. If it were the mere dispatching of pills or the clean incision of a surgeon's knife, that he might handle. But they wanted more. They wanted pity and hope and limitless love. They wanted comfort.

377

"Me. The man everybody thinks of as so supremely capable, yet I wasn't capable of living up to their emotional demands, Annie. I was afraid I didn't have it in me."

So he turned away, into the tighter, more abstract world that lay beneath the microscope. Microorganisms don't talk back. Chemical substances don't cry, don't ask for unreasonable boons.

Had he copped out? His father believed so. Very well, Seth would make it up. He would find a way to compensate for this deficiency of feeling. This secret failure. He would do it by becoming a hero in his chosen field.

Yet much as he feared intimacy, he craved it too.

"And then I met you."

Even now, the night remained vivid. He had been studying the chemistry of lipids when she burst into his life—this beautiful girl singing of the ghost of a rose, investing his world with magic.

To Seth, Annie embodied everything he lacked, all the miracles that defied analysis. "I adored you then. I adore you now."

That she knew nothing of science merely enhanced her in his eyes. Annie didn't make demands. His days were spent toeing the mark, testing his mettle against colleagues and competitors. In his private life, he sought poetry and warmth and unquestioning love.

"And I found it in you, Annie. We were a tight little package all those years, until this tragic business with the mice."

He didn't know what caused that disaster in the lab, conceivably he never would. But from the start the dreadful question had been raised in his mind: the fate of the patients in the Phase One test.

He believed in his discovery, believed that what he was doing was for the best, yet always there was that element of doubt. Night after night he tried to wrestle down his anxieties, seeking a rationale for his actions, a rationale that would put an honorable complexion on that one other vital factor: his need to win.

The answer to his moral quandary was not hard to find. One must be pragmatic, he told himself. One must balance the worst possible scenario against the great gains that might be made.

Who were these people anyhow? They didn't have faces. Or personalities or names or souls. They were not flesh-and-blood individuals, but case histories, selected to fit a computer-designed statistical profile. Anonymous beings, already shortchanged by life, who—thanks to Seth's efforts and abilities—were now being given a second chance. Beyond that, he preferred not to speculate.

And then came Annie with her nagging, her persistence, burrowing into him where he was weakest and most vulnerable. Affectionate, good-natured Annie, who never made demands, was suddenly demanding the impossible, creating scenes, pushing him up against the wall.

When she moved out, he almost breathed a sigh of relief. Now there was nothing left to hound him. Nothing, that is, except his own conscience. In the hush of that lonely apartment, his inner voice refused to drop the refrain. He had simply exchanged one nag for another.

For a hellish three weeks Seth teetered on the brink of decision. "You were never absent from my thoughts, Annie, but it was something I had to work through alone."

Then, two nights ago, the doorman had buzzed to say Vi Hagerty was in the lobby.

"She'd come to see you, Annie. Completely unannounced. And you know what my reaction was?"

"Fear?"

"Abject terror. Because this wasn't a statistic down there in our lobby, a coded entry on the computer. This was a name, and if I let her up, she would become a face, a voice. A person. This was like stepping back into the wards at Mass General. All my instincts said *run*, but I couldn't. Because I had to satisfy myself about something."

Vi Hagerty hobbled in, a brassy little blonde in a green suit, bearing a bouquet of roses.

"I just wanted to drop these off by way of saying thanks to you and Mrs. Petersen."

"How very kind."

Seth put them in water, ashamed to look her in the eye. Oh yes, she had a lot to thank him for. Thanks for playing showdown poker with her life.

Annie wasn't here, he explained. Out of town at the moment, she'd be sorry to have missed her visitor.

There was a question he yearned to ask, but it was too personal,

379

too emotive to be stated flat out. Instead, he offered her a drink.

"I was just about to send for Chinese food, Ms. Hagerty . . ."

"Vi!"

"Vi, then. I'd be grateful for your company."

She was thrilled, poor thing. Honored to spend an hour across the table from such a distinguished man, God's gift to the handicapped. However, once over her initial nervousness, she turned quite chatty.

He poured her another drink. The food arrived. By now she was warmed up and rolling. He heard about her son, her ex-husband, her friend Crystal, her computer, her legal trials, the real estate business and what a sweet lovable guy Ward Daniels was. In fact, pretty much the story of her life.

It sounded bleak enough and yet, to his surprise, she made him laugh a number of times. Street humor, a kind of tough raucous wit that Seth found engaging. But God! that woman sure could pack the booze away.

At last she seemed sufficiently relaxed for Seth to launch a few trial balloons.

"You know, Vi, there's a fifty percent chance you won't get FG-75 at all. You might get the placebo."

She knew.

"And then there's the chance that the treatment won't work."

She knew that too.

"If it doesn't," he said softly, "if the experiment fails, you realize what you are facing."

The loss of her son. The loss of her limbs. Of bodily functions. Years of loneliness and helplessness and pain.

"It was all there, hanging in the air between us, Annie. All the horrors ahead. I wanted, I ached to hear her say the words that would absolve me of responsibility. Let me off the hook. I wanted her to tell me she would rather die than live like that. In my mind, I framed the words—*Better off dead*. I was practically psyching her, trying to plant those words in her head."

"And did she say them?"

* * *

"I guess you think I'd be better off dead."

Seth sucked in his breath.

"But you see, if I lose custody of Noonie," Vi explained very matter-of-factly, "then I've absolutely gotta stick around. Because that kid's going to need me like he never needed me before. Who's going to set him straight, otherwise? Who'll keep him from getting snotty and la-de-dah if not yours truly? Jesus, I'll be fucked if I'm going to let them turn my Noonie into a brown-nosed little Wall Street grubber. No way! And then, of course"--she rolled her eyes— "what would happen to Jesse if I wasn't around?"

Jesse? Seth was puzzled. He thought he'd already been exposed to the entire cast of characters in Vi Hagerty's life. Maybe Jesse was a pet of some sort.

"Who's Jesse?"

"He's my steady." She tittered. "My Saturday night date. I'm a computer hacker, see? It's a kind of hobby, but lately I got into this thing called the bulletin board. You plug in and you can access into thousands of people across the country, other hackers. You never get to meet them in person. They're just messages on your screen, but you'd be surprised . . . you can make a lot of friends that way. They've all got different personalities. Well, Jesse lives in North Carolina. He's a vet who bought it pretty bad in Viet Nam, and now he's housebound. His big thrill is talking dirty, poor bastard. Guess that's all he can do, but I don't care. I give it right back to him. What the hell, I guess we both could use it. Anyhow, we make each other laugh. I tell him he programs with a southern drawl. So we plug in twice a week for a half hour. He's teaching me how to play chess. Next meeting, he's going to show me the Ruy Lopez opening."

Seth stared at her astonished, then leaned over and kissed her on the forehead.

"Bless you, Vi."

She stayed a few minutes longer, rambling about this and that. Then Seth called a limousine service to take her back to Jersey.

"That something?" he said to Annie, eyes brimming. "Talking dirty over a computer. What a fantastic affirmation of life! And all

I could think of, Annie, was . . . what if it were you facing that wheelchair, if it were you hanging on to life like that? What would I do? Would I take that risk if Vi were you? No. God help me, it was unthinkable. I would never chance it! Not as long as there was one tiny spark of your spirit still left, still glowing, one last breath of your love, your warmth, your soul. If it were you, I would do everything within my power to help you stay alive, to endure, to fight the darkness to the bitter end. And then I knew, my darling"— the tears streamed unashamedly down his cheeks—"that she *was* you. They were all of them . . . all of them you!"

3

HAPPY ISLANDS.

In her dreams, they were always waiting for her at the horizon. Happy islands beckoning beyond the water's edge with their promise of music and laughter and good fellowship and the warmth of a lover's arms. Now those dreams were gone forever, banished by the harsh light of reality.

Foolish hopes, those fantasies that had sustained her all these months. A fairy tale for children, nothing more.

Vi gazed across the water, squinting in the sun, but the only prospect before her was the familiar line of the Jersey shore. They would sail for another hour or two, tie up the boat, then Ward would drive her back to an empty apartment. Back to a rapidly emptying life.

She drew her gaze away from the horizon just as Ward emerged from the hatch, toting a picnic basket.

With an air of total concentration, he set about unpacking the contents. Roast chicken. Greek salad. Olives. Cheeses. French bread. A bottle of something or other in an ice bucket.

Poor bastard. She watched him fondly. He hated the water, claiming he was unusually prone to seasickness, but Vi suspected his antipathy was based on something else—a profound and irrational fear of drowning. He dreaded going under, this man who'd spent so much of his life on the battlefield.

A wave of affection surged through her. For even though the sea terrified him, he had gone about today's business with cheer and good grace. She admired him for it. Courage wasn't courage if you

weren't afraid. It was doing the things that scared you that took
guts.

As if he sensed her thoughts, he glanced up at her and smiled, a
pair of plastic glasses in hand.

"How about some champagne before we tuck in, Vi?"

"You bet."

He pulled out a bottle of Piper Heidsieck, dripping cold. With
an assertive pop, the cork flew overboard. She watched it vanish
only to emerge a minute later and begin bobbling a lazy path across
the water.

"Here's to Ward."

They touched plastic glasses.

"Here's to us," he replied, then downed his champagne in a single
gulp. A few feet away, a gull cawed disapproval.

"Vi . . ." He sat beside her on the narrow bench. "Today I'm
going to do two things I've never done before in my life. And one
of them is a major ethical lapse. I am about to breach my promise
of confidentiality, which is a heinous crime in the journalist's hand-
book. Over the years I've kept secrets belonging to cabinet members, CIA officials, Mafia informants . . . all kinds of secrets. But
this one I can't keep. It's Noonie's. I wormed it out of him that day
we went to Belmont. It's about his father, but it concerns you too."

Vi sat up very straight, fists clenched.

"Last summer, when the two of them went to Yellowstone Park,
his father got into a poker game with some of the other guys on the
campsite. Of course, Noonie was too young to get into the grown-
ups' game, but he knows something about poker—right?—so it was
a thrill for him to sit behind his dad and watch the big boys play.
Now, what you have to remember, Vi, is he thought his old man was
the most fantastic thing since Luke Skywalker. Successful, glamorous, all that shit. He pretty much idolized him . . ."

"And?" Vi's eyes widened.

"And," Ward went on, "he caught his father cheating at cards."

"Ouch!"

"You bet your ass, *ouch*. The kid was devastated. But he couldn't
say a word about it to his father, to anyone, least of all to you. In
fact, he swore me to secrecy. Don't you see, Vi?—he was ashamed.
Humiliated. After all, the man *is* his father. But ever since then, he's
been in a panic that you're going to send him away, that he'll be

forced to live with the guy. Noonie loves you, Vi. He's desperately afraid of losing you. He needed assurance. I think I gave it to him. I told him, what he has to do when he goes before the judge next month is speak his mind honestly. He understands that now, so there's nothing in the world can take him away. Not even an army of fancy lawyers. You can rest your mind, Vi. Noonie's with you for keeps."

The light started somewhere down in her toes, raced through her body, then burst through her eyes in a radiant flash.

"Oh, wow!" She glowed. "I can't believe it! Jesus, I feel like a hundred-pound monkey just got off my back."

"Correction. A two-hundred-pound ape, name of Ross Winfield."

"Oh, wow!" she repeated, then thrust out her glass. "Fill 'er up. Absolutely calls for champagne. But why the hell couldn't Noonie let down his hair, just tell me he loves me and that's that! You men"—she shook her head—"and I include my son in that category. You are so uptight, so fucking macho, always keeping the most important things bottled up. God forbid anyone should get a line on how you feel."

"It isn't easy." Ward grimaced. "Which brings me to the Number Two thing I've never done before. OK. Here goes. Vi Hagerty, will you marry me?"

"Will I *what?*" she shrieked and dropped her glass.

Her shout reverberated over the waters.

"Will you marry me? I don't know how to say it any plainer. Will you do me the honor of becoming my wife?"

In response, Vi's leg began to twitch. She lowered her eyes, unable to face him. Couldn't he see what he was doing to her?

"Please don't, Ward. Spare me that. I don't want your pity."

"I'm not offering you my pity." He took her face in his hands. "I'm offering you my love."

"Are you crazy? Look at me!" Her limbs were vibrating like leaves before the wind. "Look at me and say that you love me."

"I love you," he said softly. "The three toughest words in the language. Before I left home this morning, I went over this moment a hundred times in my mind. I didn't know if I could bring myself to actually say them. You see, I'd never had any practice. But now I look at you and they come easy to me. I love you. I love your courage, your spirit, your laughter. I love the sound of your voice,

I love the feeling of your body next to mine. Until I met you, I had nothing to show for my life except a scrapbook full of clippings. I was the loner, the man who never got involved, never let his guard down. 'I care for nobody, no not I, and nobody cares for me.' Just like the Miller of Dee in that old nursery tune. Proud of it too, I'm ashamed to say now. The night we became lovers, you got too close to me. It was scary. So I did the smart thing, I went to Alaska. I ran away, to put it bluntly. And it didn't do a damn bit of good, because the only place I wanted to be was back with you. In my life, I'd never been so lonely. There I was up in the frozen north and it began to dawn on me—I was the frozen north, too. But would I give in? No, ma'am. I was going to keep on running, Vi. I could run all my life—London, Australia, Tahiti."

"Why don't you?" Her breath came hard. "I would run if I could."

"Because I'd be running to nowhere. I've thought this thing through up and down, Vi, and there's just no help for it. I want you to fill my life the way you fill my heart. Please, Vi, marry me and let's get on with it."

"Oh, Ward . . ." She shook her head. "You don't know what you're letting yourself in for. You'll be shackling yourself to a cripple! I couldn't let you do it."

"My sweet girl." He cradled her in his arms. "Do you think you can scare me off that easily? Not this man. Listen, love. I spent four stinking years in Viet Nam covering the war. I've seen everything . . . every kind of death and suffering. Nothing physical can ever shock or disgust me. Nothing! Least of all you. Whatever happens, you'll be my terrific Vi . . . worth a dozen of those plastic Gennies. And don't ask me who Gennie is, because I still have a few secrets left. So what do you say?"

In the heat of the sun she was shivering.

"That's a lot of years we're looking at, Ward. A whole lifetime of 'em. I can't stomach the thought of being a burden."

"You know what your trouble is, Vi?" He sat back and folded his arms, the better to see her. "You're macho. Pure unregenerate macho. You talk about me, talk about Noonie, but you're the one who's too fucking proud to soften up. Vi the Invulnerable. What do you have to prove? That you can go it alone? That you don't need anything from anyone, thank you very much? Ok, you've made your case. You can hack it all by yourself! But why the hell should you *want* to? That's what beats me! What's so terrible about accepting help from someone you love, being on the receiving end for a change? Unless, of course, I've hit on it right there. Unless you don't care for me that way."

"Don't care for you?" The blue eyes began to flood. "Are you out of your mind, buddy? I'm crazy about you, Ward Daniels. Genuine bananas. You are the most terrific man I've ever met. That's exactly what scares me so. I don't want to be a milestone around your neck."

"That's millstone, love. A milestone is what I think you and I have just passed. Now do I take that to mean the answer is yes? Yes, you'll live with me? Yes, you'll marry me? And yes, you'll bring that nutsy kid of yours along too?"

What was she fighting? Why muster all her stubbornness, all her immense reserve of pride in a struggle against someone she loved so dearly? It was false pride, foolish. No, she would save this strength and energy for the real battle of her life: the battle against disease and despair. Openly, she began to weep. Happy islands. She had been blind not to see it. Ward was the happy island she had dreamt of, sought. Ward was the haven of warmth and of love.

"Yes!" She flung her arms around him. "The biggest, fattest yes you ever heard."

"Oh, sweetheart!"

He covered her face with kisses, a man who'd just won the sweepstakes, then wiped her streaming eyes.

"Hey . . . hey! I thought you never cried, Vi."

"Only for happy." She smiled through the tears. "You've gotta admit, that's different. But what about your plans? What about the book? I thought you were going to London next week with Guthrie?"

"Never argue with gut feelings." He gave a dry laugh. "I couldn't do it. I phoned him last night to break the news and when I hung up, I felt like I'd been reprieved from the gallows. Did I ever tell you, hon, about that awful lunch I had with his lordship? Everything on the menu was brown . . . this hideous brown. Now I know why. It was the color of shit. I can't eat that stuff, Vi, not even for a million bucks." He sighed for those riches lost, but not regretted. "I am what I am. A journalist. A truth teller. I can't change. What the hell, at the end of the day, you've got to live with yourself. That's all that matters. I guess Seth Petersen learned that, too. So I'm going back to my old job at *Worldnews* and the usual scramble. We won't be millionaires, my pet, but it's OK. We'll manage just fine."

"And Tahiti?" For Ward too, she knew, cherished a dream of his own happy island.

He pushed her hair back from her forehead. "You're my Tahiti."

From the north, a sharp wind sprang up, whipping the sails. Reflexively Ward pulled his windbreaker tight. "It's getting cold out here, love," he said. "So can we turn this fucking tub around and go home?"

The time had come to talk about London: Annie's debut, the accolades, the extraordinary career now open to her. As she outlined Polo's offer to tour the Orient, Seth listened astounded.

"Why the hell did you come back, Annie—to this shame and scandal? You have the world at your feet. Was it for me?"

"I came back," she admitted, "to turn you in."

Seth stared at her aghast.

"You wouldn't have!"

"I would indeed. I was convinced you were going through with the experiments come hell or high water, and I hated you for it." The memory of her standing over Scarpia's body surfaced vividly. "Yes—hated you! There was a moment when I wished you dead. The fact is, Seth, I sold you short . . . as a man, a husband. I was wrong, thank God. But at the time, I would have moved the world to stop you. So now you know. Do you think you can live with it?"

"I guess I'll have to." He absorbed this revelation. "What the hell . . . I hated myself all those months. What can I tell you, Annie? You did the right thing. And now . . . ? I suppose you'll be going off to the Orient . . ."

"I've decided not to go."

"You can't turn it down, sweetheart." Seth was appalled. "I won't let you. It's everything you've worked for all these years."

"Well, if I change my mind"—she was curious—"will you come with me? Money won't be a problem, Seth. We could live pretty high, have some fun for a change . . ."

"I don't know." He brooded. "For one thing, it would look as though I were running away. For another—what the hell would I do on the road?"

What indeed? How would he take his wife's being the "star" of the family? For if his career was over, hers was still capable of taking a quantum leap.

Yes, there was indeed a role that Seth might play: the figure standing in the wings. He could be that useful adjunct, the accompanying male, on hand to serve a dozen functions. Traveling companion. Cheerleader. Clipper of reviews. Seeker of lost luggage. That shadowy figure so often seen in the background of photos— holding the prima donna's furs or walking her poodle while flash-bulbs popped.

Not Seth! Not her Seth!

Yet here he was arguing that the opportunity was too great to pass up.

"Don't turn it down for me, Annie. Maybe the time's come for us to loosen our grip on each other," he said. "I want you with me, darling, all the way. You know that. But I have no right to insist. Ah, sweetie, if we could only turn back the clock, go back to the way we were. But I'm not the same man you married—the great white hope of modern science, the guy with the unlimited future. I don't have much to offer anymore."

No—Annie heard him out—he was not the same man. He was a better man—more human, more courageous. Like Job, Seth had been chosen above the general run of men to undergo a cruel ordeal. Like Job, he had suffered. Endured. Triumphed.

He was sitting, chin in hand, saying good-bye to the past.

"We were such a tight little island, you and I," he said. "I don't know . . . maybe too tight. No room for anyone else."

Her pulse quickened with a surge of pride and love.

"Make room," she said softly.

You who are two shall be three.

He looked at her, puzzled, uncertain of her words.

"Make room, darling," she repeated.

He caught his breath. Then blinked in wonder, then burst forth in a glorious shout.

"Baby!" He swooped her up in his arms. "We're going to have a baby . . . oh, Annie . . ." He was trembling with joy, covering her with kisses. "My fabulous Annie!"

They spent the next half hour doing nothing more profound than being foolishly, outrageously happy.

Seth gradually changed his tune from a euphoric "I don't believe it" to a gleeful "I knew it all along!"

"Rubbish," Annie teased. "You didn't have a clue."

He shook his head in contradiction. "I knew it would happen as soon as you started taking those fertility drugs. Say what you will about modern science, love, the goddam stuff really works."

"Modern science, my eye," Annie said. "I knew I was going to get pregnant nearly a year ago. I had it straight from a little obeah woman down in St. Thomas. And she didn't need a lab full of high-tech hardware, either. She does it all with chicken bones and herbs."

"Rank superstition," Seth protested manfully, then added, "But if I see her, you think she'll give me the recipe?"

They were living in the eye of a hurricane.

From the moment the story hit the streets, the Petersens had been besieged: friends, family, reporters, colleagues eager to get the lowdown straight from the horse's mouth, relative strangers with an ax to grind. To some, Seth was a villain, to others a victim. Each voice added another level of volume to the din.

Even the headwaiter at Gino's had an opinion—favorable, as it happened, calling Seth "one of nature's noblemen." But then, Seth always was a good tipper. On the other hand, a former professor of his called to demand, "How could you do such a thing?" Seth was halfway through his explanation when he realized that "such a thing" referred not to the initial falsification of data but the more egregious sin of going public. "You've cast aspersions on the entire scientific community. Couldn't you have kept your mouth shut?"

Through it all, Seth maintained an unflappable calm. The Monday following, he had gone into Medi-Tekk at the usual hour, instructed his staff concerning outstanding projects, then tendered his resignation to the board. "Are you getting severance pay?" Annie asked, uncertain what his rights were. "Nope," came the grim answer. "But they gave me this cute little bell to wear around my neck. When I walk, it goes 'Unclean, unclean.'"

The Marriners had fled to their sanctuary in St. Thomas, secure from press and public. Annie's own instinct was to follow their lead.

"Can't we slip out of town at least till the worst is over?"

But he was adamant. "I can't very well bring the whole business out in the open and then go into hiding."

Today he was in Rockville, Maryland, submitting a deposition to the FDA, and Annie had taken advantage of his absence to catch up on her own affairs.

"And so?" Madame Natasha hungered for details. "And so what did you tell Polo von Brüning?"

"Something he didn't want to hear." Annie laughed. "He accused me of being another Irina Kaminskaya. I told him I was flattered."

Madame shook her head, perplexed.

"He offered you the earth, you know."

"So he did. In fact, those were almost his very words."

"The world is yours, *ma chère*." He had called from Munich the previous day. "I give it to you—from the Sydney Opera House to La Scala, with all major points in between. I should never have let you go back to New York last week. Back to that husband of yours. I should have made love to you that night in London and we could have settled the matter then and there."

"That wouldn't have changed anything, Polo. Because at heart, we were never really lovers. Colleagues . . . friends . . . who once went to bed with each other out of affection. It was fine, it was fun. But we were never in love."

"But what does it matter?"

"To me it matters."

"Shame shame, Annie! You're an incurable romantic. I thought more of you than that. You could have been a diva . . . a goddess. Instead, you turn out to be . . ."

"Yes?"

". . . a mere woman after all."

* * *

"You think I'm mad—or don't you?" She tried to read Madame's mind, for the face was sphinxlike. "When Polo first called and offered me *Tosca*—God! it seems like years ago!—you said it was a once-in-a-lifetime opportunity. So it was. But so is this baby. So's Seth . . . so's our marriage, for that matter."

Madame smiled. "I made a different choice when I was younger than you, my dear. He was divinely handsome, a captain in the Coldstream Guards with a magnificent mustache. I went on tour and never saw him again. Who's to say what's wise or what's foolish?"

"And even if I weren't pregnant," Annie mused, "I think my choice would be the same. I proved myself that night at Covent Garden. It was wonderful. It put 'paid' to all those years of speculation about whether I had the stuff or not. Now I can truly say, 'I'm not a might-have-been. I'm an artist with world-class stuff.' "

She got up and walked over to study the photographs that lined the wall of the studio. Ponselle. Jeritza. Maria Callas. The ranks of the immortals. Then she turned to face her teacher and smiled.

"That's speaking musically. But temperamentally? I'm no diva. The role doesn't suit me. I don't want to be idolized, worshiped from afar. I'd rather be loved at close range. And then the life! You're just a high-class hobo living out of a suitcase, even if it's an alligator suitcase by Cardin." She laughed. "Personally I suspect the hoboes have it better. At least they get to enjoy the sights. A whole week in London, and all I saw were the rehearsal halls and my hotel room. At times it was marvelous—the applause, the glitter, that hothouse atmosphere. At other times, it was lonely beyond belief. Like Tosca, I have to ask—*il prezzo*. The price."

Madame cocked her head, puzzled.

"That week before the performance, I was petrified that I might catch a cold or come down with a headache on the night. I didn't even dare scream at a bellboy in case I hurt my voice. What kind of life is that? Not for me. I'm no hothouse flower, Madame. More of a garden-variety rose, thorns and all. So there we are."

"And where are we?" Madame pursed her lips in dismay.

But Annie knew.

She was going to continue with her career as planned, preserving London as a precious keepsake. This season she and Ari already had a dozen concerts lined up. Not headline events, but the two of them were a terrific team. They'd make good music, earn a few bucks into the bargain. Then after the baby was born, perhaps she'd line up some pupils of her own. With her London reviews, she might reasonably audition for whatever was available in the New York opera companies. Beyond that, she didn't care to speculate. Much would depend on what happened with her husband's career.

"And could you go back to the provinces if you had to?"

"I could," she said. "And if I do, you may be sure I'm going to be the best goddam singer in Fort Worth or Sausalito or wherever. A mover and a shaker, as they say. You were right, Madame. Success has a lot of different levels. I hope we can stay in New York, but if not—I'll always be a musician. As for that night in Covent Garden, nothing can ever take it away from me. And now"—she went for her coat—"I have to meet my husband. His plane gets in any minute."

Madame walked her to the door.

"Tell me, Annie, when you were in London, they took publicity photographs, yes?"

Annie nodded.

"In costume?"

"In full regalia, Madame. Velvet gown, jewels, right up to and including the Jeritza tiara."

"Then I would like you to give me a photograph, my dear. It belongs on that wall. I have just the space for it."

"Really?" Annie swallowed down the lump in her throat.

"Oh yes indeed!" The tiny Russian stood tiptoe to peck Annie on both cheeks. "And I shall tell all my students—all the young hopefuls who come to me with their beautiful voices and big dreams—I will tell them . . . now *there* was a *divina* Tosca."

There is a legend—Seth said—of a raja whose beloved wife has died at the peak of her youth and beauty. The young prince is desolate. In his grief he commands his subjects to build an exquisite temple in which her mortal remains will be housed. All the wealth of his realm is to be poured into this monument. Gold, jewels, ivory, marble: no expense is to be spared.

For forty years, a thousand craftsmen labor to create a masterpiece such as the world has never seen. At last the work is finished. The prince—now an old man—comes to see it. As he makes his way past golden columns and sumptuous hangings, he stops at the altar. There lie the remains of his beloved wife.

"Who"—shrieks the prince—"who has defiled the splendor of my temple with this ugly bag of bones?"

So Seth.

Once long ago, he had set out with a pocketful of ideals. To be of service was all he asked. But somewhere en route, priorities got switched, values altered or forgotten.

"It had already begun to happen," he told Annie, "even before I came to Medi-Tekk. Even if nothing had ever gone wrong with the mice, I was already treading a very fine line. Success had become the be-all and end-all."

He had been caught up in the scramble for recognition, hypnotized by the razzle-dazzle of technology. The goal had not been people, but honors, grants, the thrill of being first at the finish line. For years, he had measured his worth in raises and titles and the number of papers that bore his name. And in the course of that unrelenting pursuit, he had lost sight of the real reason for his work.

"The big question is, what now?"

He'd come back from his trip to Maryland in a reflective mood. That night, they sat late in the kitchen, over scrambled eggs and coffee.

"Everybody keeps asking what happens next."

"Me too," Annie said. "Looks like we're back to Square One."

"Not Square One, Annie. We're at a different place on the game board. Not that we'll starve." He shrugged. "I could always get a job of some sort or other, although not at what they call 'the cutting edge' of science. But even if I could, I feel I'm done with research at that level. I don't want to go on to yet another Medi-Tekk."

"Maybe Medi-Tekk was unique."

"Not typical of all labs, thank God. But not really unique, either, Annie. It's very much like most successful corporations in the kind of demands that it made upon employees. The fast track is the fast track. You either keep the pace or you don't. I don't flatter myself that I'm any better than a lot of other people who work in pressure cookers. But I don't think I'm much worse either. Look around us— people we know. Not only in other labs, but in business, in academia, in law. All hustling, elbowing. Gleefully screwing the competition. How else do you prove you've got more 'smarts'? Because in these contests, there is no second place. You win and you're god. You lose and the waters close over you. But I'm not going to let the waters close over me. I've been through hell, Annie. All that experience shouldn't go to waste. I've decided—now, promise not to laugh—to try my hand at writing a book. A sort of cautionary tale for fellow climbers."

"I'm not laughing, Seth. I think it's a helluva good idea."

"Hope so. Anyhow, it would be a healthy antidote to the usual how-to-succeed manual. You know the kind. Those best-sellers that fill you in on the latest sideswiping techniques. Results results results, they tell you. That's all that matters, and the hell with how you achieve them. You know what the big boast is in Medi-Tekk? In most of those fast-track companies? That you're tougher than the next guy. Well, I discovered I'm not so tough after all."

But he *was* tough, she realized with admiration. Tough in the right way, resilient, always seeking new solutions.

Writing a book, of all things! And if she knew Seth, it would be a superb book, informed with his warmth, with all the emotional power that had been bottled up within him for so long. It was all at his fingertips now.

"Maybe you could build a life as a writer," she volunteered.

"Maybe." He cleared away the remains of their meal. "Sit, darling. Let me clean up for a change." He loaded the dishwasher with swift, deft movements, then switched the machine on.

"The golden hands of Seth Petersen." He turned them over, examining them thoughtfully. "Annie, love . . . I'd welcome your opinion about something that may sound even crazier than the book. Because when that's finished, I'll still have the rest of my life to consider. Whatever else I may be, I'm a scientist, same as you're a singer. Annie"—he paused—"how would you feel about my going back to med school next year? Pick up where I left off, so to speak. In a lot of ways, I was a kid when I dropped out. I hope I've become a man in the meantime. They're good hands still, Annie, with a lot of miles ahead of them. I want to put them to the best possible use. What I'd like to do is obstetrics; help bring life into the world, for a change. It feels right. Well, sweetheart, what do you think?"

"I'd say"—she nearly cried with delight—"that it's an absolutely marvelous idea and that I'm only slightly surprised. I had a hunch that you'd wind up in medicine."

"You and your hunches." He laughed. "Of course, it's a long way from Covent Garden celebrity to the wife of a lowly med student. Are you sure you'd want to stick it out, and with a small baby yet? We're looking at a few hard years. Oh, darling"—he encircled her in his arms—"I wish I could offer you something better after all this time. I love you so much, I wanted so much for you. There are times when I wish we could turn back the clock, be young again. But we can never go back to what we were. That kind of innocence, that loving blind trust . . . those illusions we had about each other. We were Prince and Princess Charming. Gone forever. We'll have to take each other just as we really are."

But that was all right with Annie. Better than all right.

"We can't go back"—she smiled—"but we can go on."

"Together." He kissed her. "Always together."

They went to bed with the joy and passion of first-time lovers. At his touch she trembled, fresh with the sense of expectation. Slowly, she undressed, almost shy, yet proud of a body that had begun to reveal the emergent signs of pregnancy. The subtle swelling of her breasts, the rich sheen of her hair. Apparent, perhaps, to no one but Seth, with his loving and observant eyes.

He came to her naked and vulnerable, then drew her to him, hands sliding over her flesh, touching her lips, her nipples, her belly, the hollows of her back, caressing her with a mixture of awe and desire.

"I shall have to discover you all over again, my darling Annie."

They made love first with a blinding urgency—mouths hungering, bodies aching for an intimacy that would drive away ancient shadows forever. Then they made love again, soft and lingering with the long slow strokes of two people for whom life had begun anew.

Later, Annie lay by his side replete, turning her happiness over in her mind. Seth slept the dreamless sleep of a man who had squared himself with destiny.

Dear Seth. His devils had been exorcised. His ordeal had brought them close once again.

Without illusions, he had said. Yes, love was best without illusions.

She had believed herself married to a god, only to discover he was mortal after all.

No, they could never again be as they were. But if they'd lost everything else in the hurricane of scandal, only now had they truly found each other.

Dear Seth. He had striven so hard to make his name immortal. He had sought fame and glory, quested for mastery over life and death.

That was not to be—or if so, not for years to come. And yet, Seth—who had come so close to taking life—had created it. The new life already formed within her, growing, shaping itself to become the living proof of their love.

Their child would be his immortality.

She brushed her lips against the burr of his cheek, then placed his hand upon her belly. Without waking, he burrowed close, sluicing his body in a flow of flesh to seek out the warmth of her own. Then he resettled, content. Annie shut her eyes and went to sleep.

EPILOGUE

ONE AFTERNOON IN LATE NOVEMBER, GERALD MARRINER DIED. The end came as he lay drowsing in the Caribbean sun. He was buried in the topiary garden of Villa Narcissus, overlooking the sea. It was as the obeah woman had foretold: You who are two shall be one.

Margot's fondest wish was that she might soon lie beside her husband for eternity.

For a week, she never left the villa. "Turn the mirrors to the wall," she told the houseboy. "I never want to see my face again."

Had the Medi-Tekk scandal robbed Gerald of his last few precious months of life? Margot could never be sure. But neither could she find it within herself to forgive those who had caused him such suffering.

Seth Petersen, and beyond him, Annie. Above all, Annie, for it was her influence—Margot felt—that had tipped the scales. Such ingratitude. And she had been so fond of the girl! Had taken Annie into her heart and her home. Into her last will and testament, as well.

"And to think," Margot addressed the windswept beach pines, "that I was leaving her my jewels."

Annie could have been free, rich beyond the dreams of avarice. Had she realized that she was Margot's heir, would she have held her tongue, swallowed her qualms? Probably not. Not the Annie she knew. At any rate, the bequest would have to be revoked.

Thus, a week after her husband's death, Margot phoned the Wall Street law firm of Moresby, Palmer. "Send one of your attorneys down here on the first flight tomorrow," she said. "I've decided to change my will."

That night, she did not sleep. For hours, she sat at her little teakwood desk and reviewed the disposal of her worldly goods. Such wealth! And no one truly close to leave it to. The fortune that would have been bequeathed to Gerald would now be divided among others. She drew up lists: brothers, nephews, cousins, servants. As for the jewels, she would leave them to the Metropolitan Museum with the stipulation that they be sold and the proceeds spent in acquiring English art. That seemed an apt bringing together of her two worlds.

Toward dawn, she finished the document. It only awaited the usual verbal flourishes that a lawyer would provide. Then, once her business was concluded, she planned to join Gerald in the warm earth of the topiary garden. A simple matter, if one had no moral qualms. A handfull of sleeping pills, a final walk along the coral sands and she and Gerald would be together once again.

The following afternoon, Roger Moresby himself arrived at the villa. Margot was astonished. Such a routine matter surely called for little more than any one of the firm's hundred junior lawyers.

"It's just a will, darling," she greeted the distinguished guest. "I never expected to be offered the services of a senior partner, let alone the director of the firm."

"Dear Margot!" Roger kissed her hand. "I wouldn't permit anyone else to handle your affairs. If I can help in any way, be of any comfort . . ."

He held her hand rather longer than necessary.

"How very kind." She smiled, momentarily revived by the pleasant warmth of a man's touch and presence.

They spent the rest of the afternoon going over the details. Then, business over, Henry served them dinner on the patio. They dined by the light of hurricane lamps. Fish mousse, sherbet and an excellent white Bordeaux.

With the brandy came a certain nostalgia. In the flickering lamplight, Roger seemed unduly soft and subdued.

"I remember the first time I ever saw you, Margot."

"Yes, I remember too," she said. "It was at a dinner party at the Paleys'. What was the year . . . sixty-seven . . . sixty-eight?"

"That was when we met," he emphasized. "I was thinking of an earlier time. It was 1946. I'd just been discharged from the army. I was going to law school on the G.I. bill and I saw you in *The Pirate Princess*. A dreadful movie. But I fell in love with you on the spot."

"How sweet of you to say so." Margot was touched.

"I even wrote the film company and wangled an autographed photo of you. I kept it in my desk drawer all through Yale, rather like a talisman. I thought you were the most beautiful woman I'd ever seen."

Margot was grateful for the darkness of the Caribbean night. It would keep the invidious comparison at bay.

"The most beautiful," he continued. "Then, years later, when we finally did meet that night at the Paleys', I discovered that your pictures didn't do you justice. You were a radiance, Margot. Lovely and glowing as a goddess. I can tell you now, I adored you hopelessly."

Margot fought back a tear. Yes, she had looked marvelous, even well into her forties. Yet she rather wished Roger hadn't reminded her of glories past.

Nonetheless, what an extraordinary admission for him to make after all these years. At the time, he had given no hint of even the slightest infatuation. Had he done so, he might very well have joined the long roster of lovers.

But then, Roger had always been very much the New England gentleman, too august a personage to indulge in a flirtation with another man's wife. Was he still married? she tried to recall.

Widowed. Yes, she remembered distinctly now. Abigail Moresby had died some years ago. Not that it mattered at this late date. Surely Roger's idealization of her beauty had long since been put to rest. Or had it? He sounded almost as romantic as a schoolboy.

In the near-dark she studied him more closely. Time had dealt kindly with Roger Moresby. One could not but remark the elegant bearing. The aristocratic features. The leonine thatch of gray hair. A very handsome man indeed.

"I'm immensely flattered," she said finally. "I thought you were enormously attractive too."

"Did you!" Astonished, he put down his brandy to consider this. "Of course, now I'm nothing but an elderly lawyer. Whereas you . . . Margot, you are as beautiful as ever."

"Roger!" Her heart began palpitating. "How can you say such a thing! Why, I'm—" She was going to say "middle-aged" or some such nonsense, but what was the point? He was her lawyer. He knew exactly how old she must be. "I'm hardly the same pretty thing I used to be."

"To my eyes you are," he said. "As exquisite as ever. And as enchanting. Ah, Margot, if you could only see into my heart—" He pulled himself up short. "I know it's far too soon after Gerald's death for you to even think of consolation."

She stretched her hand across the table.

He took it, a Parsifal touching the holy grail. "Sweet Margot. Forgive my presumption, but should you ever need an adoring servant, a faithful helpmeet . . ."

"My dear Roger!" She drank in his words in a state of delirium. Why, the man worshiped her! He spoke as though she were fair and twenty. Given a hint of encouragement, he would be down on his knees. Unseemly at this point. But in another month or two?

Of course, she'd have to get her appearance tended to. A new haircut, some lovely new clothes.

What did the wives of great Wall Street lawyers look like? she wondered. What kind of existence did they lead? Splendid, as far as she had noticed. They went everywhere: charity balls, first nights, museum openings. At Roger's level, they probably dined tête-à-tête at the White House.

Her heart quickened. Personally, she had always been very fond of Roger. Why, only this afternoon she had found him a tower of strength. So firm. So knowledgeable. Yes, indeed, here was a man on whose arm one could gracefully lean, perhaps for many years to come.

"Dear Margot!" he was murmuring.

She cast her eyes out over the topiary garden. Dear Gerald. But Gerald would understand. Hadn't he always? It was proof of the happiness he had given her that she might seek such joy again. For a moment her lip quivered. Subtly, she returned the pressure of Moresby's hand.

"Dear Roger." She sighed. "Where would I be if not for friends like you?"

In his eyes, she could see her beauty reflected, amplified, captured for all time. It was the elixir of life, had Roger but known it.

"I trust," he chided, "you're not going to bury yourself away here on the island. That would be unkind. Would it be too much to hope that you will soon be returning to New York so those like me who care for you might hope to offer comfort?"

She permitted him to bring her hand to his lips.

"I intend," she said, "to return very soon."

Gene Leavitt was rooting through his files, one crisp December morning, when a piece of paper caught his eye. Not that there was anything untoward about the paper itself, a routine interoffice work order on the pale blue stock that was sent up by the ream from the supply room. It was the date that provoked his curiosity. January 4, 1968. Medi-Tekk wasn't founded until 1977.

He pulled the sheet from the folder for closer inspection. It wasn't even his, he observed, unrelated to any of his projects.

Those goddam temp secretaries, always misfiling. They spent more time doing their nails than doing their jobs. Didn't know or care which end was up.

Gene scanned the sheet. It was a memo. A set of routine instructions. At the bottom of the page were two sets of initials:

SP/ja

Seth Petersen, obviously. He presumed "ja" to have been the Dumbo Temp of the Week. Yes, definitely Petersen's stuff. He recognized the formulation. Nothing very important, just a worksheet, a memo giving the specifics of the day's medication. Different batches, different doses, the usual shit. Only the girl made a typo. 1968 for 1986. No big deal.

Christ—he shook his head—what a bunch of ditzes that agency used to send around. They finally had to switch temp bureaus. The new girls were uglier, but at least they could type.

Yup, there Little Miss Miracle had done it again. Transposed another set of numbers.

Dyslexia, was Gene's bet, seeing things ass-backward. Like his sister-in-law Margie. Marge was bright enough, mind you, but she had this hang-up with numbers. Like if she told you to meet her on 79th Street, then you automatically went to 97th instead. Drove everyone in the family bananas.

He ran down the figures more closely. Suddenly, sirens went off. There, where it said 8.1 cc.

No way! Couldn't be. Obviously the figure was supposed to be 1.8 cc. You were shooting up mice, after all, not fucking Great Danes.

Gene sat down sweaty-palmed.

Jesus F. Christ! The implications were too hairy for words.

Still, it was impossible. After all, say some dyslexic dodo screwed up on paper, that would have been the end of it. No way an over-dosage that size wouldn't be questioned by the lab associate. That was one of the things they got paid for, to see that goofs like these didn't slip by. Petersen had that girl . . . what's-her-name? the Pakistani with those fabulous forty inch knockers. Chandra something-or-other.

The one who was banging Tony Cianelli down in Purchasing. Good-looking kid, that Tony, if your tastes run to Day-Glo ties. Jesus, some couple they'd been. There was a period there when you couldn't open up a broom closet without finding the two of 'em going at it like jackrabbits.

Boy, was she frosted when Tony announced his engagement to Terry Conti. Shitty of Tony, he supposed. And to make the announcement at the office Christmas party was not exactly tactful. But let's face it—Chandra wasn't exactly the kind of gal you brought home to your nice little Italian mama in the Bronx.

Hard not to feel sorry for her, though. She really was heart-broken, all forty inches of her. Guess she expected the dude to marry her, so she could provide him with a batch of little Cianellis. Poor kid. She'd been in a state of shock all that winter. One thing for sure, she didn't have her mind on the job.

Was it possible? Gene considered. Given the circumstances, was it possible she could commit a goof of that magnitude? Not probable. But *yes!* very, very possible. She'd probably realized it halfway through.

Funny thing was, Seth Petersen didn't have a clue about what was going on inside her. Probably thought those moony eyes and sighs were all for him. For all his smarts, Petersen was a lousy judge of character.

Gene sat down on his desk and smoothed the paper out yet again. He felt suddenly sick to his stomach, wished to hell he'd never opened that fucking drawer. Could this be it—this one lousy sheet of blue paper? He just might have stumbled on the source of Seth Petersen's failure. It was the scandal of the decade, with congressional inquiries, articles being written left and right in every magazine. Did it amount to nothing more than a couple of typos and a distracted, lovesick girl?

Conceivably. But if so, that wasn't for him to determine.

Gene Leavitt reached for the phone. The thing to do was get in touch with Petersen pronto. Let him figure out the implications. Last he'd heard, the Petersens were living in the wilds of Brooklyn. Or was it Long Island? Easy enough to find out. He dialed 9 for an outside wire. The dial tone came on.

For a moment Leavitt wavered, then replaced the phone on the cradle. Why the hell should he get that bastard off the hook? What was this—a bleeding hearts convention?

Instinctively, Gene put his hand on his throat. He could still remember the press of Seth's thumb against his windpipe, still feel the weight of his body. Son of a bitch had damn near killed him.

And Gene owed him favors? Hell, he owed the man zilch!

No sir. Yours truly Doc Leavitt was not about to play white knight to the likes of Seth Fucking Petersen. Why should he? So he could win the Altruist of the Year Prize? The Dumb Klutz Medal was more like it. After all, Gene was on to some interesting research of his own these days. Why try to salvage Petersen's chestnuts from the fire?

He opened his office door and poked his nose into the corridor. No one around. Good.

With a hard tight smile, Gene Leavitt took the paper and dropped it into the document shredder down the hall. *CHOMP CHOMP CHOMP*, the mechanical teeth gnashed.

Then Gene Leavitt settled down to a good day's work.

Union College is a small but select institution some four hours' drive north of New York City.

"The heart of snow country," Ari said.

Tonight was the last leg of their college tour, which was just as well. Another week and she wouldn't fit into her concert dresses anymore. As soon as she got back to the city, she'd have to have them let out at the waistline.

Even so, she looked every bit of five months pregnant. It hadn't affected her voice, thank God, and if the audience didn't mind her appearance, that was fine all around. Even if they did, too bad.

So far, the receptions had been terrific. She and Ari had built sophisticated and demanding programs, and the students had lapped it up. It boded well for return concerts next season. They'd raise their fees, of course. Damned if there wasn't a nice career in all this.

Tonight, too, the house was packed.

A foot and a half of snow notwithstanding, a full complement of listeners—both town and gown—had turned out for the recital. Seth, too, had driven up that afternoon, straight from his publisher's office. Just before the concert, she had shooed him out of the dressing room.

"Sit way back in the audience"—she chose the most strategic location—"and make sure you clap hard."

She and Ari had been in superb form as they worked their way through first Bach, and then a Schubert grouping. After intermission, she sang the Rückert songs of Mahler. The program ended with the brisk clear taste of Poulenc.

"Best reception yet," Ari murmured as they went back on stage to acknowledge the applause. The audience was wonderful—sharp and knowledgeable. A joy to make music at this level. From the midst of the house, someone began yelling *"Bis bis,"* in the continental manner.

"Encore time. Are you ready, Annie?"

"Yup. You've got the music?"

Ari nodded.

Annie smoothed down her dress. The stage light caught the glitter of her gold bracelet. Then she stepped forward and addressed the audience. Beyond the pool of light, the theater was black, faces lost and indistinguishable, but she felt their reflected warmth.

"I would like to sing as an encore"—she smiled—"a song that has a very special meaning for me . . . and for my husband."

In the hush she could divine Seth's surprise.

She dipped her head to Ari, then began softly.

"Ouvre ta paupière close . . ."

The words spun out seamlessly, hung in the air light as gossamer. "*Je suis*"—she shut her eyes—"*le spectre de la rose . . .*"

The ghost of the rose. The ghost of that summer night when first they met.

He was listening. Remembering too. Her heart flooded with joy.

And with the music, she reached out once more into the darkness to touch him and to seal their love anew.

FREDA BRIGHT began her career as a concert pianist after studying at the Paris Conservatory. She was an advertising executive for many years in New York and London before writing her first novel, *Options*. Ms. Bright is also the author of *Futures* and *Decisions*. She lives in Montclair, New Jersey.